Nestled in each other's arms, celebrating with occasional hugs and kisses, marveling at how right it felt . . . eventually, Miranda and Jay made love again. She had never before been so aroused by a man; she had never before dared to tease and titillate, because never before had she felt so secure.

When Miranda drifted to sleep, safe in Jay's arms, she noticed that the sun was coming up. She thought how wonderful it would be waking up with him beside her.

But when she reached out for him, he was gone . . .

"A novel that could only happen today . . . romance has never been more real and wonderful."
—ROMANTIC TIMES

Berkley books by Carolyn Fireside

ANYTHING BUT LOVE
GOODBYE AGAIN

Goodbye Again

Carolyn Fireside

BERKLEY BOOKS, NEW YORK

GOODBYE AGAIN

A Berkley Book / published by arrangement with
the author

PRINTING HISTORY
Berkley edition / November 1984

ISBN: 0-425-06286-4

A BERKLEY BOOK® TM 757,375
Berkley Books are published by The Berkley Publishing Group,
200 Madison Avenue, New York, New York 10016.
The name ''BERKLEY'' and the stylized ''B'' with design are
trademarks belonging to Berkley Publishing Corporation.
PRINTED IN THE UNITED STATES OF AMERICA

*For Beverly Lewis
and Bill Grose,
with thanks to
Arlene and Shep,
Tom and Scott,
Judith and Nat*

AUTHOR'S NOTE

In applying my imagination to a recent period of time, I've taken certain liberties, both with events (the Academy Awards, say, or any number of stage productions that happened only in my mind) and with establishments (a restaurant, for instance, which may have opened a year or two earlier or later in actuality than in this narrative).

*I'd thank the Gods above
If I could only love
Somebody, not you,
But I've got you on my mind.*
—COLE PORTER

Prologue

MY MOTHER IS wearing ermine—a long er-
mine mantle arranged about her shoulders like a princess in a fairy tale. Ermine and diamonds—diamonds at
her ears, at her throat, sparkling on the slender, graceful
fingers that, when she elegantly dismisses the servant,
dance about for emphasis like a shower of stars from a
magic wand. Ermine and diamonds and satin—satin the
color of young cherries, molded to her tiny waist, spilling from waist to hem like the cascade of a waterfall.
She thinks she is alone, is utterly unaware of my twelve-
year-old presence, hidden in the darkness as I am, spy-
ing on her, breathless with the anticipation of suspicions
at last to be confirmed.

Thinking herself unobserved, she lets the ermine cape
drop carelessly from her shoulders onto a white and
gold divan, then dashes to a mirror, arranging the auburn curls that rest lightly on her alabaster shoulders,
straightening her necklace, obviously pleased with the
way the ice-glow of the jewels and the bright cerise of
her décolletage highlight the flawless skin and the unmatchable swan's neck.

Rehearsing for a rendezvous soon to come, she prac-
tices her expressions—first a small, almost imperceptible turning up of the lips, just enough to bring out a

dimple, then a little more, a little more, until she presents herself with a radiant smile, head thrown slightly back as if ready to laugh, and it is then I am fully aware of her incredible beauty—the jade eyes, bordered in sable lashes, the high arch of the brow, the perfect symmetry of the nose, the marble cheekbones, the absolute oval of her unforgettable face.

Bored with the performance, she walks nervously about the room I love so much, checking the clock on the mantel above the fireplace, striding to the window and pulling back the draperies. Seeing no one arrive, she marches over to a brocade love seat and hurls herself into it, but almost immediately jumps up and paces again, her steps luring her again to the window. She, so lovely, so worldly, so grown-up, is as restless as a child, and I catch her nervousness, even hidden away, even in the dark, and I can practically see the pulse pounding in her temples as it pounds in mine.

She is, of course, peering out the window when the door opens, and she whirls around, terrified of being surprised in her vigil by the object of it, and she is just in time, for, only an instant after she has metamorphosed from an anxious girl in love into a woman radiant with allure, a dark-cloaked figure bounds into the room and halts, struck immobile by her beauty.

Of course, it is he, just as I always knew it would be. His tall, manly figure, even under the layers of evening clothes, glows with health and great vitality. Even in repose, his muscles ripple, ready to spring or glide or bow. Sparks from the pewter eyes ignite my racing heart as they must hers, although she stands still, still and calm and ready.

Though neither moves, it is he who speaks first. Raising a hand to smooth his thick, lustrous hair, he then makes a fist, which moves to his hip in a pose of absolute challenge. "Madam"—his magnificent voice enchants as his eyes fix hers in a wondrous gaze—

"despite all, madam, I have come. Despite all, I have kept my word!"

She does not drop her gaze, yet still keeps silent.

"And so, my darling," he continues, "despite all, I expect you will keep yours."

At last, at long last, she speaks in a voice so resonant, so confident, that it belies the fright I know she is feeling. "Yes." She allows her eyes to close for only a second, gathering strength for the words to follow. "Yes, despite all, I will."

And suddenly, he is across the room, and suddenly, she is in his arms, and all I feared and hoped for so long has become as real as my fantasies and my nightmares, and the exhilaration that springs up in my heart wars with the awful knowledge of what lies ahead.

"My only love," he murmurs, and she answers, "My only love. God help us!"

And as they meet again in a last, adulterous embrace, the red velvet curtain falls, the applause thunders through the theatre, and I awake, no longer Randy, the twelve-year-old kid in the fourth row, but Miranda Lawson, a young woman who has dreamed that scene over and over through the years, for it was the last time I saw my mother alive.

PART ONE

chapter 1

Miranda
Manhattan, 1975

"IF YOU WON'T tell me who he is, Jack, at least tell me what he's like. If I'm supposed to snow him, point me in the right direction!" Miranda concentrated on her companion the laser look of a lady spy primed for interrogation.

"Keep it down, M.L." Jack Price hissed. "You can never tell who's listening."

"Oh, Jack, you're being paranoid," Miranda laughed, looking around upstairs at Sardi's. At nine-thirty, the place was practically deserted except for an occasional couple of walkouts from a Broadway show. Even the bartender was deep in conversation with some cronies at the far end of the bar and couldn't have cared less what Jack and Miranda were talking about.

"Paranoid? Paranoid?" Jack's tone was rapier sharp. "It's my future we're discussing here. And, I might add, yours, my dear!"

"Oh, cut it out, Jack! You know I can't stand it when you get self-righteous!"

"Bitch!" the young man snapped, all Bette Davis in *All About Eve*, then abruptly shifted to that darling boyish smile that made his unavailability so bother-some.

Ah, that smile! Oh, that unavailability! She had

heard about both long before she'd met him, had actually traveled up to Boston with some friends from the Yale Drama School to catch a play of his at the Loeb Theater at Harvard. The play had been dazzling, especially coming from an undergrad; it was fresh, it was new, it was powerful, and there was even a perfect role for her. She'd raved on and on about it to the gorgeous blond and blue-eyed guy she'd instantly connected with at the party, and afterward, when he turned out to be Jack Price, the playwright, she'd blushed and he'd pronounced himself charmed. They'd spent a good part of the evening together, laughing and getting drunk, until the guy he was seeing, a dark and temperamental actor, stepped in and whisked him away, but not before Jack had made sure he knew how to reach her in New Haven. He hadn't called, although she knew if things had been different he would have, and then, busy with graduation and the relocation to Manhattan, she'd shifted her disappointment way back in her feelings. When they'd met again, it had been in New York, by accident when they were both attending a production at the Public Theater. He was no longer the toast of Harvard, and she was working as an office temp and making the rounds of auditions. Neither of them was on top of the world, and both of them needed a friend, so, in the year that followed, they became inseparable.

"Between men and between engagements, kid," Jack, whose affair with the Byronic actor hadn't survived graduation, had regaled her merrily one evening the year before. *"La Bohème* and *Le Bohème.* Let's enjoy the misery because we'll never be this poor or this desperate again. Ten years from now, we'll look back on this and miss it."

"Maybe you'll miss it, Jack. I sure won't," Miranda had muttered over a splurge burger at Joe Allen's. "You didn't have to slave over a hot switchboard all day."

"No, babe, just over a cold typewriter. And I mean cold, because there wasn't any heat or hot water all day. And I'm beginning to think my agent *is* in—she just won't take my calls."

"At least you've got an agent!"

"At least you've got heat and hot water."

"Jack," she'd urged him, "maybe you *should* go to law school, or pretend to, or something. Just so your father'll relent."

"Bug off, Miranda," he'd shot back. "That's over and done with . . . And how do you pretend to go to law school, anyway?"

She shrugged idly, "Oh, Jack, I was just talking."

"You know, M.L.," Jack muttered, "just because my father's a great trial lawyer doesn't mean I inherited the talent. Maybe someday I'll write a hit courtroom drama and earn my way back into the family bosom. Naw, forget it. When I buy the co-op on Fifth Avenue, it'll be with my own hard-earned bread. Hey, how're you doing, moneywise?"

"Oh, Lord, it's practically gone. I'm so broke that a five-story walk-up's beginning to look expensive. I've been canceling the singing lessons because I can't pay for them. Something's got to happen soon!"

"Baby, you ain't just whistling Dixie! Meanwhile, let's have another beer!" He'd signaled the waiter, and they'd changed the subject, but even banter couldn't chase the blues away. Jack's almost surrealistically small room in the West Village seemed to be growing smaller by the day, but the rent had gone up. Miranda was doing the office temp work to pay the rent on a borderline tenement in Yorkville, but the work cut into acting class and making rounds, as Jack's driving a cab stole him away from his typewriter more and more hours every week. Of course, they still managed to see the best of Broadway—*Equus,* Peter Cook and Dudley Moore in *Good Evening, A Little Night Music*—but there were plenty of other things they had to pass up, and Miranda gave daily thanks to the gods of fashion that jeans still went everywhere.

Then, in February of '75, a couple of things happened. First, Jack met someone. The guy, a Brooks Brothers-outfitted stockbroker with a rather less conventional private life, had been a cab fare of Jack's, but in the course of a leisurely ride up the East Side Drive from Wall Street, where Jack had picked him up one evening, to East Seventy-second Street, where Chuck, the stockbroker, lived, the driver/passenger chitchat had blossomed into something more; Jack ended up parking the cab outside Chuck's building, where it languished until the next morning, when Jack gallantly drove him back to work with the meter off.

Miranda had expected Jack to get involved, sooner or later, and was happy for him, but she'd gotten used to his being around pretty much all the time, so the fact that he was busy gave her a lot of free nights she'd not really welcomed.

It seemed as though all her friends, gay and straight, were arranged in pairs, which made her the perennial third party. And although she was invited to everything, their Upper West Side grass-wine-and-pizza evenings, where everybody left with a special friend and she left alone, depressed her.

She didn't have work. She didn't have a man. She was twenty-four, small enough to be shorter than the average man without looking like a midget, with a body and a face Jack, at least, called striking. Her long, wild, and wavy hair was the same fabulous auburn as her mother's, her eyes the same green, but there the resemblance ended. Miranda Lawson was a cute girl with a feisty manner, but no one in the world would have recognized her as the luminous Margo Seymour's daughter.

Not that she had ever wanted to be a clone of Margo. She wanted to make it on her own, to earn her individual fame on her individual merits. Yet there were times when she had to acknowledge that beauty made things easier, legendary beauty even more so. What would her life be like, she wondered, if she looked more like her gorgeous mother or, for that matter, had inherited Margo's star quality? More even than her mother's face, Miranda envied her unmatchable aura, which had literally illumined movie screens and proscenium arches all over the world; and it was that ebullient grace, that fierce and satin sweetness that Miranda, monitoring herself on- and offstage, found lacking in her own presence. Too intense to glide, too strong-willed to murmur, Miranda had, as her teachers had told her, power and character to spare, but she would have sold it all for a modicum of allure.

It's not you, it's the times, Jack would have countered, if she'd ever unbent enough to confess her self-doubts to him, and he would have continued: Women are different now; the style of the movie goddesses, Margo Seymour included, was an anachronism perpetuated mainly in the archives of gay culture. And he would have been right, but he would also have been wrong, because the fact remained that, women's lib or not, most of the women she knew were seeing someone and she wasn't.

Was she too liberated? Too sharp-tongued? Too ordinary? Too weird? In the evenings without Jack, she pondered an endless list of depressing possibilities, searching for an explanation that continued to elude her. And then, something happened to make her failure as a seductive woman abundantly, humiliatingly clear.

Like a storm cloud from nowhere, it had burst onto a Monday that had showed every promise of being sunny. The temp agency had called her late Friday afternoon with what had to be a good omen. The assignment was only a week-long filing job in an accounting department, but it was no ordinary accounting department; it was, in fact, the accounting department of Harrington

Enterprises, the world-famous Manhattan real estate empire whose properties included luxury high rises, a constantly expanding collection of huge commercial monoliths, a couple of skyline-revolutionizing towers, a good third of the operating Broadway theatres, and a hefty piece of most of the shows in those houses. Granted, all she'd see was the accounting department—she probably wouldn't even get a glimpse of the legendary founder of the Harrington dynasty, "Old Man Sam"—but you could never tell whose assistant you might meet in the ladies' room, and whatever came of the job, it just had to be a good sign.

The Harrington Building towered, proud and cold and contemporary, above the archaically stunted rooftops of New York's theatre district, and although it sheltered a large movie theatre, two legitimate theatres, and a mammoth restaurant and bar as well as a garage, it was definitely all business. Of the forty-eight stories, Harrington Enterprises occupied the top five, and Miranda was disappointed when the receptionist on forty-eight directed her down to forty-six, which *was* the accounting department. So much for meeting Sam Harrington's secretary in the ladies' room.

When she arrived on forty-six, she found, to her delight, that fate had placed her in the middle of a conversion of the theatrical accounts onto a computer. So, from nine-thirty on, she alphabetized and filed folder after folder of figures from an amazing number of major shows, some of which she'd been taken to as a child, some she'd seen when she was in school, some still in the planning stages. By eleven she'd gotten through the *c*'s and been asked to lunch the following day by the secretary to the head of the division, Manuela, who had, according to ladies' room scuttlebutt, a unique talent for keeping her ferocious boss, Lew Steinberg, from running amok and firing his entire staff.

The new files were located blessedly near a window, and the bright light of early April streamed in, making it through the damaged air with remarkable pluck. About eleven-forty, Miranda stopped for a coffee break, reading, as she sipped, the figures for *Dream Time,* the gigantic hit musical that had been running for the last couple of years, and which had cost, to her astonishment, $800,000 in capitalization, maintained a weekly net of $75,000, and at this point, was clearing a cool weekly profit of $40,000. A far cry from even the most elaborate of the college productions she'd considered so big-time. Drifting from the *Dream Time* figures to her own personal fantasies of glory, she noticed, all of a sudden, that someone was standing over her. She looked up to find, staring down at her, a pair of astonishingly gorgeous gold and brown eyes, which belonged to one of the tallest, handsomest, broadest-shouldered, and most obviously annoyed men she'd ever seen.

"I didn't know this was a branch of the public library." The voice was as deep and wonderfully liquid as the eyes, but the tone was arctic. "I was told it was an office. You know, a place where people go to work. As opposed to where they go to sit around and read."

"I'm terribly sorry, sir." She stressed the *sir* with just the correct amount of liberated scorn. "I was on my break, which I was told all employees are entitled to. But can I help you?"

"If it's not too much trouble," he growled, "get me the *Lullaby* file."

Not even a *please!* Who was this jerk to think he could order her around? Some executive assistant, no doubt.

"Right away, sir." She inwardly cursed him as she sauntered over to the stacks of unfiled folders and began searching out *Lullaby* from the huge collection before her.

"Will you please make it snappy, miss? I'd like the figures before the end of the week."

Of course, she couldn't find *Lullaby.* Wherever it was, it wasn't around *Lament of the Harlequins* or

Lonely Too Long, and as she scrambled, conscious of his lethal and lovely eyes bearing down on her confusion, she began to panic. What if he wasn't an assistant? What if he was Lew Steinberg, the man with the terrible temper? He seemed awfully young to be running a department, but he did have the air of a man to the manor born. She prayed he would leave her to suffer alone, but instead, with consummate perversity, he sat down and stared at her as she hoisted bunch after heavy bunch of folders from one pile to another.

"What's the problem, miss?" he inquired after a hostile silence.

She wanted to explain to him that her job was to make order out of this chaos, and that he'd be better advised to yell at whomever had left things in such a mess, but all that came out was, "Problem . . . um . . . no problem . . ."

"Then what's taking so long? It's now ten to twelve, and by twelve I need those figures *and*—"

And suddenly, there was *Lullaby,* seven down in the second to the last pile. She had just begun to dig it out as she heard him add, "—the figures for an old play called *Goodbye Again.* You probably haven't heard of it, since it was done before *Hair."*

Goodbye Again. She'd heard of it, all right. From the opening night when she was twelve and sat in the audience, dazzled by her mother's utterly convincing portrait of the lover of a man who would, in real life, steal her from Miranda. Oh, she'd heard of it, had relived it in her memories and dreams for all the years after, but its stunning evocation at this particular moment shocked her so that the *Lullaby* folder flew from her hands, showering papers all over the floor.

The brute didn't even help her collect the papers, just sat there, a smug and self-righteous tyrant.

She managed to recover the papers and at the same time figure out that *Goodbye Again* had to be in the one pile she'd hadn't looked through, so that, in a matter of seconds, she was able to hand him both files, sure now that he was Lew Steinberg, even more sure that this would be the end of her job. So she was both relieved and infuriated, as well as embarrassed, when his parting words, which didn't include either "Thank you" or "You're fired," turned out to be, "And, miss, tomorrow could you please come to work more . . . more suitably dressed?" He slowly scanned her jeans-clad form—a little too thoroughly, it seemed to Miranda—before announcing haughtily, "This is a place of business, not a Stones concert," and then he was gone.

Throughout the eternity-long wait until lunch, Miranda pushed herself to continue working, sure that the ogre would return, having decided out of spite to dismiss her. Strangely, neither he nor his minions arrived to execute her downfall, and when Manuela asked her if she would mind covering the phones while she was out to lunch, Miranda agreed with the largesse of a prisoner reprieved from the chair. Surely, the evil Steinberg would already have left for lunch and was bound to get back later than Manuela, so for the next hour or so, she was safe from his scorn. The phone didn't ring, and there wasn't anybody to talk to, so Miranda spent the time brooding over Steinberg and pushing thoughts of *Goodbye Again* and Margo and Anthony and the scandal to the back of her mind. At about one-thirty, she called her answering service—keeping it was a necessity despite her tight budget—and found that Jack was urgently trying to reach her.

"Jack? How was the weekend? What's up?" she asked when she called him, hoping that Steinberg wouldn't come back early and catch her in the mortal sin of talking to a friend on office time.

"Where are you?" Jack demanded.

"At work. I guess I didn't get a chance to tell you I'm doing a week at—"

"Forget it, kid," Jack announced expansively. "Wherever it is doesn't matter, because what I have to tell you is going to make office work obsolete. Something great's happened. Something fantastic for both of us!''

"Like what, Jack?"

"Like someone's interested in producing *Up on the Heights*."

"Oh, Jack! You mean it?" She'd read the play and thought it was the best thing he'd done, but the last she'd heard his agent hadn't been able to interest anyone in it. "Who, Jack? How?"

"It's a big surprise, Miranda, and I do mean big, so I'm not going to spoil it for you. But let me say this, kid: You're part of the package."

"What do you mean?" But she knew, and her heart thrilled.

"Look, the part of Rachel was written for you, my love, and I want you to do it."

"Does the mysterious moneyman know that?"

"Yes and no. Anyway, listen. Meet me upstairs at Sardi's tonight at nine. We're taking a meeting with our future producer!"

"God, Jack! What should I wear?"

"What should you wear? What you always wear. What I always wear. Jeans. I don't know. Why?"

"I had a dress code problem with this guy at work today, and it's made me a little paranoid, but, oh, Jack, this is unbelievable—it's great. But I'd better get off the phone before the ogre catches me on it, okay?"

"All right, doll. See you at nine. And be at your most sparkling!''

"You bet, chief," and she'd hung up, sparkling already. She was still sparkling when Manuela came back and she went out to pick up something to eat, positively glowing when she walked back through the lobby, entered the empty elevator, and waited for the doors to shut. She was seeing stardom dance before her as the doors began slowly to close and she heard an all-too-familiar voice calling, "Hold the elevator!" Her decision was possibly the product of her euphoria, was certainly rash, but as her finger declined to push the Open button, she had the double pleasure of seeing the doors close on Lew Steinberg and of seeing Steinberg seeing *her* shut him out. She shouldn't have done it, shouldn't have risked agitating him still more, but with Jack's news, this crummy job no longer seemed so desperately important. If he fired her, he fired her.

She was passing Steinberg's office on the way back to the file morgue when she heard Manuela say to someone on the other end of a phone call, "Hold for Mr. Steinberg," and she paused just long enough to try to figure out how he could have beat her upstairs, just long enough to notice that the middle-aged, balding guy sitting behind the desk in the inner office didn't look anything like her persecutor, long enough to hear Manuela say over the intercom, "Mr. Grayson for you, Lew," and then Miranda continued back to her cubicle, convinced that her first impression of the guy she'd fought with was correct, that he was some nobody with a lot of *chutzpah*. She was glad that luck was finally with her, thrilled that she had closed the door in his face.

The afternoon dragged on and on, and although she'd made it through the *f*'s, her thoughts were fixed on nine o'clock and the golden destiny that waited her. She had nearly forgotten about the past until, freshening makeup in the ladies' room, she heard Manuela ask her, "Did Jay give you a rough time this morning?"

"Jay?" She stopped combing her hair, and her eyes met Manuela's in the mirror. "You mean that uppity, sexist nobody who was so obnoxious?"

"Well, I wouldn't call him a nobody."

"What do you mean? Who is he?"

"He didn't even tell you who he was?"

"No, and believe me, I didn't ask. Who is he?"

"Miranda, he's Jay Harrington. Sam's son."

"Sam Harrington's son? You're kidding!"

"No, right out of the Harvard Business School, and the heir apparent to the whole kit and caboodle. You really didn't know?"

"God, I had no idea! Is he always like that?"

"No. I mean, he's gone out with a lot of the girls in the office once or twice, but nobody's every complained about anything except that it was only once or twice. I mean, he *is* a great catch. In terms of the office, well, nobody's ever going to mistake him for Mick Jagger —he's pretty straight—but I've never heard anybody complaining that he was an s.o.b. Maybe he was having a bad day."

"That's for sure," Miranda concurred, and that was that. Curse her luck that she hadn't been able instantly to charm a man so susceptible to female charms, but what liberated woman would want a man who abused her for incompetence, criticized her for malingering, then cruised her for the snug fit of her jeans? Boss's son or no, he was a creep. Too bad he looked the way he did. Well, she assured herself, when she was famous, he'd break down walls just for the chance to be nice to her.

She'd asked Manuela if she could leave at four-thirty, promising to make up the time the next day. She was going to splurge on a cab, get home early, soak in a hot tub, and get ready for her command performance that evening. At last, when four-thirty came, she'd taken the elevator down to the lobby and dashed to the revolving doors when *he* appeared, wearing that same gilt-edged smirk.

"Leaving early, *miss?*" He lingered over the words.

"I have permission from my supervisor, *Mister* Harrington."

"Of course, you would. Still, you don't like doing anything according to the book, do you?"

She decided not to honor his remark with the dignity of a reply, just gave her hair a little toss and started into the revolving door. That was the fatal mistake, for he had paused just a second to push the door for her, but she hadn't noticed, which meant that he quickly had to step inside with her and they ended up pressed together in the same section of the door. For the brief, mortifying time that they scuttled together to make the door turn and release them, she was simultaneously aware of the powerful feel of his trench-coated body against hers, of the seductive smell of some aftershave or cologne, of how utterly foolish they both looked, and of how totally her fault this was. If she had just let him push the door for her, she would be out on the street and safe. The eternity finally ended, the door freed them—she blushing, he daring to laugh out loud.

"God, lady"—he stared her down, laughing still—"you are trouble!"

"And you, Mr. Harrington, are a pig!" She speared him with the statement, tossed back her hair one final time, and dashed off down the street.

Why, *why,* had she said it? Why had she alienated the guy once and for all? Why did embarrassment always make her blossom with rage? Well, it was over, and there she and Jack were at Sardi's, waiting for their savior to arrive. Later, she could castigate herself. Later, she could play back the scene and bury her humiliation in clouds of future glory. Now, she had to be *on,* she had to glow, because Jack, seeing someone approaching, had gotten up and called, "Hey, buddy, here we are!"

Their benefactor had arrived, and their bright futures had arrived with him, except for one thing: The mystery man was Jay Harrington.

chapter 2

Jack
1984

FROM THE TOP rung of the gilded ladder of fame, it's hard to catch a glimpse of yourself as you were back then, before everything turned golden. Tiny in memory, simplified in outline, like a comic strip figure, the young, vulnerable you, so naive, so blindly optimistic, seems like another person. Somehow, over the years, so gradually you really don't notice it, your circle of friends changes and your old haunts fade away. Too many people remember you "when," and too many interrupted dinners end in embarrassing pitches for favors. I guess that's the price of fame, but the surcharge is your innocence.

I'm tougher now. Public acclaim and a co-op on Fifth Avenue have divorced me from those early, crazy times of constant surprise. I'm still a nice guy—or so they tell me—but I'm undeniably harder, and like me, those few relationships that have survived the journey from obscurity to fame have toughened, have assumed the fiery, frozen veneer of icons, twisting and turning in lyrical patterns that embody and protect the version of the past I have chosen to allow myself. And Miranda Lawson is the most priceless icon in the collection, the woman whose life brushed mine from time to time, but brushed it with strokes of such intensity that our en-

20

counters have taken on the symbolism of painting or poetry, putting a frame around the past, structuring it.

Fellow travelers we were, Miranda and I, right from the beginning, when our similar dreams caused us to clasp hands on the dark and dangerous journey through the forest of Manhattan. Like Hansel and Gretel, we saved each other from the self-doubt that might have sprung up along the way without a spiritual buddy to hold on to. We were pals, siblings, nanny and charge, cheerleader and quarterback, lovers of each other's most intimate quirks and qualities, but never of each other.

We met after one of my early, easy college triumphs, and although I'd recognized her from a couple of dazzling undergrad performances at Yale and in the summer at Williamstown, and was aware of her notorious past, she didn't know who I was. She first appeared as a small, slight girl, as high-strung and shy as she was intense, with a face that seemed plain until she quieted down. In the relatively rare moments when she relaxed, a real and considerable beauty emerged. To those uninitiated in her elaborate history, that loveliness would evoke some resemblance that skittered too quickly through the mind to be grasped; to me, who knew better, it announced her unmistakably as Margo Seymour's daughter.

But she hid that beauty the way she tried to hide her pedigree (although, of course, she fooled only herself; everybody knew who she was), and I, only an amateur psychologist, could understand why. Beauty must have seemed, to the young Miranda, the agent of her mother's downfall. What had led to scandal and, worse, to suicide could only be a bad thing, a dangerous thing. Beauty was a curse, and stardom sealed one's fate.

Still, she definitely wanted to be a star—I could sense that right from the beginning of our association—but she also fought the impulse, because she dreaded what stardom brought. You could almost see her acting out the struggle as she stood in the middle of a crowded party, alternately charming you with her brightness and honesty and intimidating you with her overstated, unconvincing self-assertiveness. She was playing the part of a liberated woman, but she hadn't quite gotten the role down.

If she had smoked and I had tried to light her cigarette, she undoubtedly would have been insulted. If I had attempted to buy her dinner, she would have bristled. If I had complimented her on what she was wearing, she would have looked at me askance. And it struck me then that getting close to Miranda would be an exercise in strategy and tactics equal to the siege of Leningrad. In those days, I was still debating the nature of my sexuality, and that first night, when we began to have a good time and she let down her defenses, I felt some spark between us, something that happens only between a woman and a man, and I knew she felt it, too. So I took her number, but I never called. When her name came up, I always felt a pang of guilt for not having gotten in touch, but I knew that having a thing with Miranda—despite her warmth and strength and energy and wit—was a major commitment, a tall order, and I had a lot of tall orders before me in my dazzling future. So I let it slide.

Later, when we met by accident in New York and the roseate haze of academic praise was disappearing as fast as the allowance I'd enjoyed at Harvard, it wasn't as easy to dismiss an obvious soul mate. So affinity became a substitute for romance. We spent the following year together, orphans of the storm, struggling and despairing and hoping. I dreamed, then, in the good old, bad old days, that we'd be together always—wildly famous, flamboyantly rich and glamorous, I with my dazzling young lover, she with her dashing tycoon, but as we received some major honor, we'd smile across the table at each other, and it'd be something special. Which only goes to show you never know.

So when, after almost a year of relative celibacy, I took up with someone, I couldn't help feeling I was betraying Miranda. She never let on that she felt betrayed, but it bothered me. Since I had a lover, I wished for her the satisfaction I was feeling, but it didn't happen. She would allude to men she'd met—old college affairs on the verge of revival, guys she'd met in class or through friends, but something always went wrong; either he didn't meet with her approval or he took too much time from her studies. I was worried about her, and I didn't know how to help her out of her loneliness. Success would do wonders, of course, but success continued to elude us both. Until the winter of '75 was turning into spring, and everything changed . . . one drunken afternoon at the Harvard Club.

I'd run into a college friend on the street; he'd formerly been an aspiring poet but was now a fast-rising copywriter at a major ad agency, turning over substantial bucks and looking prosperous, so, when he invited me to lunch at the Harvard Club—on him—I accepted. At that point; I was in my Harvard rejection period, and I entered the imposing red-brick building on West Forty-fourth Street with trepidation, afraid that I'd be spotted by some of my hippie cronies. But after a few martinis in the bar plus a largely liquid lunch in the vast, oak-paneled dining hall, David and I were having the time of our lives, a sort of first reunion. When I mentioned a script I couldn't sell, one that seemed to me —and only me—to be my first really commercial attempt, he mentioned that he'd run into Jay Harrington on the squash courts. Jay was a mutual school acquaintance some three or four years my senior, who, being the scion of a powerful family of theatrical producers, used to make visits down from the business school to catch up on our doings at the Loeb. I remembered him as tremendously handsome but all business, an entrepreneur born and bred, a real go-getter. And he was living up to that promise, for David mentioned that Jay was starting some theatrical venture out of town and was looking for interesting scripts. When he volunteered to put me back in touch with Jay, I jumped at the chance. And lo and behold, Jay's B-school heart raced when he read my play, and he agreed at least to consider using Margo Seymour's daughter in her professional debut, so I immediately called Miranda and had her join us at our first meeting since he'd read *Up on the Heights*.

It took place at Sardi's—where else?—and Miranda was edgy, but she was also excited. In fact, she shimmered. I was beside myself, but tried to bury it beneath my customary casual bonhomie. This was grown-up. This was serious. Big money and big futures hung in the balance. I could almost hear my dad apologizing for doubting my talent as I won the Pulitzer Prize. I could see them moving the Steinway into my penthouse. I could almost see myself on the cover of *Time* as I won an Oscar, a Tony, *and* the Pulitzer Prize in the same year. But, as we sat at the bar, those visions faded before a scene that could put them all to rest: Jay Harrington, young, dashing, if a little solemn—breaking up with hysterical laughter, and Miranda, liberated woman that she was, blushing a beet-red.

chapter 3

Miranda
Manhattan, 1975

SHE THOUGHT OF FAINTING. Of bursting into tears. Of fleeing. She thought of all this as Harrington, apparently weakened by the force of his guffaws, leaned against the bar for support. Wiping tears from his eyes, he looked toward a totally befuddled Jack and gasped, "Buddy, did you *write* this?"

"Did I write what?" Poor Jack, trying to play along, attempted a laugh, then looking toward a stunned Miranda, exchanged it for an expression of desperation. "Did I write *what?*"

"This, all of this." Harrington had recovered control of himself, although he was still grinning broadly, and motioned the bartender over to order a Beck's. "Miss Lawson—Miranda—and I have met before."

"You have? Miranda?"

Jack's penetrating stare couldn't make so much as a dent in Miranda's mortified silence.

"Yeah," Harrington continued, "we met only today, while she was liberating my office."

"You . . . she . . .?" Jack gave up and ordered another Scotch.

"But, Miranda"—Harrington had the audacity to

flash a seductive grin—"if you smile, *I'll* forget it ever happened."

The temptation to hurl at him the fact that he was the one who'd behaved badly, that he was the one who should be begging her pardon, was almost irresistible, but something, maybe emanations from Jack, maybe just a newborn common sense, prompted her instead to smile obligingly.

"Then we have a deal, Miranda?" He extended his hand, taking hers and holding it for an instant too long before tightening his grasp and shaking it.

"Sure." She smiled, then turning to Jack, said, "And I'd like another white wine."

Jack, caught in the middle of a conversation from which he was totally excluded, muttered, "If we'd ordered at the same time, we wouldn't keep having to call the bartender over," but no one seemed to hear him.

Things improved after that. The drinks softened the focus of the meeting, Jack and Jay traded Harvard stories, and Miranda, although she said almost nothing, felt a relief that was close to serenity. They ended up sitting in a booth, talking earnestly about Jack's play and Jay's theatre-to-be. It was a rambling old church, on a pond, no less, in western Connecticut, near the family summer house. He'd fallen in love with the building when he was a child. The property, which had been vacant for some years, belonged to the town of Tintagel, which, given his Harrington connections, seemed willing to lease it to Jay, was eager, in fact, to bring more culture to the affluent township. Jay hadn't even approached the town until he'd raised nearly all the money he needed for his enterprise by using every link to the family business he could come up with and even persuading his father to underwrite, as a tax shelter, a good part of the capitalization for the first couple of seasons until they turned a profit. He was a comer, was Jay Harrington, a natural entrepreneur, and she had to applaud the graceful way he segued from himself to Jack.

"You know, Jack, *Heights* is a masterful piece of work. Just the kind of stuff I want to be doing. I'm not a *schlockmeister*, and I never want to be. We've got a brand-new musical pretty much set to open—you'll be astonished at the personnel, they'll get the New York critics there on the first train—and if we can manage to put together the package I have in mind, I'd like *Heights* to be the second attraction in our flagship season."

Beaming broadly while trying to appear cool, Jack asked, "So what's the next step?"

"Glad you asked, buddy." Jay smiled a catbird smile. "I've been talking to a few top directors, and I should be in a position to make a decision in the next couple of days. Meanwhile, I'm seeing Penny tomorrow."

So Jay was even on a first-name basis with Jack's agent. God, for one so young, he certainly knew how to work an industry, Miranda thought, with still grudging admiration.

"Great," Jack said. "Now, what about Miranda?"

Jay glanced down toward his glass, a signal, Miranda thought, that there was a problem. When he looked up, it was directly at her.

"Well," he began, taking a cigarette from Jack's practically exhausted pack, and lighting it. He doesn't inhale, Miranda noted, so he doesn't really smoke; he's stalling.

"Well," he began again, confirming her suspicion by stubbing out the cigarette. "I've heard only the best about Miranda's work, and if casting were my decision, I'd give her the part right now. But it's not, and I can't possibly agree to anything. What I can do"—he assumed an air of such profound sincerity that she knew it was just a snow job—"is to have the director read her as soon as I've decided who that director is going to be.

Word of honor." He reached across the table and placed his hand lightly on hers. "Really, Miranda, word of honor."

"Of course." She smiled, realizing he was right about the way things were done, and realizing that the knowledge didn't help. Letting his hand rest on hers for just an instant, she looked at him and said, "I do understand."

As the conversation, which had come to a dead stop, started again with some bumps and awkward pauses, she decided to take a breather. "If you'll excuse me, I'll be right back." She patted Jack's hand under the table to assure him she *was* just going to the ladies' room, and he moved to let her out. Dear Jack. She was happy for him, and knew he was disappointed for her but still elated for himself, and by the time she'd walked across the room, she could hear the two men's conversation picking up rapidly. In the ladies' room, staring idly in the mirror, she congratulated herself for getting up and leaving them alone so that her disappointment wouldn't queer the evening. She reminded herself that Jack was her dearest friend and, assuming Jay Harrington was on the level, this was the chance of a lifetime for him. And—who could say?—maybe he was even on the level about her. Maybe he would have the unnamed director get in touch with her. And maybe she'd dazzle whomever that was. But, she had to admit to herself, what she was really having trouble dealing with was that Jay Harrington, a man whose impression lingered, for better *and* for worse, had wandered into her life for the second time in a single day and was about to disappear again. Even admitting that she was bothered bothered her. Well, if this was a day of strange beginnings, and even stranger endings, the least she could do was finish the evening in style, leaving Jack thinking she was a good sport and Jay, that she was civilized.

She'd been gone quite long enough, so she fluffed up

her hair, left the ladies' room, and started back across the room. But when she got to the table, she realized, first, that she was a little high, because she couldn't find the booth, then saw that she *had* found it and was only confused because something was different: There was only one person waiting there. Jay Harrington must have split to avoid confronting her again. Then she saw to her astonishment that the person sitting behind two freshly filled glasses wasn't Jack at all, it was Jay.

He greeted her with one of his smiles and half rose. "Jack sent his apologies," he told her as she slid back into the booth, "for having to split so fast."

"Jack split?" She couldn't hide her surprise. "Where was he going?"

"I don't really know. He made a phone call, and when he came back, he said something important had come up and to apologize to you."

"That doesn't sound like Jack," she mused.

"Well, that's what happened." His comment dismissed the subject as he handed her a wineglass and raised his own, indicating a toast. Staring her down with those huge gold-flecked eyes, he announced, "Miranda, I owe you a multinational-sized apology for being such a beast today . . . I was fresh from a 'difference of opinion' with Dad. Sorry I took it out on you. Am I forgiven?"

"Of course, Jay," she said, despite herself.

"So," he said, as they clinked glasses lightly, "here's to meeting cute!"

But as she smiled and then sipped and then smiled, she realized that she was scared. This guy was no eccentric artist into social anarchy, no bohemian space cadet who broke out in a sweat before he lunged for you; this guy, whatever his age, was a man of the world. Knowing with all her heart that she was outclassed, Miranda felt little stabs of shyness penetrate her throat, her heart, and her head. No thoughts came, and when they did, they died before they reached her tongue. If it was up to her, they would sit in silence forever, playing with their drinks, praying for a miracle. But the next surprise, which would last the length of a long evening, was that it wasn't just up to her.

"You know, Miranda," Jay said easily, taking charge, "I wasn't just flattering you before. Your legend does precede you. They still talk about that Yale production of *The Stronger*. What's it like to be in a two-character play when you don't have any lines?"

It was, of course, the right thing to ask. She was too much of an actress not to be disarmed, too much of an egotist not to want to talk about herself, so she did, haltingly at first, but only at first, telling him how, when you concentrate, really concentrate, if the play's good and the other actress is good and the audience is with you and you play the action, speech is the farthest thing from your mind. Your reactions become your speeches, your means of communication. Conscious still that this was an interview, she let him shift the conversation from her performance in Strindberg's play to Strindberg and from Strindberg to Jack.

It was only after they'd both raved over *Up on the Heights* and the glowing future of their single mutual acquaintance that Miranda realized they were on their third round, that he made her feel sort of beautiful, and that she was dazzled by the classical portraiture of his presence: the heavy brows, which still managed gracefully to arch, enhancing the burning brown-and-gold intensity of the ebony-lashed eyes; the nose of a Roman patrician; and the requisite dark, thick hair, square jaw, and generously sculpted mouth. It was the kind of face whose strength announces itself from beneath a quarterback's face mask, at the head of a long conference table, or across a crowded room. At this close range, he was positively hypnotizing. And the spell he had cast over her was slowly defrosting her, making her carefree and comfortable. Comfortable enough to respond to his questions and talk about her glamorous childhood, when she and Margo had made the covers of *Life, Look,* and an occasional *Ladies' Home Journal* or *Photoplay.* Beautiful mother and adorable daughter, for all the world to ooh and ah over. About all the presents and the preening and the sense of privilege without end. He knew about that all too well, he interjected, and she said, yes, he must.

"But the privileges did end, Jay," she continued. "You must know that. I guess it's still a pretty famous story." And she, acknowledging it to herself for the first time, apologized for her rudeness of the morning, admitting that his mention of *Goodbye Again* had totally unnerved her. "You know, after Margo ran off with Anthony Gainsborough, there was a huge custody battle, which my father won. But, of course, once he *had* me, he didn't want me around. I guess I reminded him of unpleasant things. I was a living embodiment of his own defeat. So I wasn't allowed Margo, and my father always kept me at a distance—boarding schools, vacations with friends or relatives. My first year as an undergraduate at Middlebury, I didn't spend one single holiday at home. I was nineteen when he died, but at that point, I knew him so little it didn't affect me much, except for the provision in his will that if I became an actress, the trust fund was to stop. So that was the end of that. I got through Yale on the money Margo left me. And when I came to New York after Yale, being the struggling offspring of a dead goddess didn't pull much weight. I was just another aspiring star. No big deal.

"I guess I'm a poor little princess—what a rotten role that is. And you know, I still don't understand a lot of what happened. When Mother died, I felt the impact mostly by the fact that there weren't any of her new movies to see. And after the gossip died out, by not seeing her name in the columns anymore. I must have felt awful, I must have grieved, but I couldn't get in touch with the sadness. What I did do was turn it into anger and aim it in Anthony's direction."

"You'd known him for years, I guess."

"Oh—forever. He'd meant more to me than my own father. While Dad was alive, there wasn't any question of my continuing to see Anthony—not that I wanted to see him—but Anthony did make sure I got the money Margo left me, and when I was at Yale, he used to send me—do you believe it?—a Christmas card every year without fail, always with a five-hundred-dollar bill and a tremendously charming little note, giving me his love and begging me to contact him if I ever needed anything. I spent the money, knowing I should return it, but I needed it. And that made me hate him more, for buying me off so cheaply. Because I did hate him—I hated him for ruining my life, and for doing whatever he'd done to Margo to drive her to death. You know how she died, I guess. She waited until Anthony was away filming and then took enough pills to kill herself three times over. She left a note, but they said it was crazy and, well, I never saw it. Anyway, you can understand why I didn't answer any of Anthony's cards."

She suddenly stopped to ask herself aloud, "Why am I telling you all this?"

"Because I asked"—he covered her hand with his—"and because we're weirdly relaxed with each other."

It was true, she realized; they were relaxed, no, more than relaxed. They were really grooving together. The sexist pig and the liberated artiste had given in, it seemed to her, to being just a man and a woman considering each other with respect and pleasure. This had to be rare, at any time, but now, in 1975, with the battle of the sexes raging around them, it was too good to be true. Still, it was true, so true that when the burgers and fries arrived, she didn't even remember his ordering them, but knew instinctively that everything would taste utterly delicious, and it did, even the catsup. And, after the food, there was brandy with the coffee, which should have make her drunk but instead made her happier. She hadn't even noticed the place filling up with the after-theatre crowd, then eventually emptying out again. By the last call, they were grinning at each other like idiots, talked out but unwilling to end the evening. He made her feel so good, so sure. He made her feel like a winner.

When the check came and he got out a credit card, she didn't for once, demand to split it. She also allowed him to help her up, steer her across the room, down the stairs, and into a cab, and when he asked her her address, then repeated it to the driver, she didn't protest that she could make it home alone. Halfway there, speeding through the empty A.M. streets, privacy provided by the partition separating them from the driver, he kissed her. He didn't lunge or grope or grab. Didn't attack with his tongue or miss her mouth or clank teeth. He very gracefully placed his hand on the back of her head and gently urged her to him, his mouth so slightly open, his lips so soft, barely grazing hers but leaving their imprint on each millimeter, then moving to a sweet place on her neck and nestling there, his warm breath blending with the heat from the pulse point below to light a fire in her.

When he drew back, it was to smooth her hair lovingly, with amazing familiarity, to take up her chin with his free hand, and to smile a smile that outdid the others by light years, as he whispered, "Who would have thought?"

"Nobody." She cast down her gaze, then repeated with a grin, "Nobody," and let him take her hand and kiss the palm.

Once they got to her place, he didn't hesitate, didn't bother to ask if he could come up, just looked at her and got the answer he wanted. "I think it's only fair to warn you," Miranda told him, as they stood at the top of the steep and timeworn steps of the ex-tenement, "it's a walk-up."

"Okay, how far?"

"All the way," she apologized. "Fifth floor."

"I should have known." He laughed, kissing her lightly. "You are not a girl—um . . . woman—who makes it easy. You're like the Lady of Shalott, living at the top of the tower in exquisite inaccessibility." He kissed her again. "But you can't scare me off. I'm always up to a challenge."

"Me, too," she murmured as she drew away, fished her keys out of the army surplus bag, and led him through the two doors leading to the stairs.

"Watch for stray toys. Sometimes the kids on the second and third floors forget and leave them out. Somebody fell over a baseball bat once." And they began the ascent, trudging past the tricycles and faded travel posters, over steps planed smooth by the feet of generations. She had to give Jay credit. At the crucial turn on the fourth floor, where even kids stopped to take a breath, he showed no sign of lagging.

When they got to her front door, she said, "You're incredible. You're not even winded."

"I play a lot of tennis," he explained. "Keeps me in shape."

Tennis. Of course, he would play. All bourgeois royalty played tennis, so why not Prince Charming? He was probably the club champion somewhere. Women of all ages and political persuasions probably stood in line to watch him on the courts. Because Jay Harrington was definitely the kind of guy who did things only if he did them superbly. He *was* too good to be true, but here he was, walking into her apartment, complimenting her on the charm of the place, taking her hand as they strolled from the kitchen, which doubled as a living room, into the adjoining bedroom. The bedroom was tiny, but it had a skylight through which, tonight, you could glimpse the odd star. A foam mattress took up almost the entire space excpet for the bedspread, white as the walls and a small, low table, which held a ginger-jar lamp, a Princess phone, and a vase of white roses she'd bought on her way home to make herself feel better after her run-in with Jay at work.

"Can I get you something to drink? I think there's some beer," she said after she'd taken his jacket and was heading toward the other room to hang it up.

"Fine," he called, then added, "Can I use the phone?"

"Of course," she called back, grabbing two cans of beer from the back of the fridge and praying that there were two clean glasses. There were, and as she loaded everything on a tray and headed back toward the bedroom, she heard him checking with his answering service.

"Oh," he was saying. "Three times? When was the last time? Hmm. No . . . no message. I'll contact . . . tomorrow."

He had lowered his voice, so she wasn't sure whether he'd said he'd call *him* or *her* back, but she decided to think it was *him*.

As she entered the room, she thought she saw him frowning, then watched the frown fade as he acknowledged her entrance with a smile. He was stretched out on the bed, his tie loosened, his shoes off as if he'd been there a long time. He looked tall and supple and royal from the top of his head to the tips of his navy-blue socks.

"Business?" she inquired, setting the tray on the floor by the bed.

"Yeah, but it'll wait."

Sitting down on the edge of the mattress, facing him but not touching him, she felt a twinge of fear, a confusion about how to proceed, but again, he took care of her awkwardness simply by sitting up, leaning forward, gathering her into his arms, and gracefully pulling the length of her onto the bed beside him.

This time the kiss was open-mouthed and lasted longer, both a probing and a caress, a memorizing of intimate places, warm and perfectly executed, like a dance. When, his mouth still on hers, he spoke, it was to whisper, "Special . . . you are so—" but this time her tongue stopped his.

From then on, everything was easy, so natural, a complete sharing. For the first time in her unmemorable sexual history, she felt she was neither the aggressor nor the object. She was *with* him. They were together in a wonderful collaboration. He undressed her slowly, with leisure, learning the body beneath the clothing, preparing it for the sweet impact that would come after they had undressed him, too.

She knew—or seemed to know—exactly what he wanted, could intuit, from his touch, her reply. So they took their time, letting their excitement build gradually, exploring with an honest curiosity, finding greater pleasure for their patience. No need to rush, even when he entered her, and she felt, as never before, her body welcoming him. It was a joyride, just the way it should be, spun out of dreams and half-forgotten fantasies, hot and wet and tender. And, as he proved his satisfaction without embarrassment, her delight at his delight brought her up to his peak in an instant.

They never got around to the beer, but nestled in each other's arms, celebrating with occasional hugs and kisses, marveling at how right it felt, and when, eventually, they made love again, it was, astonishingly, her idea, a task of rapture. She had never before been so aroused by a man; she had never before dared to tease and titillate, because never before had she felt so sexually secure.

And when she drifted to sleep, safe in his arms, she

noticed that the sun was coming up. Her last thought, as sleep came to her, was how wonderful it would be waking up with him beside her. And her first thought, after the alarm went off and she reached out for him, was that he was gone.

chapter 4

Jack
1984

IT WASN'T UNTIL six years later, in 1981, in England, that Miranda came clean about what happened the night of her momentous meeting with Jay Harrington. We were taking a late afternoon stroll around the grounds of the magnificent and memory-haunted cottage whose very presence in Miranda's life suggest the most poignant of ironies.

I'd come to Britain for the London opening of *Crackerjack*. Miranda had been relaxing in the country before beginning rehearsals for an *Antigone* she was doing at the National Theatre at a fraction of her normal asking price. She'd driven down to London for the *Crackerjack* festivities but afterward had insisted on spiriting me away to the country for a long weekend *à l'anglaise*.

The renowned lord of the manor being, thankfully, in Yugoslavia, shooting a couple of cameo scenes at a stupendously inflated salary, we were alone, Miranda and I, for the first time in much too long. Alone to dine too extravagantly, to drink too much wine, in short to play *Brideshead Revisited* and reminisce until the weest of hours.

"You know, Jack"—she broke the amiable and easy silence, one of the many still moments we'd at last managed to achieve in the few days we'd spent together—"it is truly so peaceful here. Despite everything. Despite the past. Even when *he's* here and the three-ring circus commences, even then, there's a genuine serenity. Don't you feel it?"

She led me to a small bench nestled amidst the exquisitely designed riot of the English garden, the thatched gables of the Tudor house in the distance making it all seem a fairy tale.

"Not only do I feel it"—I draped my arm loosely around her shoulder in a gesture of time-honored fellowship— "but I see it. Miranda. You've never looked more beautiful!"

"Oh, Jack, you haven't changed," she laughed, pecking me on the cheek. "You always saw me in a golden glow."

"Nonsense," I snapped back. *"You* always saw yourself in a distorting mirror. But, regardless, you're perfectly lovely." And I wasn't kidding. The beige-rose hue of her turtleneck washed her alabaster skin with just enough color to suggest both health and fragility, and her green eyes sparkled—they really did—like emeralds. I was struck by how much, in the last years, she had come to resemble her mother and wondered if she knew it, too. But it wasn't one of those things you ask. Not now. Not after all that had happened.

"It's nice, being peaceful with you, Jack." She grabbed my hand and drew me up from the bench, and we wandered on, holding hands like children, intimate yet totally innocent. "In the old days, in New York, we were always so frantic."

If I observed that she talked too passionately about serenity, that her newfound calm was more performance than reality, that beneath the rosy glow was a feverish desperation, I chose to overlook it.

"You thought we were frantic back then?" I challenged her. "I'd call it impatient. Remember, back then, anything was possible, and we were just raring to get going.'' I dropped her hand to reach for, then light, a cigarette.

"Jack,'' she reprimanded me, "I thought you said you'd stopped.''

"I did.'' Replacing the lighter in my jacket pocket, I again took up her hand. "For a while. You know who got me to stop? Jay.'' If I expected a reaction from Miranda, I was to get none; her calm remained unruffled. "He kept beating me at tennis, and I convinced myself that stopping smoking would raise the level of my game. My subsequent disappointment drove me right back to the Marlboros.''

"Oh, Jack,'' she laughed, "will you never learn? You can't beat that man at his own game. Even trying's an act of self-sabotage!''

"Maybe.'' As I considered the thought, I let my mind drift backward. "And speaking of Jay and self-sabotage . . . what actually happened between you two that night we first met at Sardi's?''

"And I always thought you were too much of a gentleman to ask.''

She stopped to pick an invisible leaf or minuscule insect off her riding pants, but I wasn't to be so easily diverted.

"Hmm.'' She cocked her head away from me and down, like a swan. "Hmm . . . you know, six years ago, torture couldn't have gotten it out of me. But now, well, he is who he is, and I am who I am, and there's a lot more than an ocean between us . . .'' Suddenly, she had a thought that caused her to raise her head and stare me down. "All right, I'll tell you what happened, on one condition. That you tell me what made you bolt out of Sardi's. Consider me a lady for not asking until now.''

"Gulp.'' I pronounced the word, like a comic-strip character. "Do I have to?''

"You guys set me up, didn't you?''

"Well, I wouldn't exactly put it that way,'' I muttered as we walked on.

"How would you put it?"

"Jesus, Miranda. Okay. I was worried about you, for Christ's sake. I mean, I didn't like seeing you alone. You didn't like being alone, if you recall. So when the most eligible man in New York shows an interest in you, and goes so far as to suggest he'd like a little time alone with you, the least I could do was to oblige the guy. Right?"

"Right." She kissed me on the cheek. "I always figured it was something like that. It was sweet of you."

"So then what happened? After I split?" The sun was beginning to slip behind the house, imparting a slight chill to the air, but still we wandered.

"What happened," Miranda told me, "is that Jay swept me completely off my feet . . . Hey, want to continue this inside, in front of a cozy little fire with a glass of sherry?" When I nodded, we went inside, to the wood-paneled, book-lined study with the stained-glass casement windows—a vision, more than a vision, a stage set, and why not, considering the master of the manor? The sherry warmed us, and we snuggled on the sofa and continued to recall the past, she in her Snowden portrait-perfect turtleneck and riding pants, I in my writer's fisherman sweater and jeans.

Miranda placed her glass on an end table and took up the tale. "To continue. I was the most defensive woman in the world, right? Well, Jay broke through my defenses as if they were Kleenex—just lifted them off and crushed them. And I loved it. I capitulated immediately. It seemed like *it* to me—you know, 'some enchanted evening.' I thought this was the real thing, love at first sight with all the trimmings. There was no way I could have turned him down. I was afire for him, or something that adolescent. So he came home with me, and what followed was . . . a revelation, so flawless that it should have occurred to me that it couldn't really be about two perfectly attuned souls. I thought it was us, but I came to see it was him—the living embodiment of practice makes perfect. Anyway, when I woke up in the morning, he was gone. No note. No nothing. He even straightened the sheet and plumped up the pillow. I could have dreamed the whole thing.

"So I went to work at Harrington's the next morning, expecting him to stop by or call my department or something, but he didn't. And, with my luck, I heard some hot little number whispering to her friend that she was going out with Jay the following week. Of course, I had expected him to immediately lose interest in all other women. It was sickening.

"And then two weeks went by, and you were meeting with him or talking to him almost every day because of *Heights*, and I didn't even get a card from him. My heart was broken, and I was furious. At him, for treating me so insensitively. At myself, for getting taken so badly. And a little bit at you, for letting it happen and then withdrawing. And because you got to see him or call him whenever you wanted, and I couldn't."

"Yeah," was all I said, years of guilt contained in the word.

"So I spent all my spare time—and I had a lot of it," she continued, brushing back her hair with the glamorous mien of a star who has to fight for every second of solitude, "rehearsing how cool I'd be when I ran into him. How I'd pretend to forget his first name. Or, better yet, be with someone so fabulous he'd see how unimportant he had been to my life. Those fantasies were about all that kept me going, too, because I was truly on the verge of hitting bottom. I felt so awful about myself. I couldn't get work, you were too busy to bother with me, and I'd loved and lost within twenty-four hours a guy who wasn't remotely interested in me—personally *or* professionally . . . Anyway, a month went by, and I had completely given up hoping I'd ever hear from Jay. I didn't even bother to jump when the phone rang, and I stopped checking with my answering service six times an hour. Then one evening around eight, I was mooning around my apartment, washing my hair, actually, pretending I wasn't thinking about him, when the phone rang. I remember thinking it must be you, making your periodic check-in, so I answered with something flip—I forget exactly what—'I can't talk now' or 'Call you back,' but it wasn't you, it wasn't you at all.''

chapter 5

Miranda
Manhattan, 1975

SOAP STINGING HER eyes, dripping hair escaping from the towel she had hastily wrapped around her sodden head, she felt her way out of the bathroom and over to the phone, stopping it on the fourth ring. It had to be Jack; when he called these days, it was usually at a time when he assumed she'd be out, she was thinking, as she shouted into the phone, "Jack, lemme call you back!" There was silence on the other end of the line. "Jack? I said I'll call you back! Jack, where'd you go?"

"I'm here," said a male voice, "but I'm not Jack. You're warm, though."

"Who is this, please?" she barked, prepared simply to hang up if the guy hassled her.

"It's Jay Harrington, Miranda."

As the sound of his name brought on an attack of trembling, she attempted a vocal cool suggesting evening gowns and perfectly groomed hair. "Oh, Jay, how nice to hear from you. If you could just hold on for a second, I was in the middle of something . . ."

"Sure, but you could also call me back," he told her affably, not sounding guilty in the least.

"No, no, I'll just be a second. Hold on." Determined not to let him get away now that she had him, she placed the receiver on the table, made a pass at towel-drying her hair, and eased the remaining soap out of her eyes with the wet towel before resuming the conversation. "How've you been?"

"Out of my mind with this Connecticut thing, which is why I haven't called before now. Listen, I have a feeling I *am* disturbing you, so let me make this brief. Could you possibly have dinner with me tomorrow night?"

"Dinner? Tomorrow? This is sort of last minute," she said casually.

"Yes, I know. I'm sorry about that."

"Well, let me just check my book." She put down the phone long enought to have got her book and checked it, then picked up the receiver again.

"I do have something," she told him with utterly convincing sincerity, "but I guess I *could* change it."

"Miranda"—already the old bedroom voice was functioning at top speed—"I'd really like to see you."

"Well, if it's important . . . " Even as she said the words she was furious with herself for having given in so easily.

"It is. Listen, I'm calling from Connecticut and I'm going to be here most of tomorrow, so could we make the arrangements now?"

"Fine." What could he want so urgently after all those weeks of silence? Or was she making things too complicated? Maybe, all of a sudden, he'd realized he missed her. Maybe he—

"Why don't you come to my place? I make a passable steak. Let me give you the address."

She groped for a ballpoint, which was out of ink, then settled for a lip liner dug out of her makeup bag, and prepared to scribble on the back of her phone bill. "Ready."

"Right. It's on Canal Street, off West Broadway and Prince. Know where that is? Good. It's a loft in an old factory building, one twenty-one, a red door next to a hardware store. You just walk in the red door, and when I buzz you in, take the elevator to four. It opens right into the apartment. Okay?"

"Okay," she chirped, wondering, in fact, if she'd ever get there, and how she'd ever get there, and deciding right then that she'd take a cab. "What time?"

"How about seven-thirty? I apologize for not picking you up, but I'm not sure exactly when I'm going to be back in town, and I could use the time it would take to get uptown and back. You don't mind? Next time, I promise it'll be door to door!"

Next time! Pick her up! Boy, in her circle, nobody ever apologized for not picking you up. They expected you to meet them on street corners. He really did want to see her! "Not to worry," she said. "I'll see you then."

"Terrific." He made it sound like a caress, like the promise of something wonderful. "I'm really looking forward to seeing you."

"Well, me too. Well, goodbye," she said, and he said, "Goodbye," and then she put down the phone and just stood there, naked and freezing, the happiest woman in New York.

If, six hours later, she was too wired to sleep, it was a pleasant kind of wired, the result of having something to look forward to at last. Her head raced with what she should wear, what she should say, but most of all, with what would be the sheer exhilaration of seeing him again. And that set her wondering if Margo had felt the same way every time she saw Anthony Gainsborough, if it was that same kind of dangerous folly, "whose appetite," as in Shakespeare, "grew with what it fed upon." Had the craving escalated until it had finally driven her mother away from her family, into her lover's arms? No, this was different; there were no moral strictures keeping them apart, no marriage, no children, no scandal; they were free agents who could come together without hurting anybody else. If Jay was up to a challenge, so was she. If he was the artful dodger, she would be the supreme huntress.

An open season, after all, requiring strategy and incredible cunning, but a fair pursuit. And when she finally drifted off to sleep, she was wrapped in the memories of another drifting off, a happier time, which now would come again, and she woke up smiling.

Luckily, she had things to do all day. The acting class kept her relaxed, focused her concentration, and by three in the afternoon, when she stopped at an Indian imports shop on her way home and splurged on a dress-length aqua gauze shirt with silver embroidery, she was sure she'd done the right thing and practically skipped up the five flights home. The stage fright didn't hit until five-thirty, when she had two whole hours to kill and nothing to do. She tried a little meditation, but it was only so effective, then flicked on the news, but she just couldn't keep her mind on it. Her pulse racing, her hands shaking ever so slightly, she got through her makeup and dressed, repeatedly changing from boots to shoes and from belt to no belt, unable, at this point, to tell what looked better. At seven-ten she decided on boots and the belt, then sat around, sick with the nerves that made her heart pound and her stomach lurch a half hour, to the minute, before curtain. Well, this was certainly a performance, for better or worse. At seven-twenty, she exchanged the small gold studs in her ears for silver dangling ones, removed the bronze necklace, picked up her shawl and her bag, and not entirely conscious of what she was doing, walked through the door, locked it, made it down the stairs and over to East End Avenue to catch a cab.

But there weren't any cabs, not for long enough to make her frantic that she'd be much later than the fifteen minutes she'd planned. It seemed like hours but was probably only minutes before a taxi stopped across the street to let somebody out, and she raced over, making sure no one else got to it before she did. In a breathy voice she gave the driver the address and settled back for the long ride down the East River Drive. The cabbie began babbling about the perilous state of the city, looking for a conversation, as cabbies do, but she couldn't spare the energy, and finally, having failed to get more than a yes or no from her, he settled into slightly hostile silence. They got to Canal easily and found the red door with no trouble, and she tipped the cabbie overgenerously because she couldn't concentrate on figuring out the change. She almost tripped on the curb, but saved herself from falling, made it up the steps and through the door, her heart racing, feeling as if she were running a fever, shocked by the harsh rasp of the buzzer that admitted her. The elevator was ancient and commercial, promising catastrophe but delivering instead a harmless series of squeaks and clangings. Too slowly, too quickly, she made it to the fourth floor.

Stepping out into a vast, dim expanse, she had the impression of soft lights, huge couches, of Mozart playing and mirrors gleaming, but her eyes hadn't adjusted to the darkness and she just stood there, as he materialized out of an exotically underlit area to the right.

"Miranda." He strode gracefully over to the door, looking even better than she remembered, in jeans and a faded Harvard sweat shirt, wearing tortoiseshell glasses—she hadn't known he wore glasses—and looking utterly divine. He didn't kiss her, just came close to her and took both her hands. "You're looking great," he murmured, smiling down at her with an intimacy so clear she knew he was remembering what she was remembering. As she felt his closeness, her nervousness began to subside before the thrill of performance, before the promise of being with him for a whole night, and when she smiled her leading-lady smile, she could see it take.

"And now—" He retained one of her hands, as he began to lead her to the spot from which he'd come.

"—a surprise. Come on, just follow me."

She let herself be led into the dimness, toward the huge couches and Deco tables and lamps, and it was then she saw they weren't going to be alone at all. Two people sat on the couches. Two men. One of them was Jack, and the other—the other was Sir Anthony Gainsborough.

chapter 6

Jack
1984

"IMAGINE HOW I FELT, Jack," Miranda told me long after in England. "Imagine. Walking into what you thought was a romantic interlude and finding your whole life flashing before you. It was like drowning. I was . . . stupefied, mortified, whatever. I actually felt as if I'd lost consciousness for a split second, because I have a first-thing-I-remember image of what happened after that."

We sipped our sherries as a servant discreetly appeared, asking what time we would like to dine, and I realized that Jack as we'd talked the mellow light of that English afternoon had almost faded. We were sitting in near darkness.

"So there I was," she continued after the servant's departure, "turned totally to stone. You and Anthony both jumped to your feet, but of course, Anthony beat you to it. One moment he was sitting, the next he was standing. I don't know how he did it!"

"So while I scrambled off the couch, Anthony was already standing at attention."

"Yes," she smiled, remembering. "And he was smart to do it. I needed a little time to take him in. You know, I hadn't really seen him—live, at least—since I was twelve or so. Even though I'd seen his picture constantly since then, I still retained him in my memory as a much younger man. So, at first, it was an added shock to see the gray in his hair and the face so much older. That took about three seconds. Then the realization that I was standing opposite the man who had caused so much misery swept through me with a ferocity that made me want to leap at his throat or tear his eyes out. Then I was struck again by the charm, the elegance, the vitality—all the qualities that had made me love him so much as a child, and I wanted to run to him. Then I wanted to cry because he had, in the end, betrayed me. All those things, in a flash . . . Could you tell?''

"No," I assured her, refilling her wineglass. "No, I really couldn't." But, of course, that was a lie, and for a moment I had been afraid she'd go absolutely out of control. She didn't, of course. I was surprised—no, pleased, maybe even proud—when she smiled quite prettily and walked to Gainsborough, her hand extended. Never a man to miss a cue, he grabbed it and held it clutched in both of his, his whole person a study in delight.

"Miranda." He said it as only the most magnificent voice in the English-speaking world could—a three-noted aria—then motioned her to step back so he could meditate on her. "Now, turn around, dear girl, I want to see you all round,'' he said, making his fingers dance and twirl to suggest what he wanted her to perform, and obligingly, she did a strangely provocative little girl's pirouette. "Well, darling, you're a beautiful woman." He crossed his arms on his chest and announced, "You've grown up, and I've grown old!"

"Oh, Anthony, never!" she dismissed his remark and took his hand so that he could seat her on the couch. Anthony was bending over her; Jay was on the sidelines, watched contentedly, his hands linked behind his back in a vaguely Napoleonic stance, and I just stood there, in the middle of a frozen frame, plagued by the feeling that Miranda was only acting serene. Knowing her as well as I did, I suspected, could nearly feel, her fury—probably at me, her trusted friend, who had, once again, set her up. We were going to be fighting over this one for years.

Somehow, we all got seated, and Jay brought out the excellent champagne. Although things were still a little awkward, Miranda couldn't be faulted. Maybe it was the anger inside her that lent a kind of arrogance to her demeanor. Whether she had sensed what was to come or not, she damned well knew that every other person in the room owed her one, and she played the situation for all it was worth. The princess with three suitors. By the time we were on our second glass of champagne, we had all raved, sincerely, over the loft, as striking a study in black-and-white Deco as I'd ever seen, and Jay had explained that it was done by his sister, who lived not far away with her stockbroker husband, and had become SoHo's foremost interior decorator; that he didn't spend nearly so much time here as he should; that with this Connecticut enterprise, he felt as though he were living on the train, thereby bringing the conversation back to the business at hand.

Miranda took the amazing news that Anthony Gainsborough was directing *Up on the Heights* with what looked like genuine enthusiasm; after all, the Renaissance man of the theatre's stooping to direct summer stock, not to mention *my* play, was an extraordinary coup for Jay, and she congratulated us all round.

"Now, Miranda dear." Gainsborough had seized her hand and applied it to his knee in avuncular fashion. "Now, what about you?"

"What *about* me?" asked Miranda, a little coyly for my tastes, but it seemed to work with Gainsborough.

"I've heard so much . . . *good* . . . about your work from these two . . . " He raised his eyebrows and swiveled his head from me toward Jay and back toward her, "lugs," and he chuckled, "and I'll want to read you for the part of Rachel. You know the play?"

"Yes, I do." She gave me a comradely grin. "I'm a friend of the author's."

"Of course." Gainsborough released her hand and picked up his champagne glass, actually daring to stare at her seductively over the years. "Now, when shall we do this? How about Thursday afternoon? How does that sound?"

Miranda, also toying with her glass, took a moment to think about it, then placed the glass on the coffee table, looked him square in the eye, and asked, "What about now?"

"Now?" Jay broke in, startled. "This was just supposed to be a little get-together. Anthony, don't you have dinner plans?" That Jay so obviously wanted to get rid of Gainsborough and me was surprising. As far as I knew, that night at Sardi's had not worked out blissfully for him or Miranda; maybe I should have been suspicious when they were both so noncommittal about it. Now I was definitely getting the sense that Jay had got what he wanted from tonight's event and was eager to press on to his next appointment . . . *à deux.* Jay isn't the kind of guy who appreciates last-minute changes in his schedule, and I wondered if Miranda had realized that and was being as perverse as she sometimes could when she had been caught off guard.

"Come on, Anthony," she urged. "Jay must have at least one copy of the play around, and I'm as prepared as I'll ever be. Jack can read with me. Okay?" She looked to me, taking my lack of response as affirmative. "See? It's fine with Jack."

I saw the gleam in Gainsborough's eyes. He clearly approved of her enthusiasm. "Now? Why not? Just let me make a call to my hostess"—he stressed the second syllable in the English fashion—"to tell her I'll be late," and he rose to go to the phone as Jay got out a couple of copies of the script from a priceless Deco desk and tossed them our way.

Up on the Heights is a romantic comedy about Broadway, but I'd based it on a witty and wicked Restoration play called *The Man of Mode*. The seventeenth-century work deals with the conquest of London's most notorious womanizer by a clever young heiress from the sticks. Using a mixture of provincial common sense and such imaginative strategems as feigned indifference, the heroine, Harriet, persuades the rake, Dorimant, to give up his wild London ways and marry her.

But does Dorimant capitulate because Harriet is a breath of fresh air, a new kind of challenge for a man jaded by sophistication? Or because he's badly in need of her fortune? Or because he's burnt out on the high life? Or because, for the first time in his lascivious career, he's met his match—and fallen in love? And does Harriet set her cap for Dorimant because he's the greatest catch in London and she's ambitious? Or because she's looking for a shortcut into the smart set? Or simply because he's the man for her?

That you can't assign any single motivation to either of them gives the play a really remarkable modernity. It suggests that behavior results from a complexity of motives, some of them unconscious, some of them denied, some of them underhanded, some of them noble. It's a work I'd always treasured—and it's very funny and extremely sexy to boot.

In my contemporary adaptation, the rake is a big sixties movie star, a Warren Beatty-type sex symbol named Chris Motherwell, who's doing his first Broadway show, a lavishly mounted production of *The Man of Mode*. Every woman in the cast—in fact, every woman in New York—is dying for him, with the single exception of Rachel, the girl who's playing Harriet. Rachel is a budding actress from Minneapolis whose father, a millionaire industrialist, is bankrolling the production behind Rachel's back as a showcase for his little girl.

Since Chris feels compelled to bed every woman in the cast, he comes on to Rachel, who refuses to settle for being just another notch in his belt. Secretly, she's fallen for him, but she's savvy enough to know that giving in to him is the least likely way to win him. So as she continues to spurn him, he decides he can't stand her, and their rehearsals turn into verbal shooting matches. When he actually goes to the producer to demand she be fired, he finds out that she *can't* be fired because her father owns the show. And Chris can't quit because too much is at stake. His last couple of movies have been major flops, and the critics and studio execs are beginning to hint that he's too long in the tooth for the boyish roles that made him a superstar. He's gone through several fortunes and a couple of marriages, and he's developing a reputation as trouble because of his drinking and drug-taking and generaly inadequate sense of responsibility. He's known from the beginning that Broadway's a risk, but it's a risk he has to take if he wants to climb back to the top. So he's trapped in the production, and he's not a man to take to claustrophobia easily.

A week and a half into rehearsals, he's already having trouble remembering the blocking and learning his lines. All he needs to have his concentration totally blown is for a woman to reject him—especially the woman with whom he has a lot of love scenes. He's a baby. He's got to have his way with Rachel. To make matters more complicated, Chris's present lady, who has the juicy role of Dorimant's aging mistress in *The Man of Mode*, notices his attention shifting away form her and turns nasty.

Into this maelstrom wanders a bouquet of eccentric characters, including an American actor, Eric Gerard-Steele, who's been hanging around obscure outposts of the English theatre so long he's developed more elaborate British mannerisms than Sir John Gielgud. As foolish and foppish an actor as they come, Eric insists on giving Chris unwanted advice on his acting and attempting to direct the director. He does serve a useful function, however, for Chris manipulates him into mistakenly believing that the aging glamor girl has the hots for him. She can't stand him, of course, but his pursuit of her provides Chris and Rachel with all kinds of additional chances to be alone, scrapping and flirting and working. Ultimately, of course, Rachel, with the iron-willed determination of a woman who's found her man, resists being seduced and succeeds in guiding Chris to a wildly successful opening night—and to the altar.

That night at Jay's, Miranda chose to do a scene in which Chris, the actor, during a bitter confrontation over the way a rehearsal is going, blurts out to Rachel that her father bought her the part. Miranda and I had run through the scene before, through several drafts, to test how it played, so she knew how effectively it show-cased both an actress's comic timing and her emotional depths.

While Gainsborough made his excuses to his hostess, Miranda walked to the far end of the loft, sat down at the kitchen table, concentrated for a few minutes, then rose, walked back to us, and announced she was ready.

I'm a writer, not an actor, and although I write for the theatre, I don't comprehend the process that creates good acting. So I'll never be able to explain how, that night, Miranda managed to block out a roomful of past and present complications, even disasters, and be some-one else. But she did. With no warm-up, no props, not even another actor's physical presence to play, she soared. I had seen her get upset in life—and in the scene—many times, but never this universally upset, never with so much clarity and stature. One could sense, before one saw, each subsequent stage in her emotional explosion—it was that believable—and the fact that she had her wits sufficiently about her to play the entire scene to Anthony only enhanced my respect for her pro-fessionalism. Since I was reading her, I couldn't check my companions' reactions, but nobody moved and the scene continued to build beautifully. At the climax, she actually started to laugh at the absurdity of the situation in the play, then took three beats and proclaimed, "You know, you really hurt me. I bet you're a real champ at hurting people. It must be reassuring to know you're still good at something," then walked off calmly, and the test was over.

From my admittedly biased viewpoint, Miranda had passed with flying colors. She was all freshness and worldliness and charm, the most fetching thing Broadway had seen in years—and certainly since Margo Seymour.

Gainsborough's applause seemed spontaneous enough, but, then, why shouldn't it have been? Miranda was the best she'd ever been—and she'd always been good.

"Miranda, darling!" Gainsborough had sprung to his feet. "Dare I say . . . you *are* your mother's daughter!" and he embraced her. And as he held her, this great and terrible surprise, launched from a host of painful memories into the dead center of her dreams, I saw her face. In that instant before she set her smile and inclined her face toward him, I read in her expression the years-long disappointment, the grief at his betrayal, the anger, and the absolute refusal to be charmed again. She had trusted him once, and he had brought them all down. And that evening, that moment, as I looked at her, still clasped in his arms, I sensed it would be years, if ever, before she could forgive him. But then she smiled, and then they separated, beaming at each other, and he placed an arm around her as they walked back to the sofa.

"Dear child, you deserve more champagne," he told her, refilling her glass, then looked around at Jay and me. "Well, boys, what do you think?" and Jay and I mumbled something vaguely fatuous. "Well," Gainsborough continued, "I think you were superb, darling, simply superb—" He paused to sip the champagne. "—but . . . I'd still like you to read for me on Thursday, if you would."

Miranda must have been crushed by that, but it didn't show as she smiled and agreed. "Now," Gainsborough merrily rolled along, "do I have your phone number, my sweet? Well, I'll get it from our Mr. Harrington, and you'll hear from me by . . . let's see, this is Tuesday . . . by tomorrow afternoon. Now give us a kiss—" She did. "—and I must fly to the San Remo." He turned to me, "Price, old man, going uptown? Shall I drop you?"

"Can you drop me off, too, Anthony?" Miranda asked. "I'm exhausted."

Jay's color faded. "Miranda, we're supposed to be having dinner."

"Well," she picked up her purse and her shawl, "I hadn't counted on working tonight. I'm not exactly the life of the party after a performance."

"You don't seem tired," Jay insisted, positioning himself between her and the path to the door, as if to bar her way.

"But I am," she countered.

"Just stay for a second," he urged her, as Anthony and I discreetly walked toward the waiting elevator, out of earshot. But we saw Miranda abruptly sit down and level at Jay a remark that literally froze him in his tracks. He was still dazed as he walked over to Gainsborough and me and distractedly sent us on our way.

For so long I had wondered what she'd said to Jay that night to totally destroy his cool, and that evening in England, she finally told me. "You know what I said to him?" Miranda chuckled at the memory. "I sat down on the couch, stretched out, looked boldly into his baby browns, and asked quite innocently, 'If I put out tonight, can you get Shakespeare and Burbage to read me for Juliet?' "

chapter 7

Miranda
Manhattan, 1975

"LET THE CASTING commence," Miranda
purred. She was reclining, movie-siren style, on the all-
too-symbolic couch as Jay closed the elevator door and
turned back into the room.

"Now, just wait a minute, Miranda." He crossed to
a·spot in the center of the floor, opposite where she
reclined. "Just wait a minute!"

"Wait a *minute*? I'll wait all night—if it'll make me a
star." She stretched out a languid arm and took up her
champagne glass. "So put on some romantic music—
maybe Frank Sinatra, something from the fifties. I'm
assuming that's the vintage of your subtle sexual style."

Jay was shaken, but armed with a Scotch from the
bar on the other side of the room, he marched back and
sat down on a couch arranged at a right angle to hers.
He was bending forward, facing her, his glass clutched
in both hands. "Damn it, Miranda. You're not being
rational!"

"Rational!" She shot straight up from her siren's
pose. "Rational! I have been led on, embarrassed,
shocked, even horrified, and—it seems to me—dismissed, what else? You want more? Why in the world
should I be rational?"

"Okay, don't be rational." He took a hefty slug of

the Scotch. "But be quiet. Be quiet for long enough to hear my version."

"Oh, this should be great! Is this the standard version you've memorized for all the girls—or do I get something *special*?" She wondered if he'd caught the irony of the word, if he remembered using it with her, if it meant anything, if it hurt.

Something hurt, at least, because he slammed down the glass, stood up, and announced, "All right, you win. You're totally on target. I'm an evil producer who preys on innocent young actresses, with a list of scores that numbers in the thousands. No, I'll be completely honest. I'm worse than that. I'm a rake. I live off my vast trust fund and play like I'm a producer to get girls. I may, in your view, inveigle helpless women into my den of iniquity, but I don't, you'll be happy to know, hold them prisoner. So why don't you just put on your cloak of virtue and leave?"

"Leave? Gladly. I *wanted* to leave before, if you recall. I'll be thrilled to leave." But it wasn't true. She didn't want to go. She didn't want to do anything except make it like their first—their only—night had been, before Anthony, before all of this. She was so tired, so tired and so disappointed and so angry and so—

"For Christ's sake," Jay exclaimed, "don't start crying," but it was too late; she was sobbing uncontrollably.

Head buried neatly in her hands, she heard him through her sobs, moving down the room, then back, then sensed him standing over her. "Here's some Kleenex." His futile attempt to force one hand from her face to give her the Kleenex only started a fresh generation of tears.

"No, no, leave me alone," she gasped. "I'll be all right in a little while," but she wasn't, so he sat back down and watched her cry. Then, he was at her side again, sitting quite close to her, disengaging her hands from her face, taking her in his arms as if she were a child who needed comforting, patting her back, urging her tearstained face onto his chest. "It was just so . . ." She spoke into the sweat shirt. "I mean . . . you *know* . . . I *told* you . . . about my mother and Anthony and . . . and that night at Sardi's, you lied to me . . . you *lied* . . ." And she started to weep afresh.

"Miranda"—he was trying to soothe her, running his hand over her hair—"I didn't lie. When did I lie? I just . . . well, I felt that . . . well . . . I hadn't closed the deal with Anthony at that point, and there was a good chance that I wouldn't. If I did, I knew there'd be a potential problem with you. But if I had told you, and we hadn't gone with him, you would have gotten all upset for nothing—Oh, shit, you've got me so defensive, I'm not even making sense to myself." He paused to think. "If I *was* drawing you out about him, it was mainly because I acknowledged the existence of a problem, and I wanted an opportunity to appreciate the extent of it."

"By deceiving me?"

"By not telling you the entire truth. Look, you certainly can't accuse me of not trying to put you in the play. Can you?"

"No," she murmured.

"You're damned right, you can't," he continued. "And, besides . . . Hey, listen, what I'm going to tell you is just between us, okay?"

She nodded her word.

"There were problems with Anthony. Problems that had nothing to do with you. I really *was* talking to other directors because, originally, Anthony turned me down flat. Believe me, it took all my powers of persuasion to sew him up. Made him feel he owed it to the theatre, boosting new talent, et cetera. Then, when I was just about there, it turned out Dad was against using him."

"Why?" She looked up, puzzled.

"Why would he be against using *the* theatrical legend of our time? Beats me. He mumbled something about working with him on a production that went insanely over budget. It was one of the plays I needed the file for. *Goodbye Again*. When I asked for it, I didn't know Margo Seymour had been in it. But then''—he smiled slightly—''I didn't know who you were, so it wouldn't have mattered. Anyway, the weird thing is that I went over the file very carefully, and what I found was that it *didn't* go over budget. And it more than paid back the investors.''

''Really?'' She looked up, tears momentarily forgotten. ''That *is* weird.''

''The morning when I met you, I needed the file for a working lunch I was taking with Dad, and I was really pretty uptight about it. When I confronted him with the *Goodbye Again* figures, he admitted he had it confused with another property. But he still didn't want to use Anthony. This time he changed his tack and told me Anthony was too hard to control for a man of my limited experience. You know, intimating I was too wet behind the ears to play with the big boys. Then I accused him of being resentful because I'd managed to get to Anthony in the first place. What I couldn't say—maybe I should have—is that he's not interested in my doing anything he isn't totally in control of. I even think he's got mixed feelings about this Connecticut thing. You know, I think if I managed to get Jesus to play himself in a revival of *Superstar*, Dad would find some way to argue that it's bad box office. Anyway, over the next week, I simply out-argued him, and I told him if he wanted to pull out his financial support, I'd go elsewhere. Hey, these are my problems, not yours, and you're the one who's upset. But I was trying to explain why I barked at you. And, look, I'm really sorry you think I wasn't honest with you, but it was my professional decision, and I can't be sure I wouldn't do the same thing again. But, Miranda—'' he took her chin in his fingers and turned her face up toward his ''—I'm sorry I hurt you. I don't want to hurt you. I want to do the opposite of hurt you, okay? Now, don't you feel a little better?''

She was impassive.

"You don't? You sure look better. How would you like a brandy? It's supposed to be soothing.''

She nodded, and he slowly released her, kissing her forehead, and then went to get the drink. By the time she'd taken a couple of sips, she was able to ask, "Is there black stuff all over my face?" and when he didn't answer, she said, "Then I guess there is. Where's the bathroom? I'd like to mop up my mascara.''

"It's down there, off the kitchen." He pointed, then took her hand and led her to the large and luxurious room, complete with makeup lights, and closed the door behind her.

She was a mess, all right, but she felt better, felt that wave of peace that follows an emotional tempest, and when she had repaired her face as best she could, she walked calmly into the kitchen to see him peering deep into the refrigerator.

"Jay, you look as though you've never seen the inside of one of those before!"

He straightened up and faced her. "I promised you dinner, and dinner it shall be. But . . . I have a confession to make. I did lie to you. I don't make a passable steak. I don't make a passable anything. Even at camp, I bribed the other guys to do the hot dogs . . .''

"Do you want me to do it?" she asked, not meaning to be so obliging.

"No, no. I invited you. I don't suppose you feel like going out? There's a great French place practically around the corner.''

"No, I really don't.''

"Let me look again." He was foraging through the back of the shelves. "Hey, there is one thing I can do." He was extricating a foil-wrapped package from the depths of the fridge. "Bologna. How about a nice bologna sandwich?"

"How long has it been there, Jay?"

"Not that long," he told her, and she decided she wouldn't press it.

"And here's some bread. The cleaning lady tries to keep me in staples." He hurled an unopened package of white bread onto the kitchen table. "And here's some mayonnaise!" he announced triumphantly. "And . . . mustard . . . and for my last trick, Swiss cheese . . . and there used to be some pickles . . . right around . . . yeah, here!"

And so they dined on bologna sandwiches and champagne, and he did unearth a Sinatra record, and she found she was having a lot of fun. With his brown eyes warming her, his surprisingly boyish optimism infecting her, she felt, well . . . happy. If he made a smart-ass remark, she countered with one of her own, and he seemed to enjoy the game. If she confessed something about herself—something a little revealing, displaying a spot of vulnerability—he came up with a matching admission. She knew she'd never remember just what it was they'd talked about, but she'd always remember how they said it—lightly, playfully. For the first time in much too long, she felt at ease with herself and the way she appeared to the world. If he thought she was neat, she was neat. If he thought she was cute and smart and talented, she was. And so pleasing was this newborn state of grace that she could almost forget the evening and the past, could almost banish the thought that Jay had used her to get to Anthony, that he needed Anthony and her together because they were box office.

And when he kissed her, it was natural and nice, the way a kiss should be. And when he drew her to him, molding his palms to her back, her body remembered the first time, and then her mind remembered what had followed, and instinctively, she pulled out of his embrace.

"Hey—" He tried to draw her back. "What just happened?"

She kept quiet long enough to fight the desire to say what she wanted to ask, and to lose. "Jay, why didn't you call?"

"Miranda," he sighed, sat back and began. "I'm a workaholic. I was bred to be a workaholic, and I was educated to be a workaholic—" As if on cue, the phone rang. "Excuse me." He got up. "I've got to take this."

It could have been prearranged, because the call certainly sounded like business, and it took what seemed like hours. When he returned, he said, "I promise you, I didn't know that call was coming. But it happens all the time. Miranda, you of all people should understand what it's like to be the child of a stupendously successful parent. It's a competition, and it probably never ends to anyone's satisfaction. So you're stuck with the family trade, and I'm saddled with the family business . . . so many expectations—from my family, from the world, and from myself."

"Yes, you're right," she agreed.

"And I go out with a lot of women. Why shouldn't I? I don't lead them on or try to get them to believe they're the center of my existence. The theatre in Connecticut is the center of my existence, certainly right now. For starters, it's the only way I'll ever buy any distance from Dad. If he wants to challenge me to equal him—or to surpass him—great! I'm for it. Remember, I told you before: I'm not the kind of guy to pass up a challenge."

So he did remember that night, remembered it in detail. Curling her legs under her, she asked, "So what does all this have to do with not calling me?"

He clasped his fingers in hers and held on fast. "Listen, Miranda, I had a super time with you, you know that—you can't fake that kind of—well, you know. And I *have* thought about you, not just about you and Anthony, but also about *you*. But I've got a lot to accomplish, fast, and I just can't handle a heavy emotional commitment right now. You've got to believe you *are* very special to me, though. I love your company and

I love your talent. I don't know what Anthony's up to about Thursday, but I honestly think you're going to be a big star. And I'd like to be involved in that. I'd like very much for us to be present in each other's lives for a long time."

"As . . . *friends*?" she asked him, because she didn't understand. "As . . . what?"

"Miranda"—he took both her hands in his—"I don't really know. But I'll put money on this: Whatever we have together won't be like anything we've ever had with anybody else. It'll be as special and different as you are."

"Special and different. And nonexclusive?"

"Well, yeah, I guess." He smiled. "It'll be my first try at a liberated relationship. Let's see how I do."

As her heart took a dive, she announced calmly, "Jay, I'm sure you'll do just great!"

"I'll certainly try." He hugged her, a gracious winner consoling the loser at the net. "And now that we've got all that straightened out, feel like adjourning to the bedroom?"

"Yes, Jay, I do," she said, then followed him up a curving metal staircase into a fabulous black-and-white bedroom. "Jay—" she started to say, when they were both ensconced in the massive bed, but the phone interrupted her.

"Oh, hi," he said, sounding sheepish. "Are you at home? Can I call you back in thirty seconds? Wait, can you hold on for a minute?" Putting his hand over the receiver, he whispered to Miranda, "I've got to take this downstairs. It's business, and all the figures are down there. Won't take long. Just hang up when I yell."

"Bring back some champagne, okay?" she said as she took the phone.

"You bet," he said, kissing her lengthily, then heading down the stairs.

Sure that it was a woman, she held the phone to her ear, but Jay outsmarted her by yelling to her to hang up and waiting to hear the click before he spoke. So she'd never know for sure, but her instincts told her to be wary, lying in his bed, dying to know what he was saying, her arms around a pillow suffused with his unique and wonderful smell.

And when he returned, bearing two glasses of champagne, he was excited by the russet fan of her hair on the pillow, by the rather prim way she had pulled the covers up almost to her chin, then puzzled that she was still fully dressed, and finally shocked by the fact that she had fallen fast asleep.

chapter 8

Jack
1984

YOU'VE NEVER BEEN charmed until you've been charmed by Sir Anthony Gainsborough, and the evening of Miranda's impromptu audition, I was the all-too-willing recipient of the royal treatment. Gainsborough charmed me in the cab going uptown; charmed me at the dinner party to which he insisted I accompany him ("They've invited forty people, dear boy," he said, brushing away my hesitations about crashing a party at the San Remo. "It's buffet, you see, and one more mouth to feed won't faze thèm in the least."); and he continued to charm me, after we'd made our farewells, by insisting I come back for a nightcap to the *pied-à-terre* he was borrowing for this trip.

The *pied-à-terre* turned out to be a fabulous eyrie at the top of a Park Avenue residential hotel, a penthouse with its own private staircase and entrance, an expanse of Anglo-Italian champagne minimalism—plush palest champagne couches, a few glass tables, unadorned walls, and yellow roses everywhere—featuring a double-exposure and a patio around which was wrapped the cyclorama that was the New York skyline. I wondered to whom this perfection of understatement belonged, a person who, even in his or her absence, saw to it that the flowers were fresh and that there was plenty of champagne in the fridge. But to ask seemed inappropriate to the magical possibilities of the place and the presence that so extravagantly filled it, and soon I just sat back and enjoyed the wizardry.

Till the small hours Anthony Gainsborough entertained me. It's not that I didn't know he was interested in something other than my enchanting company. I knew he was wooing me because he had to work with me, making me his because he made everybody his, treating me like an old war buddy who just happens to be a genius because he was expertly, painlessly, extracting information from me as he simultaneously hypnotized me into carrying back a certain image of him to people he would be working with. I knew it all, but none of it mattered. If this was an interrogation, it was the most pleasant possible version of the process; if Anthony was recruiting me for his network, I was the easiest agent he'd ever turned. Merlin and Arthur I felt we were that night, and I basked in the glow of his unsurpassed vitality.

Every so often, in the middle of a brief pause between his praising my work or tossing off a dazzling and apparently self-deprecating anecdote about himself stumbling amidst the great, I started to ask him about Miranda—about what he'd thought of her performance and why he'd insisted on the second audition—but before I could form the thought, the conversation seemed to be again in full swing. Anthony clearly wasn't ready to talk about Miranda, hence the expertise with which he took us off and running on some other track. I was right about that, but I underestimated Anthony's manipulation, for before the night ended, I was to see how clever, how much cleverer than I, he was.

He was describing to me, as the clock turned to half past three and the third bottle of champagne was uncorked, a randy and hysterical show-biz story involving John Gielgud and Edith Evans during the run of a play in which the young Anthony had appeared. The punch line, a withering but affectionate put-down of Gielgud by Evans, had broken us both up, and we were still chuckling when Anthony seemed to sadden. "That was ... God ... it must have been thirty years ago ... Can you imagine a time when you'll be able to say *that*, my young friend? It'll give you pause, I can tell you."

I simply smiled, a little too woozy to conjure up a phrase clever enough to dazzle, wise enough to comfort, but Anthony, totally unfazed by the lack of a feed-in line, simply pressed on. "Thirty years, it was ... You know, boy, it was during that run of *Winter's Tale* that I first met Margo!" Just like that, he'd thrown it away, as if he were telling me the time. The one subject everybody was afraid to broach, the root of all the trouble that was muddling my own contentment at a time when I had the right to pure joy. Margo, the key to Miranda. Here was the lead-in to a lot I needed to know about my strongest and strangest attachment. Buried somewhere in the story of the adulterous lovers was the reason why, for me, and possibly for Jay, Miranda could be loved so easily—and feared so greatly. Did I really believe the sins of the mothers would live again in the daughters? Was Miranda's turbulent intensity some manifestation of what, in the classical tragic heroines like Electra and Medea, came to be seen as their doom? And I wondered if the wildness I saw in Miranda had blossomed, in Margo, as some dark and terrible power, dragging Anthony into its wake, dooming him to be the catalyst of the destruction she sought. If I followed Miranda, would the curse be broken—or would it kick into life?

And now, I'd been presented with an opportunity to start to know the secrets of the past, from the man best qualified to tell me the saddest story he'd ever heard. Anthony, after all, had survived. Anthony was a witness.

"It was just at the end of the war." Anthony rose, strode to the window, champagne glass in hand, turning his head to emphasize his magnificent profile. "Yes, forty-six, it was. I'd had a promising little acting career going before the whole bash started . . ."

In fact, Anthony had already been running neck and neck with Olivier and Leslie Howard for the title of Great Young Star, which was interrupted by a brief stint in the service. He didn't mention, but I knew, as did everyone, that he had been not only a pilot in the RAF, but an ace and a national hero as well, ending up a group captain with a large portion of fruit salad on his tunic.

"Forty-six. London." His voice was softening with elegiac elegance. "The Blitz was behind us, but things were still hard as hell. But, Jack, we had come through! It was a terribly exciting time. Everybody felt like a hero. And with the Blitz over, the relief was almost a religious experience. Anyway, in the midst of all this mad euphoria, someone at an Alex Korda dinner party suggested to David Lean, who had just confessed to a secret desire to direct *The Winter's Tale*, that he do just that. The timing was perfect for a play about hard times and happy endings. Vivien—that's Vivien Leigh, of course—then expressed an equally intense desire to play Hermione . . . why, I'll never know. Even Larry was puzzled; it's such a tiny part. Must have been the final scene—Viv was always fond of the idea of returning from the grave—and then Larry chimed in, and some others, and that was that. An all-star production of *Winter's Tale* in the West End—a victory celebration! Probably the greatest assemblage of actors ever brought together on one stage. Let's see . . . Gielgud . . . Michael Redgrave . . . Ralph Richardson did the old shepherd— fabulous work, as usual . . . Olivier, his idiot son—he was hysterical, a great character actor as well as a wonderful clown. I think his talent for comedy has always been underappreciated, but, of course, it's his own fault. I did Florizel, who unknowingly falls in love with his father's archenemy's daughter, Perdita. For

Perdita, they were courting some little thing, an American girl who, in the space of only a couple of years, had been discovered both in New York and in Hollywood. I hadn't seen her work, but I envied her desperately, since we'd all heard she'd come from money and had never had to struggle so much as a day in her life. She'd taken a break in her work to live in London with her husband, a young Boston stuffed shirt with the Allied High Command, and it was arranged one day for her to come by to read with the cast. The actress, of course, was Margo.

"I remember the first time I saw her. We were all sitting round the stage of the St. James's, smoking and stewing because she was terribly late. Inexcusably late. I'd been prepared to hate her if she'd shown up two hours early, but now I was vowing, if ever we played together, to make her existence a living nightmare. And I wasn't the only one who felt that hostility, needless to say. And just as tempers were turning ugly, in rushes this sparrow of a creature, tremendously upset, half in tears, so delicate, so fragile, and so absolutely beautiful —really beautiful, all sweetness, all innocence—that we all forgot to be angry. She never, by the way, explained why she was an hour late for a first reading, and it took me some time before I realized that she did it because she was a star, with a star's arrogance, *but* with a great actress's talent for turning any group to her side. Whether she ever was consciously aware of her superior manipulative powers I'll never know, although, of course, I'll never stop thinking about it. All of that is rather aside from the point, though, Jack. The point was that, from that first second when she ran breathless onto that stage, I was in love with her. It wasn't like falling in love, you know, because I don't remember a second of capitulation. It was as if I had always loved her—a feeling *that* assured, that deep and abiding. Remember, we were both married at the time, she to the man who would be Miranda's father"—I realized I was hearing Miranda's name for the first time just as he switched from champagne to brandy—"I to a woman I'd respected, if not adored, until that moment when I saw Margo."

I had always heard he'd enjoyed quite a reputation as a rake, but was now prepared to accept his own version of his romantic life.

"But neither of us was prepared to launch an adulterous union. No, I'm not being honest. We were acting the role of lovers, after all, being thrust together so much of the time, that I was more than willing, but although she flirted, she never presented the opportunity for me to declare myself. What happened, of course, is that we became a stage couple . . . you know, we ended up doing a couple of pictures together, both in London and Hollywood, so we became linked in the public imagination long before we . . . well . . ."

He went on to describe his befriending Margo's family, being named godfather to Miranda when she was born, languishing, all the while, for the woman he could make love to only in public. He continued through the commencement of their affair, the subsequent collapse of his own childless marriage, through the jealousy of Miranda's father, always believing his wife and Anthony to be lovers until he drove them into each other's arms, through the scandal that ensued, and the loss of Miranda, which had slowly, steadily driven Margo to a storm of desperation that ended, tragically, in her suicide.

"You know, Jack"— Anthony had returned from refilling his brandy glass and was sitting down for the first time in the long and painful recital —"losing Margo was . . . words fail me . . . twenty years of romantic obsession and great passion. I would have done anything in the world for her, but—" He raised one finger to wipe away a single tear. "I couldn't save her . . . wasn't even there when she . . . Maybe if I had been

. . . if I'd known she wasn't really better . . . Well, enough about that," and he shifted the subject before I could even step in.

"Jack," he went on, his face and tone noticeably brightening. "Jack, when Miranda walked into that room tonight, amidst the shadows and the dim lights, I truly thought I was seeing a ghost. She seemed so like Margo. That quicksilver energy! That irresistible drive! And that spirited beauty—just like Margo before . . . the breakdowns . . . I'd lost my heart to it once; how could I fail to lose my heart to it a second time? It was astonishing, as if some force were restoring Margo to me. And in the person of a woman who'd been the child I'd cherished as if she were my own. I'm mad to work with Miranda, Jack. How could I not be?"

And suddenly, despite the fact that I'd probably never decipher Miranda, certainly not through Anthony, I felt reassured about everyone's well-being. Anthony appreciated Miranda, perhaps in greater measure and for more complicated reasons than any other man ever would. In time, she'd learn to forgive him, and we'd all share the pinnacle together. I was just about to congratulate Anthony on his wisdom in casting Miranda when I heard the fabled Gainsborough voice enunciate, *"But . . ."*

I looked at him. "But what?"

"But"—he returned my stare—"there are a few little bothersome things . . ."

"Okay, shoot," I said boldly, prepared to defend my closest friend to the death.

"Let me be frank with you, Jack." Anthony, without missing a beat, had managed to refill both our brandy glasses. "I would have given her the part tonight, on the spot, if I hadn't sensed in her a certain resistance, an inability to take direction, if you will. Remember, lad, I knew her as a child. She was somewhat willful then, very independent, and though she wouldn't be *Miranda* without that, she could sometimes become utterly intractable. Tonight, I thought I saw that same defiance in her. Granted, that's probably because I am who I am. I know how deeply she must resent me and how my very presence must evoke a score of painful memories, but it's for that very reason that I want to be reasonably sure we're not heading for a clash.''

"But she's not a child anymore," I dared to suggest.

"No, she's *not* a child anymore, and I'm utterly thrilled by the extent of her talent and training. Obviously, she's done excellent work with various directors; I'm sure her reputation's top-drawer . . . But there was one thing—I can't remember the particulars, some disagreement—I believe I heard it happened at Yale . . . something about—"

And I, drunk as a skunk and no match for a master manipulator, jumped right in with, "The *Hedda Gabler* thing? That was absolutely not her fault! I know a dozen people who were involved, and it simply wasn't—" Realizing that I'd not walked but danced into the trap Anthony had set, I knew, for every instinct in my body screamed, that I had to get Miranda out of this unscathed. I'd made a major mistake; it was that simple. I had to right it.

"Anthony, listen." I girded my loins and began. "The director was impossible. He had a testy disposition, and he was the kind of asshole artiste who goes through leading ladies the way drag queens go through panty hose. And on top of that, he kept changing his mind, but he was such an egotist that whatever he felt at the time—forget five minutes ago—was law. He recast Hedda twice after Miranda left, and ended up using his girlfriend, and then the production turned out lousy!''

"After Miranda left . . ." Anthony mused. "What exactly happened? Did she walk out?''

"Ummm . . ." I knew I had to tell the truth." . . . yes . . . but from what I understand, she was totally justified.''

"How did she behave? At the time?''

"Well," I continued, "I didn't know her then. But I heard about it through mutual friends. She never mentions it, but I expect, well, she took it pretty hard. But everybody around her was very supportive, I do know that, because it really wasn't her fault. She didn't have a choice."

"Of course not." Anthony patted my knee, as if, with that gesture, he turned my thoughtless betrayal into an act of faith in the woman I'd smeared. "It happens to everybody. I'm glad to know it was through no fault of her own. Don't worry, Jack, I believe you. And if that's the only time she's ever had trouble, she sounds—" he laughed heartily "—if anything, too stable for the business. Truly, Jack, your honesty has reassured me . . . as I hope mine has you. I felt I owned you an explanation of why I wanted a second audition, and now I've given it you. And won't you—and our young producer—be interested in seeing me direct her in a scene?"

"You bet," I added buoyantly, ready again to take on faith the words of a man who had just set me up.

"And," Anthony continued, "speaking of our young producer—what do you make of him, Jack? That was quite a surprise he pulled on *me* tonight—springing Miranda on me like that! I'm actually a bit annoyed at him. It seemed the callow action of an overprivileged youth who's apparently never lost anyone or anything he didn't want to lose."

That one took a bit of thought, but sipping my brandy, I managed, at least I thought I did, to organize my ideas. "Well, Anthony, I guess you're right in a way. But if it wasn't polite, it was effective. Miranda didn't know you were involved, either. Who knows if this meeting ever would have happened—or *what* would have happened—if you two had known? Look, if it helps, I'll apologize for Jay, but really, Anthony, he's a terrific guy. Very smart. Very fair. He certainly has been in his dealings with me."

"And what about in his dealings with Miranda?" Anthony's eyes narrowed just enough to alert me to the fact that this stage was critical.

"Oh, Anthony, I don't know anything about that. He took her out once. He's never mentioned the evening. *She's* never mentioned the evening."

"He was certainly not casual about getting her alone tonight," Anthony challenged me.

"Maybe he felt he owed her an apology for his tactics in bringing the two of you together."

"Perhaps . . . but it was more than that. I hear, of course, that Mr. Harrington is quite the gay blade with the ladies."

"Well, yeah . . . "

"That icy seductiveness, it's very effective, you know. Very dangerous. No, I could never condone a match between Miranda and that young man. I tell you, Jack, I hope he soon moves on to the next platinum-blond showgirl!"

"Miranda can take care of herself," I said firmly, only half meaning it, for Anthony's concern for Miranda had reawakened my own fears.

"And, Jack"—Anthony was visibly upset—"I'm interested only in Miranda's good, I swear to you. If I cast her in your play, they'll be thrown together, and I'm worried about that eventuality. Miranda's very high-strung, as you know, very sensitive and fragile, so much like her mother. I suspect she *hurts* more than the average person, and I suspect she can't tolerate a lot of pain. I would rather die than see what happened to her mother happen to her, and to prevent that, I must protect Miranda—and you must, too." He threw an arm about my shoulder in a gesture of common cause. "You, who know her better than anyone, who are closer to her than anyone, must help keep her safe. Agreed?"

Of course, I agreed, tremendously flattered by Anthony's enlisting me as his aide-de-camp, as well as by his having chosen me as confidant. Innocent adorer of the great as I was, I felt he didn't often let down his guard, and his rare openness and honesty had earned my respect. And Anthony wasn't one-hundred-percent wrong in what he'd sensed about Miranda; she did have an undeniable tendency to reject any outside limitation on her spirit. It had marked her personal life and could mushroom into a professional problem; in fact, a guy she'd briefly dated in school had actually told me she needed a lion tamer, not a boyfriend, and I'd known what he meant. Well, Miranda would simply have to grow up, and learn to give and take as I had to, and despite what had happened long ago between her and Anthony, I looked back to earlier that very evening when her talent had filled my heart, as I was sure it had Anthony's, and I was thrilled at being part of this great enterprise.

And as Anthony and I shook hands and said good night—although the sun was rising—I felt incredibly close to the complex, deceptive, supremely confident and deeply suffering institution that was Anthony Gainsborough. Our bond filled me with pride and trust. And that's why, when I arrived at the rehearsal studios in the Harrington Building on Thursday afternoon, I was surprised when I was told that Sir Anthony Gainsborough had requested I wait outside.

It only took a minute for my shock to subside behind the revelation that the man who was my hero, my buddy, and with luck, my mentor, had just barred me from the reading.

chapter 9

Miranda
Manhattan, 1975

SHE WAS EARLY, and he, of course, was late. By now, judging from the graduated build of her anxiety, she guessed half an hour had gone by. The large, long room, mirrored along one wall with a barre, and with two walls of windows facing the street, was empty except for four folding chairs, which had been set up across from the mirrors in the center of the room, where she had been ushered by some smartly dressed young woman seated at a desk outside the rehearsal studio. So she sat and sat and sat, staring at herself in the mirrors across from her—a plaintive figure, despite her attempts at a proud posture, stomach afire, temples throbbing. She had to sit up straight, couldn't relax for a moment, because at any second Jay and Jack and Anthony could walk through the door and catch her unprepared. She had to be up for this, wanted it more than anything, but if somebody didn't show soon, she was likely to bolt. When the door did at last open, it was only the receptionist coming to tell her that Sir Anthony had called to say he'd been a bit detained but would be there shortly. She gasped some kind of thank you, then was left alone, sitting straight up still, wanting to scream.

The last few days, starting with the scene at Jay's, had been crazy. She'd gotten up early the next morning and crept out of his place without waking him, both embarrassed and amused at the newest strange twist their relationship had taken, wondering if her falling asleep had ended things between them. She'd been rewarded the following afternoon with an extravagant bouquet of white roses, borne by a delivery boy who had clearly not enjoyed the five-story climb to her eyrie. Enclosed with the flowers was a note that read, "To a constant surprise. I'll never forget you—believe me." It had been scrawled with a fountain pen, in semilegible executive penmanship, and she wondered if it was an insult or compliment.

Jay had called later that day to set the time for the audition. By then, with the coming crucible uppermost in her thoughts, she had been pleased to hear his voice but surprised that Anthony hadn't placed the call himself. Still, it was all arranged; the audition was set for three-thirty in the afternoon, and both Jay and Jack would be attending. Jay didn't allude to their truncated night of passion, just accepted her thanks for the flowers and rang off with a minimum of banter—all business during business hours, no doubt. It was hard to deduce his private feelings, but if he didn't seem ardent, he didn't sound icy, and besides, she'd see on Thursday.

Thursday! The day on which she'd find out an awful lot! Whether she was desired or declined. A star or a reject. On noon of the fateful day, her fretting and fussing and deciding what to wear had been interrupted by the ring of the phone. When it turned out to be Anthony, she had been taken aback, even more unsettled when he asked her, simply dripping charm, if she could possibly make it to the Harrington Building by one o'clock. Oodles of apologies, but he'd had a complicated schedule change. She had wanted to scream that she couldn't possibly be there that fast, but didn't. Not after the message that Jack had carried back from Anthony for her. He had slipped in the warning amidst an elaborate recitation of all the wonderful things the older man had said about her. The gist of it was that Anthony feared she might have a little too much spirit, might be a little too inflexible and hard to control, given their history; she might, Jack lectured her, try to defer to Anthony's superior experience and authority and act like a grown-up.

Act like a grown-up! He was a fine one to talk! Jack's rejection of his heritage and his family was so intense and undigested, she sometimes wondered if he'd turned gay simply to deprive his father of the pleasure of grandchildren. Jack Price, only kid, spoiled rotten and just as rebellious as she, but quieter about it. Absolutely likeable, even lovable, the kind of guy about whom people say "What's to hate?" So warm, so interested, so talented, and—although she probably knew it better than his constantly changing string of lovers, his college and theatre cronies—so afraid to be deeply touched. Like a kid demonstrating his autonomy by wiggling out of a parent's embrace, Jack danced away from involvement and into brief encounters. She thought she might be the one exception.

For she and Jack definitely had an attachment—buddy-buddy, brother and sister, Cathy and Heathcliff, whatever it was, it really *was*. He was almost always there for her, as she tried to be for him, and they knew each other too well to fool one another. When he said she looked good, she knew she looked good; just as when she told him she liked his work, he knew she liked it.

But, still, Jack's ambition, fueled on the fire of his private war back home, set an aspect of him apart, even from her, who knew him intimately. His desire for success exceeded hers, and it was far more urgent than anyone who met the easygoing, attractive playwright would ever dream. That was the part of him, the rage for fame, that she feared when she was feeling paranoid, as she was now, and his seeming to have fallen so quickly for Anthony's double-edged wiles exacerbated her unease. So did the fact that he'd been all too willing to be Anthony's messenger. But she had accepted the advice and agreed to be docile. She'd be the best little girl in the world, submissive and sunny. And now it was Anthony who was being erratic, who was asking too much and taking unfair advantage. Damn his lousy schedule! Why the hell did she have to suffer because something more interesting had come up? How could he be doing this to her?

Still, recalling her childhood and his unpredictable yet magical descents on her life, she understood how he could act like that; he always had. The unscheduled outings to the zoo, to F.A.O. Schwarz, to the Palm Court for ice cream—Anthony was like that, and his mercurial nature had always been a major ingredient of his enormous appeal. Well, today, years later, it was a pain in the ass, but, she had to admit, at least the change meant she'd had less time to work herself into a frenzy.

Throwing on a pair of jeans, sandals, and a pretty peasant shirt, she had grabbed her purse, raced down the stairs, flung herself into a cab and over to the Harrington Building, making it by ten to one. Now, with what seemed like half an hour gone by without Anthony, she was livid. *He'd* called *her* and changed the time to suit his blasted convenience, and she had broken her ass to get over here, and now *he* was keeping *her* waiting, leaving her to suffer silently as she pondered whether he had done all this on purpose and why. When she was a child, before the trouble, she'd been convinced he was without flaw—a knight on a white charger. It was as if he'd come into their lives, into their home, especially to amuse her. And he had. Amused her. Enchanted her. And made her fall in love with him in the way that little girls first fall in love with grown-up men. He was her hero, and she was his charge, and he'd escort her through the rigors of adolescence and make her a beautiful, gracious woman.

But she'd been wrong. He had flaws, all right, and they were bad ones. He'd stolen away the mother whose presence guaranteed she always be treated like a precious princess. And worse, he'd crept away with her heart, with her loyalty, leaving her with a fear of loss that several fabulously expensive shrinks couldn't even begin to treat.

And now, just as she was beginning to make a go of her life, just as she was beginning to get the past under control, he had returned—an omen, and hardly a good one. That the incredible anger she felt toward him might be compounded of tantrumlike rage, guarded joy, and the desire to stun with one's own radiance occurred to her, and she was trying to deal with it. But now this! Keeping her waiting and changing the rules. Trying to unseat her for who knows what crazy reason. Well, screw him. If she was going to lose out, she would go down fighting. Tooth and nail. Screw him. She was going to be strong. And calm. And ready for him.

And yet, ten minutes later, she was at that point of anxiety when she was starting to feel drowsy; her eyes were almost closing and her thoughts drifting off as the door burst open.

Framed by the doorway, Sir Anthony Gainsborough posed with the classic grace of the eternal leading man. Clad with consummate taste in some fabulously customed arrangement of Irish tweed, Egyptian cotton, French gabardine, English cashmere, and Italian leather, he was a study in how a gentleman dressed for an afternoon audition should look, the greens and browns and beiges picking up the glints in his chestnut hair and the sparkle in his dark-green eyes, the jacket held in one hand and casually slung over his shoulder. He dazzled, dazzled as much as, or more than, he always had, now that the years had given him character, now that the graying hair had added stature. The body, as lithe as, but more substantial than, in his youth, suggested stores of energy still to be manifested, and as his initial expression of harried concern metamorphosed into pure delight, she melted—as she always had, even as a child, and . . . as her mother had, as millions had. She still adored him. But she'd never trust him.

Having allowed her a few moments to contemplate him, Anthony strode rapidly to where she sat and took her hand, drawing her to her feet, then embracing her with an easy informality. "My dear, I'm so awfully sorry about the screw-up. So awfully sorry . . . " Releasing her from his embrace, he took her chin in his hand and asked plaintively, "You will forgive me, won't you?"

"Oh, Anthony, of course." She made as if to dismiss the fault altogether, fuming and captivated at the same time. Good old Anthony. The man destined to control her future—as he had shaped her past. The man who made caprice an art form.

"I'm so glad—" He took her hand and motioned that they both sit. "—because I want so much for us to work together."

She tried to smile demurely. "When will Jay and Jack be here?"

Sheepishly, she thought, he answered, "They're not going to be here for quite a while. Darling, I felt it would be better if we got reacquainted . . . you know, on a one-to-one basis." Another double whammy. She trembled to think what was next. "Well"—he patted her knee—"are we ready?"

"As ready as I'll ever . . . " She let the cliché drift off, reaching into her bag for her copy of the script.

"Oh, you won't be needing that. Not right now, at least, darling."

"Anthony"—she felt her awful will reasserting itself—"I haven't memorized the script. I need it."

"No, no, darling. I didn't assume that you had

memorized it. I simply felt it might be nice, might be . . . interesting for both of us . . . to try something else first.''

Her heart thudded against her breast. "Something else?"

"Yes, darling, just for starters. Just to test the range. I thought we'd try a little scene from *Hedda Gabler*."

She thought she could not have heard him right. "*Hedda Gabler*?"

"You know the play, of course?"

"Of course." She knew the play all right. She'd actually been cast as Hedda in a directing project at Yale. The director had been a real Method jerk who'd left school shortly thereafter to pursue a highly lucrative career doing TV commercials. But he'd stayed around long enough to brutalize and bully her, insisting Hedda be played as an arch-villainess, a witch out of a Walt Disney movie; she knew he was wrong, knew that such a characterization would be too bombastic to make sense, too simple to be interesting, but, although they'd argued, she'd gone along. Everybody said the guy was a *shmuck*, but she'd still feared it would be a black mark on her record, having to walk out. She had to suspect that Anthony knew about the incident, but how? Could Jack have mentioned it to him? No, that didn't sound like Jack. Had she? No; when would she have had the chance? So it must have been Jack. Had Anthony hypnotized him that night she was falling asleep at Jay's and wheedled it out of him? *Hedda Gabler!* Goddamn Anthony! Was he casting her—or gaslighting her?

"One last thing before we start, darling," he told her. "I have an ironclad rule about situations like this. What we two do here is just between us. We won't discuss it with anyone outside, will we? I think it's vital, that sense of creative privacy. All right, sweet?" He placed his arm around her shoulder and gave her a hug, and she smiled and said, "My lips are sealed."

"Goodo. Now—" He extracted two identical paper-

backs from his attaché case and handed her one.
"—I've marked the pages. It's the last scene, you know,
in which poor Hedda has been entrapped by the evil—"
He twirled an imaginary moustache. "—Judge Brack.
You'll recall he knows she has given the poet Lövborg
a gun with which to take his own life, convincing him it
is the supreme sacrifice, the *liebestod*, love and death,
and he, Brack, is using that knowledge to blackmail her
morally. This is the moment when he demands her total
submission. Right?"

"Right," she almost sighed, knowing that she was
going to fail utterly, but committed to going through
with it.

"Now, darling, I'm going to read with you. So let's
set up these chairs . . . You sit here." He placed one of
the chairs in the middle of the room. "All right, it's
page one sixty-seven in this edition . . . ah . . . you have
it . . . Read it through a couple of times . . . take as long
as you like . . . " She read it through, remembering all
too well, then took a deep breath. "Okay."

"So we'll start at the point where I'm bending over
your chair. You husband's somewhere in the room, so
we have to pretend we're having a pleasant little social
chat. All right. We'll start with, 'Have you looked to see
if both your pistols . . . ' "

"Fine." She nodded, then got into position, staring
into an imaginary fireplace, feeling doom come closer in
the presence of the lowering figure standing behind her.

She concentrated hard. Tried to wipe out of her mind
everything but the warmth of the fire, which gave her no
warmth. Everything but the panic that was flooding her.
Everything but the freedom she'd always dreamed of in
the midst of her boring and constricted life, but which
was giving way instead to an even more horrible sub-
jugation. Everything but the dreadful smile that she
knew illuminated the face of the man standing behind
her, although she could not see it. Then he spoke, the
magnificent voice full of irony. "Have you looked to

see if both your pistols are still there?"

Picking up the script almost without realizing it, she answered resolutely, not bothering to turn to him. "No." She let her hand fly to her throat, felt herself choking then forced the hand into her lap, playing with a fold in her gown.

"You needn't bother." He was bending over her. "I saw the pistol Lövborg had when they found him. I recognized it at once."

Slowly, gracefully, she raised her head so that she was looking up at him, two profiles, perfectly matched. She could have been acknowledging a compliment as she asked, "Have you got it?"

"No, the police have it."

She quickly turned her head back to the fire, the color draining from her face, although no one could see that except for the man who was apparently idly combing his pockets for a match with which to light his cigar, all false levity, asking and receiving her permission to smoke.

"What will the police do with this pistol?"

He chuckled for the benefit of the other man in the room, then said softly, "Try to trace the owner."

"Do you think they'll succeed?"

"No, Hedda Gabler." He actually allowed his hand to brush her shoulder as he sought to grasp the back of her chair. "Not as long as I hold my tongue."

Suddenly, she arose, crossing downstage to the window in front of her, forcing herself to laugh, as if they were gossiping. Immediately, he was by her side, unwilling to let her stand alone, chuckling again as she asked him, "And if you don't . . . hold your tongue?"

And so it continued. The evidence growing blacker, the promise of a scandal, her resolution that she would rather die than be so compromised, and his challenge that people who threaten suicide never do it. And as the judge, whom she had refused to face as he built his ironclad case against her, continued to murmur threats as if they were love words, her heart sank. He did it all so civilly, so brilliantly, that that poor other person busying himself in the far part of the room would never know the course of her damnation.

"Well, luckily," the judge crooned, "there's no danger as long as I hold my tongue."

Finally, she faced him, repulsed, trapped, doomed. Shrinking back, despite herself, she gasped, "In other words, I'm in your power, Judge. From now on, you've got a hold over me," and she jerked herself away from him, swathed in layers of despair, and it was through that great horror that she heard him say, "Hedda would never do that!"

"What?" She was rattled by the break in her concentration.

"Let's stop for a moment, Miranda dear. Come, let's sit down." He led her off to the two chairs still in their original places.

What was the problem? How could he stop her in the middle of the final build, knowing he would destroy whatever she had going? But she kept all that inside as he looked at her and said, "Let's think of it this way. Hedda only fully realizes her inevitable end—suicide— when she is forced to acknowledge the fact that she and Brack, for whatever complicated social and dramatic reasons, really *do* belong together. Granted it repulses her—in fact, it kills her. But . . . and I stress this *but*—she realizes she is as damned as he only when she is forced to face the fact that she is attracted to him. It isn't his words that wound her. It's the opposite, it's his attractiveness. She wouldn't pull away instinctively. It's when she *doesn't* pull away that she knows what her end will be.

"You see, my dear"—He took her hand and moved closer to her—"Brack is the only man in the play who's strong enough for her, who *challenges* her. Who leads her to the brink, which is where she's always wanted to be. That's the dramatic situation."

"I'm not sure . . . I . . . " She couldn't agree, would never agree. She just didn't see it that way. "Don't you feel that she would have preferred a romantic double suicide with the poet but lacked—"

"Let's just try it this way, dear. Just this once?"

"But I—"

"Come on, just this once. Let's try."

Burying her pride, she got back up, and they began again. This time, it was different. Every time she got going, he stopped her, telling her to wait to turn, stopping her when she laughed at what he considered the wrong place: "Too early! If you do this so far up in the scene, you won't have anywhere to build to!" He physically moved her around, restraining an arm as it poised in midair: "Minimal gestures, my sweet, minimal gestures . . . Remember, her husband's in the room . . . what's happening is a perfectly polite public cuckolding of Tesman . . . and she's still laboring under the illusion that she's going to outsmart the judge. She'd never give herself away in so fluttery and hysterical a fashion. Hedda's not a flirt, remember; she's a siren, a Garbo. All right, darling, once more."

Some incalculable amount of time had passed, lost forever in the endless repetitions and shifts in word and tone and movement. She was exhausted, defeated. She didn't know what he wanted anymore. She couldn't understand. What little strength she still had was focused on putting an end to this travesty. She raged to be through. She hungered to get out. The entire expanse of the room had contracted into a small and deadly square in which she was being utterly vanquished. He ordered her around, wore her down, made her grovel, made her less than she knew she could be, attacked and slashed and cut her confidence to the quick. She was sick of this, sick of everything—especially of this terrible past that had come back to punish her for the sins of others. What had she done to him, what had she evoked in him, that made him bludgeon her so? And finally, there came a moment when she knew she could not go on, when she was willing—more, was yearning—to capitulate, and that was when it happened: She got it right.

They had started yet again, and suddenly she understood. Hedda *was* a siren. And the only exercise of her power, in the world of this play, was to seduce. To control men. Only when she was controlled *by* a man was she doomed. And so she laughed and sat still, let her head fall back only slightly to catch his dreadful remarks, meant only for her ears. To Tesman, preoccupied in another part of the room, she was simply being Hedda, making another conquest, while only she and Brack, that Brack whose presence she felt invading her, defiling her, conquering her, knew the real action of the scene being played out. She had crossed downstage, staring out the invisible window. He was beside her. "And suppose they trace the owner?" The unspeakable question followed, from his lips, by the most obscene word of all.

"There'll be a scandal, Hedda." He didn't even take a beat, just let it glide out, smooth as silk. "Yes, a scandal, the thing you're so frightened of . . . " And, turning away from him but smiling still, she began with a flirtatious levity. "Oh, Judge, we both know I had nothing to do with—"

He said something, but she only barely heard it because she already knew what it was, and she was fighting madly, searching for some last line of defense, until she heard him say, "Luckily, there's no danger as long as I hold my tongue."

"As long as *you* . . . " She repeated the words without thinking, without knowing, hearing them with all their hideous reverberations, with all their resonant power. For the first time she faced him, prepared to be repulsed. And, for the first time, their eyes met in an act of mutual comprehension, an acknowledgment of their perfect understanding. And in that moment, as he dared to grasp her hand and she let him grasp it, both of them sure in the knowledge that Tesman would never look up—that he *had* never looked up in all those years when she courted danger to get attention—she felt a stab of sexual excitement. Danger, even death, held her hand in his, and she hungered for it, hungered for more than just a handclasp, damned in the knowing and the wanting to be damned.

Breathlessly, she spoke. "In other words, I'm in your power, Judge. From now on, you've got your hold over me," and as she heard herself murmur the words, as she wished with all her being to surrender to his terrible embrace, she knew, with a feeling that was both despair and relief, that she was lost.

He drew her hand to his lips, lips soft and cool, but promising more than warmth, promising fire, and he whispered, "Hedda, darling, believe me." With his back in Tesman's directions, he could undress her with his eyes, an erotic rehearsal. "I'll never take advantage . . . "

His hand gently traced, without touching, the fine line of her neck. Sensing the loss of herself, wanting not to sense it, she murmured, thinking aloud, "But I'm still in your power. Subservient to your will . . . and your demands . . . . And . . . not . . . *free*. Never free again . . . " And then she found within herself the strength to leave, to go and not to care what she left behind, and that courageous resignation took the form of utter calm, utter confidence. No longer a girl, she was, in her last moments, a woman. Drawing back her hand from that nearly irresistible grasp, she looked at him and simply said, "No, it's not possible. I can't agree to this," and as she moved to part from him, he held onto her hand, still hidden from her husband's view, and said quite sunnily, "Most people get resigned to the inevitable, sooner or later."

And standing there, knowing that this was the final scene of her life, she told him, "Possibly," then walked to the door, to the other pistol that awaited her, her head held high, in triumph. But as she was about to exit the room, she felt, all of a suddenn, his embracing her, and through the fog of her exhaustion, she heard him shout, "Smashing, old girl, simply smashing," then it was Anthony's hand slapping her briskly on her bottom as he told her, "Now, let's get down to work!"

chapter 10

Jack
1984

IF YOU'RE LOOKING for a magical place, a world where past and future have come to terms in perfect harmony, try Tintagel, Connecticut. A real estate copywriter's dream town, nestled in the western part of the state, a couple of hours' drive from Manhattan, it combines the undeveloped beauty of hills and woods and mountains with the lavish restraint of exquisite Yankee houses some three hundred years old and the great homes of more recent vintage. In Tintagel, you can experience a garden party comprised of the exclusively rich and eminent while, only a quarter of a mile away, a neighbor's cows and horses graze, unimpressed by guest lists. The town itself is a perfect set of a New England village complete with a village green and clapboard buildings glowing with fresh white paint. Not even a master Hollywood designer could recreate this ambience in California; it's a reminder to the confirmed Easterner that palm trees do not a paradise make.

Jay's theatre was at the end of town, past the bank and the post office, the high school and the liquor store. It was to be named after Shakespeare's Globe, with some irony, it seemed to me, since, in such a blue-chip neighborhood, the nobles would outnumber the groundlings ten to one. The season was to open on Memorial

Day weekend with the musical Jay was so excited about, and we were to come in as the second offering, a month later. That's what we were supposed to do, but, the second to last week in April, everything changed. I was sitting in my tiny apartment, loving it now that I was sure I would soon be leaving it for grander surroundings, when Jay called to tell me there were problems with the musical. They'd just fired the director and one of the principals, and there was no way they'd be ready to open in a month. So, having consulted with Anthony, who had nearly completed casting *Heights*, and with the set and lighting designers, whose plans were fairly firm, Jay had decided to open with us. I gulped, gagged, my heart pounded, and I broke out in a cold sweat. My future, my dazzling future, was about to be slapped together in about a month and hurled half-baked at a demanding public. Jay attempted to calm me by saying that Anthony Gainsborough, who had more experience than all the rest of the personnel put together, would never have agreed to an early opening if he wasn't confident that he could pull it off. A good point, I had to concede. As for Miranda, she was chomping at the bit, raring to go. And she had every reason to be. She was going to be smashing. I'd been 100-percent sure of that on Thursday, the day when Anthony finally admitted me and Jay to the closed reading from which we had been so precipitously barred some hour and a half earlier.

Of course, it was worth the wait. She and Anthony did the same scene from *Heights* that she'd auditioned with at Jay's, and of course Anthony's participation added something my calling out the words from the sidelines hadn't. But it was more than that. She was just *better* . . . better than better—she was great, or showed that she could be, that she would be. Whatever process of mind-bending or hypnosis or just tremendously good instruction on Anthony's part had been required to calm her down and enhance her concentration was worth it; she knew it, and Anthony knew it, which is why, I assumed, he'd decided at the last minute to make us wait until he was good and ready to display her. Whatever Anthony had put her through in the audition, and she refused and still refuses to disclose exactly what happened, it had certainly produced results. So the four of us celebrated her getting the role with champagne in the Algonquin lobby until everybody was high, including Jay, who, I noticed, kept trying to grab Miranda's hand—with only intermittent success—as the drinks progressed. Eventually, at Anthony's suggestion, we all moved on into the dining room for a bite of supper, as merry a band as you can imagine, egged on in our pursuit of a good time by Anthony's pizazz. It must have been eight or nine when we finished coffee and brandy, and since Jay was attempting to move closer to Miranda, I assumed they were about to fly off together. Anthony, as usual, beat him to the punch.

In the twinkling of an eye, the older man had helped Miranda up from the table, announced, "Young lady, you've had quite a day! I insist you go home and get some sleep. And to insure that you do as I say"— his voice was light, but I wasn't the only person who picked up the edge of command —"I'll just put you in a cab!" With that, he steered her across the lobby and out the door, leaving Jay and me sitting there—me with a head full of booze and confusion, Jay with the massive tab for our meal and the verge-of-tears look of a little boy lost giving way to the icy glare of a Mafia hit man.

chapter 11

Miranda
Manhattan, 1975

WHEN JAY CALLED from Connecticut to say he was running late and wouldn't be there until nine, Miranda took it with calm, but only outwardly. For Christ's sake, she didn't see him so often that he could afford to behave with such familiarity: If they had been going together in the conventional sense, if they spent three or four nights a week together, being over an hour late wouldn't matter. But it wasn't like that.

Granted, he was busy, but she was busy, too, especially since the play opening had been pushed up, and yet *she* had plenty of free nights. Even with Anthony dragging her to parties and openings and thousand-dollar-a-seat benefits, she still had time, would have made time, to see Jay. But he obviously didn't feel the same.

And she said nothing, couldn't complain, just accepted the fact that for whatever reason, they'd still made love only once. Their "romance" was limited to drinks or hasty dinners sandwiched between her rehearsals and his endless business appointments. Because he had finagled her into agreeing to an "open" relationship, she couldn't make any demands at all. He threw out the crumbs, and she consumed them ravenously. At this point, she was grateful for anything, had actually been thrilled when he'd called early that afternoon from Connecticut to ask her to dinner and gone so far as to suggest he had no one to see afterwards but her.

Fool that she was, she'd leaped at the chance to have him all to herself; had said yes, she happened to be free, and fine, she'd expect him at seven-thirty, and had hung up the phone, scarcely believing her luck.

Jay was her obsession, the sole threat to her concentration. Even when she was memorizing lines, her mind drifted off into fantasies of where he was and what he was doing and why he wasn't mad to see her, of how she would put him down if he ever called her and what it would be like to make love to him again. Only during rehearsal and for as long as an hour at a time in Anthony's company could she forget Jay. Jay, who moved in mysterious ways, like his close relative, God. Only recently she'd decided—one night when he'd stopped by rehearsal and been, she thought, cool—that when he called, she'd absolutely, definitely not see him. She had to make the break. He was not the man to give her what she wanted, and the hunger was driving her crazy. But then he'd called, and at the sound of his voice her vow had died.

She couldn't help it! She was on top of the world at the thought of seeing him. She'd rushed home from rehearsal to clean the house, change the sheets, and wash her hair, and was finished in record time. When he'd called to say he'd be late, she was getting ready to step into the shower.

She was just getting out of the shower when the phone rang again. Sure it was Jay wanting to make it ten, she was relieved when the caller turned out to be Anthony.

"My dear! I'm frankly surprised to find you at home."

"Well, I am going out, Anthony. If the gentleman ever shows up!"

"Sounds like our Mr. Harrington. The man on the run!" he said, innocently enough.

"How did you guess?" Her voice held more than a tingle of bitterness.

"Sometimes I think that young man's too busy for his own good! Now, darling," Anthony continued, "should your plans fall through, let me present you with the wonderful opportunity that I was ringing you about in the first place. Ran into Hal Prince on the street late today, and he asked if I'd like to come to drinks—he's having a few friends in. I'd love to escort you—then I thought perhaps we could have a little supper, just the two of us. We haven't done that in years, Randy. Remember when we used to go to the Plaza when your mother and dad were busy?"

"Oh, God, Anthony, dinner's impossible. But let's see, it's six-thirty, and I guess I could be out of here in . . . um . . . forty-five minutes. Jay's not coming until nine, so maybe I could stop by the party and then come back here—No, that won't work, there's just not enough time!"

"It's up to you, of course, darling, but I do think you should make an appearance at the Princes'. Tell you what, think about it for half an hour and then let's talk. I won't be leaving until then. All right, sweet? I'll expect to hear from you."

"Of course, Anthony," she told him graciously. "But I don't want you to count on me."

"I won't, I promise, darling, but think about it."

"I will," she'd said, and she was—thinking about it. Anyone in her position—and in her right mind—would decide in a second in favor of the Prince party. Harold Prince was one of the top producer-directors in New York. But she wasn't in her right mind, she was crazy— crazy about Jay. So it wasn't even a choice for more than a couple of seconds. Too bad, it would have been nice, but she put the regrets aside and concentrated on what to wear for him. Jeans. Jeans and a red-and-white striped T-shirt . . . jeans and a—

When the phone rang again, her premonition

sharpened, and this time she was right.

"Miranda, this is Jay," he began.

"I know who it is."

"Yeah. Listen, I feel really awful about this, but I'm not going to be able to make it."

"What?" She honestly thought she'd heard him wrong.

"I'm just not going to be able to see you tonight, Miranda. I'm involved in something I figured I could take care of in a couple of hours, but it's a lot more complicated than I thought. So, I don't see how I can—"

"You're canceling? You're canceling—now?"

"Miranda, believe me, if there was any way I could see you, I would. But I can't." He sounded perfectly pleasant, perfectly at ease, and she couldn't understand why he didn't have the grace at least to pretend he was sorry. "I can't get free."

As close to speechless as she ever came, she managed to say, "I see," then was reduced to silence.

Neither of them spoke for a moment or two, and then he asked, "Are you there?"

"Yes."

"Are we still friends?"

"Friends!" she repeated, summoning all the fury she was feeling. "Why shouldn't we be friends? Good night," and she slammed down the phone without giving him another chance to jolly her up.

Tears of outrage and of stunned disappointment balled in her throat until she thought she couldn't breathe. Squeezing her fingers into fists so taut she could feel her nails digging into her palms, she stood, rooted to the spot, eyes closed, overcome with despair, wanting to die, and the phone, when it rang, startled her. Hoping against hope that Jay had devised some way to come, she waited three rings and grabbed the phone. It was Anthony.

"Time's up, darling." His cheerfulness was an affront to her misery. "Are you coming with me?"

Marshaling her scattered emotions, she said, "As a matter of fact, Anthony, I *am*!"

"And what, may I ask, happened to young Mr. Harrington?"

"Oh, the evening got too complicated, so I backed out."

"Well, needless to say, *I* couldn't be more pleased. And you've made a fine choice, my dear, as you'll see in little more than half an hour when I pick you up. Can you be ready?"

"Sure!" she agreed, glad for an opportunity to drown her sorrows in celebrity.

"Randy, darling, we'll make it a real night on the town!" he promised, his charm in highest gear. "Now, why don't you wear that lovely mauve silk shirt with the portrait collar that we picked up at Bendel's." The Lagerfeld; he'd paid but let her promise to pay him back when she could. "And the silk pants we bought to go with it . . . and perhaps your hair up, you know, with just a few tendrils . . . "

Visions of her last night with Jay still danced in her head when the limo arrived a half hour later, but if anyone could brush them away, it was Anthony. If Jay was the dream lover, Anthony was the dream escort. Jay, when he actually materialized, could make you feel beautiful. But Anthony could make you feel like a star.

In the weeks since they'd been in rehearsal, both onstage and on his whirlwind circuit of parties and events, his attention, comprised liberally of both loving criticism and restrained praise, had changed the way she felt about herself. And, God, he was charming! Watching Anthony work a room was like going to charm school. She was far from forgiving him completely for the past, but she had to admit that for whatever reasons, he was doing his utmost to ensure her a stellar future. Anthony so thoroughly enjoyed being himself that you inevitably caught the enthusiasm; he gave an absolutely perfect performance as a man with no self-doubts. He showed her how confidence looked, provided her with a role model, and she'd proved to be a fast study. On his arm, in the best places, forcing herself to chat and smile and shine and pose, she'd made a bit of a splash, especially with the young, available men she inevitably encountered. All of a sudden, a lot of people wanted to know her better, not including Jay, who seemed to want to know her less. It was his growing private indifference in the midst of social success that she couldn't understand, and it tortured her.

Tonight Anthony guided her through the beautifully decorated, high-ceilinged rooms of the Princes' East Side town house, steering a course from group to group of Manhattan's most talented and affluent guest list. Seeing Robert Redford was a thrill, making small talk with him even more so. She'd wished she smoked so she could see if he would light her cigarette, but she didn't, and she had to settle for his bringing her a second glass of wine from the bar and resuming the conversation, until some heavyweight investment banker, whose kids went to the same private school as Redford's, broke in and took him away. She almost collided with Bob Fosse at the hors d'oeuvre table, and he, after looking her up and down, presented her with a smile that definitely indicated she'd met with his approval. Stephen Sondheim actually conceded her a good point in the middle of a spirited conversation. She watched Anthony embrace an endless stream of superstars from Angela Lansbury to Beverly Sills to Walter Cronkite, and basked in their reflected glow.

She had just been cornered by a middle-aged and over-celebrated novelist when, as if by magic, Anthony appeared, making her excuses to the writer, whisking her by their hosts to say good evening. They were quickly out the door and into the limo, and Anthony was giving the driver an address way downtown.

"Anthony," she said, a little high on wine and budding stardom, "where in the world are we headed?"

"To what I've been told is the new 'in' restaurant. It's a French bistro sort of place in SoHo, called Raoul's. I realize I'm much too elderly to make the new 'scene,' but I couldn't resist the impulse to dine out with such a lovely young lady!"

"Oh, Anthony, stop that. You're the best person in the world to be seen with, anywhere, as you well know," and she smiled sweetly. "I've been to Raoul's. It's a lot of fun."

As the limo made its way downtown, Anthony took her hand and said solemnly, "Miranda, we have so much to say to each other. So many grievances to air, so many misunderstandings to try to clear up."

"Oh, Anthony, let's not—" She felt good, very good, and she had no desire to come back to earth, but he broke in with, "My dear, I have no intention of dwelling on unpleasant things for the rest of the evening. Still, I feel I must say this. Miranda, you must never doubt your mother's love for you—or mine. Remember, you were very young when all that happened, and sometimes the very young misunderstand the actions of adults. Margo wanted you with us desperately, and I wanted you, more than you'll ever fully realize. We both fought to have you—in the courts, through a long and bitter struggle. It broke her heart when your father wouldn't permit her any contact with you whatsoever. She didn't forget you, Randy, far from it."

"Anthony, I really don't want to have this discussion."

"And so, my dear"—he patted her hand and smiled —"we shan't. This is the last thing I have to say: I pray every day that someday you'll forgive me, if that's possible. I hope it is. But more than that, even more than that, I beg you, Randy—implore you—to forgive Margo." He was so touching, so persuasive—you could see his face age with sadness, and with pleading. Who could doubt his sincerity? Who could doubt his love? It took all her strength of will to remind herself he was the greatest actor in the world, a man of complex and disturbing contradictions, a genius at make-believe.

Torn between wanting to trust him and the fear of being rooked again, she placed her hand lightly on his arm and told him she would honestly try.

The cab made a sharp turn, and she saw that they were on West Broadway. Formerly a ghostland between Greenwich Village and Wall Street, SoHo had recently became a bohemian center of artists' lofts, galleries, smart boutiques, and hot bars and restaurants. SoHo was where the smart set was moving. It was where Jay lived. In fact, it was Jay who had taken her to Raoul's.

"Ah, yes, that is it. Up ahead." Anthony was indicating a neon sign at the end of a narrow, curving side street.

As the limo pulled up at the curb, Miranda forced herself into the spirit of the evening and told Anthony, "I'm really looking forward to this. I think you'll have a wonderful time."

"Being with you, Randy"—he was actually kissing her palm—"how could I help it?"

The maître d' recognized Anthony and escorted them with a certain fanfare through the press of patrons crowded around the bar and on into the dining room. She scanned the diners, but saw no one she knew. It was only as they were being seated at a back banquette that she looked up and saw Jay, in a very private booth directly across the room, in a terribly crucial meeting with a bottle of Beaujolais—and a very striking brunette.

chapter 12

Jack
1984

ON A SATURDAY afternoon in May 1975, I was sitting in the orchestra of a little gem of a country playhouse called The Globe, entranced by the creatures of my imagining come wonderfully to life on the stage before me. Watching the rehearsal was confronting my future, but seeing Miranda up there, saying my lines, I found my thoughts wandering back into the past. So much had changed in the last couple of months that I looked back on March as if it were a dim memory from childhood. March. The last time things were simple. The month before Jay decided to open the Globe with *Up on the Heights*. Before Anthony decided to play the role of Eric, the vain actor—a great cameo as well as a lure for Globe subscribers. Before rehearsals had started in New York and we all became monomaniacs. Before the move to Connecticut only a few days before. Although my presence was not absolutely required, I'd finally explained to my New York circle, including a set designer I'd been seeing on a casual but stormy basis, that I was utterly useless in town and hightailed it up there. Jay had rented a huge, rambling house about ten minutes away from the theatre and stashed everybody in it. Anthony had been planning to stay there as well, but the offer of his own wing in the house of some extremely eminent friends had been too gracious to refuse; he arrived and departed via a neat cream-colored jeep in the style of Viscount Montgomery at Alamein. Jay was in and out so much I wasn't sure where he was staying. I suspected he slept in his office at the theatre because he couldn't bear to leave it, but of course he had access to his parents' exquisite house, and would occasionally invite the cast for tennis or a picnic or—when the weather got warm enough—for a swim. He spent a fair amount of time around the cast house, mixing with his people, making himself available to everyone on a regular-guy basis, and doing a pretty good job at it. It was a pleasure to work with him. Jay has always been the kind of man who engages people's attention, and at that point, with his looks and bearing and a boyish enthusiasm that took the hard edge off his overwhelming drive, he was playing the young king to a 'T': easy to talk to, properly respectful of the actors' and technicians' superiority in their chosen fields, always at ease with everyone in the company, with one exception—Miranda. The new Miranda.

For she was transformed—and suddenly radiant. A fairy-tale princess, but with the common touch. Her work with Anthony—and since that night at the Algonquin, he had pretty much preempted her—had given her confidence not only on the stage, but in the world, too. She was much more outgoing, much less intense and defensive, even spending what little free time she had making friends with the kids in the show. She looked different, too. She had become, all of a sudden, lovely, poised, a newborn temptress. And, quite frankly, she owed it all to Anthony. Through his monied female connections, he located the perfect hairdresser, the perfect gym, the perfect place for a facial and a massage. He taught her how to be snapped by the *paparazzi* who hang around outside the exclusive restaurants, "in" shops, and celebrity-studded apartment buildings. He honed her "struggling young actress" style to something smarter. Miranda was becoming, under Anthony's tutelage, a budding young personality amongst the Beautiful People, and once you saw her photo in a column or a magazine, you remembered her look and enjoyed it.

Naturally, the columnists had picked up on the story behind the story of Miranda and Anthony's reunion; given the bonus that she did resemble her mother, the two of them made great copy, and of course, great publicity for their coming theatrical endeavor. Their relationship, never clouded by innuendo, was a poignant one, both to the public and to those friends, like me, who knew her well. They weren't lovers; they weren't friends. It was as if Anthony had resumed the godfather role that had been assigned to him at Miranda's birth, righting the wrongs that had, for so many years, prevented the exercise of his duty. "I'm just so happy to be working," she'd told me, but I knew it was more than that. She had always dreamed of becoming a star, but had also feared it—with good reason, given her past. Now, for the first time, the dream seemed achievable, and in light of that, the fear receded. In a sense that seemed largely benevolent, Anthony Gainsborough was her dictator as well as her deliverer. He laid down the law, and she obeyed, and admiring the blossoming of my friend under his sway, I had to say more power to him. But if Miranda had become Anthony's Galatea, she had simultaneously become Jay's bête noire. One could easily deduce this from the fact that, around her, he behaved with the stilted politesse of someone in chronic discomfort.

Even before we'd moved to Tintagel, it had been obvious that Miranda and Jay weren't getting along. They didn't exactly avoid each other, didn't fight, but even when they were standing next to each other, it was as if they were glaring at one another across a frozen tundra.

Once we were all ensconced in Connecticut, thrown

together in a smaller, tighter community, more like a village than a city, their animosity was much more apparent. I'd suspected that Miranda was the instigator in the argument, that Jay's hostility was really counter-punching, but naturally I didn't ask. Finally, I didn't have to.

It happened one evening, after the conclusion of a marathon rehearsal that had lasted until nine. Everyone was famished, and plans were being made for a company pizza-fest at a place down the road, when Jay took me aside and asked me if we could talk privately. I said sure, then started to call ahead to the others to say we'd meet them at the restaurant.

"Um . . . Jack, I was sort of thinking about a longer discussion. Would you mind if we went someplace else and got a beer?"

It was, I think, the first time I'd ever seen Jay ill at ease. Telling the gang not to wait for us, we walked in uneasy silence the half block to the nearest watering hole.

It was the kind of place that hadn't changed in thirty years—even to the bartender-owner and the few elderly patrons, who must have started going there as young men and aged with the joint. There were red plastic booths and a jukebox that alternated Frank Sinatra singing "New York, New York" and "My Kind of Town," apparently for free—you never saw anyone play the machine. The three locals at the bar stared silently, like something from *Godot*, at the blank TV screen, waiting for The Game. Still, I was aware as we sidled up to the bar that, without glancing our way, they were checking us out.

The bartender himself took his own skeptical time in tearing his attention away from the blank TV. When he asked what he could get for us "gentlemen," I didn't think it was meant as a compliment, but ordered a Beck's. They didn't have it. We settled for a Bud. Jay outdid me by ordering a "Stoly-tonic," which sent the guy into a state of total bemusement. But Jay didn't give up, and labored until he finally made his order clear. Then he, too, settled for a Bud. But after the first two beers, when the conversation got serious, we added shot glasses of anonymous bourbon, thereby earning our stripes.

I had let Jay steer the conversation around to Miranda and how well she was doing in rehearsal, when he signaled for another round. Then, studying his glass, not me, he said, "I guess you've noticed that Miranda and I aren't getting along."

When I confessed to picking up a little friction between them, he looked at me point-blank and asked, "Does everybody know?"

"I have no idea, Jay. What's the difference?"

"Jack, friction in a company—it's a bad thing, a very divisive thing. All we need at this point is factionalism! God." He massaged his forehead with his fingers. "Why this had to happen . . ."

"Okay, Jay." I finished my bourbon and got down to business. "What *is* 'this'? What had to happen?"

"This . . . this feud with Miranda. It's a mess."

"What started it?" I asked him, feeling powerful because I was getting close to someone no one got close to.

He heaved a sigh. "Listen, Jack, I never talk about my personal life or the women I've been involved with. Never. But I've got to talk to someone about this, and you're the only one who can possibly help me."

"All right," I told him, "and it'll stay strictly between you and me. You have my word." I meant it. I liked Jay and I liked his confiding in me. This was male bonding—in the Redford and Newman sense.

"Thanks for saying that, old buddy." Jay slapped my back with unusual informality, and I realized to my shock that he was getting drunk.

I had lit a cigarette, my fifth in twenty minutes, when,

wrenching his concentration from the matter that preoccupied him, he leaned his elbow on the bar and looked sternly at me. "You really got to stop those cigarettes. They'll kill you."

"I know, Jay. But, come on, what happened?"

"What happened—" He laughed bitterly. "What happened was the ultimate nightmare! See—" He downed another shot glass, which the bartender was now refilling without asking. Had we wandered into some time-honored barroom ritual of male romantic confessions? With the never-empty glass as a major part of the ceremony? "See. Uh. Well, Miranda and I . . . well, we had a . . . um . . . thing after Sardi's . . . and then . . . well, things got complicated. You know, we started working together, and I guess I couldn't decide if it was best for the theatre and the company for us to have a thing that might not work out. Plus, I haven't been sure I wanted to take the responsibility of hurting her. Know what I mean?"

"Yeah, actually, I do."

"You know," he said as if the idea had just struck him, "it would have been a lot easier if Anthony hadn't hired her. Or maybe it wouldn't. Anyway, I decided to back off a little, but—I don't know—that wasn't working either." His handsome features were beginning to blur with booze and distress. "And—shit, Jack—I *like* her, and I like . . . being with her. Know what I mean? And I thought, maybe I rationalized, that keeping my distance wasn't the answer. So a couple of weeks ago, right before we moved up here, I called her for dinner. And she said yes. And I had the whole thing planned. We were going to have this great evening together. Maybe Lutèce. Maybe some place in my neighborhood —the whole package, when I'd pick up all the tabs, whether she liked it or not. So, I raced back from Connecticut and was getting ready to get dressed when—this is the truth, Jack, I swear it. There's this girl I used to go with. But she wanted the big commitment, and I didn't want to make it. So we broke up about six months ago, before I met Miranda. So the phone rang, and it was her, Stephanie. Very, very upset. She was crying and said she had to see me and she was coming right over. She sounded so upset I said, sure, come over, and I called Miranda to tell her I'd be late. But when Stephanie got to my place she was totally hysterical. She said she was suicidal, that my leaving her had driven her over the edge. I felt terrible. Really guilty. It took a lot—more than I wanted to give—to calm her down. And then, after what we'd done, I couldn't just get up and walk out, and Stephanie was begging me not to leave her that night, so I . . . um . . . called Miranda and canceled. What could I do, Jack? I mean, the woman was desperate!"

"So you lied to Miranda?"

"Not really." He gulped down his bourbon and continued. "I didn't really lie. I never said I was still in Connecticut. And I never said the problem was business. Maybe I didn't tell her the entire truth, but I didn't lie."

Deciding on a shortcut, I asked, "So how did she find out?"

"You're so shrewd, Jack." He slapped me on the back again. "You guessed she found out! You know how she found out, Jack?" He was leaning toward me, his arm still drunkenly draped around me. "She found out by walking into the restaurant where Stephanie and I were eating. Isn't that something? Do you believe that? Out of all the restaurants in New York, who would have believed that she and Anthony Gainsborough would pick that one?"

"That's some coincidence."

"Some coincidence, Jack, some coincidence. But—" and he leaned closer, lowering his voice to a conspiratorial whisper "—I don't think it was a coincidence. I think Anthony arranged it.'

I was shocked. "Jay, you're knocking back those bourbons too fast. How could he have? That's paranoid."

"Maybe." He took another slug. "Maybe not. I do know this: When Stephanie called, I was on the phone for a long time. Then, when she arrived, I turned on the service, but I heard the phone ring. Anthony had left a message that he was trying to reach me, but that the line had been 'engaged' for a long time. I don't know what he wanted, but I know what he found out—that I was home in New York, not in Connecticut, at six-thirty. He must have called Miranda about dinner *after* he knew I was in town, and she must have told him I was detained in Connecticut. He obviously didn't tell her different, but he knew she was assuming something that wasn't true—with my help. Okay, so he takes her out, and where do they go to dinner? To a place in my neighborhood, miles from where Anthony's staying, a place where I'd actually wanted to take him, back when we were negotiating. *Then*, it was too far downtown for him. Not the other night, though. He *knows* it's my favorite restaurant in SoHo. See the case I'm building, Jack? Obviously he couldn't have been positive they'd run into me with another woman, but it was a damned good shot."

"Really, Jay? You're sure you believe that?" I was honestly dubious.

"As sure as I can be. Since he's entered the picture and been wafting Miranda off to Wuthering Heights, he certainly can't be accused of trying to bring us together. I don't know what he's got against me . . . Something . . . " He fell into a silent brood.

"So?" I started up. "How did you handle things?"

"That night? I didn't even see them until we were walking out. I acted like a total asshole. I waved and kept on walking."

"What did you say to her the next day?"

"I . . . I came by rehearsal and drew her aside and

told her how terrible I felt. That . . . uh . . . that Stephanie was an old friend's girl friend, that my friend had dumped her and that she'd needed my help very badly. She took it with an absolute lack of reaction, very calmly, which I took to be a good thing. But when I volunteered to change my plans any time in the next week, Miranda said she was busy and walked away, and you see the results. She won't pay any attention to me."

"Bad break, Jay." I was beginning to slur my words, but through the haze, I did feel bad for him.

"She makes me so *mad*, Jack!" He slammed his fist for emphasis on the bar. "She disorients me. She makes me do stupid things. Like trying to make her jealous. And even that's totally futile because nothing makes her jealous. She just stands there and resents! I don't know what to do!" And he lowered his head into his hands, then lifted it. "Hey, listen, I'm going to the men's room. While I'm gone, figure out what I should do," and he rose and walked shakily into the Stygian depths of the room.

"You boys from the theatre?" For the first time, I became aware that the bartender and his customers had switched their attention from the TV screen to our conversation. They were galvanized. "You boys from the theatre?" one of the old codgers repeated with a southern New England twang.

"Yeah," I replied.

"Thought so," he said, and his cronies emphatically nodded their heads in agreement.

"Too bad," said the bartender, "but she'll get him, all right," and then they turned back to the TV screen. When Jay returned, it was as if the interlude had never been. He sat back on the stool, unaware of our audience. "One last round. Bourbon and sympathy." He chuckled at his own remark. "And then, to bed. So, Jack, what's the good advice?"

I had to wing it. "Jay, stop being angry. You're hurt. And she's hurt. You're not really mad at each other, you're just mutually wounded. Now, I know Miranda pretty well, and I think that, basically, she's a very forgiving person—if you don't approach her in anger or do anything to get her dander up. I'd just watch my temper and be as friendly as can be and ask her out to a movie or something.''

"She wouldn't go," he said glumly.

"Never hurts to try. I think she likes you, too, Jay. Just promise me you won't get mad at her.''

"I will, old buddy." He slapped me one final time on the back, pulled out a roll of bills, and slammed them on the bar. "In fact, I'll give you my word on it. I have no reason to be mad at Miranda. From now on, I'm going to be gentle as a lamb.''

But Jay was wrong—about having no reason to be mad at Miranda, among other things. As much as I'd grown to like him, and I had, too, over the rocky rehearsal period, I was aware of the dangerous self-deception implicit in his seemingly boundless confidence. He was more than just mad at Miranda, he was outraged over a lot of things he hadn't yet come to terms with, and he took it out in insensitive ways. Chief among the irritants, naturally, was Anthony. Jay had been making good progress with Miranda at first. But, enter Sir Anthony Gainsborough, Jay's golden banana peel, and suddenly, Miranda was transported away from Jay, to the stars, glamorized and heading straight for the cover of *Vogue*, adored and escorted by the world's greatest charmer. Up against Anthony's *éclat*, Jay felt like a beginner, in life as in art, and the awkward adolescence that his excellence had spared him surged to the fore.

Next to Anthony, he had no manners. Compared to Anthony, he was a crass and callous womanizer who was mainly out to win the pussy sweepstakes. As opposed to Anthony, he had no credits—theatrical, business, even military, since Anthony had been a hero in a "good" war whereas Jay's status as a student and a

Harrington had kept him out of Vietnam; instead he had staged antiwar theatrical events. Jay had been a leading man until the master scene-stealer appeared on the set. And Miranda's surrender (maybe mine as well) to the fabulous Gainsborough touch gave credence to Jay's worst fears about himself. Far from blaming him, I empathized. I couldn't help it. Not when I saw his perfect features blur with confusion and hurt when Miranda allowed Anthony to open doors for her, to hand her into limos, and to help her on with her wrap. With Jay, after all, she had behaved like a liberated woman who could damn well open her own doors, while, with Anthony, she'd become an eighteenth-century lady of the court. To Anthony alone she accorded the largesse of her proffered hand to kiss; to Jay she granted the meager gesture of a disinterested buss on the cheek. She and I talked as often as ever, if we saw each other less outside rehearsals, but when we talked, we never talked of Jay.

That silence, following peculiarly as it did on the heels of an initial rapture, was less confusing to me since Jay's disclosure about the debacle at Raoul's. Still, what *did* Miranda want? From Jay or Anthony? And if she was playing hard to get with Jay and using Anthony as the bait, the game was dangerous. Since Miranda rarely appeared on *his* arm, Jay had compensated by stepping up his conquest of the gorgeous female population of New York, one by one. Six-foot-tall models of indeterminate age (were they minors?) and startling beauty began appearing at the end of rehearsals, pressing close to Jay and dashing off with him to what clearly promised to be another in a series of long evenings of fun and games. In a matter of weeks, Jay had collected enough incomparably lovely women to start his own modeling agency. His bevy of beauties had become a running joke in the company, since no one could miss noticing. No one, that is, but Miranda. And, at odd moments, I thought I could see Jay notice her not noticing, could sense his disappointment, could almost feel his frustration. Miranda was now the "hot" person, a budding star before we'd even opened, while Jay was just another handsome rich kid. By the time we moved to Connecticut, her indifference and his feeling of intimidation had produced rage. But since Jay had called me in to save the day, I felt things would be better. He wouldn't act so angry, for starters. He'd given me his word, and his word was good, and that's why I was so surprised when, that May afternoon, at the end of rehearsal, I saw him stalking toward me.

"Jay," I said softly, "how's it going? With Miranda?"

"Miranda!" He was afire. "Miranda . . . Jack, if you know what's good for your little friend, keep her away from me, because, if I catch up with her, I'm going to strangle her."

chapter 13

Miranda
Connecticut, 1975

THE REHEARSAL HAD gone especially well. Miranda had felt it, from herself and from Steve, the young actor playing the leading role of Chris Motherwell. The action was flowing so naturally, she knew they were at least halfway there, that by opening night they'd be better than ready. Anthony, too, had seemed more satisfied than usual, breaking in less, smoothing out the rough spots fast and easily. As rehearsal ended, Steve asked her if she wanted to go down the street for a beer, but Anthony hurled his arm around her and marched her outside toward the jeep. Ever since rehearsals had begun in New York—no, before that, since the night at the Algonquin—Anthony had worked her like a demon. And it was hard to mind. He was magnetic and brilliant and as amusing as he'd been to her when she was a child; it was amazing how quickly they'd fallen into old habits, how their relationship seemed a natural continuation of those intense, exciting childhood times.

And then there was Jay. Jay, the spoiled brat who thought he was God's gift to the girls. Jay, who expected it all. Jay, who was all business and all pleasure, who wanted to be just friends and just lovers with every woman in the world. Jay, whose ambition made him capricious, whose single-minded dedication to himself made him a no-win emotional risk. Jay, who was currently engaged in seducing her best friend in the company, Charlene, the costume designer. Jay, who was even now marching toward the jeep, scowling.

"Jay, my boy!" Anthony called amicably as he prepared to hand Miranda into the jeep.

"Anthony"—Jay was very serious—"I've got to talk to Miranda. Now."

"Can't it wait, Jay? We were on our way to conferencing a scene." Anthony flashed a charming glance Jay's way, but it didn't make a dent in Jay's fury.

"No, I'm sorry. It can't wait." He was addressing his remarks strictly to Anthony, not even honoring Miranda with a look.

"Well, all right." Anthony relented under the firepower of Jay's anger. When he had retreated, Miranda flinched from the blowup that was obviously coming. She had seen Jay Harrington annoyed, out of sorts, but she'd never seen him mad.

"Darling," Anthony called as he jumped into the jeep and prepared to move out, "call me at home when you're finished with your . . . little talk." And blowing Miranda a kiss, he shot off, leaving her alone with Jay.

"So?" For some strange reason, she found herself with a smile frozen on her face as her body turned to stone, a rigid jeans-clad statue in the middle of an empty parking lot. "Jay," she asked, "what's this all about?" Her hand fluttered to her cheek. "I really don't understand."

He grabbed her wrist, wresting her hand from her cheek and gripping it tight. "Miranda, we're going to have a fight. A big one. Now."

"You're hurting my wrist." All the frustration of being so close to him, and of knowing that whatever was wrong must be her fault, diminished her voice to a whisper. In response, he loosened his grasp and led her to the black pickup he tooled around in. "Let's get out of here."

"Why? So no one can hear me scream?" All the stored-up anger over Charlene and his desertion rang out in the phrase.

"No. So no one can hear *me* scream! Get in!" He released her wrist and walked around to the driver's side.

So they drove and drove and drove. Down country lanes where, behind thick hedges, a hint of a mansion would sometimes appear, past lush fields and verdant foothills, sometimes driving in circles, but always in silence. When, abruptly, he turned down a path off a main road, she saw ahead of them his parents' house—a great, sprawling expanse of white clapboard and green awnings surrounded by expertly manicured lawns, with the tennis court stretching behind on one side, the swimming pool evident only when he made it up the driveway and turned off into the grass. It was that late afternoon hour when the sun gilds the edges of everything. With the trees already rich in foliage, the grass already a summer green, the setting was serene, glowing with affluence and meticulous care. She had been here before, but only with the company, although she had often daydreamed of being here alone with him. Not like this, though.

She watched him turn off the engine, then sit very still, bent over the wheel, fuming. Suddenly, he said, "Get out," and they both did. When he strode past her, she followed him, made obedient by her uncertainty, and they ended up on the patio behind the house, next to the swimming pool.

When he turned toward her, she could see the anger even plainer than before. Coming close to her, he said, "All right, Miranda. Let's just have it out, okay? No tears this time, right? Because this time, it ain't gonna work. Okay?"

With confusion and a vague kind of fear melding into scorn, she shot back, "Jay, if you want to have a fight, I'll be more than glad to take you on. But let's play fair.

You've got a gripe. So share it with me. What's the big problem?''

"The big problem, as you so casually put it, Miranda, is this: If you don't like me, don't like me. You're entitled to like who you want. I don't really understand the trouble you seem to have with me, but okay, so I don't. However''—and he visibly stiffened—"what you don't have the right to do is to undermine my professional competence.''

"Undermine your—what? Jay—'' She stared him down, eyes blazing. "What in the world are you talking about?'' But underneath the righteous indignation, she knew, all of a sudden, exactly what he meant, and with the knowing came a stab of betrayal and humiliation. She was caught. Trapped by her own naiveté and petty jealousy. Nailed, indicted, and sentenced to the chair. Maybe her face hadn't given her away, though, and she could still brazen it out.

But Jay, rigid with anger, fists clenched, pressed on. "And don't play dumb, Miranda. You're lousy at it.''

"Jay, please.'' She continued on her course, regardless, aware he might very well be beating her at her own game. "At least give me a chance to defend myself. Even in Russia, they tell you the charges.''

He wasn't moving, not a muscle, his rock-bound fury pinning her to the spot as well. In the old days, less than two fragile months ago, when they'd stood this close it had been exciting, an enthralling beginning. Now it was about fear, and embarrassment, and magic come to a screeching halt.

His brown eyes boring guilt into hers, he fumed, "Miranda, I'd like to know why you attacked my professional competence to Charlene.''

All right, the jig was up, and she had to think fast. To figure out how to salvage something from her moment of adolescent folly.

"I'd like to know,'' he continued, "how you felt justified in telling her I was . . . let me quote: 'unreliable, unprofessional, irresponsible, and a baby!' ''

Her resolve broken, regret sweeping through her, she could only murmur, "Oh, boy."

" 'Oh, boy'? Is that all you can say? Taking it upon yourself to pronounce judgment on my work—work that, I suspect, you know little or nothing about! Weakening my position with the people who work for me! Weakening the company, who you need as much as I do! If we're talking unprofessional here, I think you outran me forty ways to Sunday!"

And, suddenly, she got mad. "Now, wait a minute, Jay. Maybe *you* think it's professional to mix business with . . . pleasure . . . but a lot of people don't!"

"Just what do you mean by that, Miranda?"

"I mean—" She knew she shouldn't be doing this, knew she was losing control of her temper, but she welcomed the loss. "—I mean, when you cancel a business supper with Anthony, your director, and me, the leading lady—and you plead some super-important business meeting . . . and then it turns out that the 'big meeting' is with the blond bimbo in the box office—"

His eyes still blazed, but sheepishness had crept into his face.

"And don't *you* play dumb with me, Jay," she snapped, aping him. "*You're* lousy at it. Four people in the company saw you delivering your little package of goodies back to the house—at eight o'clock in the morning!"

"Oh, yeah?" He presented the words like a taunt, but half-heartedly.

"Yeah," she hurled it back at him. "Yeah. And Charlene—"

"Was one of the people who saw me with Janice. And she told you she saw me. And you lost your temper. And you told her exactly what you thought of me, right?"

"As a matter of fact, yes."

"So you really got mad."

"Of course I got mad!" She had some instinct that the tables were starting to turn, and giving her dramatic skills full rein, she sizzled. "Anthony and I needed to talk to you!"

"About what?"

"About money. About a new backer Anthony found. We needed you to talk about money, which is what you're supposed to be good at. When you're not riding in the thirty-eight C sweepstakes! Or am I wrong in thinking that another hundred thousand dollars wouldn't come in handy? From one of Tintagel's most distinguished citizens, who'd just happened to have invited us all for dinner!"

"Okay, Miranda." He shifted slightly, and his eyes narrowed with concentration. "If the dinner was about money, why didn't Anthony tell me? He didn't. I thought I was in for one of our fantastically interesting evenings for three where you hang on Anthony's every long-winded word and I just sit there feeling like a jerk!"

"He *did* tell you. You just didn't listen!"

"Bullshit, Miranda! He did *not* tell me."

"Well, maybe he wanted to surprise you!"

"Maybe." He paused, as if a thought had hit him. "Goddamnit, Miranda, I—don't—want—to—talk—about—Anthony Gainsborough. I've had it up to here with Anthony Gainsborough. I'm—I'm *bored* by Anthony Gainsborough."

"Bored? By Anthony?" She felt a stab of blind rage, or blind instinct, or the dawning of an insight. "I don't think you're the least bit bored by Anthony. I think . . . I think—" She was making a move, heading into the eye of the storm, heart suddenly pounding. "I think you're jealous of him!"

He met her gaze and growled, "You're damned right, I'm jealous!"

"I don't accept—" She stopped, shocked by what he'd admitted. "You . . . you are?"

"Yeah." He stood there, repentant, hands at his sides, eyes cast downward. "I'm jealous because . . . " Slowly, he lifted his gaze to her, his eyes softened, their golden flecks glowing. " . . . because, ever since Anthony arrived on the scene, I'm, like, not in the play anymore."

"Oh?"

His whole manner had relaxed; his fists had unclenched, and his hands reached out for her. "Miranda, please don't storm away until we finish this, huh?"

As if she could have, as if she would have.

"Look, I thought we had a . . . a good thing going, you and me, and then all of a sudden you start treating me like a slow-learning leper—and all over a silly little misunderstanding about a broken date! Quite frankly, Miranda, I don't think that *was* the reason. And I also think there's another factor here—the one person who's always involved in the fuck-ups: Anthony!"

"Jay, that's not—"

"Look, Miranda, I can understand the thing with you and Anthony. I mean, with your past and all. And I can certainly understand why you'd rather be going to A-list parties than hang out with me. But I just want you to appreciate the fact that there's one thing I can give you the big time can't."

Her hands still clasped by his, she murmured, "What?"

"This," he exclaimed, taking her in his arms and kissing her before she had a chance to push him away.

It was a young, white-hot kiss, demanding and imploring, and, oh, had she missed it! In the midst of it, consumed by it, she felt entirely safe, entirely sure of him, as if she were the only woman in his world. After the kiss, he just held her the way she needed to be held, his face buried in her hair, his arms clasping her close.

"Miranda, I've got a confession to make."

"Oh." She tried to pull back, but he held her fast.

"No, stay here. I was trying to make *you* jealous with the blond bimbo. And . . . um . . . with Charlene, too. And it hurts to admit it."

This time, when she tried to move back, he let her. "Really?" she asked, surprised.

"Yeah, really. And, look, don't blame Charlene for ratting on you. I got her drunk and forced it out of her. I practically threatened her. She felt terrible."

"Well . . . " She hesitated long enough to make him worry, before telling him, "Okay."

"Great."

"And Anthony's bringing our hosts by the theatre to meet you; the money's practically yours. Anthony's a great fund-raiser."

"So all's well that ends well, huh?"

She smiled at him. "I guess so."

"You know, kid"—he chucked her chin—"you play a great hard-to-get!"

"Coming from a master, that's high praise," she giggled.

"Hey," he said as a thought struck him, "before the bell rings for the next round, there's something I want to show you."

He led her into the house from the awesomely up-to-date kitchen through the exquisite nineteenth-century parlor, and beyond, into the center of the house, into what she now saw was a different structure, smaller, more primitive. "This is the original house," he told her. "It's really old—1700's. The additions were done in three or four stages—the last being ours. But this part was always my favorite."

They walked out into a tiny hallway, toward a narrow winding staircase. "Watch your step," he cautioned her. "The stairs take a funny turn, and they're tiny. Our ancestors must have had tiny feet to match the steps, like little kids. When I was a kid, I loved it. It was built to my scale. It was my own secret place. Come on."

Up the winding stairs they proceeded, and when they reached the top, they stopped before a closed door. "What's there?" she asked.

"My old room. From when I was a kid. I've been bunking here lately. I wanted you to see it." And he opened the door and admitted her.

It was a different world, one she'd never glimpsed before—a boy's room, a special kind of shambles, years in the making: Jay's museum of his own youth. Fading posters of baseball and basketball and football players, of rock stars and movie stars plastered almost every inch of the walls of the small, cozy room. Abounding on tabletops and windowsills were trophies for sports, lots of them, awards from school and college and camp for being the best of any number of things, photographs of senior proms and college festivals, the silvery gleam of sound equipment, shelves full of records, some full of books that must have been in place and unread since high school, two old-style black phones (had he always needed two?), a globe draped with a football jersey, a few framed pictures of Jay and beautiful girls, all of them dating from the sixties, a tiny TV set on top of the dresser, tennis rackets, tennis balls, barbells and hand-stretchers littering the perimeter of the room, and in the distance, an open closet filled to bursting with football helmets, boxing gloves, basketballs and footballs and baseballs, bats and badminton rackets, hockey sticks, golf clubs, sneakers, ice skates, and roller skates, all hurled into the closet at random. Clothes were squeezed together to make room for all the sports gear. The single bed, covered in a possibly twenty-year-old, brightly colored pattern of football players passing and receiving, was, at the moment, littered with papers. Stacks of more papers, but neatly arranged, were on the table at the foot of the bed. In the mock-ups of ads, propped against the wall, she glimpsed her name—a note of familiarity in an environment so male it was alien.

"You're the first non-family female who's been in this room since I smuggled Barbara Ann Henderson up here one night when I was fifteen."

"Oh?" she asked, turning from a black-and-white poster of Richard Widmark looking coolly psychotic. "How did it go with Barbara Ann?"

"Not as well as I'd hoped. Turned out she just talked big. When put to the test, she split—which was easy, because she was sixteen and had her own car."

"And that's really the last time a woman's been in here?"

"Well—" He contemplated the question as he tried to clear the bed so she could sit, since the room's single chair was piled with discarded clothes. "My parents always kept a place in the city, and after my sister and I went away to school, they moved there pretty much full time, so nobody's been around on a regular basis. The maids don't feel comfortable straightening up this room, mainly because I always intimidated them about losing something valuable. They'd change the sheets and get the hell out fast. Even my mom and my sister always felt that this was sort of off-limits. I guess it was."

Seating herself on the bed, she motioned him to sit beside her. "Well, I'm flattered."

"You should be." He grinned, kicking the empty soda cans out of the way. "I usually *don't* let people see this much of me." He had taken her hand in his, had interlaced his fingers with hers in a tight clasp. "Because . . . see, I've always been successful, you know, and I guess it's spoiled me some, but I'm—well, there's a large part of me that is solitary, that wants to be solitary and refuses to share. Maybe all guys are like that—I don't know. But, at least until now, that loner part of myself has always been very precious to me. And you threaten it."

"I do?"

"Yeah, and the thing is, the way you get through to me scares me, but it also makes me want to be . . . more scared."

All he had to do was touch her, and she fell toward him, floating through space, hoping he would catch her, thrilled when he did. Her fear, a mirror of his, transformed itself into intense desire, and on top of the faded football players, amongst the relics of a legacy she could never truly understand, they made love, laughed and trembled and talked a little dirty and sighed and tickled and clung, driving the fear away. As the afternoon turned to dusk, as the room grew darker, they binged on pleasure, wondering if the waiting and the hostility and the crossed signals and the fantasies had only enhanced their delight.

Finally, as they lay in each other's arms, happily forced into an embrace by the narrowness of the bed, he told her, "God, Miranda, what a time you picked to appear in my life. Just when I needed a nice, uncomplicated affair, you land in my lap, sparking and ready to explode." He hugged her, kissing her hair. "You drive me crazy, and you challenge every move I make. You're as stubborn as I am and just as unyielding. You're a total pain in the ass, to be frank about it, but I have to say no one has ever managed to penetrate my cool like you have. You make me mad, make me hurt, make me vulnerable, and I hate it, but I like it. Look, I still am who I am, and I'm not sure if I'll ever completely conform to what you want me to be, but I promise you this: I'll try. I'll try because . . . because as scared as I am of having you, I think I'm more scared of losing you."

"Oh, Jay," she whispered, wondering if it could all be that simple, if there were really happy endings, then, coming back to reality, she saw that the clock by the bed read seven-thirty. "Oh, no, look how late it is! I've got to call Anthony!"

"Sure, here's the phone." He picked it up from the floor and handed it to her.

With the phone resting on her stomach, she looked over at him and said, "Jay, I really do feel terrible about that thing with Charlene. Whatever happened, the least I can do is set her straight. After all—" she couldn't help a giggle "—we can't have people thinking you're a baby."

"You don't have to bother," he told her, picking up his jeans and heading off in the direction of the bathroom. "It's been taken care of."

"Taken care of?" she asked, suddenly wary. "What do you mean?"

"I took care of it." Although his tone was casual, his meaning was not.

"You took care of it?"

"Yeah, I took care of it last night." He was halfway out the door, but he turned back toward her. Raising his eyebrows in a Groucho leer and flicking an invisible cigar, he asked, "What else could I do to prove I was a grown-up?"

chapter 14

Jack
1984

MIRANDA AND I HAVE always referred to the opening of *Up on the Heights* as The Great Blur. Even at the time, at the apex of our delirium, we must have suspected that we'd remember little of the most important night in our lives. Still, over the course of the years, so many nuggets of memory have popped into our minds, fuel for the fires of our nostalgia, that together we've arrived at a fairly accurate reconstruction that, to this day, chills and amuses us both. I do vividly recall how we careered through the last two weeks of rehearsal, exhausted with anticipation, thrilled by terror.

We were to open on the Sunday night before Memorial Day—black tie, mind you—to what was shaping up to be a full and celebrity-studded house. Jay was proving himself a damned good CEO. With opening night and the following two performances the next day all sellouts, and the season subscriptions coming in at a rate that exceeded even Jay's most optimistic predictions, we were building an audience, if all went well, not only from the neighborhood theatregoers, but also from people as far away as Boston, New Haven, and New York.

The fact that we didn't have to worry about playing to an empty house should have relieved us, but it seemed only to sharpen our fear that all those people would snore or jeer or walk out, never to return. Given the accelerated rehearsal schedule, we weren't having previews, and Anthony had insisted on a closed dress rehearsal, so we were going into the lists untested. Still, given the rigor of those final days, we would certainly be battle-ready.

By the last week, the countdown was definitely in effect. The set was being finished around the actors as they rehearsed; then, when they completed a scene, they would rush off to a costume fitting, rush back for a lighting rehearsal, get the last-minute script changes that Anthony had suggested after the previous rehearsal and that I would have dashed off to write, then once more dash off to learn the lines. We were all dashing somewhere, racing toward The Great Blur with a frenzy that kept us too wired even to worry about physical collapse.

By the Friday before opening, I was up to three packs of cigarettes a day, had lost ten pounds, and was a classic nervous wreck. I guess the ditzed-out playwright is a time-honored theatrical tradition, though, because everybody was very gentle to me, as if they were afraid I'd have a breakdown or kill myself before Sunday at seven. Fat chance! Despite my haggard appearance, I was humming with excitement, overflowing with energy. Nothing existed for me but Sunday night, not world events, not art, not sex. At that point, I had no private life. My love object was *Up on the Heights*, a passionate obsession that made my days and nights fevered but pure.

Not so Miranda. Whatever had happened between her and Jay the day he wanted to strangle her seemed to have changed them both for the better. With work consuming them, they appeared, nevertheless, to be closer than they'd seemed before the preopening frenzy began. A couple of times after rehearsal, I saw him whisking her off in the pickup before Anthony could claim her, had actually observed them sitting together by the pond one afternoon, not even holding hands, but seeming very intimate, but that was about it. Whatever Jay and Miranda had worked out, they were definitely being discreet about it.

Yes, they were very discreet, but not discreet enough for Anthony. With that splendid second sense of his, he seemed to have intuited the very moment when Jay and Miranda got together. Despite the secrecy, he guessed, and he wasn't pleased. He had invited me to have a drink with him late one evening, and I'd been pretty sure it was to press me about Miranda, which, of course, he did, in so concerned and sincere a fashion that it took all my willpower not to squeal.

With remarkable consistency, I'd ended up in the same bar where I'd gone with Jay to talk about Miranda, but with Anthony involved, it was a different experience.

If the bartender remembered me, he didn't indicate it or, at least, didn't bother to acknowledge it. Anthony was, once again, stealing the show. What a crowd-pleaser! There was no room in the world Anthony couldn't work.

The bartender, seeing Anthony and me approach one of the tables opposite the bar and sit, immediately abandoned the baseball game on TV and came right over. If Jay and I had tried to get table service, we'd probably still be waiting to order. But Anthony's magic had transformed the man into *mein* host. He was courteous, he was attentive, and he even managed to come up with a bottle of better-than-average brandy. Whether he and the other old codgers actually recognized Anthony as Anthony or whether he was a famous face to whom they couldn't assign a name or whether he just radiated stardom, he was clearly the most luminous presence ever to patronize the establishment. And the regulars rose to the occasion: They suddenly had developed too much class to eavesdrop. We were allowed the luxury of absolute privacy. Anthony waited until we had each downed a second brandy to begin the interrogation.

"You know, Jack," he began casually enough, "sometimes I wish I were a youngster again. Given the extravagant bouquet of nubile American womanhood with which I'm surrounded, only the sad awareness that I am more than old enough to be the father of these beauties keeps me from being an absolute rake. But if I were your age, or Jay's . . . By the way, what's happened to that petite flirtation between him and the little costume girl . . . Charmaine, I think it is."

"Charlene," I volunteered.

"Charlene. Yes, of course. Charlene."

"I don't really know, Anthony."

"But I don't see them together."

"No," I concurred. "I guess it didn't work out."

And then, RAF ace that he was, he dive-bombed in with, "And who's he seeing now? Come on, Jack, don't squirm. Just because I've got a sir before my name doesn't mean I don't dish the dirt like the common man." He was fairly twinkling with charm. "Where I come from, gossip's an ancient and honorable activity. Americans feel some guilt about gossip that Europeans never do. Now, who is Jay's current lady fair?"

I sipped my brandy, trying to look dispassionate. "I think . . . nobody special. Gosh, I don't know any more about Jay's private life than you do, Anthony." And it was nearly true. I only suspected more. "But, God, Jay's certainly got a lot on his mind right now. Maybe he's taking a break or something."

"Do you think so?" Anthony signaled for another round, which, given the fact that the room was already beginning to swim very gently, would make my performance that much more difficult.

"Perhaps you're right," Anthony was saying. "Perhaps you are. I must say, I'm rather relieved that his little romance with Miranda seems to have come to nothing, aren't you?"

Sloshed as I was, giving what I'm sure was a ludicrous

burlesque of a sympathetic nod, I was convinced that Anthony's relief was a posture. His real feelings had nothing to do with relief—they were comprised of suspicion and hostility.

Still, I was puzzled by his purpose in quizzing me. Was he looking for confirmation or denial of the affair? Did he seek the truth, or did he want to be lied to?

"So"—Anthony shrugged—"we have to believe it's all for the best. And you must agree the young man has certainly proved to be the roué I warned you he was. Hardly a good candidate for stability, and Miranda must have stability. Especially when she must expend every ounce of her energy and passion right there on the stage of that theatre. In fact, for the next few years, until she really matures as a talent, I suspect any kind of intense emotional involvement would be a dangerous distraction for our Miranda. You know, having the kind of talent that she does—and, of course, you do know, my boy—is a mixed blessing. At least, when it comes to leading a normal life. Awesome, the sacrifices that talent demands!"

"So you can't be great *and* happy?" I articulated each word carefully to avoid slurring.

'Well, it's extremely difficult, my boy. I'm loath to make this point, but I must: Miranda's mother was a victim of that truth." His eyes misted over; I could see that clearly, even in the dim light. "She thought she could have both, greatness and happiness—no, that she *deserved* to have both. It was her fatal folly, all that trying and failing and blaming herself. And there was nothing, nothing, I could do to make her realize the error of her aspirations. Finally, it drove her mad. Finally, it killed her. You know, it would kill *me* to see Miranda pursue the same treacherous path."

And then, despite my stupor or because of it, things began to make sense, and I felt my compassion flowing out to the dazzling but disappointed man across from me. Of course, Anthony's concern about Miranda was a refraction of his distress over Margo! It was that tragic history and the unspeakable fear of its repetition in her daughter that so plagued him. I wanted to ease his pain, wanted to convince him his fears were overblown by his personal past, and that that past had embittered him and twisted his perception of reality. I wanted to assure him that Miranda's relationship with Jay could be good, could be benevolent, that the contentment she was sharing with him made her glow, offstage and on, and that, if anything, they got along better when they were both busier. I wanted to point out that Miranda hadn't missed one rehearsal, hadn't ever come in late or underprepared, either before she and Jay got back together —for I was sure they had—or now. I wanted to convince him that if Jay loved her, he loved her talent, too, because it was so much part of her, and that he would nurture it. I'd already watched him at rehearsals, beaming with pride and pleasure at her brilliance.

So I wanted to implore Anthony to trust them, and not to worry, but something stayed me, some instinct that plugged up my declaration before it could come spewing out. Suddenly, I found myself struck with the notion that, in ways I'd probably never be able to substantiate, Anthony *had* played a hand in driving Miranda and Jay apart, just as Jay claimed, and although it had been done for the best of reasons, I didn't want it to happen again. I doubted that Miranda suspected Anthony's involvement, doubted that even he himself suspected it, at least consciously, but I had no desire to open up old wounds again.

I likewise kept quiet about repeating to Miranda Anthony's veiled warnings about the sacrifices required of greatness. In fact, I made it my policy to convey no messages and ask no questions. What Anthony only suspected couldn't hurt him or anybody else, and confirmation of those suspicions only risked turning the opening night jitters of the greatest actor in the world into a Shakespearean tempest.

And so, when I heard the bombshell news that, at 7:00 A.M. the day of the opening, Anthony had called Miranda at the cast house and been told by someone who happened to answer the phone that she had last been spotted heading off in Jay's pickup late the night before and still had not returned, I expected an answering salvo from Anthony. And I wasn't to be disappointed. Even so, I would be stunned by the force of that response, for, yet again, Lord Gainsborough was preparing to unleash a thunderbolt that would strike us all.

chapter 15

Miranda
Connecticut, 1975

"HOW DO YOU FEEL?"

"Funny. How do *you* feel?"

"Funny."

"Funny how?"

They had both awakened at the ungodly hour of six-thirty on Sunday morning to find themselves clinging to each other with ferocity. "Like at eight o'clock tonight, I'm going to my coronation or my execution or both," Jay said. "And yourself?"

"Queasy. Wired. Terrified. But you make it better." She confirmed the compliment with a kiss. When he kissed her back, it was with serious intent.

"How about one last anonymous roll in the hay before we become celebrities and get our names in the columns every time we so much as walk down the street together?"

"I'll deny everything." She pressed her body hard against his.

"They'll never believe you," he whispered back as he rolled her gently under him.

"Wanna bet?" She raised her arms, encircling his neck, urging him down to her.

"Depends."

And, as they kissed again, she ran her hands slowly down his back, savoring the power of his body, feeling it calm her even as it excited her. "Umm, you feel good." She had inclined her head ever so slightly so he could nuzzle her neck. "You're better than Valium!"

Raising himself above her, he smiled and said, "And you're better than—" but the shrill of the phone stopped him.

"Oh, Christ!" He dropped down beside her, reaching for the receiver, obviously panicked by the prospect of a theatre in flames or a death in the cast. "Hello! Hello!" The bed was so narrow and the voice on the other end of the phone so unmistakable that Miranda could hear every word that Anthony said.

"Jay, Anthony Gainsborough here. Sorry to be calling so early. Hope I'm not waking you."

"No, no, I was up. What's wrong? Is something wrong?"

"No, not really. Nothing major, in any case. Actually, I was trying to reach Miranda and was told she might be with you. Could I speak with her?"

"Sure, Anthony."

The terror in Jay's face had subsided; now it was she who was shaken. As he started to hand her the phone, she emphatically shook her head no, then silently mouthed, "Call me."

"Uh—just let me call her." Jay picked up the cue, then shouted as if to someone in another room. "Miranda . . . " then waited, then called again, then announced, "Oh, here she comes!" After allowing time for a person to cross the room, he said distinctly, "It's Anthony. For you," and gave her the phone.

"Anthony!" She tried to sound slightly out of breath.

"Darling Miranda! I've been looking all over for you! They told me at the house that you hadn't yet come in." His voice churned with concern.

"Oh, well, you know, I just wanted to be by myself last night, and Jay was kind enough"—she arched her eyebrows at Jay in self-mockery, feeling sheepish and silly—"to offer me the use of one of the guest bedrooms here."

"Well, dear, I hope you got a good night's sleep and that I haven't disturbed you too dreadfully." He sounded as if he'd bought her story. "Now, what I wanted, sweet, was to change a bit of business in the first-act curtain. Came home from the dress, fell into the soundest sleep of a lifetime, woke up with this positive brainstorm, and am mad to try it out. Could you meet me at the theatre straightaway? I'm leaving right now."

"Of course, Anthony," she said. "I'll be there in . . . in about half an hour."

"See you then, darling."

"Yes, see you then." She hung up the phone and reached for Jay, who was sitting up on the edge of the bed. When he didn't respond, she was puzzled. "Jay," she urged him, but he didn't turn around, and when at last he did, his playful mood had vanished. "What's wrong with you?" she teased him lightly.

"I'm pissed, Miranda. I'm really pissed."

"Why? Just because of that interruption? It's nothing. You know what he's like—"

"I know what he's like, all right, I know what he's like, but sometimes I think I don't know what you're like."

"What do you mean?"

"Miranda, why do we have to lie and sneak around and act like adulterous lovers to please Anthony or spare Anthony or whatever it is? I don't know why this has to be such a big secret! There's nothing illegal or immoral about our seeing each other. We're not married to other people. We're not even involved with other people. In the ordinary world that I come from, people celebrate things like this, they don't hide them! Why do we have to?''

"Jay—" She grabbed his hand. "It's just until tonight. After tonight, it'll be fine. We won't have to pretend. I just—well—I get the feeling that Anthony is more confident right now thinking that there's nothing in my life but this performance. He's very big on conserving energy. But you'll see, after tonight everything will be different."

"I don't think so." Frowning, he avoided her touch. "I think that tonight, there'll be another reason why we shouldn't tell Anthony. And after that reason, there'll be a different reason. And on and on. Jesus Christ, Miranda, can't you resist him? Did he hypnotize you or something?"

"You seem to forget, Jay"—she heard her voice growing stern—"what Anthony and I have been through together."

"I couldn't possibly forget, even if I wanted to, Miranda. You keep reminding me." He got up, grabbed some underwear from an open suitcase on the floor, and his jeans, which were slung over a chair, and started dressing. "You and Anthony are more dedicated to the painful past than you are to the future. Well, the past is over, Miranda; it's over and done with. Let it run your life if you want to, but I'm not going to let it run mine."

"Just what is it you're trying to do? Force me into making some kind of crazy choice?"

"Goddamnit, Miranda, it *is* a choice! And it isn't crazy. And it also isn't something I could force you to do, even if I tried. Because I really don't believe you're ever going to risk doing anything you think might displease Anthony—you're too damned intimidated by him. Jesus, for somebody you loathed a couple of months ago, he certainly ranks high on your list. But, look, maybe I'm wrong. I hope I am. Because if I have to continue to sneak around behind his back every time

I want to see you, I'm, going to get very angry, and eventually, I'm just not going to be there. I feel like I'm committing treason just by holding your hand! Miranda, I'm trying to change—for you. The least you could do is return the favor!''

"So this is an ultimatum?"

"Yes, I guess it is. Make up your mind, Miranda. For once." Engrossed in tying his sneakers, he didn't even bother to look up.

"Well—" She rose in a huff. "—you certainly did pick a fine time for this. As if I'm not nervous enough!"

"And I'm not? It's *my* fucking theatre, Miranda. And don't worry about getting too upset to perform just because of a trivial matter like us! Just go see Anthony. He'll incant a magic spell, and all your cares'll fly away." He grabbed a T-shirt and his car keys and walked to the door. "And you'd better step on it," he told her as he disappeared. "We wouldn't want to keep Anthony waiting!"

Somehow, Sunday passed. It both crept and flew by, bathing the company in a fevered glow compounded of impatience and dread. Catching the reflection of her own heightened state in everyone around her, buoyed by the commonality of feeling, Miranda took courage and pressed on. So, somehow, Sunday passed, despite its troubled beginning.

The ride to the theatre that morning with Jay had been made in hostile silence. He brooded while she simmered, but neither of them seemed to have any more words left in them. In the short and tempestuous time that they'd been with each other, she'd feared that their every time together would—by some dreadful stroke of karma or temperament—be their last. She had feared losing him long before she'd really had him, was sure that every demand she'd made would send him straight out of her life. That it hadn't happened, that he'd stayed, had boosted her personal confidence as much as Anthony's extraordinary instruction had enhanced her professional pride. They had come, she'd felt, to a place where the pressures lessened, where an easy trust had allowed them to be themselves in the best way. And now, out of the blue, Jay, the artful dodger himself, had turned it all upside down by demanding from her some gratuitous proof of fidelity.

Maybe he even had a point. Maybe, looking back, she would one day appreciate that his demanding was an act of love, and further, that the conflict had to happen when it happened because one aspect of intimacy is the freedom to fight it out personally in public panic situations. But she still resented his timing; this was the one day of her life when she had earned the right to have it all.

As they'd approached the theatre, she asked him if she would see him later and was shocked, after so long a silence, by the sound of her voice. He'd been very distant, told her there was so much to do; the caterers were coming to set up the opening night party at his parents' house, and he'd probably be running back and forth all day. When she'd asked him if he wanted to grab something to eat in the late afternoon, he'd told her not to count on him, then, after allowing her to peck him on the cheek, he waved at Anthony, who was waiting on the front steps, and drove off, leaving her feeling weepy.

After Jay's ironbound indifference, Anthony's verve and energy were a joy. He strode to meet her and caught her in an effervescent embrace. "And how are we feeling?"

As he released her, slipped his arm around her, and walked her into the theatre, she'd told him, "Anthony, I feel like I've never been on a stage before!"

"Oh, my darling," he'd chuckled, "that's how one's supposed to feel! Trust an old trouper like me! I could

write a scholarly monograph on stage fright, believe me
. . . You know, Randy"—her childhood nickname, so
unfamiliar for so long, was now such a comfort—
"people say that without stage fright there wouldn't be
performance. Over the years, I've come to agree with
that."

"Really? Why?"

He paused at the back of the spanking new, still
darkened auditorium. "Because I've finally accepted
that the jitters are a massive buildup of artistic juice
that actually propels one into performing, that sends
one onstage raring to go, bursting with energy, and
needing the release of creativity. So, dear, get as nervous as you want, because you *have* been on stage
before, no matter how you feel right now, and you'll
be on countless stages from here on, but you'll always
feel like a neophyte on opening night. Randy, there are
no stars ten minutes before curtain—everyone's a rank
amateur!"

He'd turned on the houselights, then marched down
the aisle and jumped gracefully onto the stage, disappearing to turn on the stage lights. That done, he walked
to stage center, opening his arms toward her. "Come
on! Time's flying, and we've got work to do!"

He was a fabulous man, posing fabulously. The khaki
gabardine slacks over Lobb loafers, the simple oxford
cloth blue-striped shirt with the sleeves perfectly rolled,
the baby-blue cashmere tied casually about his shoulders—he was classically handsome. If Jay was a photograph from a smart men's magazine, Anthony was a
painting from a great collection. Shorter than Jay, but
tall for an actor, he was fit—and tested; you could see it
in the fine lines of his strong and aristocratic face, in the
silver streaking at his temples. He was a man who had
pleasured and suffered, who had grown wise with fame
and the pain of living, whose humor was seasoned,
whose manners were natural. God, how she'd missed

him all those years! She hadn't even realized how much until now, until these moments when his very presence warmed her, making it all better. It was like being a child again, for nobody then—and nobody now—could contain her fears as Anthony could.

They worked all day, on fixing the first-act curtain, on some other last-minute reblocking, on a brilliant inspiration for a lighting change, on a costume fitting, on a million tiny corrections and completions that, necessary or not, gave them something to do. Anthony's phenomenal intensity allowed him to concentrate on three or four things at once, and through the whole frenzied day, he was always there for her, bolstering her spirits, lavishing on her the breadth and scope of his experience. How she adored him! How could she wound him, especially in the childish fashion that Jay was so bent upon? Yes, upon reflection, *childish* was the key. Anthony was a grown-up, and Jay simply wasn't, and it was a man's support she needed today. So the fact that Anthony was the one by her side, while Jay kept his distance, seemed appropriate. For today. By tonight, when the performance was over and the jitters were gone, she could convince Jay that things didn't have to be so black and white. Things *would* work out, she knew they would. And when four o'clock came, she felt better, slightly more calm than she'd expected. But, at four-thirty, when she and a bunch of people, including Anthony and Jack, went down the street for something to eat, she was first annoyed by Jay's failure to join them, then upset that he hadn't stopped by during the meal, and, by the time they all headed back to the theatre, crushed by his absence.

As if reading her thoughts, Anthony chose then to ask, "And where's our Jay?"

"Jay?" She tried to say it lightly, as if the question of his whereabouts hadn't occurred to her. "I don't know. Probably locked up in his office or something."

"Uh-uh-uh, my girl!" He shook a finger at her, reproving. "Don't try to feign indifference with me! Have you two had a spat?"

She sighed, glad to be able to talk about it, "Yes. Yes, we have. We always seem to be having . . . spats."

"Well, Randy"—he took her hand affectionately as they strolled—"I just don't want you blaming yourself. Jay is, let me say, one of the finest young men it's been my pleasure to work with, *but* . . . but he is . . . *cocky*. Shouldn't think he'd be at all the type a strong and spirited woman could easily get along with!"

Cocky. That was true, Jay was cocky. And arrogant, spoiled, and willful. The kind of guy who expected a woman to do his bidding. Well, she wasn't prepared to be anybody's slave, that was for sure! Screw him! Now, only now, she was beginning to understand the real significance of his apparent capitulation to her demands. Sure, he'd agreed to being her—oh, God, "boyfriend"! —but only in exchange for her submission to his being the boss. Once a male chauvinist, always a male chauvinist. Remembering their first, terrible encounter at Harrington's, she condemned herself for forgetting what he'd shown himself to be the instant they met. Well, if he never spoke to her again, it would be a blessing, a profound relief. At least she could be her own person again!

Still, when she climbed the stairs and entered the dressing room she shared with another actress, she was disappointed that, although there were lots of flowers and notes and telegrams waiting for her, there wasn't anything from Jay. As she applied her makeup and bantered with Sue, the other actress, she tried to make herself not think about Jay, but every time someone came to the door with more flowers she started, hoping they were from him. They weren't.

At about six-thirty, when she was sitting at her makeup table, staring into space, one of the kids appeared with two bouquets of flowers, one for her, one for Sue, both from Jay. The notes were identical, wishing them love and luck, and although Sue was thrilled at being remembered so personally by Jay, Miranda felt deeply slighted.

By the time it got close to seven, her dresser had helped her into her opening costume and she was sitting quietly, breathing deeply as she sipped the honeyed tea Anthony had prescribed for the sore throat he had accurately predicted would develop forty-five minutes before curtain. A few moments before, Sue had given her a warm good-luck hug and disappeared, graciously allowing her a chance to be alone, and now, the knock on the door startled her. She was sure it would be Jay, but it was Jack, his ashen face frozen in a rictus smile, looking fragile but darling in his dinner jacket. They hugged each other, wordlessly, each feeling the other trembling, hanging on for dear life. When they parted, he took both her hands in his and said, "I love you. *And* you're going to be great!"

"I adore you, and your play. And your genius. I'm gladder that I know you than you'll ever know."

"It's mutual," he replied warmly, "and it's maudlin," he added, dismissing the affection. "See you later." He pecked her lightly on the lips. "And break a leg," he called from the doorway, blowing her a final kiss, then turning to go, tripping over something or other, righting himself, making a clown face, and disappearing.

Anthony arrived on the heels of the first call, in full costume and makeup, wreathed in smiles.

"So here we are! All ready to go!" He grabbed a folding chair, placed it opposite hers and sat. "You look radiant, my dear. Radiant." He took her hand and kissed the palm, then gazed up at her and murmured, "Now, we'll remember that new cross to Steve at the end of Act I? And the little speech Jack gave us this P.M. We won't forget that, will we?"

"Of course not, Anthony. Please don't worry. At

school, even the directors who didn't love my acting worshipped my memory. I'm famous for it. You needn't be concerned," she reassured him.

In response, he tossed back his leonine head, laughing. "You see, darling. You see: I'm every bit as terrified as you are! Probably more so!" Patting her hand, he crooned, "But many thanks for the assurance."

"And Anthony"—she met his gaze—"thanks for being . . . everything you are." The love and intimacy and shared hope in their mutual glance made her want to be good for him, to be great for him. It was such a pleasure to please him.

"And now, darling . . ." He broke off that very private moment by reaching into his jacket pocket. "I've a little something for you." Fishing out a small package wrapped in red tissue paper, he announced, "This is the present I gave your mother on the opening night of the first play we did together, *The Winter's Tale*. It was my first gift to her, and I know she'd want you to have it as much as I do."

She accepted the package, looking from it to him and back. "Oh, Anthony," she exclaimed.

"Well, open it, Randy!" And slowly, carefully, she did, to find the thinnest of gold chains, from which were suspended tiny interlocking gold comedy and tragedy masks, inset with chips of diamond and ruby. Her obvious joy delighted him, for he veritably preened as he told her, "One of a kind! I designed it myself for your mother! But don't be worried about the value—it's mainly sentimental, since the stones are only chips. Later, as one grew more solvent, the stones got larger. But this was at the beginning, and so it seemed utterly appropriate for you, a brilliant young actress soon to follow in her mother's sublime footsteps. Here, let's put it on you. Let's see. Perfection! Oh, darling, Margo would be so proud of you!"

"Anthony—" She sensed they were both close to

tears, both celebrating and mourning a past as they stood on the brink of a whole new future. "Anthony, this means so much."

"As you have come to mean so much to me," he said softly, seeming to move toward her, then to pull back, until his momentary indecision resolved itself into a brave, new embrace. "Just let me hold you, my darling," he murmured. "I promise I won't muss your makeup. Just let me hold you tight!"

She closed her eyes and felt him clinging to her, knowing that it was both her and Margo whom he held, happy to provide the comfort and relieved that, for the moment, she didn't have to stand alone. And it was in that moment, that last bit of benevolent surrender, that Jay appeared, surprising them in each other's arms.

"Am I interrupting something?" he called from the doorway. Immediately, she and Anthony broke from the embrace, and Anthony, looking none too pleased, said, "Actually, Jay, you *were* interrupting something. A time-honored thespian rite to be exact." He was smiling merrily now. "The pre-curtain hug was probably a tradition when they opened *Oedipus Rex* in ancient Greece. Now, what can we do for you, my boy?"

"I'd like to talk to Miranda, Anthony."

"Dear boy, we're only moments away from curtain!"

"I'd like to talk to Miranda. Alone, Anthony."

"Jay," the older man persisted, "I have to caution her against any encounter that could prove upsetting."

"I want to see Miranda."

"And I don't want—"

"Anthony," Miranda broke in, "I can handle it. Really, I'll be fine."

In return, Anthony shrugged his shoulders grudgingly, preparing to withdraw. "Well, if you must. But don't be long about it."

"No, I won't. I promise. See you down there!"

Jay had moved out of the doorway to let Anthony

pass, and as he prepared to leave, he muttered to Jay, "Don't you go getting her upset!" and then stalked out.

Jay didn't go to her, just shut the door and stood beside it, tall and tanned and dinner-jacketed, looking like a million dollars. "So how're you doing?"

"As well as can be expected," she said, smiling. "How about you?"

"Ditto." And then began a long, awkward silence, which she, despite her nervousness, broke by rising and motioning him to come to her. "Jay, I'm really glad you came."

"You are?" He looked surprised. "I . . . um . . . I . . ." He paused, then, at the same time, they both blurted out, "I'm sorry about this morning," then laughed at their walking on each other's line.

"Bet I'm sorrier than you." His fingers traced the lines of her features without touching them.

"Bet you're not." She stared him down, then laughed, "Oh, God, let's not fight about it!"

"Yeah, let's not." He placed his hands lightly on her shoulders, drawing her closer, but with their bodies still not touching.

"Is it going well?" she asked, surprised by the depth of her concern for him.

"Yeah, that's what's so frightening. It's all too smooth. Mom and Dad just arrived, and we've been downstairs greeting the celebs . . . God, Miranda, there're a lot of celebrities down there!" It was then, for the first time, that she saw the nervousness beneath the cool manner, felt the fear he hid better than anybody, and the youth and the vulnerability, and with that vision came a rush of unexpected affection.

"Just don't tell me any famous names or I'll vomit!" she joked.

"Not in my theatre, you won't. I'd never allow you to throw up on my sets and my costumes."

"No?"

"Definitely no."

"Okay. You win. So?"

"So can I kiss you with all that gook on your face?"

"Well," she mused as she came into his arms, "since you're the boss, I guess I'll have to permit you a light peck on the lips."

"Better than nothing," he grumbled, but the peck turned into more than a peck, and when they separated, she looked at him and broke up. "Hey, you look great in my lipstick!"

"Huh?" He panicked, checking himself out in the mirror. "That's all I need. To greet the patrons wearing makeup!"

"I'll get it off," she calmed him, searching for a Kleenex and the cold cream. In the process, she caught a look at herself wearing Margo's necklace. "I guess I can't wear this onstage," she said. "Would you undo the clasp?"

"With pleasure." He grinned, seizing an excuse to kiss her neck.

"Do you like it? Anthony gave it to me." She dipped a balled-up Kleenex in the cold cream and was reaching up to wipe the makup off his lips. "Don't cringe! It won't hurt . . . There. See, it's all gone. Now, I'd better fix my own face."

As she was reapplying lipstick, Jay was examining the necklace. "Present, huh?"

"Anthony gave it to my mother on opening night of the first play they ever did together. I was very moved that he would give it to me."

"Yeah," he said noncommittally, then placed the necklace on the dressing table, gave Miranda's shoulders one last loving massage, and kissed her neck again as she finished correcting her makeup. "You'll have to wait till afterwards for my present."

"Oh, why?"

"Why?" He seemed surprised by her surprise.

"Frankly, after my little talk with Anthony, I didn't see any point in bringing it. After hearing a message like that, it took me a couple of hours just to get up the guts to stop by your dressing room."

"Message? What message?" She met his gaze in the mirror.

"See, you forgot already! I knew you didn't mean it!"

"Mean what, Jay?"

"Mean the message that you sent with Anthony—that you refused to see me before the show."

chapter 16

Jack
1984

"TO THIS DAY, I'll never really know how I got onstage that night," Miranda told me later that peaceful evening in England as we took a moonlight stroll around the grounds before turning in. "I keep retracing in my mind the steps I must have walked down, the cables backstage I must have been careful not to trip over. I can see the technicians clear as anything, and John, the stage manager—remember?—and the other actors crowded in the wings and all that, but I can't remember for the life of me being part of it. It was like being invisible, you know—like being a ghost. Didn't you feel like that?"

"Sort of." I considered the question carefully. "But, primarily, once the lights started to come down, I thought I was going to die. No, no, really *die*. I was so pumped up, my heart was racing, literally thudding against my chest, and I was sweating, alternately cold and hot, and my stomach was mimicking cholera symptoms. The headache felt like the beginning of a stroke, and when I reached out to shake someone's hand, I was sure I looked palsied. I was even envisioning the concise and tragic headlines—I still remember them: Playwright Succumbs During Masterpiece Premiere—Twenty-six-year-old prodigy Jack Price collapsed and died last night during the first performance of his play, *Up on the Heights*, which is already being heralded as a classic of twentieth-century dramaturgy.''

Laughing heartily, Miranda nodded. "God, I remember how you looked when you stopped by my dressing room! I was worried myself."

"Now that you mention it, I've seen *you* look better." I couldn't resist that.

"Agreed. Anyway, I guess I was lucky that I was onstage when the curtain went up. At least I didn't have to make an entrance. Because I'll always wonder if I wouldn't have bolted at the last minute."

"Bullshit! You're too much of a ham, darling!"

"Yes, you're right, but I certainly would have been tempted. You know, Anthony had given me a lecture on stage fright that day. It was extremely perceptive. It actually did propel me onstage that time, and I still use it to get through the worst of the jitters. So I took my place onstage. I was sweating before I hit the lights, and the heat once I was in place was simply overwhelming. I could feel my makeup baking under the sweat. And I thought I was going to die, too, because at that point, the audience had become one with a firing squad. I was in such a heightened state that I thought if I got any higher, I'd explode or my heart would stop. It seemed clear, anyway, that, for many reasons, I wouldn't be living through the next five minutes. And then the curtain went up, and I could hear a sort of hollow roar as the audience applauded the set, and then—as Anthony predicted—all my nervousness turned into energy that simply sent me off, and by the time Steve entered and we'd played a couple of scenes, I could actually feel myself taking off, springboarding off the stage fright. I was there, I was Rachel, I was angry at Chris, but I was still me. Like astral projection . . . or possession . . . I was two people at once. And I imagine that's when the audience really began to be with us. At least, it was that moment that we bridged the separation between us and them. And then Anthony entered, madly eccentric as Eric Gerard-Steele, and the crowd went wild with applause, thrilled by the presence of a great star, and I shared that thrill. I totally forgot my personal feelings —including some recent resentment and confusion—for Anthony the man.

"From then on, I think we all knew that we didn't have to work *for* the audience; we were working *with* them. And that association is . . . becomes . . . part of the performance and, during the first-act curtain scene—Anthony's last-minute changes were brilliant, of course—I really soared, and I could feel the audience response building along with me—they were laughing at the laugh lines!—and that was a dream, a joy, because just as I peaked, the curtain came down, and the audience started to applaud, and I just knew that they meant it."

"Yeah." I added my two cents. "Even in the middle of my authorly throes, I was part of the audience. Even walking up and down with Jay at the back of the house, I could tell it was working, because we could hear the laughter, but we didn't say anything to that effect. Just kept walking around, circling each other, like an elephant's death dance. We didn't want to jinx what we thought was happening. And I sort of steered clear of as much of the crowd as I could during intermission. Nobody knew who I was anyway, so it was easy to sneak off and smoke about three thousand cigarettes in relative privacy. Jay told me afterward that everyone had been extremely enthusiastic during intermission, but he didn't tell me that at the time. I guess he was afraid they were just being polite and he didn't want to build up my hopes."

"Oh, that intermission!" Miranda sighed. "It seemed longer than the first act. I was up, I was flying, and I didn't want to lose it—or the audience. I was afraid the intermission was so long that they'd all be drunk for the second act and fall asleep and wake up feeling testy and hostile. And then . . . oh, God, it makes me sick just to think of it . . . I was in my second-act costume—you know, the black satin gown from the play within the play, and as I was leaving the dressing room, one of the prop people was coming the other way, and somehow, he stepped on the train and the whole skirt pulled away from the waistband. I froze . . . just froze . . . couldn't move. I was so still a crowd collected, and someone screamed for the costume people, and they were tacking the skirt back on as I was walking down the stairs—in a coma, I think—but somehow it got fixed and the curtain went up."

Yes, the curtain went up, and the audience didn't seem drunk, as Miranda had feared, and I watched Jay walk up and down the back of the house, utterly poker-faced, and the good feelings I'd developed during the first act seemed to slip into a miasma of doubt. And the doubt slowly built to frenzy. In my delirium, I could feel the audience losing interest, the cast losing energy, the whole thing going up in smoke. Why had Anthony insisted on rewriting the one scene I'd felt loath to change? He was wrong, clearly wrong, and the audience's silence definitely gave testimony to my side of the argument. But it was too late now. The die was cast, and my excitement flip-flopped into a despair so profound, I contemplated suicide. So deep was I in my own disappointment that I was stunned when Jay suddenly grabbed my shoulder and I saw that he was beaming. "Listen!" he said. "It's happening. The whole fucking audience is in tears, exactly when they were supposed to be!" He was right. I'd written the scene to move, to produce tears, and it had worked like a charm. And I'd missed the whole thing.

"Let's sit down," Jay urged for the first time that evening, so we took our seats in the last row and watched Miranda and Steve move a whole audience to sniffles.

"And then," Miranda went on, that day in England,

"and then it was over, and the applause started and grew and grew and we just looked at each other, not knowing what to feel, but knowing that we had to get ready for the curtain call. And then, God, Steve gave me a quick embrace before the curtain rose, but I started to move away or something, and anyway, his foot landed on my skirt, and it ripped again, all the way across the back. So I took my bows standing straight up, with one hand behind my back, holding my costume together. Remember?"

We both laughed because, of course, I did remember. When Jay had walked me backstage into the wings and then pushed me on, insisting, without asking, that I share a curtain call, Miranda held out her free hand to me and made a place between her and Anthony as—I'm not too modest to admit—the crowd began a new wave of bravos. And then Anthony abruptly walked off the stage, to the confusion of Miranda and Steve and me, and the audience too, I'm sure, and came back, literally dragging Jay. And so we all stood there, applauding him, as Anthony shook his hand, and the good fellowship from audience to stage and back glowed like a nova. We were linked together in a common bond of ecstasy, all animosities forgotten, loving each other and loving the realization that this was the happiest moment of our lives.

How could we have known, as the lights bathed us in a grand and generous glow, that our dream of glory would turn, before too many hours had passed, into a nightmare?

chapter 17

Miranda
Connecticut, 1975

IT WAS ALMOST eleven-thirty, but the millions of strings of colored lights crisscrossing the verdant grounds of the Harringtons' estate shone on the crowd like a midnight sun. Caught up in the music from a dance band far off by the pool, sipping champagne as they wandered from famous face to important name, the guests seemed jolly, blessed by inclusion in so grand a celebration.

Jay had gotten to Miranda first when the curtain fell for the final time. He'd seized her hand and run off with her, into a dark place behind a stack of flats, looked at her with joy and hugged her to him with exhilaration.

She could almost literally feel the heat of his body as it glowed with triumph, could, as their bodies touched, feel his powerful heart beating in rhythm with hers. "Oh, Jesus, you were—" he began, but she stopped him with, "We all were, darling," then realized it was the first time she'd ever called him that, then forgot that and clung to him, sweaty and wilted and incredibly satisfied. When they parted, he had asked how she was getting to the party, and she had told him that she and Jack, the oldest of friends, were bent on arriving together, and he had smiled his approval. "That's great. Anyway, I've got to get back now. I have to be at Mom and Dad's to greet all my once and future investors. But—'' He smiled as he ran his hand down her back and over her ass. ''—we'll have our own private celebration later. Is it a date?''

In response, she'd molded her body to his, touching every part of him, and murmured, ''Wouldn't miss it for the world!'' And as they parted, he said, ''And your present! Aren't you curious?''

''Curiouser and curiouser,'' she told him as she blew him a kiss and ran toward the stairs to the dressing room. ''See you later!''

When she returned to the dressing room, having been stopped on the way a thousand times with hearty congratulations from so many people she lost count, Sue was out of makeup and about ready to leave for the party with Steve, whom she'd been dating. They embraced sincerely, with mutual happiness, and Sue congratulated her and told her she'd see her at the party. By the time Anthony made his appearance, Jack was already seated in a chair, smoking and laughing and aiming wisecracks at the screen behind which she was dressing.

''Well, my dears . . .'' caroled Anthony, resplendent in a dinner jacket, success having subtracted years from his face. ''I think we've got it!'' he finished in a mock Rex Harrison voice. He shook hands with Jack and called to Miranda, ''I suspect, my dear, a star is born.''

It was only then that Miranda remembered Jay's words, that Anthony had told him she refused to see him, and she said, ''Oh, Anthony, I've got something to talk to you about.''

''And I've got something to talk to you about, my dear. You and the whole cast. But not tonight. We'll have notes in the morning!''

''No, it's not about the show.''

''Should I leave?'' Jack asked from his chair.

''Oh, no, my boy.'' Anthony took over. ''Miranda and I will have plenty of time on the way to the party.''

"Oh, Anthony." Miranda appeared from behind the screen, wearing Margo's necklace and the sleeveless, scooped-neck green silk gown she'd spent a small fortune on. "I've asked Jack to escort me."

Anthony looked exasperated for only a moment, then brightened and said to Jack, his eyes never leaving Miranda, "Well, Jack, I hate to think the best man won, but certainly, one of the best men did. Congratulations on two counts. See you children later."

"See you later, Anthony," she called as he turned to leave. "And thank you."

So her entrance to the party was made in Jack's frail, rusty, green beetle, but it could have been a limo, so ebullient were they both. "Tell me, M.L.," Jack said, as they drove along. "It's true, isn't it? It's not a mass hallucination? We are a hit?"

"I *think* we *are,* Jack," she told him, "but at this point, I'm too excited to know for sure."

"Well, I think I know for sure. Isn't it weird, getting what you want?" They were turning off the road toward the Harringtons', and already they could hear the music and the melodious banter of a large-scale extravaganza. "I mean," he continued, "I still think I'm dreaming."

"Yeah," she'd said, patting his cheek, "yeah, but I'd rather be here than anyplace else. And I'm glad I have you for a best friend," she added as they pulled into the parking area.

"All right," he announced, handing her out of the VW. "You look like several million dollars, and you're on your way to the stars. Now get in there and work that party!" And she had. Through groups of admirers, some famous, some merely rich, she floated, accepting the accolades, smiling, offering her hand, posing gracefully for all to see. Millions of lights sprinkled the trees, illuminating her and Jack, the two happiest people in the world; the champagne offered by the circulating waiters was only a pale echo of their effervescence; the attention of a host of major celebrities could shine only so brightly against the dazzle of their own glorious success.

There was a band playing something from Rodgers and Hammerstein, and a few people were ballroom dancing by the pool. Suddenly the music ceased and another band struck up "Satisfaction," and she knew, as she had never known before, exactly what that felt like. Somehow in the midst of the melee, Jay found her. "God, you look gorgeous," he said, putting an arm around her shoulder. "Feel good?"

"Feel great!" she answered. "It's a hit, isn't it?"

"More than you know, my beauty." He bussed her lightly on the ear. "But in time, all things shall be revealed."

"Jay, you creep! So many secrets! And I want my present!"

"Don't be impatient, Miranda," he chided. "It's bad for the concentration. Hey, I want you to meet my parents."

Making their way across the lawn, they stopped to accept the congratulations of the likes of Mike Nichols, Lauren Bacall, Liza Minnelli, Jay and Lewis Allen, Bob Fosse, Sam Cohn, Candice Bergen, Neil Simon, and an assortment of Nederlanders, Minskoffs, and Trumps. An array of obviously wealthy couples, effusive in their praise, turned out to be major backers, and Jay handled them with a graciousness and professionalism she found impressive for a man his age.

"Hey, *boychik,* not bad for a kid!" called a gruff yet jolly older man, and Jay immediately headed in his direction. "Thanks, Uncle Al. From you that means a hell of a lot!" He shook his hand. "Miranda Lawson, I'd like you to meet Albert Goodman, an old and dear friend of my family's."

"You were lovely, my dear," said one of America's best directors, and added, "Your mother would have been proud of you." He topped off his words by kissing her hand.

"It's a pleasure, Mr. Goodman." Miranda beamed, flattered and touched by the gesture. "I hope some day we'll meet again—preferably on a rehearsal stage."

He smiled, as Jay beamed proudly at them both. "So, Jay, let me say again how pr—"

"Ah, there you all are! Good to see you, Al." Anthony appeared from out of the crush, grabbing Goodman's proffered hand and shaking it heartily.

"Memorable, as usual, Anthony," Goodman replied, then, grinning at Miranda, added, "Remarkable what a little talent can do!"

"Yes, she's a marvel, isn't she? So like her mother, don't you think?" Anthony added as, simultaneously, he managed to take Miranda's hand and turn her toward him. "I've got to borrow your star for a moment, Jay."

"Could it wait, Anthony? We've been trying to get to—"

"Only a minute, Jay. I'll deliver her into your hands in no time at all," and with that Anthony whisked her away. He led her to a surprisingly deserted place under some trees, by a stone bench, and they both sat.

"So, dear," he patted her hand. "You wanted to talk to me?"

Suffused in the glory of the evening, Miranda had all but forgotten her resentment at Anthony's interference before the show, but now it came back, a tiny pinprick of irritation. "Anthony," she began, "why did you tell Jay I refused to see him before the show?"

He didn't drop his gaze, just looked at her with a strange kind of sadness before replying, "Oh, Randy, dear, I thought that must be it. Before I begin, just let me confess to my guilt. I did indeed tell him that. And, to be frank, I'd do it again, if the occasion demanded. You simply fail to remember, my treasure, how upset you were at Jay this afternoon. It troubled me. It would trouble me anytime, but right before a curtain, it plagued me. I was worried, Randy, pure and simple. I was afraid he'd hurt you, my dear, on the most important night of your life. And I couldn't let that happen. If you can't forgive me, at least try to understand that my action came from the depth of my concern for you."

And, of course, she did understand, regretted immediately her anger and her distortion of his generous intentions. "Anthony, I do understand. But you didn't have to do it. I'm a big girl. I can handle my own problems."

His expression was beseeching. "Tell me I'm forgiven," he urged her, chucking her chin and beaming when she nodded yes. "That's wonderful. Now, shall I apologize to young Mr. Harrington?"

"Oh, no, Anthony, don't bother. We straightened it out before. Let's consider the entire incident forgotten!"

"Fine." He rose as a waiter approached with a champagne-laden tray, helped himself to two glasses, handed one to Miranda, and announced, raising his own, "A toast. To us, dear Miranda. To a tremendously happy reunion. And to a long and prosperous future—together!"

"I'll drink to that!" She raised her glass to his, and then sipped.

"Now, darling"—he was helping her up—"there's someone you must—"

"Hey, guys!" Heading toward them was Jay and a sleek-looking, middle-aged man who was unmistakably his father. The legendary Sam Harrington bore little physical resemblance to his son. Short where Jay was tall, stocky where Jay was lean, he was less handsome than enormously commanding. Tanned, silver-haired, with penetrating eyes that seemed not merely to see but to fix his attention with a view as deep and sweeping as a CAT scan. But his manner was Jay's, as was the power he radiated and the bearing that announced that power from far away. The Harringtons were royalty, all right, and Jay had been groomed for his father's throne. Two such strong wills, she could well imagine, must inevitably clash in a home. In an office, they must be dynamite.

Jay and his father had reached them, and Jay was saying, "Anthony, you remember my dad!"

At the sight of Sam Harrington, Miranda had sensed Anthony almost visibly stiffen, and Harrington himself had briefly allowed those martinet's eyes to broadcast something dark. For whatever the reasons—aesthetic differences, past business problems, or instinctual dislike—there was no love lost between the two men. Still, Anthony, with his customary instant recovery, immediately drew his emotions in check and extended his hand. "Sam! It's been years!" He shook Harrington's hand with the gustiness of an old war buddy.

"Much too long, Anthony!" Sam graciously allowed. "It's good to have you on a Harrington payroll again. By the way, the show's superb!"

"And we have this lady to thank for it." Anthony put his hand on Miranda's back as if to bring her to Sam's attention. But she already had it; once she had caught his attention, it hadn't wavered.

"I don't need to be introduced," Sam told them all. "I'd know her anywhere. My dear, you look so much like your mother, it's startling."

"I only hope I have her talent," Miranda responded, aware that this was the first time anyone but Anthony had said that, wondering if success, or love, or both could really make you beautiful.

"What do you think, Dad?" Jay broke in. "Wasn't she great?"

"She was remarkable." Sam took her hands in his and smiled with a warmth she had doubted he possessed. "You have a dazzling future to look forward to . . . " As he spoke, his eyes spied the necklace

Anthony had given her, and lingered on it. "That's a charming piece . . . very charming."

"Thank you," she smiled back. "It was a present from" —and she turned back to Anthony— "my director!"

"Very charming," Sam repeated, then turned back to Anthony. "A perfect gift."

"Sam! Jay! There you are!" A tall, white-haired woman in a white crepe evening gown was walking in their direction. "Sam," she told Jay's father, "Carol Channing's been looking for you. Anthony! You were wonderful!"

Kissing her on the cheek, Anthony took her hand. "Helen, you're looking more beautiful than ever!"

And indeed she was lovely, tall and elegant and exquisitely coiffured. She must have been a really striking beauty when she was younger, Miranda thought; she would have had Jay's dark hair, and still had his liquid brown eyes.

"You're the same old flatterer you always were, Anthony! How I've missed it!" Helen Harrington joked, then turned to Miranda. "Hello, dear, it was a pleasure to watch you tonight. I'm Jay's mother."

After the requisite few minutes of small talk, it was Helen Harrington who took the lead. "Sam, Anthony— let's leave the young people alone. Besides, an old friend of yours has been waiting to see you, Anthony."

"And who would that be?" he asked jauntily.

"Paul Scofield. He was in New York, and Sam persuaded him to come up for the opening."

"Paul! My God, I haven't seen him since . . . Well, my dears, I'll catch up with you later!" and Anthony and the Harringtons began to move away.

"Oh, Jay!" Helen Harrington turned back. "Have you seen Stephanie's parents? No? Do try to say hello, dear. They simply adored the show and were so disappointed Stephanie couldn't make it. So you'll do that?"

Jay, obviously taken aback, promised he would, and

Miranda felt a moment of fear. Who the hell was Stephanie? Well, whoever she was, she wasn't here, and Jay certainly didn't seem to care, so she wouldn't.

"Your mother's so beautiful!" Miranda exclaimed to Jay.

"She's a good lady," he told her, pleased. "We always got along. But what'd you think of my dad?"

"God, Jay, he's awesome!"

"Well . . ." and he paused before going on, "you've experienced the presence, so you can imagine what I was up against. He was always a little too much to live up to."

"But you're doing fine at it." She kissed him lightly. "Just fine. This is certainly a victory party!"

"Yeah," he murmured, "I guess it is. I guess we're all launched."

"So," she began, changing the subject, "where's my present?"

"Don't you want to wait till later, when we're alone?"

"Alone? Where?"

"How about that little inn, you know, the Gilded Rose, a few miles from here?"

"That gorgeous little place with the swans in the—"

"The very one! I booked a room for the night, if it's not too tacky."

"Tacky! Oh, Jay, it's the most beautiful place! When can we leave?"

"Not just yet. I *am* the host of this thing. The reviews aren't going to be in the papers until Tuesday because of the holiday, but nobody thinks we're going to get anything but raves. Walter Kerr was all aglow."

"I know. He smiled at me. I almost fainted."

"So give me a little time, okay?" They were walking back through the crowd, and as they reached a group including the stage manager, Steve, and Sue, they paused. "I've got to see some money people with Dad," he told her quietly. "I'll explain why later." Extracting a Tiffany box from his pocket, he said, "Here's your present, but you're not allowed to open it until later, okay?"

"Cruel, but okay," she replied, slipping the box into her gold evening bag. "Hurry back," and she waved goodbye as he headed to the house, wondering if this was what Helen Harrington had gone through all her married life—meetings in the middle of parties, sudden disappearances, and urgent phone calls at inconvenient times.

So the evening flowed. Feeling like a star, she floated, she bantered, she graciously accepted compliment after compliment, was introduced by Helen Harrington to Jay's sister Marilyn, a smart-looking matron in her late twenties, very Bendel's and very snooty, with the best nose job in the world, but who, under what must have been Helen's instructions, couldn't have been more polite. Marilyn's husband, a tanned and dapper cardiologist, seemed to pay a little too much attention to Miranda, and she wondered whether he always paid too much attention to other women and whether Marilyn's attitude was only a façade covering a mass of marital insecurities. Only in passing, it occured to her that romance was one thing and marriage another, that intimacy was a struggle that never ended, then she put the thought aside and gave herself up to the celebration.

By two-thirty, the crowd was finally beginning to thin out, the band had stopped playing, and the bar was shutting down. She had taken advantage of the winding down to sit on a patio chair by the pool, but all too soon her privacy had been invaded by a rich young backer who was too drunk to realize he was groping for her. She had gracefully made her escape when, out of nowhere, Jay appeared.

"Did you have a chance to talk to Anthony?"

"About what?" she asked.

"About us."

As a chill seized her, she told him, "Actually, I started . . . just when you brought your father over. I haven't had a chance since. He's never been alone."

"But you will?"

She looked at him, steeling herself. "Yes, Jay. I will."

"You know, I've got to talk to him, too. And you should be there. Let's find him." So they made the rounds, hand in hand, released from their pretense of impersonality by the headiness of triumph and the lateness of the hour, wandering dreamily, like high school lovers. They found Anthony talking to Sam and Helen Harrington, and when Miranda and Jay approached, he had apparently just reached the punch line of one of his famous anecdotes, for everyone was laughing broadly.

"Jay," Sam Harrington greeted them, "and Miranda, it's time for us old folks to call it a night." Everyone exchanged warm pleasantries, and Miranda thought she caught a look of approval passing from Helen to Jay. He must, she thought with surprise, have told his mother about her, and his mother seemed pleased. Helen and Miranda kissed lightly, and Sam bussed her on the cheek, and they were gone.

"Anthony," Jay said, "I'm glad you're alone. I've got a few things I'd like to talk to you and Miranda about."

"Righto, old boy. And where shall we *take* the meeting, as you Americans say?"

"How about right here?" He indicated three wrought-iron chairs by the pool. "It's as good as anywhere. Let me try to get us something from the bar, and I'll be back."

As he disappeared to fetch the drinks, Anthony, more energetic than she and twice as excited, grasped her hand. "You still look aglow, Randy. Have you and Jay made up your row?"

She hesitated, afraid to tell him what she had to.

"Yes. Yes, we have," she began haltingly.

"Well!" He sighed broadly. "That's a relief! I do so hate to see you unhappy."

"Yes, I know you do, Anthony." She patted the hand that held hers.

"Am I then to be led to expect that this is a . . . a serious involvement?"

She was terrified to agree. "Serious? I don't really know what you mean by—"

"Ah, Jay, the miracle worker, comes through again!" Anthony exclaimed as Jay returned with three champagne glasses and Jack in tow.

"One last toast," Jay insisted, pulling up a chair for Jack, "and then down to business." The toast was made, the champagne downed, and Anthony asked, "So, what's the big news, my lad? What awaits us?"

"Well"—Jay's expression grew suddenly serious—"I know this is premature, and I shouldn't even be talking about it but . . . *But*. If the reviews are as good as they promise to be, and if the backers we talked to don't lose their enthusiasm . . . well . . . if everything goes as planned, in October, we'll be bringing *Up on the Heights* to Broadway!"

"What?" Jack gasped.

"To Broadway?" Miranda breathed at the same time.

"You heard me." Jay nodded. "I can't believe it either, but we've got the backing, and tonight I got the theatre. So it looks like, barring unseen misfortunes, we'll all be together on the Great White Way!"

"Oh, Jay!" Miranda beamed. "How wonderful!"

"I can't believe this is happening," Jack murmured. "Did somebody put acid in the champagne?"

"No, it's for real. I promise you," Jay replied.

Of all the people seated together, only Anthony seemed less than thrilled. Miranda noticed and felt suddenly afraid, although she could not tell why.

"Anthony," Jay said eventually, "why so grim? If

you've got another commitment, we *can* get another actor to play Eric, although, of course, it won't be the same. But the direction won't—"

"Jay, my boy," Anthony broke in, assuming a grave tone, "I wasn't going to mention this tonight—it didn't seem pertinent—but now I feel I must. I won't be able to direct your play, nor star in it, and, regrettably, neither will Miranda."

"What are you talking about Anthony?" Jay asked, while Miranda, shocked into silence, felt her happiness begin to crumble.

"Well, my friends," Anthony began, "this is a matter of good and bad news. The bad news, as I've told you, is that neither Miranda nor I will be in a position to stay with *Heights* when it comes to New York. And the good news, the very, very good news, is this: for years, Larry Olivier has been after me to do *Lear* at the National Theatre, and I always turned him down, pending my discovery of the perfect Cordelia, but his invitation has always remained open. So today, I called him and told him I *had* found my Cordelia—" He glanced glowingly at Miranda. "—and that I was ready to do the play. So, I'm afraid, Jay, by Christmas of this year, Miranda will be starring on the stage of the National Theatre in London!"

Jay had, during the speech, turned ashen, and now his voice shook with suppressed rage. "Well, I certainly won't try to change your mind or dissuade Miranda from doing what she wants. I'll just wish you the best and say good night and good luck," and he got up and walked away.

Instinctively, without caring about manners or decorum, Miranda ran after him. "Jay, Jay—please!"

"Why didn't you tell me, Miranda? Why did you set me up like this?"

"I didn't, Jay. I didn't set you up!" Her voice was pleading as she grasped for his arm.

"Are you telling me you didn't know about this?"

"I didn't. I swear I didn't, Jay. Jay, I lo—I care too much for you to—"

"Then you're not going to do it?" He stared her down, and his eyes were stone.

"I . . . I don't know what I'm going to do," she confessed, sick at his hurt and at the hideous timing, but, in some part of her that deserved to be respected, thrilled at this miracle of good fortune. "Jay, even if I do go to London, it won't be forever." She was throbbing, churning, torn and desperate, hoping for a way out, fearing there was none.

"You're going," he told her. "You're going with Anthony, and that's that, right?"

"Well, that's not *that*."

"But you're going, aren't you?"

"Jay . . ." She was desperate for him to understand. "My God, Jay, *you've* told me over and over that your career is the most important part of your life. Why can't you believe that's true of me, too? Why can't you take me seriously as a professional? How can you expect me to make an easy, simple choice in an impossible sit—"

"So you're going with Anthony?" he cut her off curtly.

"Since you've forced me into an instant decision," she responded, angry and hurting and lost, "yes. Yes, I guess I am."

And suddenly, he turned cold, a perfect stranger, his father's son. "Well, fine. It's been good knowing you. And, by the way, take a look at the present, and when you're through looking, just toss it in a mailbox."

In parting, he didn't reach for her, didn't utter a regret, or sigh a sigh, just walked away across the lawn and into the darkness. Watching him disappear, desperate and wanting to die, she felt for the Tiffany box, still unopened in her purse. With shaking hands, she extracted the blue velvet case and opened it.

Inside was a solid gold key on a ring, to which was attached a golden disc. On one side it was inscribed "121 Canal" and on the other, "M, Wanna room together next semester? Love, J." and it dropped from her hand onto the grass as her triumph drowned in a tidal wave of grief.

PART TWO

PART TWO

chapter 18

Jack
1984

SO THE THUNDERBOLT had come crashing down upon our heads, altering all our destinies in one godly masterstroke. Since mine was one of those destinies, it's a tribute to Anthony Gainsborough that I can recall his actions that night with a sort of detached admiration. Ethics aside—and I couldn't begin to guess what farrago of motives had directed his fine strategic hand—it was awesome to watch him decide so many futures in one perfectly staged moment. It was said he'd done a legendary Prospero some years before, but surely this performance outshone that one by light years. He had finally conjured up a tempest that would rage about us all for years to come.

Without both Anthony and Miranda, *Up on the Heights* now lacked the big-time cachet it had had before Anthony's announcement. And that meant a whole lot of disappointments, mine among them. Without our superstars, my play was once again a very promising work by a young artist. I wasn't back to square one, but I had to face the fact that I wouldn't be pricing co-ops for a while yet. I'd get to the Great White Way, but probably not this year.

Still, if Anthony's announcement was a disappointment to me, to Jay it was a devastation. Dashed were his hopes for showing his father he could leap to Broadway with his first effort, for being an under-thirty mogul with both a hot theatre out of town and a New York hit, and for claiming as his own the hottest young actress around.

That's only a surface interpretation, for I felt Jay was hurting with a more private pain as well. His fervent need to prove his independence from his father had taken a massive step backward, given the fact that Sam's warnings about Anthony's capriciousness had proved right on the money. If Anthony hadn't actually proved Jay a fool, he'd certainly not made him look like a solid businessman, one who could deliver on what he'd promised his investors. And that was far from all: Early on, he'd made him feel like a loser over Miranda, alienated him from her in a haze of glamorous possibilities and sweet memories. Jay and Miranda had gotten back together by skirting public acknowledgment, had hovered on the border between infatuation and commitment behind his back. And when he found them out, he parted them. It was that simple. So, for Jay, Anthony had become, in an instant, the symbol for the gulf that had yawned between Jay and everything he craved. I could sense the anger and the grief, and I wondered whether the bitter animosity that had sprung up in him toward Anthony would ever be, could ever be, healed. They had started this glorious, gruesome evening as associates and ended it as adversaries. I wondered what would happen when their paths crossed in the future.

And then there was Miranda, who hadn't been spared the sad fallout of Anthony's edicts, despite the fabulous turn her career had taken.

Oh, there would be stumbling blocks and small setbacks in the next few years—a first film she shouldn't have done; a play in New York she wanted but didn't get; a couple of fractured romances with men of sufficient celebrity to have the breakups noted in print—but nothing that would seriously impede her meteoric rise.

But the mistakes she'd made had been on her own, without the benefit of Anthony's experienced and expert counsel, and although I doubt he ever held that up to her, it soon bound her even more closely to him. For it was clear that when he chose an agent, it was the right choice; when he cautioned against a relationship, it was for profound and convincing reasons; when he read a script, his unfailing nose for a hit (luckily, including one of mine) or the perfect part always steered her toward glory.

With Anthony at the controls, she could have—would have—nearly all the magical advantages of success, including a host of admirers with famous faces or solid millions. She could desire and get, sooner or later, billing above the title, the cover of *Vogue* and *People*, Paris gowns. All her wishes could come true—except for Jay. Because that was how Anthony wanted it.

Why he wanted it, and how much actually had to do with Jay as Jay, would remain for far too long a mystery to me. To Jay himself, it was a challenge to battle that grew with the passage of time. After all, he would rise too, amazingly quickly. If he harbored bitter feelings about Miranda, he never articulated them to me after that night, just as she never spoke of him, but on the subject of Anthony he was considerably more blunt. "You know, Jack," he told me over dinner at Elaine's some six months later, "I'm going to be a power in this town, and not just because I'm Sam Harrington's son. Because I'm good at what I do. And because I love and respect New York and the New York theatre. And someday, someday when I've got it all sewed up and running smoothly, when Anthony Gainsborough comes up against me, I'm going to crush the motherfucker!"

So all the hurt and murderously bad feelings and misconceptions that would stain our dealings in the years ahead had sprung to life that night in Tintagel, at Anthony's bidding. It was Anthony who had swept us up, borne us to the stars, and then sent us crash-landing back to earth. And I, finding myself standing on the IRT local to fame when I'd expected a compartment on the Orient Express, was caught in the middle of everybody else's misery. I felt for Miranda. I felt for Jay, and God knows, I felt for myself. Surprisingly, I even felt for Anthony, for some secret and solitary sorrow that drove him to do what he did, with such deadly panache. Much, much later, I was to discover the source of that sorrow, but only when it was perilously close to too late.

chapter 19

Miranda
Manhattan, 1979

"OH . . . I'M THRILLED. Absolutely
thrilled." Sipping her wine, Miranda paused for a moment, then let her eyes dart happily around the serene
dining room of the Carlyle Hotel, then move gently
back to the young man sitting opposite her. "Such
glowing reviews for my first major movie—well, it's just
too good to be true!"

The lunch with the guy from *Rolling Stone* had been
endless and difficult. He was little and dark and sar-
donic and ambitious, and she knew she had to be careful. The reporter from the *Times* had been polite and
pleasant, asking only decent, serious questions, which
she answered easily and as truthfully as her position
allowed. But this one was probing, prying, trying to
get her to say things she didn't mean to say, looking for
her vulnerable places. And if she slipped for only a second, the cover piece could turn out to be an unspeak-
ably bad piece of publicity. This guy wanted *the story*;
he wanted to make *news*; damaging her would be in-
cidental. She knew she'd better charm him, and charm
him good.

First, she suggested, could they clear up the myth that

she was an overnight success? Four years was faster than six or ten, but it was still four years, and she was far from being a household word yet. There was a whole group of very promising young actresses now, all around her age, well-trained and with terrific range. No, it hadn't been all good notices and champagne, she said, smiling, and went on to regale him with a few well-chosen anecdotes of failures, making the stumbling blocks seem minor ones, engaging him with her humility and spirit. All that aside, she admitted she was, of course, proud of her achievements, and considered herself blessed to have had the showcase that *Smitten* provided her. Sure, if she got an Oscar nomination for it, she'd be honored, but that was months away . . . it was too soon to get nervous. Over the tiny portion of cold lobster, which seemed to take hours to come, she'd declined a second glass of wine—trying to get her drunk, was he? No way she'd fall for that. She said that, of course, she was a New Yorker, despite her time in London; she was planning on getting an apartment here so she wouldn't have to stay in hotels, although staying at the Carlyle during this publicity trip was no cross to bear. And, after all, *Smitten* had been filmed in New York as well as London. "I guess you can call me bicontinental, but New York will always be home." How had she decided to do this film? Well, when she was doing the new Peter Shaffer with Anthony Gainsborough in London, her great buddy, Jack Price, had sent her this little film script he'd written, and she'd fallen in love with it; so had Anthony. It was funny and romantic and had a great part for an ingenue, and as it turned out, the adorable Patrick Grace as the star, plus top director Luke Dawson. How could she turn it down, especially when Anthony consented to do a cameo? Well, sure, they'd all been a bit surprised over its massive success, but what's better than that kind of surprise? Were Jack and she an item? Did they plan to marry?

"Oh, Mr. Raskin," she smiled, "my private life is private. You can't expect me to tell you that." She wondered, as she said it, why it was that she had less of a private life than any reporter would believe.

Over coffee (she declined brandy), he broached the subject of her mother, and she gracefully suggested that a famous parent was always something of a mixed blessing, a definite boon if you believed in genetic legacies, but a lot to measure up to; actually, she'd started pretty much at the bottom professionally and was proud of her own accomplishments. Of course, Anthony Gainsborough was more than a help; he had been a benefactor and a joy.

Raskin's ferretlike eyes were beginning to gleam, and she could see him readying himself for the kill.

"So, do you forgive him for the scandal?" he asked brashly. "You *are* convinced he was not responsible for your mother's . . . um . . . ?"

Drawing herself up to her full height, she met his gaze and answered, "Mr. Raskin, you're asking me to solve family mysteries that I can't even begin to unravel. Doesn't your family have ghosts, Mr. Raskin—things you'll wonder about your entire life and never be able to know?" It was working; his eyes had softened.

"Yeah, maybe," he was forced to admit. "But still . . ."

Pulling a cigarette from a pack in her bag—a delaying trick she'd learned from Jay—she held it until the guy lit it. "The past is the past, Mr. Raskin . . . or can I call you Mitchell?"

He nodded, flattered, then murmured "Mitch," and if he could have blushed, he would have.

"I don't dwell on the past. I'm interested in the present—and the future."

"And the future doesn't include marriage?" he asked, with an attempt at a sophisticated grin that missed by a mile.

"Not the immediate future. Of course, I'd like to marry and have a family, just like any other woman. But, right now, I'm devoting so much time to my career, I don't think I could handle marriage. It wouldn't be fair—to my husband or to my kids."

"So, right now, you'll have to settle for glamor and celebrity, huh?"

"Mitch, don't put words in my mouth. I'm a long way from the top, and it's already getting lonely. I've had relationships—I'm sure you've read about some of them—and when they broke up, I grieved. But they broke up because of my work—funny hours, in different cities. I'm in a business where it's very hard to settle down." She paused a second and then smiled, "All of which is not to say that if 'the right guy' came along this afternoon, I wouldn't totally change my tune."

Somehow the bit about her love life had turned him on, had lit his libido and compelled his gaze toward the apex of the V made by the slightly plunging neckline of her blue-striped shirt. Adding fuel to the fire, she casually raised her arms, causing the décolletage to expand slightly as she moved her fingers to the upturned collar, pushing it perfectly erect. Apparently, he saw what she'd wanted him to see, the necklace Anthony had given her, delicately arranged around her neck.

"That's an interesting piece," he said. "Is there a story behind it?"

"I'm glad you asked, Mitch." She smiled, stubbing out the cigarette, which had been burning in the ashtray. "Yes, there is. This was Anthony's first opening night present to my mother. It was a very emotional moment when he gave it to me. We laid a lot of ghosts to rest that night." And she paused, casting her eyes demurely down to the table, then looked up suddenly, as if she had just remembered something. "Oh, God. What time is it?"

He checked his watch and reported, "Two thirty-five," and, as he did, she could detect the disappointment in his voice. She was a celebrity, and people liked being with celebrities—especially creeps like this guy; it made them glow, made them feel important.

"God, Mitch, I totally forgot. I've got to be in midtown in fifteen minutes. Where are you going? Can I drop you?"

"Well," he retorted, a little miffed, "I'm going to . . . farther downtown. Can I drop *you*?"

Desperate to escape from the creep, she'd suddenly decided on a visit to Bendel's. It'd been so long since she'd had any free time to shop, and even longer since she'd been able to pick and choose amidst the gilt-edged merchandise of her favorite store, solvent and unintimidated by the prices. "Fifty-seventh and Park would be ideal."

"Groovy," he replied, the fool. "Have your coat?"

"I've been living in London long enough"—and she smiled at him—"to think a fairly balmy May day in Manhattan is like the end of June. I think this sweater will be fine," and she put on the pearl-gray cashmere cardigan that looked so right with the light gray flannel pants that Anthony's tailor in London had made for her.

So he paid the tab with a credit card and took her arm as he escorted her out of the dining room and through the perfect little parlor where tea was served, through the narrow strip of lobby, and out onto Madison Avenue.

He hailed a cab and steered the driver over to Park Avenue, then he turned on his tape recorder and began the final interrogation. Her next project? She wasn't absolutely sure what she was going to do next. Anthony had a play he was thinking of doing with her in London, and then there was . . . At this point, it remained to be seen . . . Oh, yes, Anthony was due in tomorrow, mostly publicity, but some business . . .

As they sped down Park, past the building where she'd lived as a child, the child of a star, she thought of what her life had come to be. How she'd captivated critics and ensorceled patrons, not in *King Lear*, which she suspected Anthony had never meant to do until much later in his career, but in a stellar, sold-out production of *The Duchess of Malfi*, then with the Peter Shaffer, and now with *Smitten*. How the last four years had been spent becoming known, becoming recognizable. How Anthony had dealt with her as if she were an athlete and he were her coach, stripping down her social schedule, making her practice, making her stretch. How she had dazzled and won acclaim, while the delight of her professional triumph contrasted ever more sharply with her private loneliness.

And when her thinking got to that point, she always circled back to Jay. Jay, her single great regret, her crushing disappointment. She'd spend four years now, fantasizing casual meetings with him on street corners or in expensive restaurants, where he would instantly see the light and realize how much he'd missed her and decide to try again to woo her. Jay, whose bright fortune had paralleled her own, who was building buildings and producing plays at a rate and of a quality that made him, before the world, a most worthy heir to the Harrington empire.

He had finally brought *Up on the Heights* to Broadway with a new director and a different aspiring actress, prettier than she, and possibly better in the part; as she'd lovingly explained to Jack, she'd never had the guts, during the filming of *Smitten*, to check it out. She had read about Jay in all the columns, producing like crazy, financing charity benefits, lunching at 21 with politicians and magnates, the darling of the New York Democratic Party, and appearing at fund-raisers with his unending assortment of lovelies. Jay, who had touched her too deeply, for whom she might have given it all up, if he'd only wooed her properly. Jay whom, ironically, she'd *never* run into—except in print—and whom she didn't have to think about, but who was there, in her mind, almost all the time, as if her every moment was being lived just so she could tell him all about it someday.

Raskin was jawing, and she was responding smoothly, mechanically, and then they'd made it to Fifty-seventh and Park, and the cab stopped.

"Well, Mitch—" She smiled, returning to the present. "—it's been . . . er . . . you're a tough marker but . . ."

He smiled with an attempt at seductive charm and told her, "I hope I hear from you when the piece comes out . . ."

"If I dare call you," she demurred.

"Oh, you will. Don't worry about it." He leered, obviously sure that he'd bought a date with a hot ticket.

"Mitch," she murmured, "great to meet you."

"Same here," he said, starting to move toward her, but before he got there, she was out the door, blowing him a kiss, and practically running down Fifty-seventh.

Past little antique shops, past Tiffany's, where she waited for the light, past I. Miller's, loving Manhattan, realizing how she'd missed it.

Now, up ahead was Bendel's, and as she headed toward its doors—and the familiar doorman who looked as if he would "call for Philip Mor-*ris* . . ."—she heard someone call out her name.

Some instinct told her to keep on walking, to duck into the "safe house" of the expensive store, but the voice fixed her steps, and she wheeled around.

It was Jay, of course. Jay, tall and lanky, but a little older and a little solider and not quite so much a boy. Jay in a blue pinstripe for which Giorgio Armani must have charged him thousands. Jay, just standing there, as if he had been waiting for her for every moment of the four years that separated them.

"Jay!" It came out choked, like a strangled scream, but he didn't seem to notice.

"Miranda," he repeated to himself, as if he were trying to convince himself it was really she. "This is . . . this is amazing," and he flashed her the old sexy smile, which still broke her heart and challenged her will. "God, you're looking great. Hell, you're *doing* great, and it shows!" They were standing very close to each other, he towering reassuringly over her, right outside the door, so that shoppers had to walk around them to go inside, but it never occurred to either of them to move.

"Hey," she told him perkily, "you're not doing so bad yourself, from what I hear!" She was sure she was blushing.

"No." Some trace of reality must have flitted across his mind, interrupting his happiness, for she saw the sparkle fade for a moment from the luscious gold-flecked eyes. "No, I'm not. But you . . . wow!" He impetuously grabbed her hand, making her want to stand where she was forever, with him holding her hand, a long and deserved vacation after a dreary time.

"So, listen," he continued, still grasping her hand, "can we . . . would you like to . . . get together for lunch or something? Where are you staying? How long are you going to be in town?"

She was on the verge of telling him when he abruptly dropped her hand. A cab had pulled up at the curb and out had dashed a dark-haired, gorgeously attired young woman. She wasn't beautiful, but she was striking . . . in fact, she was the striking brunette Jay had been with at the restaurant in SoHo, four years ago. Now, she was heading across the sidewalk right toward them, right toward Jay.

"Darling!" she called to him as she proceeded, not

even focusing on Miranda, reaching him and pecking him on the lips. "Guess what! Guess what I found in a little shop on upper Madison. The perfect dress! The very perfect dress!" And then she stopped and checked out Miranda, with a combination of awe and confusion. "Jay, dear," she suddenly said, "aren't you going to introduce me to your friend?"

And, without hesitation, he did: "Miranda Lawson. I'd like you to meet Stephanie Greenwood, my fiancée."

chapter 20

Jack
1984

BY THE SPRING of '79, I had become a full-fledged *mensch*, but a full-fledged *mensch* with a problem. Now that I was the author of a hit play *and* a hit movie, Broadway and Hollywood both seemed to be laying down a red carpet for me that stretched clean across the country. All of a sudden, I was inundated by more social invitations than I could handle, walking into restaurants and getting the best table, being interviewed and wooed and called at funny times from important places in different time zones. I'd moved to a two-bedroom luxury apartment with a river view on Fifty-second Street and had actually hired a decorator to do it right. And if my professional life was surging forward beautifully, my private life was almost keeping pace. But my private life was very private. Somehow, the press called me a bachelor, although they must have suspected that was a euphemism, and I suppose it was my constantly keeping company with Miranda that kept them in the dark. I'd gone to see her *Duchess of Malfi* in London, as well as the Shaffer play, been royally treated by Anthony, and, in fact, encouraged to paint the town red with my best friend. During the shooting of *Smitten* we definitely made the rounds—went to fancy restaurants with great wine and indifferent cuisine, to gambling clubs and dancing clubs and jazz clubs, to country weekends and openings and benefits. I even bought a dinner jacket to complement her evening gowns.

We were photographed at Wimbledon, at Ascot, in Malibu; on people's yachts, at people's dinner parties, and once, and only once, at a golf tournament attended by a couple of genuine royals. Frequently Anthony was hovering in the background of the shot, smiling benignly on our union. It was a fake, Anthony's invention, but as a result of it I became known as a great escort, and I went out every night—with ladies who appreciated my cachet or my wit or my manners. I'm not complaining; I enjoyed every minute of it.

So then, you might ask, what was my problem? My problem was that I had two dear friends—friends I treasured and loved—and they were enemies. So much so that, although I tried repeatedly to find a way to tell Miranda that Jay and I were friends, I hadn't succeeded. And I wished I could have come clean with her; I wanted to share with her the truth—that, over the course of several years and some successful professional dealings, I had become the closest male friend in Jay's life, and he in mine. He'd been the first producer to take a chance on me, and that the risk had been wildly successful had created the bond between us. I respected his talent, and he respected mine.

Either because he was too enviable or because he was too busy, Jay didn't seem close to a lot of men, and I saw he needed an easy kind of alliance, a buddy relationship, just as I sought a male bond without sexual strings. So there it was. It's not that I didn't envy him— it was tough not to—but I wasn't intimidated, as he wasn't intimidated by my being an "artist." I was proud of our friendship, but I couldn't share that pride with Miranda.

I also couldn't share with Miranda—because I'd given Jay my word—the fact that it was Jay who'd arranged the financing for *Smitten*. Covertly, so that neither Anthony nor Miranda would know, he'd put the right people together with the right people, had even planted in the ear of somebody important the suggestion that Miranda play the ingenue. But, since he'd made me promise, she would never know; Jay discreetly had his finger in countless income-producing pies, and even I was unaware of most of them.

If things had been different, and I'd been less afraid of distressing her, I would also have suggested to her that Jay casually asked about her much too often to be casual; that, although he swore he never thought about her, never regretted how their affair had ended, I simply wasn't convinced. But, with an empathy that could be interpreted as cowardice, I didn't broach the subject.

For Miranda refused to admit that Jay existed. Whether Anthony had totally brainwashed her or whether eliminating Jay from her conversation was some female protective tactic, I couldn't begin to fathom. But I was sure that, if I had mentioned him, she would have found some excuse to change the subject or leave the room. And, when Jay at last capitulated to the wiles of Stephanie and the will of his father, who wanted the marriage, I simply couldn't bear to be the messenger bringing Miranda the bad news. She certainly wouldn't hear it from him, either, but she'd hear about it soon enough—from party chatter or in the columns.

So, in May, when Miranda was in New York on a publicity tour and Jay called, suggesting I, the professional storyteller, concoct some way to get them together, I was prepared to decline, fearing her wrath and the disturbance of a very delicate karma. But I couldn't help detecting the unusual strain of urgency in Jay's voice, and from that deduced that something mysterious had happened that altered things I'd never understood anyway.

For some reason, I decided to trust his instincts, so I went along: I hatched a plot and set her up for a chance encounter whose false spontaneity wouldn't have fooled a six-year-old. And, as I plotted, I even daydreamed that everybody—now that we were grown-ups—would be pals again, all thanks to my peacemaking. But what I should have suspected was the far greater probability of what would happen when they met again: big-time, long-term trouble.

chapter 21

Miranda
Manhattan, 1979

SHE HAD TOLD Jack firmly no, that she had no intention of going to a backers' audition that afternoon. There was no possibility of her spending three prime hours of her brief Manhattan fling cooped up in somebody's studio while she could be . . . But he'd told her that the word on the show was excellent, that friends of his were involved, that potential backers are always impressed by the presence of celebrities, and that this was the least she could do to help dedicated theatre people trying to raise the financing for a show that would be their breakthrough.

"Forget it, Jack," she had grumbled, not bothering to hide the crankiness. "I want to be alone."

"Oh, come on, Ms. Garbo, be a sport."

"Cute, Jack, but no way."

And yet, unrelenting, he'd appeared at the hotel to find her languishing and in a foul mood. It was worse than a foul mood. It was anguish and rage and cataclysmic disappointment. It was embarrassment and longing and loneliness. It was Jay and that hideous encounter in front of Bendel's.

"Oh, come on, Princess, run away with me. I'll tell you what. We'll have a burger at Joe Allen's, just like the old days, and then dash to the show. It'll take your mind off your troubles."

"Troubles? What do you mean, troubles? I have no troubles," she'd snapped.

"Fine, my mistake." Jack had presented his most engaging grin. "Then come with me, and you won't acquire any. Come on!" He grasped her hand and pulled her up from the couch where she'd been reclining, staring blindly at a game show on the huge TV.

"Oh, all right," she'd agreed. "Just to get you off my back!"

"And look good. You're money in the bank to my friends!" he'd called as she disappeared into the bedroom.

She chose a black cotton Saint Laurent safari shirt, beautifully oversized, rolled up the sleeves, added a great pair of olive drab pants, alligator loafers, and a rust-colored ivory bangle. She piled her hair on top of her head and paled her makeup. She hoped the effect was Katharine Hepburn. Then she grabbed her trench coat and a Vuitton clutch, and presented herself for Jack's approval.

When he whistled, she knew he wasn't entirely kidding. She looked good. She looked glowing. Because she was ready to go public, and in public, stars have no bad moods.

They cabbed it to that block of Forty-sixth Street between Eighth and Ninth called Restaurant Row. They had crossed Central Park, then headed down through the theatre district and over to the randy borderland of Eighth, and as they walked the half-block to Joe Allen's, she reveled in the vivacity of New York's down-and-outness. Although it was a Wednesday—matinee day—and Joe Allen's was filled to overflowing with the pretheatre ladies, they didn't have to wait for a table. Unlike the old days, the maitre d' shook Jack's hand enthusiastically as soon as they entered, called her by her name and made a little bow, and promptly escorted them to a table from which, clearly, someone else had been bumped when Jack called at the last minute for a reservation. People obviously recognized her, but no one bothered them, and when a few professional acquaintances came over to say hi to Jack, they greeted her with a kind of respect; she had arrived. By the time Jack threw down his credit card, paid the bill, and escorted her back outside, she was feeling as good as she looked.

"Cab?" Miranda asked jauntily.

"Nah, the theatre's only a couple of blocks from here. Let's walk." He steered her west toward Ninth Avenue.

The day was bright and sunny, but a little cool for May, and the trench coat protected her just enough. Through the tough terrain of Hell's Kitchen they strolled, noting the ages-old street life as well as the first stirrings of the renovation that was taking place all over the city. "Am I wrong, or is this neighborhood starting to change?" Miranda asked. "I'm afraid when I come back in a couple of years our bad old neighborhood is going to be gorgeous."

"Then don't stay away so long." He squeezed her hand briefly. "And you won't have to go through the culture shock."

Culture shock. Interview shock. Jay shock. New York just never let you know what it was going to pull next.

They arrived at the theatre a half hour early, so Jack suggested they run across the street to a theatrical pub for coffee. But the place was packed, so they settled in at the bar. "Perrier?" Jack asked, but she decided, since the glass of wine at lunch had definitely lifted her mood, that she might have part of another. By the time they left for the audition, she was up for the performance as herself that she would shortly have to give.

And she did it well. Up the winding stairs to the

rough-hewn barn of a lobby, teeming with people, few of whom she knew, although everyone nodded to her and Jack. Into an equally rough-hewn house, with a stage built along one end of the room and the seats, bleachers really, rising sharply up to the far wall. The crowd was pouring in fast, rich people looking for an investment, a fancy bunch, personally invited for their money.

They found space about halfway up the seats, and Jack, ushering her into the row first, took her coat, and moving next to her, placed the coat on the space that bordered the aisle. "What if someone wants to sit there?" she asked.

"So we'll move it," he said casually, then looked up and waved as a bearlike young man in his late twenties, jeans-clad and grinning broadly, dashed up the aisle and extended his hand to Jack, who rose.

"Harve, how's it going, old buddy?" Jack shook his hand, then turned back to Miranda. "Miranda Lawson, this is Harvey Resnick, the so-called composer of this piece of garbage."

"It's a real pleasure to meet you, Miss Lawson." He said it with feeling.

"And I hear only wonderful things about your show. I'm really looking forward to hearing the score."

"Thanks. And thanks so much for coming. I know how busy you must be," he told her, then knelt down by the bleacher to talk to Jack.

"How's it looking?" Jack asked.

"Not bad. Paramount's coming. They might be good for a bundle. Word has it Jimmy Nederlander might consent to appear. Our producer says someone's accepted from the Shuberts. And, if we're real lucky, we'll get Jay Harrington."

Suddenly the glow faded, suddenly her heart sank to her stomach. Oh, no, please . . .

"But you never know with these guys," Resnick was

continuing. "They say they'll be here, then they never show. Jesus! What a business! Why didn't I go to medical school like my mother wanted? Anyway, guys—" He rose and took Miranda's hand. "—I hope you enjoy it. I'll be at the keyboard, by the way. And, for Christ's sake, when you see me afterwards, *be honest*—but not too honest." And, smiling weakly, he climbed back down the steps.

At once she turned to Jack, furious. "Why didn't you tell me Jay was going to be here! Just whose friend are you?"

He turned to face her. "Look, Miranda, I don't keep Jay's schedule for him. How in hell am I supposed to know if he's coming or not? You heard what Harve said. They *don't* come three fourths of the time. And if I did know he was coming, how could I possibly tell you? You refuse to talk about him."

"Oh, come off it, Jack," she whispered so the rest of the audience couldn't hear. "I'm not a teen-ager. I can—"

"Handle Jay?"

"Oh, forget it. I don't want to talk about this anymore."

"See?"

"Oh, screw you!"

And then the performance began. Harve played the score, and the author of the musical's book read the bridging material. The actors walked onto the set, which was for the show that was playing the theatre at night, with their scripts in their hands, and began to go through the scenes. The property the audience was here to judge was a musical version of the great movie comedy *Bringing Up Baby*, with Cary Grant and Katharine Hepburn. Done in the thirties, the film had lived on as the ultimate screwball comedy, complete with jungle cats. Harve's version was called *Animal Magnetism*, and it started out fresh and lively, with a charming score and promising numbers. Even in a semi-staged reading, it revealed itself early on to be a crowd-pleaser; you could tell by the audience's enthusiastic attention.

But to Miranda, giving an award-winning performance as a rapt member of the audience, it wouldn't have mattered if she were seeing a backers' audition for *My Fair Lady. He* hadn't come, which meant he probably wouldn't come, but if he did, at least he'd be sitting on the aisle next to Jack. After forty-five minutes she was sure he wasn't coming. Thank God. It was over and done with, a false alarm. But when she faced the fact that she wouldn't see him, she found herself close to tears. The time dragged by with agonizing slowness, and by the time the act break came, she didn't know how she was going to keep up her facade during intermission.

Jack immediately dashed off to call his date for the evening, and she wandered to the ladies' room, waiting her turn at the mirror to fix her makeup for . . . for no one . . . There was one moment, as she finally stood before the mirror, with everybody watching, when she allowed herself to see the distress surface, but she recovered so fast she was sure no one else noticed. Then, turning back to the prospect of a large, crowded room full of people who would call her by her first name, although they'd never met her, she breathed a sigh and strode out the door.

He was there, standing in the dead center of the room so you couldn't miss him, talking to Jack, a cute young press agent, and a couple of Wall Street types. The first thing that struck her was that he was wearing a dinner jacket in the middle of the afternoon. The second thing was that he was the best-looking man she had ever seen. And the third thing was that she was turning to run. But before she could move, he was there at her side, too quick for her, as always.

"Jay." She tried for an imperious tone, and extended

her hand. "Twice in as many days! What a coincidence!" She suspected this second encounter was less coincidence than collusion.

"Yeah, it's amazing." He beamed innocently.

"Miranda! Jay!" Jack called, as he walked jauntily over to them. "Hey, you're actually speaking to each other!"

She shot him a look that she hoped was withering, but he gave no sign of noticing. "They're starting again," he said, and herded them both back to their seats.

"I feel awful about being so late," Jay said, "but I couldn't—"

"Don't worry about it," she heard Jack whisper, as they filed toward the seats. "You're *here*! They're delighted!"

By the time they got to their row, Miranda, who was in the lead, realized that she was going to be trapped next to Jay. There was no way of switching seats. It was too late. He was sitting down. With no seat arms on the bleachers to separate them, he was sitting down very close to her. Very close.

The second act began with a flourish exceeding even the buoyancy of the first, and this time the audience was already prepared to love it. "Good stuff," she overheard Jay whisper to Jack and wondered how he could tell. She couldn't. All she could tell was that, even after four years, her body still yearned for him. That she was excited by the accidental brush of a knee that hastily retreated. Was intoxicated by his smell and the heat of his presence, which made her nerve endings come alive. With or without physical contact, she was his. And she wished with all her heart that the play would never end, that they could be here, with him next to her, in a haze of memory and desire, no fiancée, no Anthony, nothing at all to challenge her absolute possession. Well, she wasn't that blessed. Nobody was. What she had was half an hour, tops. And no more. Ever.

So she prayed each number would be reprised, applauded loudly to guarantee there would be encores, laughed at the laugh lines, giggled at the lyrics, performing some actress's voodoo to keep it from ending. She was doing great, giving a terrific performance, all for the man who was seated perilously close by, and she was gratified when he whispered in her ear, "God, you've really changed! I've never seen you enjoying yourself so much!"

Bending slightly to whisper back, feeling, for a second, the soft skin of his neck, she responded gaily, "I *am* enjoying myself! This is going to be a huge hit!" Then she turned her apparently riveted attention back to the stage. But, all too soon, the final curtain happened, the piano finishing with a flourish against the chorale of actors' voices. Jay reached for her hand in the darkness and held it, and suddenly, without warning, from some strange and foreign place inside her, in passionate counterpoint to the gaiety she'd taken pains to radiate, came the tears.

chapter 22

Jack
1984

IT'S A SINGULAR feeling to be a bystander in a grand passion, especially an interested bystander. When you're not interested, when you're, for instance, walking down the street and you see two strangers kissing, it's fun and removed, like a scene from a poster of Paris. But when you're sitting next to two people you know very well, as I was the day of Miranda and Jay's reunion, and you feel the heat radiating from them, when you're both drawn to and denied access to their utter closeness, it makes you feel at once embarrassed—like an unwilling eavesdropper—and excited—like a voyeur. Well, writers are supposed to be voyeurs, right? Anyway, the bottom line is that, stellar as the show in front of me may have been (and it was to become a very major hit), it ran considerably second to the drama unfolding to my right.

Admittedly, it was through my own clever machinations that I was currently being seduced and excluded. It wasn't the exclusion part I minded. That very night, I was seeing for the third time a young actor who reminded me of a famous British movie star and who charmed me as no one had in a long time.

But there were other feelings playing in my head that afternoon, weird feelings, born more of instinct than of knowledge. Dark feelings accompanied by a realization that, until now, had eluded me. Maybe it was because Anthony had planted the seeds of unease in me some years ago. Or maybe not. For whatever reason, it was with an insidious dread that I contemplated what now seemed to me a grievous error. Before today, I had always seen Miranda and Jay's relationship as trouble, but trouble in the style of romantic comedy—crossed meetings, misunderstandings, meddlings, all easily resolved by the final curtain. Trouble, yes, but cute trouble. Though destiny had crossed their stars and made it tough for them, love could still prevail. But now, sitting in that theatre, and having my heart pound with the intensity I could pick up from them, I knew that their shared passion was more than trouble. It was dangerous.

chapter 23

Miranda
Manhattan, 1979

SHE'D STANCHED THE tears by sheer force of will before the houselights came up. So her breaking down had been just a momentary, and probably imperceptible, lapse of control. Whatever damage might have been done to her eye makeup was easily camouflaged beneath the sunglasses she always carried in her purse and which she slipped on just as the lights went up. If Jay had even noticed her "lapse," he'd chosen to ignore it, allowing her hand to escape from under his as he began to applaud the show. By the time they stood up to leave, she was as effervescent as before.

Jack and she had stopped to congratulate Harve Resnick and his associates, while Jay was drawn away by the producer for a private discussion. Then they were down the stairs and out the door, she and Jay and Jack, and then back in the pub across the street for a drink. She slipped away to the ladies' room, hoping her eyes weren't a mess, and was relieved to find only the trace of a smudge, which she fixed, then practiced smiling, repeatedly, to put the still-threatening tears to rest.

Why had he come back into her life—why now when he couldn't be part of it? When all they could be to each other was uneasy acquaintances—if Princess Stephanie allowed even that—maybe distant friends because of mutual friends, but no more. And how could they be friends when even his nearness made her mad to touch him, when his grasping her hand was an act of greater physical intimacy than some of her sexual encounters in the years since they'd last been together? But it didn't matter, none of that mattered, because that was about tomorrow and the days after. What mattered was that for the moment he was here, sitting at a table, waiting for her—and she had thought he would never be there again. For a while at least, for minutes, maybe longer, she could bathe in the comfort of his presence. So the urge to weep retreated as her joy advanced to conquer it, and she smiled one final time, her best smile, her dazzler, observing herself as he would see her, and returned to see his eyes light up as she approached.

"Of course, I'm interested," Jay was saying to Jack, "but I know what Dad's going to say. No stars. A bunch of kids nobody's ever heard of. Nothing bankable about the property but talent! And they want to go into the Bankhead next fall. It may be too big for the show; I'm not sure. Anyway, there's no guarantee it'll be available . . . Well, that's all I've got to say right now."

So they talked, killing pleasant time over a couple of beers, but knowing he was going somewhere that required black tie, Miranda watched the huge clock over the bar move from five-thirty to six forty-five, and she felt her elation slipping away. He was there, now, but soon he would be gone, and that would be that.

But it wasn't. When, at seven, Jack apologized for having to leave, pleading an important engagement, Miranda prepared to have it end. But Jay had other plans.

"Can I buy you dinner?" he asked, smiling.

"Well, actually, yes. I left tonight free just to relax. But . . . aren't you going somewhere? I mean, you're dressed . . . "

"I was going to a fund-raising thing, but we've already made a major donation so I'm sure I can bow out. Just let me make a phone call, and we can take off.''

She watched him walk to the bar to ask the bartender where the phone was, then checked him out as he disappeared down some steps. He was magnificent—graceful and fit and ablaze with energy, and as he made his way across a room, women's heads turned. Oh, people had looked at *her* when she'd run down to the ladies' room. She was recognized; she was a star. But she was a star because she was known, because she'd been in a hit movie, because she was featured in newspapers and magazines. But Jay was a natural star. You didn't have to see him on a screen to know it, you just knew. Lots of people wanted her attention, but it was because she had earned it—with years of training, and of practice and of striving. But lots of people didn't want Jay's attention —*everybody* did, from cab drivers to composers to all the women in the restaurant. But tonight, tonight, he would be with her, and she would be the person he was paying attention to—a star intimidated and enchanted by a star.

"Done!" He reappeared. "No problem. You need to make any calls?" He offered her a dime, but she declined it. Although she might have called the hotel for messages, she decided not to bother. There could certainly be nothing urgent enough that she couldn't wait to find out about it. Anthony was flying in from London some time tomorrow, but that was tomorrow. So she was free.

They hit the street to find night falling fast and a mildness in the air that hadn't been there during the afternoon. It was a perfect spring evening, with a breeze that titillated more than chilled, and the fading light was soft-hued as it blended into the deep purple of the coming night.

"An enchanted evening!" she exclaimed, feeling safe, feeling secure.

"It's us. We always make them happen," he told her, slipping his arm around her for a moment in a hug.

They strolled at their leisure, over to Eighth Avenue, now hectic with the arriving theatre crowd, and headed uptown to Columbus Circle, where the traffic was bustling in a roughed-up version of a Parisian scene, then they walked along Central Park West, not talking much, surprisingly easy in their quietness.

"Hey," he said after a while, "I'm getting hungry. How about you?"

She wanted to say that his being with her had caused her to transcend hunger, that she was too high to care what she ate, but, instead, she answered, "Yes, ravenous. Any ideas? The way I'm dressed and the way you're dressed—we certainly don't look like we got out of the same limo!"

"My dear, this is New York! And anyway, tonight, anything goes. Besides, I already picked a place."

"Is it close?"

"We're practically there." He squeezed her arm. "I never do anything by accident."

"So I noticed," she told him tartly.

"I'll let that pass." He smiled, guiding her across the street.

At eight forty-five, both dining rooms of the Café des Artistes were packed with smartly dressed patrons, and the sounds of clinking glasses, laughter, and conversation filled the place with the music of refined pleasure. They were ushered, by a maitre d' who knew Jay, through the two rooms—the first a triumph of dark wood and flowers and decorative glass, the second a blur, to Miranda, of pastel friezes with dancing nymphs —and thus to the bar, hidden behind the restaurant itself, another dark and sparkling place, but more intimate, obviously Jay's favorite, and up to a table in a section one level above the bar.

Time passed as if there *were* no time, as if the hours

were measured in glasses of champagne and the spirited banter she'd missed so much since he'd not been in her life. The subject of Stephanie never came up, by an unspoken mutual pact; for the time, at least, she didn't exist. Instead, they bragged about how successful they'd become, and agreed that success hadn't made them arrogant.

Jay had made the Globe a raging success, an established proving ground for Broadway. He had made a bundle bringing *Up on the Heights* to Broadway—and why hadn't she seen it?

She confessed what she'd already told Jack: that she hadn't seen *Heights* because she was afraid the actress who played Rachel would be better than she had been. He assured her she had been twelve times as good as her replacement, at least. Yes, she told him, *Smitten* had been a blessing, coming just at the right time; thank God Anthony had urged her to do it. And, okay, he acknowledged, Sam Harrington was being forced to take his son seriously—how could he not, since everybody else did?—but, of course, the problems between them were far from resolved.

When the entrée came, she picked at it, oblivious to what it was. He was holding on to her free hand, yet managing to eat everything on his plate; it was the first time she had realized he was left-handed.

There was brandy and coffee, and then they were in a cab, heading across town. They got out at Seventy-second, strolled up Fifth, then over to Madison and up to the Carlyle.

It was then, as they walked down elegant streets lined with town houses, spellbound in the misty magic of the streetlights, that her joy began to fail her. They had, in the course of a long and leisurely evening, quite intentionally talked of nothing intimate. Tacitly committed to pretending they still were the way they had been, they had rolled along easily, demanding nothing but the comfortably steady stream of interested conversation natural to two friends after a long separation. But suddenly, all that had changed: Now, as his arm went around her shoulder, it wasn't casual, and as her arm, in response, slipped around his back, she felt a kind of fear coupled with intense desire. She didn't know what he wanted anymore than she knew what she expected, but what she did know was that it was up to him. She would protect herself this time, present him with no opportunity to reject her. This time, she'd be smart. But as they at last stood in front of the hotel, close together but unmoving, waiting for some cosmic force to make the decision for them, her will collapsed.

"Come up for a drink, how about it? The fridge in the kitchenette is overflowing with champagne, and there's Scotch and some brandy and we can order coffee and—"

"Miranda—" He cupped her chin in his hand and looked down, deep into her eyes. "—Miranda, it's late. I think I'd better be—"

"Oh, come on, Jay. How often do we see each other, after all? We might not get together again for four more years. Don't you think this is a special enough occasion to miss getting eight hours of sleep?" She was pushing him, despite her best intentions, pushing hard, but she couldn't stop it, anymore than she could hide the desperation in her eyes, in her voice. "Come on, be a sport!" And she tried for a jaunty smile, seeing, all the time, how hard he was resisting what she was begging him to do, but not knowing why, and not caring.

"Um . . ." He was obviously trying to say no without hurting her and having trouble coming up with the right line; she could feel that. But she thought she could also feel in him a desire mirroring her own. "Um . . . okay, but don't let me stay too late."

"Far be it for me to be a bad influence," she told him happily. As they entered the lobby and walked to the elevators, she could sense his nervousness at being spotted. It bothered her, but once they were in the elevator, she forced it from her mind. After all, he was almost a married man, and what they might or might not be planning to do would be construed only one way by any friends of Stephanie who might run into him.

Once inside the suite, his relief was obvious, and she wondered if her newly born anxiety was as apparent. A little awkwardly, she asked him what he wanted to drink, and when he said it didn't matter, she decided they'd both have brandy. While he used the phone to get his messages, she prepared the drinks, returning just in time to hear him bill a call to his credit card number, then wait, then say, "Darling, hi, what's up? You called so late. Oh, great. Yeah, yeah, sounds perfect. Sure. Yeah. Stephanie, Stephanie, it's one o'clock in the morning; it's too late to talk about the color of the flowers. No, I'm not mad, I'm just tired. We'll talk about it tomorrow. Uh, oh, I didn't go, actually. Had dinner with some friends . . . nobody you know . . . "

She handed him his drink and sat next to him on the floral print sofa, listening to him lie. Wasn't he worried that somebody might have spotted them at des Artistes? No, of course not; that was why they'd sat in the very dark, very covert bar, to which the maitre d' had led them without prompting. Was that where Jay always took his girls? But that wasn't fair of her, she admitted. Four years they'd been apart, after a bad and final break, and what in hell could she expect—for him to have waited, when they'd agreed there was nothing to wait for? So, when he finally disengaged himself from the phone call, looking a little sheepish, she didn't comment.

He did, though. "Yes, that was my fiancée. If you're wondering why I was on my own tonight, it's because she's at the family manse in East Hampton, with Mums, planning the wedding. The wedding's going to be out there. I'm sorry you had to hear me lie. But, well . . . "

"I know, Jay," she said, pretending to be all-wise and all-forgiving. "Enough said." And she moved closer to him.

"No, Miranda." He took her hands in his, sadly. "Not enough said."

"Why, Jay?" She smiled as she said it, but she didn't feel at all like smiling. "We're grown-ups. I have some sense of the ways of the world."

For a moment, she was sure he was going to catch her to him, could already feel his hands remembering her back, could feel his lips on hers with maddeningly sweet intensity. Instead, he got to his feet. "Miranda, I'm going now."

"Jay!" She was on her feet as well. "Don't! Don't go!"

"Miranda, I can't do this!"

"So you mean," she said wryly, "that physical attraction fades? I thought absence made the—"

"Damn it, Miranda, you know that's not it. Jesus, I wish it was!"

"Then what is the problem, Jay?" She was pleading her case, trying to be calm and reasonable, Portia in *The Merchant of Venice*. "All we're talking about is—"

"A one-night stand. That's what we're talking about. And I don't want to do that. Not with you."

As her heart plummeted, she demanded, "Why? Because I'm so . . . so . . . *special*?" And she thought she could sense her barb wounding him.

"Yes, because you're so special. And because . . . seeing you so unexpectedly . . . it surprised me. After you left for London, after the rage subsided, I thought I'd forgotten you, but all I forgot were the good parts. Seeing you, spending this evening with you, made me remember. We got close, Miranda. I think, toward the end, we really began to sus out each other, and that's rare. I missed it, and I didn't even know I missed it. Now that I do know, I'd go a long way toward compromising my pride—I'm not good at taking rejection,

Miranda—if we could be . . . friends. I don't want us to have to ignore each other for the rest of our lives because of something that happened when we were different people."

"Different?" she asked him. "Are we different?"

"Yeah, both of us. Four years ago we were young and free. We didn't have strings. Now we do." They were standing close to each other, maybe too close, for suddenly he said, "Miranda, I'm going. I'll call you tomorrow morning and we'll make a date for lunch."

"Jay," she said to his back, "do you love her?" and he turned to move toward the door.

His silence was the only answer. She didn't move for a moment, then walked toward him with deliberation, and when they were once again standing very close, she said, "Jay, kiss me just once. For old times' sake."

"Miranda—" His hands stayed at his sides. "Miranda . . . "

"Then *I'll* kiss *you*," she told him, as she reached out, grasping his arms, then standing on tiptoe, making her hands travel softly up to his neck to pull him down to her. He didn't resist, but he didn't consent, just allowed her lips to brush his, her hand to caress his cheek. And then, slowly, she felt his hands on her back, as she'd dreamed, and his lips returning the kiss. And as his tongue found her tongue and she felt the urgent pressure of his body against hers, she knew a thrill of pleasure that turned her legs to jelly and took her breath away.

When they parted for a moment, he looked at her with such longing that she knew what was between them could never fade and, no matter what, must not be lost.

"Jay," she murmured, "Jay, please."

"Oh, God, Miranda, I don't—" But then she was in his arms again, and then his jacket was off, and his tie was undone, and they had passed the point of reason and were happy, carefree lovers, with time to kill and old intimacies to recall. So when the doorbell rang and a lilting Jamaican voice called out, "Room service," they both started to laugh at the ridiculousness of the error. But the guy wouldn't go away, insisting it was flowers for Miss Lawson, from a gentleman who insisted they be delivered personally. So, still smiling and shrugging at who they might be from, Miranda, hair disheveled, shoes off, padded to the door and opened it.

And there stood Anthony, loaded down with flowers, the smile frozen on his face, his glowering, glittering eyes pinning them with rage.

chapter 24

Jack
1984

IT WASN'T UNTIL much later, during that evening in England, that Miranda revealed the cataclysmic conclusion to her evening with Jay. Rather timidly at first, almost embarrassed, she described the anger in Anthony's eyes, the way the frame froze for a moment before the master actor recovered himself. Thrusting the flowers into Miranda's arms and bussing her soundly on the cheek, he'd bounced into the room, all icy smiles, offering Jay his hand.

"*Mister* Harrington!" he'd exclaimed. "What a lovely shock to see you!" Then, clapping him on the back, he added, "And a thundering great success you've become, too, my lad, since last we met."

"Anthony." Jay's manner showed remarkable cool. "Miranda and I were just reminiscing over old times."

"Yes, I can see you were." Anthony then turned his attention to Miranda, clutching her to him in a jaunty, fatherly fashion, then stepping back to address both of them. "Accept my apologies for bursting in as I did. You must forgive an old man's impetuosity. Mad I was to get to New York," and with the old Gainsborough twinkle, he added, grasping her hand, "to get to my

Miranda, so finding myself with a free dance card in London today, I rang up those lovely people at Galaxy Studios, who obligingly booked me a flight one day earlier. I'd been ringing you for hours, without success, my dear, so, when I finally found the line engaged, I assumed you had come in from the evening. That's when I decided to pull my little stunt with the flowers. Do forgive me!''

But he'd given no indication of leaving, Miranda told me, just arranged himself in an armchair and asked her for a brandy. "Now, am I interrupting your reunion?"

"Someone had to tell him he wasn't, and Jay, damn him, was the one who did. So the three of us sat there for what seemed like hours, while I prayed that Anthony would leave and that, somehow, Jay would stay."

"Another sherry?" she asked me, and when I nodded, she took my glass and hers and refilled them before continuing.

"But, of course, Anthony was too clever to allow that. He regaled us with delightful stories so lively and long that it was positively perverse. He wasn't just punishing me; he was torturing me.

"You see, it was as if he knew that, for the space of the two days since I'd seen Jay again, I'd forgotten about *him*. And he was making sure, one, that I would never risk reprisal by forgetting about him ever again, and, of course, two, that what Jay and I had started would not be consummated.''

"So what happened?" I asked, patting her knee as acknowledgment of the frustration and anguish her retelling had stirred up.

"So, at last, Anthony yawned and stood up to go, suggesting, of course, that since he was down the hall from me, he could walk Jay to the elevator. And Jay went right along with it, probably with relief at having been rescued from the devil's grasp. With the determination of an armed guard, Anthony escorted Jay over to me for a peck on the cheek, then out of the room, and . . . '' She sighed '' . . . out of my life,'' she concluded softly.

chapter 25

Miranda
Cambridge, 1979

SHE AWOKE IN sunlight—bright sunlight streaming in the bedroom window. It took her a second to realize that she was in Cambridge and that this was Saturday—a free day, her first all week. She and Anthony and Patrick Grace had come up to Boston on Wednesday, done interviews for every medium, and finally packed it in on Friday. Patrick and Anthony were off to New York, and thence to Southampton for a celebrity-studded weekend at somebody eminent's house. Anthony had wanted her, commanded her, to come, but she'd refused. She had the use of a beautiful apartment in Cambridge and enough old friends in Boston to keep her tied up and occupied for a weekend, she'd argued, and he had given in with relatively little argument. Actually, he'd been much less dictatorial with her since they'd had it out over his finding her with Jay.

The confrontation had taken place the next morning, over breakfast in her suite. At first, he'd been all joviality, never even alluding to the night before, but she, for once, had been too upset to go along with his charade.

"Anthony," she'd begun, "about last night . . ."

"Oh, my dear, don't be harsh with me. I know I stayed too long and I do apologize." He smiled benignly.

"No, no, that's not what I wanted to discuss with you," she murmured, trying to control herself. "No, it's . . . it's . . . " She lowered her eyes, then looked at him. "I met Jay by accident—at a backers' audition. Then he took me to dinner. And then he came up here because *I* insisted. He didn't want to. I made him come up, and I'm embarrassed about that. Because, Anthony—" She was on the verge of crying. "—because all he wanted to tell me, what he finally got across to me, is that he doesn't want me. It's over for him."

"Oh," Anthony replied quietly.

"And I guess I haven't been honest with myself, or with you, or with anybody about him. I guess I haven't gotten over him. I guess I won't. But it doesn't matter, Anthony, because he doesn't want me. Whatever you thought you walked into, it was . . . it was . . . the end," and the despair that fell over her prohibited even tears. "Anthony," she said slowly, painfully, because it hurt so much, "he turned me down, if you must know. He turned me down."

He was instantly at her side, dropped to his knees, cradling her as if she were a baby. "Oh, Randy, Randy, how you must hurt! I wish I could make it better, but all I can tell you is that time, if it doesn't heal, does help. I know you won't understand me now when I tell you it's all for the best, really, dear. Let him have his dull conventional life and some dull conventional woman! God, you were always too much for him, Randy! Too damn much, too damned strong and gifted. But, darling—" He drew back to be able to face her. "—you must promise me this: that you will work on forgetting him, as you work on preparing a part. It's hard, Randy, terribly hard to do, but you must try. Don't let yourself be torn apart by a dream, darling; it's too perilous a course. Now, will you promise me, Randy? Can I trust you when you tell me you will try?"

"Oh, Anthony," she said, desperate.

"Let me look into your eyes, Randy. I've known you

so long, I could always tell when you were fibbing. Still can. So I want you to look at me and promise you will put aside all thoughts of Jay Harrington."

And when she met his gaze, tears glistened in her eyes, and her voice shook at first, as she told him, "Yes, Anthony, I'll do as you say. I have no choice. I'll forget him," and the tears flowed unchecked.

"Oh, my poor darling, I do believe you. It'll be fine, Randy, really. Now, enough tears." He gently dried her eyes with his handkerchief. "I've got some very exciting things to tell you."

And for the rest of their time in New York, he'd kept her busy, rushing her from lunches to drinks to cocktail parties to dinners, with great panache. He had obviously decided that keeping her on the go was an effective tactic for preventing depression. She went along with it, trying to be delightful, wearing a Halston one evening, a Valentino the next, charming successful young men who bored her silly, and graciously accepting the compliments of older ladies who repeatedly told her how much she reminded them of her mother. She had gone along with New York, as she'd gone along with the whirlwind pace in Boston, and she was exhausted. But the weekend would take care of that. The weekend would leave her feeling fresh and alive. And the weekend started now. So, stretching languidly, she rolled onto her side, toward the window, then bent over and, very softly, with her lips, grazed the perfectly muscled, bare back of Jay Harrington.

Jay hadn't called after the scene at the Carlyle, so finally she'd called him—after three days of silence, when every ring of the phone made her jump, when every message promised joy and delivered disappointment. One bitterly depressing late afternoon, she'd realized several things: that she had to see him; that he would never be the one to take the step; and that she had lied, cold-bloodedly, to Anthony. There was no way she could dispense with Jay, absolutely none. Even when they were apart, he had been constantly in her thoughts, assuming the role of an alter ego. When she was angry at herself, she would rail against him; when she attempted to charm, it was him she was really charming; it was him she went to bed with in her fantasies, him she'd sought to impress with her professional excellence, and it was his memory that had invaded her heart, holding it willing prisoner, rebuffing all assaults by other suitors. She had been prepared never to see him again, knowing she would, knowing she must; now that she had, the intensity of her passion, which had built greatly during his absence, had burst into flame. She was afire, like Phaedra; like Medea, she was possessed.

And as her desire for him grew, so did her resentment of Anthony. For several years, she'd repressed it, grateful to him for the giant steps he'd made possible for her. But now, those other feelings burst into her consciousness with astonishing power: It was Anthony who had kept her from Jay in the first place, when she could have had him; he had even concocted a scheme to separate them permanently. That the scheme had led to her success seemed less important now compared to the great loss, the unbearable loss of Jay. It was Anthony who had thrust her into a vast loneliness, and she could not forgive him. How could she, then, feel guilt about the lies? If it weren't for his past machinations, she wouldn't have had to lie at all.

So, she'd called Jay, terrified he wouldn't take her call, mortified at the prospect of rejection, but driven to risk it. She'd called him at the office, around six, afraid he'd left but almost hoping that he would have.

He took her call immediately, as if he'd been expecting it. She'd wanted to talk to him, she'd said, because of the crazy way things had been left the other night— unfinished, to say the least. He'd been silent for a moment, then agreed, but it was from her that the suggestion for their meeting came. She knew how busy he must be, she'd told him; she herself was on the verge of going out, and anyway, sometimes it was hard to talk on the phone. Could they get together? He'd answered, with a hint of pleading, that evenings were . . . um . . . tough . . . and she'd said she understood. Lunch then? He couldn't. What with the New York projects and the Globe opening in a few weeks, he just wasn't free. How about an afternoon?

An afternoon it was, then. A stolen hour snatched from busy schedules, it was like playing hooky from school, titillating disobedience. She suggested the Metropolitan Museum, where they'd never see anyone they knew. She dressed like a student, hair concealed under a floppy hat, no makeup, jeans. She'd gotten there first and sat outside, scanning Fifth Avenue from the top of the steps, seeing him approach in her mind but not in actuality. He was ten, then fifteen minutes late, and she was sure he wasn't coming. Cabs pulled up at the curb far below her, many, many cabs, but none of them containing him. Frenzied, convinced he'd stood her up, she rushed inside to telephone the hotel, expecting a message that he couldn't make it. But there wasn't any. He was now twenty-five minutes late, and she was shaking. But just as her anxiety was about to escalate to hysteria, he appeared, from inside the vast central lobby, where he'd been waiting for her for half an hour. That they had misunderstood each other's directions broke the ice, eased them into the old intimacy. They left immediately, stopping at a tremendously dark bar on Madison in the Seventies, where no one recognized them and no one cared. And it was there, over an intense and emotional two hours, that she'd made him fall in love with her again. Without touching, simply sitting across a table, she'd made him need to be with her. And so, with her help, he'd fabricated a trip to New Haven to see a set designer in order to be with her in Cambridge. When they'd left the bar, she'd put him in a cab, with the lightest of kisses, then walked the few blocks to the hotel, high as a kite. There was still a chance for them.

He'd called her every other morning, early, so no one would catch them at it, always sounding a little guilty but always calling. And over the days, they'd made their plans for enjoying a Cambridge he hadn't checked out in years. Maybe a stroll through Harvard Yard, dinner at Durgin Park—it would all be accomplished with delicious undergraduate stealth.

He had arrived at the Cambridge apartment at 10:00 P.M., on time to the minute, sparing her the agony of waiting. She'd picked up wine, champagne, liquor, and some cold food, arranged flowers in vases around the apartment, whose classically gray walls showcased the exquisite timelessness of chrome and black and glass mixed perfectly with colorful patterns and Oriental rugs.

She'd done her hair wild and free, then slipped into a rose silk Sanchez chiton, long and straight, flowing, yet clingy when she moved, with a virtuous V-neck and loose sleeves. It was so virginal, yet so suggestive, that it presented just the right hint of sexuality; it glowed with allure.

But she felt funny in it; it was too much of a costume, another identity she could assume only because of her training on the stage. So, looking at a clock and seeing it was ten minutes to ten, she'd taken off the negligee and thrown on jeans and a big, black, gorgeous Sonia Rykiel sweater, so understated you'd never guess it cost three times as much as the Sanchez, and—a subtle erotic touch—located and fastened into place the gold ankle bracelet she'd never before had the guts to wear. She decided to go shoeless, and redid her hair sort of messily, piled on top of her head so it wouldn't look as though she'd spent hours doing it.

As she changed, she was planning how she would adjust her life to his without sacrificing her career. London wouldn't be possible, but, then, it probably wouldn't be possible anyway, after they'd broken the news to Anthony. So she'd work in New York. And movies—well, he could fly out on weekends or she could fly to New York. Or they'd alternate. It would work out. A lot of married couples did it. It was going to be fine. It had to be.

And right then, hearing the doorbell, walking to the door, thrilled and terrified, she vowed she would make it work.

He didn't wait to be admitted, just barged in, in jeans and sneakers and a Yankees sweat shirt, presenting the flowers he'd brought, then crushing them when he moved against her, kicking the door shut, just like in the movies.

She just clung to him, willing his kisses never to end, wanting to be wearing nothing, feeling the contours of his body, kissing him again, dizzied by desire.

"I'm weak," she whispered in his ear. "Hello."

He was the same lover, the one she'd dreamed of, but better, more in control, leaving her powerless as they somehow moved from the door to the bedroom. There they made up for lost time, taking their time, with the lights on and the street noises echoing below. And then she drew back to undress him and felt herself shaking, but undressed him anyway. All the years she'd rehearsed for this moment had paid off, had prepared her for the state of sublime readiness in which she let him help her off with her clothes, then felt him move against her, wonderfully heavy, speaking but only to her body, every inch of it, till she trembled and was meant to be his. And then he was with her, and she was sighing and laughing and safe, meeting her personal destiny rhythmically, perfectly, knowing that Anthony was wrong and she was right, and Jay was her joy. She wanted rapture instantly, but he wouldn't give her her way, suggesting, with his body, that she was in a hurry, that love was patience, and now was much too soon. If she had no patience, he had enough for them both, and she learned, that night, subtleties of pleasure that made her gasp. He was hers, he was the only one, and she knew he'd craved her as much as she had him—their mutual cries confirmed it—and that they could never again be really apart. They'd saved each other by a hairbreadth —it was a miracle. It wasn't too late.

It had been four years since they'd shared a bed, four years since they'd fallen asleep in each other's arms, probably longer since they'd gone to sleep before midnight. But they had that night, and now, it was the next morning, another beginning.

And so she kissed his back, with the light streaming in the windows, and felt him stir so quickly she suspected he'd been awake already, and watched him turn toward her. His eyes were wide open, and he smiled at her as she nuzzled his chest. "You're a great wake-up call," he teased her, drawing her to him and kissing the top of her head.

"Gee, thanks. Think of all the money you'll save. I'm a good investment!" She started to kiss him when she felt a newborn resistance in him, a veiled warning, but she chose to ignore it. What she couldn't ignore was his own kiss, warm and loving, but clearly not meant to lead to anything else. Instead, he held onto her tight and buried his face in her hair, saying nothing.

When at length he spoke, it was to say, "Miranda, I want to tell you some things you don't know about my life."

"Jay! Not—" She was suddenly frightened, and the fright turned to dread when he gently separated them, facing her, his profile turned toward hers on the pillows.

"No, Miranda. Please. Before things go any farther. Please."

She was obediently quiet.

"First, I want to apologize to you because I think, in the last week, I've been misleading you."

Oh, God. "What do you mean?"

"I've been . . . uh . . . pursuing you when I didn't have the right. I couldn't help it, I guess, because I hate resisting you. But I think I painted an unrealistic picture of my situation."

"How?" She sat up in bed, bolstered by the pillow, staring at him. "How, Jay?"

"Well, to begin with: I didn't just meet Stephanie."

"I know that. Remember? That time in SoHo?"

"Yeah, right. But I hadn't just met her then, either. See, we've known each other since we were kids. We grew up near each other, went to the same schools. Our parents are friendly, and have been since we were kids. They're very big in the Manhattan construction business, one of Dad's prime contractors, in fact. Well, there's been a lot of pressure all my life for Stephanie and me to end up together."

"A merging of dynasties! How royal! Were you childhood sweethearts, too? The whole thing?" She was beginning to stir with anger.

"No, not exactly, but, look, I know this sounds very sexist, but . . . well . . . I think she set her cap for me very early on."

"And it's finally paid off, all those years of scheming. Good for Stephanie!" She was livid, at herself for being such a fool, at him for going along with her folly.

"That's not fair, Miranda," he had the nerve to say. "Stephanie is Stephanie. She's not you. She's an assistant buyer at Bloomingdale's, but she doesn't want to run the store. She wants to be its biggest customer. The career she's interested in is being a wife."

"That sounds stimulating!"

"Marriage isn't supposed to be stimulating, Miranda. It's supposed to be steady, steady and habitual, with as few surprises as possible."

So she'd been wrong. It *was* too late. It *was* all lost. And this past week, when she'd believed she could have it all, when she'd been genuinely happy for the first time in four years, had been a mistake.

"I want you to know, Miranda," he continued, his words making only a dull impact on her pain, "that I wasn't seeing Stephanie when I met you. That night in SoHo, she called me. I didn't instigate it. I wouldn't have. Believe me. We'd broken up about six months before, after I told her I wasn't ready to get married, and I thought that was that. I wasn't even thinking about her. I was thinking about you.

"That time when you and I were together, I was totally involved. You were very different from Stephanie, very different from any of the girls I'd gone out with. They were safe; they couldn't surprise me. You were a risk, and I loved the excitement. You helped me a lot, you know, more than anybody else has ever been able to. You made me brave—less conventional. Maybe if things had worked out differently . . . but they didn't.''

"So you're saying I had one chance at you, and I turned you down, and I don't get another one?" She was looking away from him.

"If that's what I'm saying, then I'm still dealing off some old resentments." He reached out for her shoulder, but she shrugged off his hand. "I'm not aware of that. I hope that's not what I'm doing."

"So you're marrying her?" she asked him, face turned toward the wall.

"Yes, I am," he said solemnly.

"And you had to come all the way to Boston to tell me that?" She turned back toward him, eyes blazing.

"I had to see you alone. In private."

"Last fling before the wedding, huh?"

She was preparing to get out of bed, but he stopped her. "Miranda, I fucked this up, and I'm really sorry. Maybe that's our karma. I always end up disappointing you, hurting you, when all I really want is for us to be—"

"Friends?" She was beyond anger, on the verge of despair. "Friends? You must be joking! Do you really expect us to be friends? Why don't you invite me to the wedding, that'd be fun! No, Jay. I assume I'm enough of a professional to work with you—if it should happen. But I don't think we'll ever be friends.''

He looked at her with such sadness it made her want to cry, but she wouldn't give him the satisfaction. "So let's just get it over with," she said. "The thing it took us four years to say. Goodbye.''

chapter 26

Jack
1984

IF WE'D THOUGHT we were successful in '79, we were dazzled by what we'd become by 1980. All of us —Miranda, Jay, me.

Jay had brought the musical we'd seen auditioned, *Animal Magnetism*, to Broadway the following fall. In a season that would prove to be the New York theatre's hottest in decades, he'd made *Magnetism* a superhit, and it had ended up collecting Tonys the way honey collects bees. Our movie, *Smitten*, had made an incredible bundle and been nominated for six Oscars—best screenplay, best director, best director, best actor, best supporting actress (Miranda), best supporting actor (Anthony), and, heart-stoppingly, best picture.

That late April afternoon, we'd arrived at the Chandler Pavilion in a threesome, Miranda, Anthony, and I, all dressed to the nines, although I was sure I was going to sweat through the layers of my evening clothes and appear on the stage—should I win—dripping wet. Miranda, cool and poised, was resplendent in a pale green gown of some floaty stuff in layers, her hair loose and flowing, and looking astonishingly like her mother.

For she had, in these years, fully grown into her heritage. Whereas when I'd first met her, the resemblance to Margo had gone largely unnoticed by the world, now, no one could miss it. It was as if her father's genes had been totally overpowered by her mother's. Yes, she was every inch Margo Seymour's daughter, judging from the Margo I'd seen in movie revivals, from her wit and charm and worldly cuteness to her sensitivity and healthy sexuality. She was better than a carbon copy of her mother; she had inherited the good traits and apparently been spared the inner fever that, in the end, had consumed Margo's ebullient levity and driven her to destruction.

In contrast, Miranda, as she approached her thirtieth year, just glowed. Fame had come to her as a blessing, and she wore it as such.

What was most gratifying to me, personally, as a peacemaker, was the fact that she was now able to work with Jay. Whatever had happened after the meeting I'd arranged must have been for the good. She seemed to have accepted his marriage, and although she could hardly be called a close friend of the Jay Harringtons, she could attend a dinner party or an opening with them and not seem bothered by it.

Best of all, she'd leapt at the chance to do the movie of *Up on the Heights* despite the fact that Jay was producing. Anthony definitely hadn't been anxious to work with Jay again, but Miranda urged him to do it for her —and for me. He went along pleasantly enough, although he must have been furious at Jay for getting to her. As for Miranda, the movie of *Heights* was a great follow-up to *Smitten*, and at least she'd have me around to keep her from making Jay mad.

We'd been in LA shooting the Hollywood stuff—I'd added a lot of it to the screenplay—and the interiors, and Jay had been in and out for a few days at a time. Marriage and impending fatherhood (Stephanie had, of course, almost immediately proceded to fulfill her duty and produce an heir) seemed to have sobered him. He turned in earlier these days, after supper with me or with me and Miranda, retiring to the house he was using in

Bel Air and appearing on the set early in our workday. We even managed to get in an occasional tennis game, which he traditionally won, even when he tried to let me win. He wasn't distant; that wasn't the word. He was, rather, more private—an enormously successful man for whom family and business came before social pleasures.

Miranda, too, was living quietly. She'd rented a house in the Hollywood Hills, that part of the Hills that overlooks everything from Grauman's Chinese to the ocean. I, writer that I was, had been loaned a beach house in Malibu, which meant a fair amount of driving to and from the set, but I learned to like it all, and traveling the long leisurely stretch of Coast highway always started the day off pleasantly. Since Anthony's role in *Heights* was small, he wasn't around constantly, but when he was, he saw to it that he was ensconced in a suite at the Beverly Hills Hotel, where he added a certain touch of class to the Polo Lounge.

During his visits, someone was always throwing a lunch or brunch or dinner party for him, and Miranda and I went along. We were, by then, considered an established item. I greatly enjoyed the role of Miranda's swain, but I was puzzled that a woman who could have had a truly dazzling personal life chose to have none at all. Over the last few years, the press continued to report on men she was said to be seeing, some here, some in England, but as always, nothing ever seemed to come of it. "I work eighteen hours a day," she told me that afternoon at Anthony's manse, "do you really think there's room in my life for a grand passion? If I were a man, you wouldn't even bother to ask the question!" She was right, of course, and since I treasured her company, I was glad I got as much of her attention as I did. Someday, she'd meet a guy who would sweep her off her feet, the way Jay had, but this time she'd be ready, and I'd lose her. So, part of me wished Prince Charming II would take his time arriving.

All in all, I felt pretty damn good as we crossed the plaza toward the Chandler Pavilion on that early April afternoon. We had come a long way together, Miranda and I, and it was right that she was by my side that day. Anthony, who'd won an Oscar twenty years earlier, played the seasoned pro to our anxious young contenders, and I was happy that he was with us. It was Anthony, after all, who had played such a major role in my career, as well as Miranda's. And Miranda seemed only to have blossomed under his rigid supervision. I felt for him, sure he was remembering an earlier time, in a different setting, but for the same celebration. Then, the Oscars were presented at the Pantages, downtown, properly at night, before TV and the great importance of Eastern Standard Time. Then, he had been a mainstay of that glittering foreign colony that had been taken up by Hollywood during the war and afterward. Then, his companions would have included Olivier and Vivien Leigh, Douglas Fairbanks and Charles Laughton and Merle Oberon and Leslie Howard; Garbo and Dietrich and Charles Boyer and Billy Wilder and Ernst Lubitsch and David Niven and, above all, Margo Seymour. They would have driven in from the Malibu Colony or the San Ysidro Ranch or rushed over from dinner at Ciro's or the Brown Derby. He would have been young and fit, glowing with his total belief in his own ability to win; Margo's presence on his arm would have confirmed that, if his will faltered. Now that world was relegated to bad prints on late-night television. How he must have regretted its passing. But he must also have thought that however mixed his luck, it had been good enough to give him back Margo in the person of Miranda. She was the beloved child they'd never had, and her uncanny resemblance to her mother must have been to him a priceless gift left by Margo to ease his loneliness. So perhaps this night was also a sort of celebration for him, and he jollied us along with a rare ebullience.

By the time we were in our seats, half blinded by the

glaring TV lights, our view of the stage partially blocked by TV crews and cameras, I was clutching Miranda's hand and Miranda was biting her lip. Anthony leaned over to whisper that we might be on television at any second and to keep up appearances, so we breathed deeply and did our best.

We continued to do our best during the opening hullabaloo, which seemed to go on forever and to be terribly unfunny, although we had to laugh, to the first couple of minor awards, which I didn't even hear. And then came best supporting actor. The presenters were Diana Ross and Roy Scheider. Diana couldn't get the envelope open, and Scheider made some crack, and then she announced . . . Anthony. For the TV camera, he smiled in a dignified fashion, kissed Miranda, stopped on the way down the aisle to shake the director's hand, then bounded up on the stage as the crowd gave him a standing ovation. When they quieted down, he cleared his throat and said, "You know, it's been decades since we've been together. Next time, let's not make it so long," and the audience laughed, and he thanked a lot of people, especially me and Miranda, and the crowd rose to its feet again, and he bowed and left the stage.

I, by the way, didn't win. A bigger script, with more serious intent, took the award away from me, but afterwards, everybody assured me I'd be up there next year or the year after, and sure enough, I was.

I had, that night, to be content with the knowledge that, at my tender young age, I'd gotten a nomination for my first movie script from people who'd been doing it a lot longer than I had. Sure, I was disappointed, but I would've been a fool to be crushed. So I immediately shifted my disappointment to the anticipation I was feeling for Miranda.

Anthony hadn't returned to his seat because he was scheduled to be one of the presenters for the best supporting actress award—either a good omen or a bad one, it was impossible to tell. As he and his copresenter,

Joanne Woodward, came on the stage to great applause, Miranda grabbed my hand and held on for dear life. I patted her knee, which was below camera range, and we both stopped breathing. The banter from the stage, though charming, was unbearable, endless, irrelevant. The reading of the nominees' names seemed so protracted, it felt as if they were reading the phone book. But then the envelope was opened, at first try, and Joanne Woodward gave it away by glancing up at Anthony before announcing, "Miranda Lawson."

Miranda's hand continued to clutch mine for an instant while the impact registered, then freed itself to caress my cheek as she lightly kissed me. Then she rose and floated down the aisle to the stage. Anthony took her hand to present her to Joanne, who reached over to kiss her cheek, then let her turn back to Anthony. It was a haunted moment, as the images of Anthony and Margo again shared a stage. But the spell was broken as Miranda fell into Anthony's arms, and they hugged each other tight, for all the world to see. When they broke apart, the Oscar was hers, and he started to back away, but Miranda clearly urged him to stay by her side while she made her speech. We could see him decline, insisting the moment was hers alone.

As she walked to the podium, her smile was dazzling. She spoke only briefly, honored by the Academy's honoring her, never forgetting the great tradition that had helped take her there, invoking her mother's memory with dignity, then thanking a few people, with a special debt to me, and of course, to Anthony. With a final thanks, and great poise, she left the stage. I have never been so proud of anyone, including myself.

By the end of the evening, Patrick Grace had added Best Actor to our trophies, giving us three Oscars—a guarantee that *Smitten*'s business would perk along for the next few months.

"You should have gotten this, not me," Miranda said when we were filing out of the auditorium.

"Shut up, beautiful," I whispered in her ear. "Nobody's complaining!"

Anthony, too, was beaming when we met up with him again. "*Up on the Heights* is the one that'll win it for you, boy!" he told me as the limo delivered us to the official party. "Wait and see. I know this town pretty damned well, even after all these years." He would turn out to be right, of course.

The party was less a party than a gorgeously attired mob scene, wall-to-wall people, some famous, some obscure, and a din so thunderous it gave me a headache. I remember having my hand shaken by the likes of Burt Lancaster and Julie Andrews and Steven Spielberg. I remember seeing Miranda embraced by Goldie Hawn and Liza Minnelli and Francis Coppola. I remember feeling what it was like, for the first time, to be at the top of the top, high on a drug more powerful than coke, loving the world and all its creatures. It could have been minutes, it could have been hours, that I was trapped in the midst of this glittering press, hot as a son of a bitch but not caring, mopping my forehead with one hand as I continued to shake more eminent ones with the other.

After some unspecified time, when people were just beginning to leave, Anthony rounded up Miranda and me and suggested we move on to Swifty Lazar's and then on to a late-night bash. But, once we were back in the limo, Miranda seemed changed—perhaps only exhausted, but I thought preoccupied. Pleading too much excitement already, she asked to be dropped at her house. She'd give the world, she said, to be alone for a while and then just go to sleep.

Anthony started to balk, but finally relented, promising to make her apologies to everyone. When we dropped her off, I walked her to the door and asked her if she was all right. Perfectly, she said, just suffering from a little too much strong emotion. "Look," I said, "want me to check on you later?"

She almost jumped when I suggested that, then made

me give my word I wouldn't. "It'll just spoil the rest of your evening, Jack, and besides, I'll be asleep in half an hour."

I trusted she would be, but despite what I'd told her, I did stop back at her house in the wee hours, hoping to offer some comfort if she couldn't sleep, to find that the lights were out—and her car was gone.

chapter 27

Miranda
Los Angeles, April 1980

THEY HAD BEEN lovers for half a year.

Jay'd gotten married and she'd gone back to London to play *Miss Julie* and to make a sexy historical art film, which had turned into an international cult movie. When they ran into each other, in the fall of '79, in London, she'd been considering a West End play and a Hollywood script. She wanted to do the play; her agent and Anthony urged her to do the film: *Smitten* had been an even bigger hit than the studio had projected, and it had made her a genuinely hot property. At this point she could pick and choose, and if she picked wisely, she'd soon be able to write her own ticket.

On two continents, people whispered to each other when she passed, and she was finding it more and more difficult to travel alone. Somehow, there was always an entourage—demi-friends, hangers-on, the regular cast of characters that hover around the rich and famous. She went out with men, often, and stayed late, but it was never a twosome; there were always at least three other people, whom she couldn't have shaken if she'd wanted to. As it was, she didn't much care. Jay—or the memory of Jay—had ruined her, once again, for anybody else.

The actual scene of their meeting was a house in

Hampstead, the occasion, a closing night party for a long-running play starring Edward Fox.

She had heard Jay was in town, talking to Trevor Nunn about importing a Royal Shakespeare Company production to New York, then she'd heard about the party, and fusing the two occasions together in a moment of heightened perception, she got herself invited, even bought a dress—a plum-colored Jean Muir, almost medieval in the way it traced the body, and with it she wore burgundy boots and a brocade vest.

The house was large, as was the party, and she'd slowly made her way through two rooms, greeting profusely and being roundly greeted, and made it out to the terrace, although it was chilly, before she saw him, standing alone in the cold. The expression on his face, when he saw her, wasn't shock, wasn't delight; neither smiling nor solemn, it was the calm look of utter concentration. His gold-flecked eyes studied her serenely, his features shone with the perfect beauty of a classical statue's, at peace with eternity. And seeing him focus on her that way, she wondered if he'd willed her here; he certainly could have, he had the power.

Her eyes never leaving his, she walked to him and said, "I'm sorry about Boston."

"So am I," he answered evenly, looking down at her.

"I didn't mean what I said. About goodbye."

"It doesn't matter. It's out of our hands," he'd told her. "Let's go," and taking her elbow to steer her back through the crowd, he led her out. They went back to his suite with the river view at the Savoy, and, there, clinging to each other with a relief that was ecstasy, they celebrated the overwhelming conquest of their judgment, their reason, and their honesty.

After that night, her professional decisions became easier to make. She did the movie because it was being shot in New York and Jay was in New York. She did a two-week guest spot in *Saint Joan of the Stockyards* at Yale, ostensibly as a gracious alumna, but really because Connecticut was a good place for her and Jay to meet. The filming of *Up on the Heights* was a dream come true.

They met socially—with distance but amiability—had even dined together with Stephanie and Jack. Anthony, stuck in London where he was directing at the National, called almost every day, buying the casual manner in which she infrequently mentioned Jay, because she always alluded to men she was dating—and to Jack's consistent presence, which must have soothed Anthony's fears.

She'd sublet a loft in New York, miles from where Jay and Stephanie lived. She guessed he'd given up his own loft, but for some reason never asked him. Her place was gorgeous—a new style in a new neighborhood, with levels and pillars and platforms, incredibly sunny and high-ceilinged, very chic. It was way downtown, near City Hall and Wall Street, where Manhattan announced its seventeenth-century roots, and she liked that, pretending it was London.

They met when she wasn't filming, at odd times, for a couple of hours, but there were some rare weekends when Stephanie had retired to her parents' house in the country and Jay had pleaded being too busy to go.

Those were the best—those stolen Saturday nights or languid Sundays, the times when she really grew to know him. She knew the way he liked his coffee and his steaks and whether he preferred his bagels toasted, which network news he watched and what was wrong with his tennis game. She knew by inference that he'd made a fortune in downtown real estate, as she'd suspected, by buying early and cheap, before the boom. She alone had heard him articulate his fondest desire— to own a major sports team, preferably in the NFL. She knew where and when he got his hair cut, how many power brokers he'd lunched with at 21, and what clothes to buy to please him. But she knew nothing about his marriage, and she never asked, just as he never pried into what she did when she wasn't with him. By a mutual unstated agreement, the imminent arrival of Jay's firstborn was never mentioned.

She'd been witness to his rages against his father, had often been made the object of their acting out: If he had a bad morning, she felt it in the afternoon. But that was fair. That was intimacy.

She never called him, because of his schedule and the complications of his life. He called her every day and usually met her three times a week. They'd spent her birthday, December fourth, together, but only for the afternoon. He'd given her an Yves Saint Laurent evening gown of black tulle and sequins, which he made her promise to return if she didn't like it, but of course she loved it, and it fit her perfectly, he knew her body that well.

His birthday, January twenty-sixth, they had the evening and much of the night together, every night that week, because Stephanie was in the Caribbean. Giving him a present was a problem, because it might be noticed at home, so she bought him the most expensive robe in the history of Paul Stuart and he left it at her place. It was all he left, because he never spent the night; he had to go home because of the servants. She had little or no concept of his relationship with Stephanie, but she felt, in what brief time they snatched from their lives, that she knew him better, in more intimate detail, especially since they were always alone. Just the two of them, time out of time, and their meetings were affected by no one but themselves. She never fantasized more to the relationship than she already had; she didn't dare to hope for longer hours together. She was unbelievably lucky to have him at all.

And then, thank God, had come California, and *Up on the Heights*. When he was on the Coast, he came to her house, leaving early, or occasionally she would spend the night with him at the house in Bel Air that he had rented; there were no servants who slept over, and if

Anthony called her place at the crack of dawn, she could always claim to have been taking a dip in the pool—he knew she couldn't hear the phone from there.

The morning of the Oscar presentation, aflutter with nerves, she'd prevailed on Jay by phone to fly in that night instead of the next morning. She needed him, she said, whether she won or lost.

He responded by repeating what he always said when she demanded his presence as necessary for her survival —that she didn't *need* him there; rather, she *wanted* him there. He wasn't keeping her afloat. He adored her and treasured her, but she was a big girl now, and it was her own strength that she *needed*, not his.

Conceding the point, she went on to insist that this was an extraordinary circumstance. How often did you get nominated for an Oscar? She agreed that she didn't require him to sustain her through a disappointment; she'd been disappointed before, alone, and muddled through. But, if she won, then it would be paradise if he were there to share it.

He pleaded appointments, which she knew were valid, but she didn't care just then. This was one unique time when tomorrow wouldn't do. He demurred. She pleaded. She stopped pleading and sulked slightly. He considered ways of changing his plans. She said, reluctantly, that she would understand if he couldn't do it. He sighed, and capitulated. He would squeeze in his appointments before he caught the flight. Assuming the plane would be more or less on time, he'd be waiting for her call in Bel Air as soon as she could get away from the post-award parties. She ventured a goodbye. He told her his fingers were crossed for her, then started to sign off, pleading lots to do if he was going to make the flight. Feeling the same wound open in her heart that she always felt when he left her, she said goodbye, she'd see him soon.

She'd called the Bel Air house the second she got

home with the Oscar, and he'd answered her on the first ring. The excitement in his voice made her thoroughly happy for the first time that crazy evening. It was as if her winning hadn't been real until he confirmed it. She had been all set to get off the phone and race to Bel Air when she realized what she really wanted.

"Let's go for a walk on a beach. I want to walk by the ocean with you, just like in the movies." But Malibu was too far, given the hour, Pacific Palisades not their line of country, so they settled, hastily, for the strip of public beach that begins quietly in Santa Monica and gathers steam and action as it turns into Venice. She suggested they meet by a giant black rock near the waterline in Santa Monica, directly across the board-walk from a smoky seafood restaurant they'd risked dining at several times, at late hours. After dinner, they'd walked along the water, pausing at the black rock, and it seemed to her their spot.

Not bothering to change out of her gown, pausing only to place the Oscar carefully on the fireplace mantel in the living room, she threw on a trench coat against a possible chill, grabbed her keys, turned out the lights, and practically ran out the door to the Toyota. At 1:00 A.M., the freeway was relatively empty, and she made good time, breezing along, wrapped in the sublime security of knowing that, for the moment, she had everything she wanted. The Vivaldi mandolin concerto sparkling on the tape deck, her hair ruffled by the rolled-down windows, she drove fast and well, savoring the getting there, drunk with the anticipation of him.

Luck was with her, for she found a parking place easily, on first try, half a block from the beach. Running as fast as her high-heeled sandals permitted her, she reached the boardwalk, still enlivened by casual strollers, apartment lights, and the bustle of open shops and restaurants; she wasn't worried, then, about being recognized: No one was celebrity-hunting this late, and even if they were, she'd be the last person anyone would expect to see in Santa Monica, the very night she'd won an Oscar.

In the distance, across the boardwalk, she saw, to her delight, that a figure waited by the black rock. Knowing she'd make better time barefoot, she took off her shoes and ran to him, across the deserted beach, toward the dark and sparkling water. He didn't move as he saw her approaching him, was leaning against the rock, perfectly still, shadowed by the mixture of darkness behind him and the boardwalk lights ahead. He was wearing jeans and sneakers and a V-neck tennis sweater over bare skin. He had on the glasses that, over the last few years, he was seldom without. He was smiling, but, as she came closer, he put out his arms, and she ran to him, dropping the sandals in the sand as she fell into his embrace.

Holding him as tight as she could, she was flooded with the realization that he, Jay, was her single source of complete contentment. Jack, Anthony, her friends, and her associates gave her so much, so unceasingly, and without them her success would be far less wonderful. But Jay—Jay was so much more. Jay gave meaning to that glory; Jay was her devotion, her reason for succeeding. Jay, whose unique blending of flesh and spirit, mind and body, made him everything for her. That she could have him only seldom was a sadness, granted, but that she could never have him was, by now, unthinkable.

"God, I'm so glad you're here!" she said into his chest, unwilling to release him, even for a kiss. He didn't answer, just stroked her hair, as the water washed gently up on the beach and the noises from the boardwalk softened to a distant murmur.

At the same moment, they released each other, longtime lovers who had grown to know intimately the way their bodies worked together. Looking up at him, seeing in his eyes joy touched with a sadness that she'd always sensed, and always dismissed, she was simply grateful: He was here, he was holding her, he was kissing her, delicately, his lips brushing hers. He was kissing her more firmly now, and she was kissing him back, recklessly, uncaring of who spotted them. His hands slipped inside the trench coat and caressed her chiffon-clad back, his touch firm against the delicate cloth, crushing it in his urgency to feel her body. Then his hands were on her shoulders, then slowly, deliberately moving over her breasts, then gliding to her neck, lifting her head toward him for another kiss.

"You're absolutely radiant," he told her when the kiss finished. "Radiant."

"Shouldn't I be?" She smiled at him. "Tonight, right now, I have everything I ever wanted. Really."

"Miranda, I—" he started to say, but she stopped him.

"No, don't. You *are* a major part of everything, Jay. I wouldn't be this happy if you weren't here to share my happiness."

He said nothing, just looked at her, the tenderness of his expression his only declaration of what he felt for her. For she had come to be the one who declared. Madly in love, she defined for him—in laughter, in words, in sighs—the precise nature of that love. On him she bestowed paeans of rapture, yet she felt she had never said or shown enough to express truly the extent of her emotion. Granted, it was he who established the intensity of their physical passion; it was she who always had to make the leap to equal him. But in every other way, she was the ardent one, he was the love object.

She didn't care. Jay was the way he was. She was the lover, undivided by her glorious obsession, feeling no guilt, under-appreciating his own. What they had was illicit, perhaps, but it was pure to her, the purest thing in her life, pure and totally good. That she had lied to Jack and Anthony seemed a minor sin, given the fact that her love for Jay was better, higher, than the world would ever understand.

And so they walked by the water, in a state of bliss, while he carried her shoes and made her describe every moment of the evening, until she was performing. Laughing, joking, she told him everything as they walked, his arm slipping around her when she wasn't in the midst of an extravagant gesture. Eventually, they headed back to the boardwalk and found they had arrived in the middle of the honky-tonk hurly-burly of Venice. Even at that late hour, the way was crowded with a mob so various, so lively and desperate and high and mischievous, that they easily lost themselves among it. As they walked back toward Santa Monica, the crowd began to thin out, and soon they stood before the seafood restaurant across from the black rock.

His Mercedes coupe was parked across the street from her car, and pausing for a final kiss, they separated, and she followed him back to Bel Air.

The house he'd rented was nestled in the green, curving lushness of the hills, lit at night by tall welcoming lamps. He drove into the garage; she parked in the tiny circular driveway. Then, arm in arm, they walked into the elegantly silk-paneled entry hall, past the softly pastel living room, where eighteenth-century antiques danced a graceful minuet with modern pieces, and on into the master bedroom.

With one whole wall a window gazing out over the galactic glitter of the LA panorama, the room was like a dream of perfect sleep in outer space. Mirrors on the other walls picked up the glowing view in a fabulous cyclorama, and the long, low furniture, almost Japanese in its simplicity, offered sensual peace. Banks of candles glowed with multicolored flame on the tables by the bed, lit by some now-departed servant, offering a magical, trancelike glow. A terra-cotta wine cooler containing a bottle of champagne stood at the side of the bed, along with two glasses. They toasted her, toasted themselves, toasted everything before they stopped, suddenly staring at each other, transfixed.

Slowly, she reached out her hand to touch his chest, then, with the other hand joining it, she maneuvered his sweater off and over his head, and she fell against him, kissing him over and over as if in disbelief at the priceless gift of his being there with her. He sighed and moved on top of her, and she savored his weight on her, loving its familiarity, needing its silky pressure.

This was the best ever, for them and for her. Weightless with giddiness, she could float and fly and turn and discover even now, after so long, new things about him. He held her closer than before, feeling her with more passionate fingertips than before, lingering longer than ever, savoring every inch of her. And when they were together, she was dizzied with the joy, and only for a moment, sad that it couldn't be this way forever, that she couldn't have him with her, in her, for longer than just now. But that quickly passed, as their rapture built, and she thought, *whatever happens, this has happened, a perfect night, with all the universe in order*. And as he began to come, he murmured her name with such ardor it made her one with him, and they stretched it out and made it last as long as possible, and fell asleep, at peace in each other's arms.

And her last waking memory, something she would have told him had she not been so close to sleep, was how sure she was that, in the quiet night, she'd heard a car slowly pull up outside, idle, then, finding something it sought, drive rapidly away.

chapter 28

Jack
1984

THERE ARE THINGS you do in your life, actions so completely out of character that they make you wonder if you ever knew yourself at all. If only briefly, you're forced to see yourself with a kind of objectivity, the clarity usually reserved for seeing others. That never lasts, of course. It doesn't take long for the aberration to weave itself into the texture of your ordinary being; in short, to become part of your life. But, before it does, you watch yourself with the bemused distance of astral projection.

The night of the Oscars was one of those times I took myself entirely by surprise. There were plenty of reasons for doing what I did, some noble (concern about Miranda's welfare and a nagging fear of the truth), some literary (eagerness to solve a mystery in which I was involved, to uncover a secret drama), some considerably less flattering (my possible disgruntlement over not winning an award, subconscious resentment at Miranda for having won, plus the perverse compulsion to discover that a loved one is deceiving you). And there are more factors, I believe, but none of them add up to a satisfactory explanation of why, after seeing Miranda's car was gone, I didn't just give up and go home.

I went, instead, in pursuit of her, to the place I was

suddenly sure she could be found. Motivated by an overwhelming craving to know the truth, I was also impelled by rage; as I drove I was horrified by how they both had lied to me. Miranda and I had been the closest of friends for years now, had shared secrets of utmost intimacy and never knowingly betrayed each other's trust. But, now, it was clear that she had needlessly deceived me, for who knows how long. She'd made me feel like a fool. And he, the only scrupulous power at the unscrupulous top level of an unscrupulous town . . . he, whom people wanted to find some fault with, and couldn't . . . he, if what I strongly suspected was true, was the worst sort of hypocrite, using his unbesmirched family-man image as a cover for his mistress. Probably he was no different from all the other baby robber barons, handing out payoffs and bribes as his daily currency! Obviously, loyalty meant nothing to him; he could abandon it as easily as a deal he had lost interest in. I had adored her character and admired his, and I had been wrong. To my fevered brain, they were no better than a gangster and his moll.

As I drove, I thought with pain of moments I'd perceived so wrongly: Miranda parting from me before eleven so many evenings, assuring me that she had to have rest because the filming was so strenuous or because she needed the time to be by herself and think. Her renewed embracing of solitude, which I'd accepted as a growth in discipline and maturity, was far from that. It was simple; she was meeting her married lover.

And I was outraged. Only later could I see that outrage as a complex and infantile jealousy. Jay's hold over her, I'd decided, was sexual; it was the reason for her betrayal of me. Yes, sex was the reason, all right; it was sex that had driven a wedge between Miranda and me— otherwise, she and I would have been enough for each other. That I wasn't thinking clearly, was actually out of my mind, never occurred to me. At that moment, I imagined I was thinking with perfect clarity. It was all for sex, their risking of other people's happiness, and that made Miranda a whore. And it made him scum.

Some months later I was dining with the Harringtons, on one of Jay's rare free nights *en famille*. The baby had turned out to be a boy, of course, named Jonathan, and he'd been doing something astonishing, like crawling, and after we studied him doing it as if we were watching the Superbowl, Stephanie picked up the child and whisked him off to his nanny, waiting in what almost could be called the other wing of the vast apartment. Jay, looking as young as he did when we first met, in jeans and a sweater, was idly sipping a Black Label, his thoughts fixed on something. When he spoke, it was to me, but half to himself.

"You know, Jack. The one thing I'll never understand—how you're supposed to make major life decisions—business, family, major things—when you're too young to be experienced. How can you be expected to look down the road and see anything at all? Deciding right has to be as much of an accident as deciding wrong. So where are you supposed to go for help? I guess you look to your heritage, your family, as a guide. But trusting your heritage—God, that's just as tricky as trusting your own inadequate powers of judgment. It's blind faith."

Stephanie had returned at that point, and the conversation switched to something else, but I wondered afterward just what Jay had been referring to. That evening I thought he was mediating on new fatherhood and the awesome responsibility of raising a child. But later, years later, in light of all that had happened, it occurred to me that even then, he might have been talking of himself and Miranda. And I felt sad for him. But as I drove through the eastern gate of Bel Air on Oscar night, I wasn't giving Jay any quarter. I approached the white house stealthily, noting that a pale light shone from the back quarters while the rest of the place was in darkness. Slowing down as I reached the front entrance,

I spotted her car, wantonly parked in the driveway—an open admission of betrayal, a billboard of her falseness. With my worst fears confirmed, I sped away, dizzy with my realization—and with the power that knowledge gave me.

I had some decisions to make, now that I had shouldered this particular burden. The first was that I would continue to behave as if I still knew nothing. And I came to do it well.

That evening, when Miranda and I were sipping sherry in Anthony's library, playing at *Brideshead*, the past we were chatting about was a mutual fiction. Why I didn't confess to her that night that I knew about her affair with Jay, why I didn't use the brutal tool of honesty to make us truly friends again, why I didn't offer some desperately needed help was the result of my second decision as I drove away from Bel Air.

And that was that someday I would reveal my jealously guarded secret, but only someday—when it was time.

chapter 29

Miranda
Paris, 1981

THE BELLE EPOQUE hall was the size of a
ballroom or a barn, but given the crowd filling every
inch of space on the floor on both sides of the runway
and the hordes of photographers and bright lights and
standees and video crews, it was difficult to tell what
function it had actually served before today.

Today, in this huge place on the Right Bank, it was
the arena for the new Yves Saint Laurent collection.
Miranda was seated in the front row, staring up at the
runway, which was lit like a landing strip. Around her
was a mob of gloriously appointed, carefully selected
potential customers—the rich, the famous, and the in-
fluential. That she was here, and in a seat so coveted,
had come as a complete surprise.

A week ago, she'd been rehearsing for *Antigone* and
living in Anthony's house in Belgravia, when her agent
had called from New York. He'd broken the news that
Vogue wanted to photograph her in the new Saint
Laurent models. Lots of pages, and Avedon was going
to do the shoot. She said she couldn't possibly do it, not
with the *Antigone* rehearsal schedule. He told her she
was doing it, period, if they had to shoot it backstage.
So great was *Vogue*'s interest, he'd continued, that they
were going to make sure she got to Paris for the show

the following week, and she'd have both terrific accommodations and the best seat in the house. He had
told her they could arrange it so she missed only one day
of rehearsals and that she should make sure to take
notes on the dresses she liked. As for the money, it was
good, but the PR value was priceless. So she'd gone
along, flown to Paris for one day and one night, so exhausted from the rehearsal schedule that she'd had to
take a diet pill to keep alert.

She hadn't been in Paris since she was in college, and
it seemed a shame not to stay for longer, but she just
couldn't. In college, of course, she'd shacked up with
a bunch of other flower children in a hostel, a far cry
from the gilt-edged celebrity circus that was the
Plaza-Athénée. She could easily have walked, but
Vogue had sent a car to pick her up and deposit her at
the front door of the show. She'd been met by some of
the Saint Laurent people, even merited a shy little nod
from the preoccupied maestro himself, then had been
escorted to her seat.

The clothes were dazzling, and the numbers she noted
down were always the ones that got the applause; she'd
picked the winners, was even considering buying the
fitted black dinner suit. The rock music blared, the heat
of the lights and glittering movement of the mannequins
as they danced up and down the runway dizzied her. She
really was up on the heights.

In the time since she'd gotten the Oscar, her life had
raced along a golden path, with more job offers than
she could handle. *Heights* had been a box-office hit and
they'd racked up a number of Academy Award nomina-
tions, more than *Smitten*. Since she would be doing the
play in London Oscar night, she wouldn't be there in
person to hold Jack's hand, or to see the joy in Jay if
they won, but her heart would be with them. Much
closer at hand, though, and most exciting of all, was
that when she got back to London, Jay would be there,
for two weeks. It was a business trip, of course, but he'd

managed it so that he could attend her opening at the National. With Anthony still doing a film in Yugoslavia, and not due back until the day before the opening, they'd be able to spend more than a week together with no explanations to anybody. He had booked the same suite at the Savoy, while she was staying at Anthony's flat in Belgravia, but to be discreet, she had rented, through a friend of a friend, a flat in Notting Hill Gate. It was a good-sized one-bedroom on the second floor of a prewar row house, with a fully equipped kitchen and all the comforts of home, although she could swear that the place had never had a permanent resident; it had a strangely empty feeling. Still, it wasn't in the least depressing, and the neighborhood was one in which their chances of running into anyone they knew were negligible.

In the interests of personalizing the flat, she'd begun bringing over a few things—perfume, a robe, jeans and a couple of sweaters, scripts she had to read, and the like. Now, the place was adequate; with him there, it would be perfect. Cozy and covert.

Only twenty-four hours and they'd be together, she mused. Twenty-four hours . . . Her attention snapped back to the runway then, as a burst of applause greeted the show's final flourish, a flame-red velvet evening dress—no traditional wedding gown to close the show this time—strapless and torso-hugging, but flaring below the hips into a series of watered-silk flounces shot through and edged with gold. The model disappeared amid more wild applause, and then the din of conversation erupted.

Rising from where she sat, smiling at the many people who recognized her, she was about to make her way, accompanied by a woman from *Vogue,* who had joined her, around the runway and to the exit. It was tough to escape, given the milling hordes, half of them faces she could either identify or knew she'd seen somewhere before. She imagined, for a panicked instant, that she'd be trapped here forever, suffocating from the overabundance of privilege, which consumed all the air for itself. That she, never given to claustrophobia, should feel such dread seemed a kind of precognition; she had to get out before the impending menace found her. But already it was too late. From several steps behind her, she heard someone calling her name, and knowing she shouldn't turn, she turned anyway. And what she saw was someone fighting her way toward her through the patrons that separated them.

"Miranda Lawson! I've been—" Stephanie Harrington's opening was abruptly cut off when some exquisitely clad young lady steamrolled past her, knocking her slightly off balance and hurling her against a distinguished man of an uncertain age. "Oh, Al, I'm . . . " Miranda didn't hear what Stephanie was saying to Al, but it was obvious he was with her. Then, as the gap between them closed again, she heard her say, "We've lost Laura! Oh, no, there she is!" Then, as they began to approach the exit, Stephanie called, "Miranda, see you in the lobby!"

So her intuition had been valid, but had come too late. Now she couldn't flee. Having bid the woman from *Vogue* a breathless goodbye, agreeing to speak with her later that day, she had to wait only a few moments; when Jay's wife wanted to catch you, you could consider yourself caught. Flanked by her entourage of two, Stephanie moved purposefully, totally self-confidently through the crowded lobby. She was a princess with her court, sable-clad and Diored. Her crepe print dress hugged a silhouette without flaw, revealing neither the telltale spread of childbearing nor the overgenerous curves of the unexercised. Stephanie definitely took care of herself. If her face was not beautiful, it was resolutely stylish: The makeup was masterfully applied, obvious but not garish; the permed and hennaed pre-Raphaelite pageboy suited her; she had the best manicure, the best fixed nose, and the most fabulous capped teeth in an exhibition of plastic perfection. It was as if her will were so strong she would not consider anything less than perfection; after all, she hadn't been willing to settle for anyone but Jay.

Miranda hated her. They'd met plenty of times over the years, when Miranda's guilt always dissolved before her bitter resentment of a woman too ambitious ever to love, or need, with passion. They traveled in different circles, came from different places; Stephanie was a respectable matron, while Miranda was not only an actress but the infernal enemy, a woman who had decided against a vine-covered cottage. But Miranda had had to learn to get through the occasional evening when Stephanie was present, and to act as if she and Jay were simply professional acquaintances. It was all worth it; anything was worth it for Jay.

With Stephanie chattering all the while, she and her two companions surrounded Miranda and whisked her outside, where they stood, still chattering, unconcerned that they had secured a good part of the sidewalk onto which people were pouring.

"Darling," Stephanie said to Miranda, "are you here alone?"

"Yes, but I've got a flight back to London early tomorrow."

"Now, Miranda"—and Stephanie shook a finger at her—"no one should be alone in Paris! It's bad luck!" Suddenly an idea seemed to strike her. "You're going to have dinner with us tonight. Don't even bother protesting. She's coming, isn't she? Al? Laura?"

"Oh, Stephanie, I'm sorry, I can't—" Miranda began.

"Of course you can. I insist. We're going to have a fabulous time, aren't we?" And she drew emphatically enthusiastic nods from her friends, who, it seemed, were Alan Jessel, chairman of the board of Manhattan's biggest, busiest department store, and Laura Burlingame, an aspiring socialite from the pages of *W* who was married to the CEO of something or other.

"Really, Stephanie . . ."

"Hush, darling. We simply will not take no for an answer. Now, we've got to go. Al's made a drink appointment with somebody crucial or other, and first he's promised to take me to Givenchy's workroom—on the sly. We've booked a table at this little two-star *nouvelle* place everybody's raving about. It'll be easy to change the reservation from three to four, won't it, Al?"

Al nodded an affirmative.

"So why don't we phone you at your hotel with the address and time? Where *are* you staying?" When Miranda told her, she thought she saw Stephanie's nose wrinkle the tiniest little bit, as if disappointed in her taste in accommodations. "Um, the Athénée. I'm at the Ritz, as always, at least since I married Jay. His family's been staying there for God knows how many generations! It would simply be sacrilege to stay anyplace more entertaining. Anyway, we'll leave a message with the desk if you're not there when I call, but it'll be around nine, won't it, Al?"

Again the nod confirming.

"Say you'll come."

And Miranda said yes, capitulating to the other woman's force of will, succumbing as well to some perverse need to know what terrible turns this fateful encounter might take.

She tried to contact Jay in London when she got back to the hotel, but he wasn't at any of the several numbers he'd given her, and she didn't want to leave messages. Without talking to him, she was left frustrated and totally in the dark by the appearance of Stephanie. If the woman was in Paris, she was probably either coming from or headed for London. But Jay had told her he'd definitely be alone on this trip. She'd talked to him in New York the day before, and he hadn't mentioned any change in plans. In fact, he'd seemed amused and pleased to hear she'd found them a love nest, and had said that he couldn't wait to be there with her. Maybe he didn't know Stephanie was in Europe. But how was that possible? He was married to her.

She'd thought he might call before dinner, but he didn't, and when the phone rang, further jangling nerves already shredded from a diet pill and the events of the day, it was the woman from *Vogue*. The next time it was Stephanie, giving time and place and effusions of expectation. Having dinner with a star! It always put a twinkle in her conversation.

Dressing with care, she decided on a black cashmere sweater worked with a million paillettes, silk gabardine pants, and a white tuxedo jacket by Perry Ellis. She drew up her hair and clipped on big pearl cluster earrings, then tried Jay one more time. No success. She would have to go it alone tonight, and as she walked to the elevator, she was overcome with a dread mixed strangely with impatience. It was, she realized, stage fright. Accepting the cab that the attendant summoned, she gave the driver the address of the restaurant, Le Déluge, which was somewhere off the Quai Voltaire on the Left Bank. The cab ride took her along a glittering route that would normally have left her breathless, but tonight she could not submit to the city's romantic mood. By the time they crossed the Pont Neuf and turned left along the Seine, she was too anxious to notice. And when the cab pulled into a side street and came to a halt, she took a second too long figuring out the currency equivalents.

There was no mistaking the address, which was clearly marked above the door of an old house. Opening the door and striding boldly through, Miranda found herself entering what looked like a magnificent stage set of a Paris restaurant. Even as a child, when she had been dragged to the best restaurants in this and many other cities, she had never felt such wonder at sheer decorative perfection. It was ironic, the loveliness of the setting, and the unpleasantness of her own role in it. The dark mahogany of the heavy Belle Epoque doors and occasional paneling gleamed in contrast to the bleached wood of the moldings above the paneling and the rosy beige of the walls themselves. A bar, ebony and rattan, with Art Nouveau mirrors, ran the length of the moderate-sized dining room; columns covered in splintered, golden-tinted glass demarcated four subsections, each consisting of four or so tables, most of them filled. Soft spot lighting, hidden in the molding, bathed the whole place in a subtle *pêche* glow, contrasting with the dramatic blossoms of light from the elaborate, candlelit chandelier, which was suspended from the center of the ceiling. Greenery in pots—some plants were the size of small trees—was placed around the pillars and afforded the tables at the rear of the room some privacy, so much so that Miranda couldn't tell if her party had arrived.

Immediately, a handsome maître d' in a blue business suit and tie came up to her, smiled, and told her how pleased Le Déluge was to have her, then, hearing the name of her party, he escorted her along the bar and to a table hidden behind the plants.

Stephanie was sitting alone, a champagne glass in front of her. She was a study in New York chic, dressed just perfectly in the simplest dove-gray frock, enhanced only by a string of small pearls that glowed so radiantly, they had to be worth a fortune. This afternoon's sable rested about her, forming a sort of frame for her. As she waved, Miranda caught the glitter of the gigantic but somehow tasteful diamond on the fourth finger of her left hand, and immediately felt both over- and under-dressed.

"Miranda, dear." Stephanie held out her hand as the maître d' seated her. "I'm so glad you're finally here. It's going to be just the two of us." She leaned forward and lowered her voice as she said, "Laura's not in the best shape in the world. In fact, she was just too upset to go out, and Al, dear Al, consented to stay with her."

"Is it . . . is she ill?" Miranda asked.

"Oh, no, not ill. More—oh, I really shouldn't talk about it." She smiled. "Not right now, at least. Maybe, when I'm under the influence of a few more *kir royales* . . ."

"Oh, I wasn't trying to pry—"

"Darling, I know. Let's just forget it for now, all right? What would you like to drink?"

"Oh, *kir royale* is fine," Miranda said—actually, it was her own favorite—and immediately, Stephanie summoned the waiter and gave him the order.

"Well," Stephanie went on, "we're so lucky to be here at all. They're booked weeks in advance, you know. Thank God Al has the connections he has, *n'est-ce pas*?"

Miranda laughed politely, wondering what had really happened to Laura and Al and if their absence was at Stephanie's instigation. They chatted relatively easily about the YSL collection over drinks, and ordered another round before their first course came—salmon mousse *en croute*. They ordered a white wine recommended by the maître d', and it was as she started a second glass of it that Stephanie asked her for details about the *Vogue* assignment.

Her anxiety unabated, her food swallowed but untasted, the wine only heightening her temperature and her nervousness, she tried to give a good performance of a person at ease. "How did you know I was here for *Vogue*?" she asked.

"I saw Jack Price a few days ago and he told me you might be doing it."

So Stephanie had known she would be in Paris. She couldn't have shown up on purpose, though—it was sheer, adolescent paranoia even to contemplate that.

"Sounded like fun. And speaking of Jack, Miranda, dear—" Stephanie's voice lowered to the girl-talk level. "—I've always hoped you two could get together. He obviously adores you."

Resenting Stephanie's intrusion for a million reasons, she tried to cut her short. "And I adore him, Stephanie. But . . . well . . . you know he's gay!"

"I know everybody *says* he's gay, but I don't believe it. He doesn't seem the least bit gay to me."

"Stephanie, you don't have to wear a dress and makeup to be a homosexual!"

"Well, yes, of course, but I've always been sure I picked up something . . . some *je ne sais quoi* between the two of you."

"Stephanie—" and Miranda drained the wineglass— "the *je ne sais quoi* is friendship. Really. The other thing is never going to happen."

"If you think like that, it won't, for sure," Stephanie advised.

Ah, the irony! If it was irony. Unless it was all deliberate. "Oh, you need more wine." Stephanie motioned to the waiter to refill Miranda's glass.

"I think I'm a couple ahead of you." Miranda noticed Stephanie's half-empty glass.

"Oh, I really don't drink, to speak of. But you, please . . ."

"Sure, it's superb." Miranda smiled, lifting her glass and sipping. "Now"—and her heart pounded at the approach of the question—"how come *you're* here?"

"Oh, well, actually, I'm here on a madcap adventure! Ah, here's the next course!"

After they were served and she had attacked the two tiny circlets of veal in some kind of exquisite but, at this moment, unimportant sauce, Miranda pressed her. "So tell me about your madcap adventure!"

"Well . . ." Stephanie sighed coyly, playing with her lamb. "Laura's been depressed, very depressed. And I and other friends of hers have been trying to shake her out of it. So I suggested that she do something wild, totally uncharacteristic, such as taking the *Concorde* over for the Saint Laurent show. I have to admit I was inspired by your plans. Laura has the connections to get a great seat—God, she wears Saint Laurent's stuff practically exclusively. 'You must be his best English-speaking customer,' I told her, 'so why don't you just do it?' So, she called me back and said she'd go, if I'd go with her. And I said, absolutely not. But then I thought, well, Jay's going to be away, anyway. And Jonathan's old enough to be without me for a few days . . . You should see him, he's getting so big. Everybody says he looks like me, but I think he looks like both of us! Anyway, I just up and flew over here on a whim, with Laura! Running into Al at the Montana show yesterday was such a fantastic stroke of luck!''

"How long will *you* be staying?" Miranda asked, as the waiter refilled her glass.

"Till tomorrow morning," Stephanie cut her food in little tiny bits, and rarely interrupted her conversation long enough to get one to her mouth. The meeting was even worse than Miranda had imagined it would be, a showcase for Stephanie's position in society; the suspicion that it was deliberate, that the wife was lording it over the mistress, played in Miranda's mind.

"I'm sure Jonathan will be thrilled to see you back so soon."

"Actually"—Stephanie had managed two bites in a row—"I'm not going right back. The second part of my madcap scheme is to surprise Jay in London."

So that was that. The end of London. That terrible karma striking again.

Beaming with her own cleverness, Stephanie went on to describe how she'd made sure that, when Jay called home, Nanny would tell him she'd gone to a super-secret health spa, where no incoming calls were allowed except in an emergency, but to add that she called in three times a day to see after Jonathan. When he called, Nanny would take his number and promise to have her call him.

"And it worked?"

"It did! So, tomorrow, I'll just show up at the Savoy. I can't wait! It'll give Jay and me a chance to spend some time together. In fact, I had this wonderful thought of stealing him away to a charming little country inn, but I didn't know how to begin to find such a place. Then something occurred to me. So I picked up the phone, called Jack, and demanded Anthony's number in Yugoslavia, and I got it. He answered the phone himself. Such humility, a man like that, answering his own phone! Of course, he couldn't have been more darling or more helpful. He even swore that if he saw Jay, he wouldn't breathe a word about my coming over!"

Ah, Anthony, Miranda thought, once you hurl down the gauntlet, the duel never ends.

"And he *did* know the perfect inn and absolutely insisted on booking our reservations himself. And it certainly sounds ideal. Secluded and picturesque. We'll go for long walks and get to know each other again. Maybe make another Jonathan. Jay's such a wonderful father, but I wish he had more time for us. He's the busiest man in Manhattan! I keep telling him I only see him in a dinner jacket or pajamas. London will be like a second honeymoon. I can't wait."

"How long are you going to be staying?" Miranda asked, all the unshed tears of crushing disappointment balled in a burning mass in her throat.

"I'll go back when he does. Ten days or so," and the innocence of her expression alerted some danger signal in Miranda. This was different, stronger than her suspicions. This was deep instinct: Stephanie knew about them, and she was torturing her.

While Jay's wife sipped coffee and Miranda finished

the wine, Stephanie asked a question or two about her work, but mainly confined her conversation to clothes, interiors, and restaurants in London. Miranda half listened, aware, for the first time that evening, that she was drunk and trying desperately not to show it. It was a bad high, nauseating and nervy, built on a base of diet pills, but at Stephanie's urging she kept on drinking. The more she drank, the greater the space from which Stephanie's words seemed to come, and it was as if from a huge distance that Miranda heard her say, "Poor Laura. I just can't get her out of my mind!"

"Laura? Oh, your friend who couldn't make it."

"Yes, I'm so concerned about her, Miranda. I've simply got to talk about it. Can I count on your confidence?"

Almost before Miranda managed to nod affirmation, Stephanie had launched a tale she was clearly dying to tell. "Oh, it's so depressing. Laura's just found out her husband's . . . fooling around. Everyone else has known for ages, but she, of course, was the last. And he wants a divorce. She's terribly upset. We're worried that she'll try something . . . oh, I don't even want to say it."

The shot, from wherever it came, made a direct hit. Miranda's whole body went rigid. "What is she going to do?" she asked, dazed.

"What is she going to do? She's such a fool! She won't make trouble. She says she loves him and she'll let him out of the marriage easily. I've told her—we've all told her—she's out of her mind, but she won't listen. It's just heartbreaking, isn't it? A man makes a complete fool out of you, and you reward him for it." Suddenly, beneath the fashionable amiability, something sharp and deadly began to emerge. "And the children," Stephanie continued, signaling the waiter once again to fill Miranda's glass. "She's got two children, both under ten. It's going to be hell on them, if the marriage breaks up. Imagine putting a child in the middle of a custody fight. It must maim them for life!''

Miranda's misery must have been apparent, for
Stephanie immediately broke off. "Oh, Miranda, darling! Excuse me. Of course, you know all about *that*. I
simply forgot. You know"—and she smiled warmly—
"I never think of you as Margo Seymour's daughter,
just as Jack's friend. I'm so sorry. That was thoughtless."

It wasn't thoughtless at all; it was coldly premedi-
tated.

"It's all right," Miranda murmured, hating the
woman for so many reasons, disarmed in a female form
of battle she had never understood, much less mastered.

"I suppose I should consider myself lucky," Stephanie continued over the coffee and raspberries, "that
my husband's mad affair is with business. At least it's
not another woman. You know, I think it may be because he's afraid of me. Because of Jonathan, I've got
him, for a long, long time."

So Stephanie had laid down the law to her, in terms so
final, so unyielding, that she had to fight back the urge
to weep. "Stephanie," she said, making a show of
checking her watch, "this has been so nice, but I've got
an eight-o'clock flight back to London in the morning,
and I want to get some sleep."

"Of course, dear." Stephanie caught the waiter's eye,
the check was brought, and the gold card placed on top
of it. "No, no!" Stephanie stopped Miranda as she
drew out her own card. "My treat! And certainly my
pleasure! We'll have to get together in London to
celebrate your opening. You and Anthony and Jay and
I. Why don't I throw a small cocktail party? It'll be—
jolly! And it was so terrific finally spending some time
alone with you!"

Downing the last of the wine, like Socrates, sinking
deeply into despair, Miranda was about to thank her
nemesis when Stephanie broke in.

"And Miranda, dear, now that we're on the road to becoming friends, I'd like to mention something I have no right to say." And the woman who had bested her placed her hand on Miranda's and bent toward her. "I say this only for your own good, darling, but I think you'd better watch the drinking. Sweetheart, you finished the entire bottle!"

chapter 30

Jack
1984

IN EARLY SPRING of 1981, Miranda was in London rehearsing and I was in Manhattan, brooding. As everybody knows, spring in New York is only a moment between winter and summer. Still, although it isn't spring as people from the normal world experience it, it's made remarkable by the fact that the painful cold of the winter is gone from the air and the stifling summer is still hard to imagine. It's the only time, outside of a few days in the fall, when it's bearable to take on the masochistic task of attempting to get a cab at rush hour.

Granted, that was no longer my problem, getting cabs on street corners. Now there were much better alternatives: radio-dispatched taxis that came to the door or, better yet, limos, so that with ease I could dash from cocktail party to play opening to dinner and then to Studio 54 or a downtown club to dance till dawn.

And that was only part of the luxury of my new life as Jack Price, nice-guy, big-time writer. I had to admit, the living was easy. But I was miserable. My new play was going about as smoothly as my new love affair—they were both rigorous, demanding, stop-and-start, suffused with the free-floating unease that had been attaching itself to every possible aspect of my life.

My new lover was a shrink, and a respected one, and

I'm sure he did his patients worlds of good. Unfortunately, he had his own intimacy problems, and they made him behave like a fourteen-year-old. He wanted a major commitment from me—this after our knowing each other only a couple of months—was putting pressure on me for us to go public as a couple; and was beginning to drop little hints about wanting us to live together.

I didn't see things his way, not at all. I liked living alone; I liked being a free agent. Given the good times I was having, "settling down," as he put it, was the last thing I would consider. But he persisted, and I resisted, and despite the fact that I liked the guy quite a lot, I was becoming obsessed with finding a way to ease out of the relationship without the requisite hysterics on his part and lingering guilt on mine.

Still, my love affair was a bed of orchids compared to my new play. The thing fought being written. Every morning when I sat down at my antique manual with a mug of coffee and two packs of cigarettes, it was as though I were going into battle. Only after several weeks of being totally unable to coax the characters out of my head and onto the page did it occur to me that, for the first time in my life, I was suffering from writer's block. Ironically, although my loving shrink should have helped me over it, he was, if anything, making it worse by pressuring me about commitment.

So, it was finally getting to be spring, a glorious time in New York, but I was desperate to get away from the place. In fact, I was counting on it. In recent years I'd always attended Miranda's London openings; it had become a sort of tradition with us, and as superstitious as anyone else in the theatre, Miranda had come to consider my presence on opening night as supreme good luck. We had even devised a little game around my coming, and we'd played it in London when I'd been there not long ago. She'd suggested casually that perhaps I could wait around, spend some time in the country, and then attend the *Antigone* opening. I told her, no, I couldn't, there were too many things happening in New York, among them the closing of my Fifth Avenue penthouse. Next, she urged me to fly back over for a day or so, and I hesitated. The game continued until she was practically begging me to be there, and once begged, I relented. It was all silly; there'd been no doubt at any point that I would be there, but it was one of the rites we practiced together, the heritage of a long, close friendship.

Of course, I'd be there. I had to be, since I was her good luck charm, something that Jay could never be. Admittedly, despite my revulsion toward their clandestine relationship, the affair did offer me certain advantages. With her heart and mind fixed on Jay, Miranda wasn't about to get romantically involved with anyone else, which gave me constant access to her. More than Anthony, more than Jay, more than any director or producer or leading man, I was the one she could relax with, the one she needed to talk to, the only one with whom she could always be herself. I knew more about her secret rituals, her magic ceremonies, her bedrock craziness than anyone else, but they all pleased me. In a way, I had what I wanted: I had *her* when I wanted, but I was spared the responsibility of hurting her. Jay, behind my back, had assumed that awesome duty, and more power to him.

So there I sat, one gloomy spring day, staring at the typewriter but thinking of Miranda and London, when the phone rang.

It was her. Sounding rather chipper and telling me not to come. It was time she started acting like a grown-up, she told me. She had to know that she could go on without me, that I was infinitely more to her than a good-luck amulet. "Please, Jack"—she was at her most beguiling—"Don't come. I'll be stronger as a result of it."

And I might even have been impressed if I'd thought

she was being straight with me, but she wasn't. Because I knew that Jay had made spur-of-the-moment plans to go to London, that the reason she didn't need me was that she was going to have him, and I smiled and smiled and played the villain, and said great, it was a load off my mind, and then I went to work to punish her.

It was surprisingly easy to find an opportunity. It happened only five days later, at the opening of the Vreeland show at the Metropolitan Museum. I was escorting a rather celebrated socialite whose husband happened to be in Europe on business. Caroline and I lunched occasionally, usually at her behest, and I often took her places when Ed was away. He reciprocated in his own fashion, by investing heavily in my theatrical endeavors. It was a dandy arrangement, and I enjoyed my forays into high society, which hadn't yet grown dull.

That night at the Met, I had just left Caroline in the capable care of Peter Martins and begun to cross the great marble and flower-filled entrance hall toward the bar. Caroline was drinking Scotch, not champagne, that night, and at an admirable rate, and I was getting her a refill when I saw Jay, deep in conversation with another young mogul, Donald Trump. I'd walked over to say hello, but whatever they were discussing must have been of extreme importance, for Jay seemed incredibly abstracted. Agreeing to call me the next day for lunch, he turned back to his conversation and I to Caroline's Scotch. At the bar, I ran into Stephanie.

"Jack, how are you? We haven't seen you in months." She was stunning in a crepe de chine sheath of palest rose, the diamonds at her throat and on her ears picking up the pink glow from the dress and illuminating her face.

"Weeks, Stephanie." I took her hand, then kissed her lightly. "God, you're looking fabulous!"

"Thanks for noticing," she said, her expression gracefully changing into a pout. "Jay didn't. He's so damned preoccupied, he wouldn't have uttered an 'oooh' if I'd come here naked.''

"Ah, but everyone else would," I said, smiling. "Hey, what's bothering Jay? He does seem out of it.''

"Who knows what it is? Some business with his father, probably. He's becoming a complete stranger. I wish I could whisk him off somewhere and get his attention.'' Whatever the trouble with his father was, I was inclined to dismiss it less lightly than Stephanie.

"And how's Jonathan?" I asked, as much to change the subject as anything.

"You haven't seen him in months, have you? We've got to remedy that. The same ordinary prodigy. Brilliant. Handsome. Destined to win the Nobel Prize for physics and a gold medal at the Olympics in the same year. Of course, Jay tells everybody that's a completely objective opinion.''

We proceeded to cut to ribbons the people we'd run into at the party, then she asked what I'd been doing to make myself so scarce. I told her I'd been in England and that I'd spent some time with Miranda.

"How *is* Miranda?" Stephanie asked, with a kind of subtle scorn implying criticism of Miranda's heedless ways. "Has she found a man yet?"

"Oh, you never know with her," I said lightly. "She falls in and out of love so fast, the items in the colums are usually out of date before they go to press.''

"I simply cannot understand any woman wanting to live like that," Stephanie continued, and I had to smirk inwardly. "Living in other people's houses, with no steady man, and no stability in her life! It seems so . . . so unnatural.''

"It may seem unnatural, Steph, but it certainly isn't hurting her career! In fact, *Vogue* wants her to do some fashion stuff. They're even flying her to Paris for the Saint Laurent show.''

"That does sound like fun," Stephanie admitted. "When's that? Next week, isn't it?"

"Yeah, and then she has to rush back to London. She's opening in *Antigone* early next month."

Stephanie's mien was beginning to show the strain of focusing on one person for too long, but she gave me her attention. "Jay'll be in London then," she said. "We must make him go to the opening and tell us all about it." She spoke rather deliberately, as if unpleasant connections had just occurred to her.

"So Jay's going to be in London?" I repeated innocently, then appeared to have been struck by an inspiration. "Stephanie, I've just had a grand idea! I'll be in London, too." And I had a pretty good idea that I would, despite my conversation with Miranda, if my scheme worked out. "Why don't you surprise Jay in London? We'll have a great time, all of us together! Come on, dear, you must come!"

"But Jonathan!"

"Stephanie dear, Jonathan hasn't kept you from La Costa. And besides, that's what you pay the nanny for. I insist! London won't be the same without you." And how I meant that! "Couldn't we have a fabulous time? Anthony and you and I and Jay and Miranda." At the coupling of their names, Jay's and Miranda's, her eyes narrowed, and for only a second, I wondered if she knew about them and was formulating her own battle plan, as I was formulating mine. The moment passed, leaving my suspicions unconfirmed.

"It does sound delicious, Jack," Stephanie mused. "I actually think I might do it! I'd just love to surprise Jay! It gets harder and harder to do. But, you know, darling—" she pecked me lightly on the cheek and whispered in my ear, "if you ever try to take credit for the idea, first I'll call you a liar, then I'll wring your neck!"

"Stephanie, dearest—" and I kissed her neck—"our secret is safe with me."

Other luminaries appeared at this point, pulling us off in opposing directions, but as I blended with the crowd, I felt satisfied that if the adulterous lovers thought they were going to have London to themselves for as long as a night, they were sadly mistaken. I had planted the seeds of grave disappointment, and I'd done it well. After that, I began to enjoy myself.

I enjoyed myself even more when, three days before the opening, Miranda rang up, apologizing profusely for her last-minute jitters, but begging me to come for the opening after all. I balked, she begged, and as usual, I agreed. I wouldn't have missed it for the world.

And I did enjoy myself in London, where I watched my mischief work to a 'T'. But what a strange kind of enjoyment. In the rare moments when the old, decent me thrust through the miasma of my malcontentedness, I felt tremendously guilty: Miranda, in the midst of the greatest artistic success of her career, was, to my practiced eye, suffering like the damned, but those crises of conscience never lasted long enough.

In Jay, too, I sensed a desperation, although I'm sure only Miranda and I were aware of it. Before London, he'd had her, and he'd had Stephanie; now, he had both of them—together. I had to laugh: It must have been perfect agony for him—a romantic torture out of Fellini, or out of a bedroom farce. He deserved every second of it.

Once in London, circumstances had actually improved my scenario, for we all ended up spending vast amounts of time together, thanks to Stephanie—Stephanie, whose unyielding insistence on being in the best places wouldn't take no for an answer. She glommed onto Anthony as if her life depended on it: There was not a hostess in London, no matter how tony, who didn't die to have Anthony on a guest list. And since her magnificent triumph opposite Alan Howard (on loan from the RSC) in *Antigone,* Miranda was equally sought after. The pair of them were social magic; wherever they went, the right people followed, and Stephanie, with a warrior's sense of purpose, endeavored to be always in their entourage. When the flashbulbs flashed, they flashed on Anthony, Miranda, me, Stephanie, and Jay, all smiling. *Women's Wear Daily* took to calling us "the Gang of Five." Indifferent to the animosity between Jay and Anthony, Stephanie was like a character from Henry James or Edith Wharton—a rich American matron plowing across Europe with an unquenchable fever for status, and a passion for crowned heads. Her superhuman will consumed everyone else's. Not wanting to go, we went.

We went, and we played our parts, and we were quite a company. Anthony, when asked his feelings about Stephanie, let his eyes shoot instantly heavenward, but to her face, he was the perfect gentleman. It was as if his gracious manner was a curse; his inability not to charm had brought Stephanie's overbearing presence down upon him. I secretly suspected that he had another, more devious reason for his marvelous civility: It must have driven Jay crazy to hear his wife ooh and ah over his old adversary. I could imagine—and I'll bet Anthony could, too—Stephanie singing the great man's praises all over town, dropping his name and confirming their friendship to anyone who would listen. Poor Jay. How ironic. Who would have thought there'd come a time when he'd be dining out on Anthony Gainsborough? It must have killed him to be enveloped in Anthony's aura, to chat and smile across innumerable tables, over interminable meals, while he and his lover had to play at being old acquaintances.

And they were good at it. No one could have guessed from the way they related to each other—with just the right amount of friendly interest—that they were anything other than warm associates who had once been more than that, but who, over the years, had drifted apart. They were so convincing, I had to believe they'd managed to fool even so masterful a pretender as Anthony. Had they fooled Stephanie? I wasn't sure, for I knew her to be shrewd, and not past pretense herself, if it served her own interests. They certainly would have fooled me—if I hadn't known better.

Admittedly, mine was a privileged position from which to observe the passing parade of strategems. I alone could sit and dance and gamble and dine with them, appreciating the artistry of their deception. And, in those rare moments when my jealousy ebbed, appreciating their hopelessness as well. It was at those times that I pitied them for their pain.

But you would simply never have known they were suffering. They never overplayed their hand; they never got careless, except, perhaps, for one night, when we were having an after-theatre supper at Mr. Chow's in Knightsbridge. The rest of us had been to the Royal Court Theatre in Chelsea while Miranda performed in *Antigone* across the river, and she had arrived palpably upset. Crediting her mood to an off night at work, she ordered a glass of wine and said she'd soon be fine. And she might have been if Anthony hadn't noticed she wasn't wearing Margo's charm. At first, she claimed to have left it in the dressing room, but that seemed unlikely. She always wore it, except onstage, and if for the first time she had actually forgotten to put it on after the play, then her performance that night must have been shatteringly bad. And I doubted that. As did Anthony, who, before long, had gotten out of her the wretched confession that she'd lost it.

"Anthony, dear God, I simply don't know how it could have happened," she explained, close to tears. "You know, I guarded it with my life. It was so strange, I can't understand it. When I left the dressing room, I was wearing it. And when I got to the car, I wasn't. I retraced my steps several times, and everyone helped. But it just didn't turn up. I'm . . . crushed."

Anthony, of course, jumped in with valiantly high spirits. Taking her hand, he said warmly, "Miranda. Please, darling. I know it wasn't due to your carelessness. I know that. And how are we to say it won't turn up in the daylight? I'll wager, by tomorrow noon, you'll be wearing it!''

No one, of course, believed that, but everyone heartily agreed, and by common consent, we decided to change the subject. Unfortunately, the next order of business wasn't much of an improvement on the evening's beginning. Jay, it turned out, was not going to be able to spare the time for Stephanie's excursion to the country. Stephanie was furious.

"Oh, *Jay*!" She pouted, playing with the pearls at her neck. "You *promised*!"

"Stephanie," he shot back, "this is a business trip. *I* came here on business."

"But, it was going to be—"

He seemed visibly to soften. "Steph, I can't do it. Next time, we'll plan a trip in advance, so—"

"Oh, it won't matter," she moaned. "Something will still come up. It always does." Then, either playing the good sport or making a double-edged point, she turned to Miranda. "See what it's like being a business widow! It's worse than being cheated on!"

"But wait!" Anthony broke in. "I have a solution to your problem, dear lady," and he seized Stephanie's hand across the table. "I offer you—and any guests of your choosing—a day trip to one of England's stateliest homes!"

"A stately home? Really?" Stephanie's curiosity was piqued.

"Well, it's stately to me." Anthony flashed a winning smile. "It's my house." Placing his hand on his breast, he intoned, "My castle!"

"Oh!" Stephanie's excitement was palpable.

"In fact, my dear, it's quite a lovely drive there. We'll motor down in the morning. It's only a few hours away, through beautiful countryside. Then we'll inspect the house and the grounds and perhaps stop by and see some friends who live in the neighborhood. Homes in the National Trust, you know. How does that sound?"

"Utterly divine!" Stephanie beamed.

"In fact, why don't we all go?" Anthony urged. "Jay? Jack? Miranda? It'll be jolly!"

Jay thought a moment. "Depends on which day you choose . . ."

"Jack? Of course, you'll come, old boy!"

"Oh, yes!" Stephanie warbled. "You must come, Jack. You always have such wonderful, droll things to say. I won't take no for an answer."

Somehow, I found myself agreeing to go; it was as hard for me to turn down Stephanie—not to mention Anthony—as for anyone else.

"Miranda?" Anthony said.

"Look, guys," she said, smiling, "I think you'd better count me out. If we go on a day I'm performing, we'll have to rush back. And my one free day *has* to be spent resting. So it's really impossible."

"Oh, darling, that is too bad." Stephanie fairly chirped at the prospect of having all the men to herself.

"Now, we must choose the day." Anthony turned to signal the waiter for another bottle of Corvo. "I, for one, vote for Friday. How's Friday with everyone?" He scanned the table. "Jack? Good! Steph? Fine! Jay, what about you? Don't tell me *you're* free!"

"Maybe," Jay replied. "I've got a breakfast date, though."

"That's hardly a problem," Anthony said. "We'll simply leave afterward."

"My God, it's a miracle," Stephanie commented wryly. "Friday will be delightful, Sir Anthony," she caroled.

When the food arrived, the conversation turned to other matters. It was not until we were asking for the check that Jay chose to remember he couldn't make the trip after all.

"What is it? What is it that's so important?" Stephanie demanded. Anthony, too, looked less than pleased.

"I can't believe I forgot something so important. Jesus, I *am* working too hard. I'm taking a meeting with some Dutch money people. They were supposed to fly in Thursday, just for the meeting, but their representatives here called to change it to Friday. They called just as we were leaving for the theatre—remember, Stephanie?"

"How could I possibly remember? Somebody or other's calling every two minutes!"

"No, this is too important. There's no way I can miss it. I'm sorry, really. But please, you go ahead."

"Now I feel better," Stephanie said sourly. "For a second, I thought you'd been possessed by the soul of a normal person. Well, you two," she said to Jay and Miranda, "you're going to miss a wonderful time! Aren't they, Jack? Aren't they, Anthony?"

I nodded amiably, from where I sat on the sidelines, out of the danger zone. Anthony, though, appeared to be annoyed. He had wanted things to work out *his* way, and was it only accidental that he had arranged to have Jay and Miranda in his sight? But he had failed, and perhaps it seemed to him that Miranda's losing the charm had broken his power over her.

And I, for one, could only marvel at how they'd beaten us at our own game. Despite everything, the two of them had managed time alone together, time to lust and laugh and congratulate themselves on their cleverness. For they had thoroughly outsmarted us—and, to my amazement, part of me was glad.

chapter 31

Miranda
London, 1981

SHE GOT TO the flat twenty minutes early, although she'd planned to be exactly on time. The hour just wouldn't be killed, and the harder she tried to divert herself, the slower the minutes had passed. It was now nine-forty, and he'd said he'd be there at ten. How ironic that it was Anthony who had made this day possible for them: Even now, he and Jack and Stephanie were racing toward the country house.

Jay's breakfast appointment was genuine, but he'd left the rest of the day free. As for Miranda, she'd left Anthony's flat shortly after he took off in his silver Rolls. Pretending she'd be seeing friends and doing some shopping, she'd dressed the part, in a tweed suit and silk blouse, but once in the flat, she changed into jeans and an oatmeal-colored cashmere sweat shirt. Putting on a Bob Marley tape she'd found near the stereo, she opened some of the champagne she'd chilled days before and a can of orange juice, made herself a mimosa, and tried to relax.

She couldn't. She couldn't concentrate on anything; the anticipation was consuming her. Luckily, Jay was there by ten to ten. At the sound of his ring, she felt some emotion so intense that she nearly fainted when she got up. But she got to the door, all right, and was overpowered by the impact of seeing him there.

He was dressed in a business suit of a glen plaid so subtle as to be almost imperceptible, and he wore a trench coat, which she took from him. She was turning toward the closet when his arms reached out for her and embraced her from behind, his hands braceleted at her waist, and she dropped the coat on the floor. Then his hands slowly began to move up her torso, as if they were dancing, he turned her, so that she faced him, and they clung together, exhausted from days of pretense.

"God, it's good to finally touch you," he murmured, then he kissed her. "Hey," he said, pulling away, "I forgot! You're the toast of London. Does an ordinary peon just walk up to the toast of London and kiss her? Maybe it's not done."

"It's done here!" She kissed him back.

"Speaking of here," he said, "this place is nice."

"Yes. Look around some." She broke away and headed for the kitchen. "Want a mimosa? I was just making one."

"No," he called from the bedroom. "Too early for me!"

"Sure?"

"Sure," he said as he walked into the kitchen, minus his shoes and his jacket and with his tie loosened.

"Can I get you anything else? Tea? Coffee?" she asked as she finished making the drink.

"You," he told her, turning her gently toward him. "You and your attention. Come on in the other room. No, on second thought, let's make it the bedroom." And she obeyed.

It was when they were making love that he first noticed something wrong. She was too desperate, too hungry, and trying too hard, barely keeping control of what he sensed was hysteria. She denied it when he mentioned it to her afterward, but she knew she wasn't fooling him.

She asked him for champagne, and he obliged by getting out of bed and making the trek to the kitchen. When he came back with the bottle and two glasses, she saw a jewelry box on the tray as well.

"Your champagne, madame," he said, pouring it into both glasses and handing her one. "Now, to the most ravishing talent in London! Who I happen to think is pretty cute." And they toasted. If he was less than happy, he didn't show it; he was more boyish and charming than he'd been in months.

"When are you going to ask who the box is for?"

She grinned. "I was waiting for the presentation."

He put the box in her hands, and she opened it to discover the most delicate platinum chain she'd ever seen. And from the chain was suspended a charm the size of her little fingernail, and so light it appeared almost to be made of platinum wire, forming the unbroken double curves of the infinity symbol. "It's a replacement for the one you lost. And it's the only one in the world. If you feel you can't wear it around Anthony, wear it when you're with me or when you're alone, when you take a bath, whenever . . ." As he removed the necklace from the box and was fastening it around her neck, he told her, "To you, from me. Forever."

She kissed him for the love so evident in the gift, clutched him to her as she told him she adored it—and him—but she held him too tightly, for it provoked him to ask, "Miranda, what the hell is wrong?"

"Nothing. Just nervous about tonight. I'm still not into the run." She smoothed his face and smiled at him. "How's your business here going?"

For a second, a shadow of seriousness fell across his face, then: "Fine. It's going well." And he left it at that, and reached for her and nuzzled her neck, and it was then that she asked, "Wasn't it strange that Stephanie just happened to turn up in Paris?"

"Oh, who knows?" Jay groaned. "It sounds like her. Costs a fortune and is totally pointless. Why?"

"Because . . . " She offered up her glass for more champagne. "Because . . . I don't think it was coincidence. Jay, I think she knows. About us."

"Knows about us?" He stared at her, then shook his head. "No, no, she doesn't. She doesn't have a clue. She doesn't even think we like each other much."

"Maybe she's pretending . . . "

"Miranda, what is wrong with you? Why would Stephanie do something so totally out of character?"

"I don't know. Maybe she's trying to catch you in a lie or a mistake or something. Maybe she's trying to build a case. Jay"—and she reached out for his hands—"it scares me."

"Miranda, you're being hysterical."

"I'm not!" she insisted, but she was growing more and more upset as she approached the heart of the matter. "She does know. That dinner in Paris, it was a warning. She was sending me a message. She was ordering me to back off. She was doing it at dinner the other night, too. Couldn't you see that? It was so obvious."

He set his champagne glass on the table by the bed and moved near her. "It wasn't obvious to me, Miranda."

"Because you didn't want to see it! You don't want to see it, even now."

"Miranda—" He took her hand. "There's nothing to see. It's your imagination. Listen to me, Miranda." She had turned her face away from him, but he forced her to look at him as he said, "She doesn't know."

"Jay," she insisted, "she does. And she's going to do something about it. Soon. Something awful!"

"Like?"

His calm was incomprehensible to her; his ability to

ignore reality was driving her mad. "Like . . . filing for a divorce."

"Well, you know, Miranda"—he continued to be calm, even casual—"that wouldn't be the worst thing in the world."

"How can you say that?" She was shocked by his cavalier acceptance.

"Look—" He had moved farther up the bed, still closer to her. "I planned on having this talk under better circumstances, but . . . I've thought about this a lot, for a long time. In fact, I've agonized over it. And . . ."

She started to speak, but he stopped her.

"Shut up, Miranda," he told her lightly. "It's my turn to talk. Okay?"

She nodded, but felt her emotions shrinking back from him, afraid of what he would say.

"All right." He gathered his thoughts and began. "*I* don't believe Stephanie knows, but if she does, well, it's irrelevant. No, I'm talking. It's irrelevant because . . . I *want* a divorce."

"Jay!" She was shaking, she realized. "Jay, you can't!"

"I can't? Why can't I? Because my father says I can't? Because my background says I can't? Because the people who write the columns say I can't? Do I—do we —have to be punished for the rest of our lives because I made a mistake before I knew better?"

"Maybe we do," she replied, downcast.

"Maybe we don't, Miranda. Miranda, our life together is hell; at least, it is to me. If I hadn't already thought it, this London sojourn would certainly have convinced me. It's been ludicrous, ludicrous and painful. You know, I never felt guilty about this 'affair' until the last few days. I hate deceiving these people, and the longer we do it, the lousier I'm going to feel. And, frankly, I don't have the time for all that guilt, so . . . ahem . . ." He straightened an imaginary tie.

" . . . want to go straight and get married?"

She couldn't believe she was hearing it. Here. Now. What she had once craved and then dismissed as impossible and then craved and then . . .

She was silent for an endless moment, then, knowing she had to speak, she told him, "Jay, how can you put me in this position? How can you ask me to be the agent of your destroying your life—and Jonathan's life?"

"Ah, Jonathan . . . I should have known."

"You should have known what, Jay? That Stephanie told me in Paris that her hold over you was Jonathan? She'll take him away from you, you know. She will. It'll be a messy divorce, and you'll lose him, Jay. Forever. And he'll lose you."

"Why are you so sure? I know Stephanie better than you do, no matter what she says when she's on a tear. Miranda, the marriage hasn't worked; it didn't work any better before you and I started seeing each other than it did after we got together. We don't fight. Or throw scenes. We just don't mesh, and I think she knows it as well as I do. It's not just my work that keeps me at a distance; the distance is simply *there*. I don't hate her, and I don't think she hates me. She must feel there's something missing, just like I do."

"I don't think so."

"Miranda, you're not in a position to know. And for God's sake, don't start feeling sorry for her. She's not going to have to move to a basement apartment. She was a wealthy woman before she married me, and I'll be more than generous. Besides, she's still young and attractive, and God knows she's determined. I guarantee you, she'll marry again. Someone who'll appreciate her a lot more than I can."

"Don't you care about your child? Don't you, Jay?"

"Miranda, can't you see you're overidentifying with Jonathan because of your own history? Sure, it was bad. I can imagine how bad it must have been—"

"No!" She was practically in tears. "No, you can't. You cannot have any idea of how bad it was. Or how it maimed me."

"Maimed you?" he stared at her. "How are you maimed? I don't see it."

"But I feel it, Jay. I have to live with it—*inside*. You can tell me about a lot of things, Jay, and I'll trust you. But I won't trust you on this, because you don't have the experience to know what you're talking about. *I* do!"

Her point had registered; she had stopped him—if only for a moment. "I'll give you that, Miranda. I don't have your experience in these matters, but I also don't accept the fact that just because it happened to you, it'll happen to Jonathan. *And* I emphatically do not believe that Stephanie would try to prevent my seeing him."

"And if she did?"

"She won't."

"But if she did?"

"God!" He paused. "Okay. Jonathan is one of the dearest things in my life. So are you, by the way. But he isn't my life, not the sum total of it. It wouldn't be fair to him to make him into that. It'd do a lot more damage than joint custody."

"She won't give you joint custody!"

"We won't know until we ask her, will we?"

"Then, it'll be too late."

"Okay. Let's look at your scenario. What do *you* want to do?" He started to put his arm around her, but she moved away, wanting to think independent of his protection.

She couldn't say it—not what she *wanted*, but what had to be. It was because she loved him that she had to save him from a fate she knew far too well.

"All right," he began again. "Let's try it from another angle. Once and for all—and I mean that, Miranda —will you marry me?"

"Jay—"

"Yes or no?"

She didn't think she could say it, didn't believe she could gather the strength to get the word out, but she did. "No."

He said nothing, just looked at her, and it hurt her to see the depth of the disappointment and hurt; when she saw the anger come to his eyes, she was relieved.

"So you really are willing to go on living like this? Skulking around? Cheating?"

Beyond tears, she met his look and told him, "No. Over the last few days, ever since Paris, I've had to make a decision, too, Jay. An unspeakable decision. I can't go on seeing you. At all."

"Oh, God" was all he said.

"Jay—" Now that she'd begun, she found it possible to continue, despite the pain. "This hasn't been any easier for me than it has for you. And I would have done anything not to have had to tell you this. But there's nothing else to be done. I refuse to ruin your life and my life and the life of your son. I refuse to let history repeat itself."

Removing his hands from her shoulders, he sat back on the edge of the bed, slumped in defeat. "You know, Miranda," he said tonelessly, "where I come from, the past is supposed to teach you wisdom. Bad times are supposed to make you strong and brave and willing to risk things."

"Nothing bad has ever happened to you, Jay. How would you know?"

Suddenly, his shoulders lifted, as if he'd considered things and come to a conclusion. "So this is it?"

"Jay, darling, I—" She reached for him, wanting to memorize the way he felt so she could remember it for years, wanting him to share in the pain and the grief and the sacrifice. But he drew back, almost with a flinch.

"Okay, if that's the way you want it. But then again,

that's the way you always want it.''

He got up from the bed and began dressing. When he'd finished, she got up, too, prepared to go to him.

"Jay, let's not end this thing in anger. It's not about anger. It's not even about fear. It's about love. Real love. It's just that sometimes love isn't—''

And when he turned to her, it was to cut her off with a ferocity of which she hadn't known he was capable.

"You're a goddamned coward, Miranda. Damn you to hell.'' Then he was gone.

chapter 32

Jack
1984

LOOKING BACK LATER on that wild time in London, it seems like the beginning of a long term of trial. By 1982, the boom that had been Broadway only the year before fizzled. Oh, it wasn't just the New York theatre that was suffering; the whole economy seemed to be sliding into the basement. The big guys in Washington swore we were on the road to recovery, but that remained to be seen.

With Broadway, though, there were special problems: skyrocketing ticket prices, for one, based on the huge expense of mounting productions, plus producers' well-known greed. Sam Harrington was one of the innovators of the forty-five-dollar ticket, although the Harringtons, like others at the top of their profession, never seemed to need the money. Jay, on the other hand, didn't go along with Sam's thinking, and when, in one of their own smaller theatres, Sam charged a blanket forty-five dollars for every seat, including the balcony, Jay took him on in an argument that became legend. They didn't speak to each other for weeks afterwards, people whispered on the street. No one challenged Sam Harrington, not even his son. I was waiting for the shock waves.

They would come with Sam's second revolutionary decision: to sell two neighboring Broadway theatres to a huge international hotel chain. The chain had in mind to raze the theatres and erect an enormous luxury hotel in the middle of the theatre district. To people who loved the theatre, and who loved irreplaceable landmark buildings—people like Jay—the decision was treason. It was turning away from an old and honored art form and a sense of the past. That it was financially sound, and given the state of the theatre itself, it was, was irrelevant to the theatre people who picketed the Harrington building, and to Jay, who didn't. At least, not obviously. But, as the deal came closer to completion, there were reports of raised voices from Sam's office, and a couple of people had actually seen Jay storm out. War had come to Olympus.

The conclusion of that war was difficult to imagine. Jay was a power in Manhattan and beyond, no doubt about it. He owned and operated a highly successful try-out venture in the Globe, he had produced an Oscar-winning motion picture, and he was considered one of the shrewdest and most honorable of the real estate and theatrical overlords. Still, it was the Harrington standard he carried and the Harrington capital with which he made his deals. Jay was the heir apparent, and a golden one, but Sam still ran the show. Even now it seemed hard to believe that Jay would do anything to endanger his succession. But they were at loggerheads, and Sam had made it clear that if Jay tried to countermand him, it would be over his dead body.

Jay didn't discuss his troubles with me—I heard much more from gossip than from the primary source—but I remembered Stephanie alluding to them over a year before. As the situation degenerated, so did Jay's accessibility. We still got together occasionally, but he had become considerably more withdrawn. No great talker to begin with, except when he was making a deal or kidding around with friends, he had grown so private, you felt nostalgia for some old, warm quality that no longer seemed to be part of him.

Something had died, maybe simply his boyishness, but with that loss had come a toughness, possibly even a ruthlessness, that the young Jay had lacked. They were his father's qualities, and they were qualities he had always despised. When I ran into Stephanie at various functions and asked after Jay, she would shrug as if I were asking about someone she hadn't seen in years. Their relationship had altered, too, in the aftermath of London; they had become intimate strangers.

I suspected that Jay's new hard exterior might be a mask for real unhappiness, and I had to believe that was related to his involvement with Miranda. Whatever their arrangement, it hadn't brought them peace. I assumed the affair continued, but, at this point, I couldn't figure out how they managed. Even with a considerable amount of subterfuge, their paths couldn't have often crossed. But that was only an assumption. The one sure thing was that he had changed.

And so had she—and not for the better. It had happened gradually, since London, had happened despite her still soaring career. Hers was a dream success, following her mother's but perhaps surpassing it: She was a star, but she was also respected as an artist. Once you saw her perform, you never forgot her. She was sheer energy, pure feeling.

Her beauty, at thirty-one, had fully flowered, and the resemblance to Margo became even more pronounced, now that she burned with her mother's dangerous fever. She must have been missing Jay's more frequent presence in her life, I thought then, must have been starved for more than she was getting, more than she would ever get, for I was sure that Jay prided himself on his respectability too much to risk the scandal of a messy divorce. She was drinking a couple of glasses of wine too many at dinner, was doing a lot of high international living—

and, I suspected, a lot of the drugs that were part of that scene. She was living fast and high, driven to it by a love affair that could only wound her, just as Anthony had predicted. I'd last seen her in February when she was passing through New York on her way back to London, fresh from wrapping up a film in LA.

We'd met for dinner at the Odeon, a downtown *moderne* cafeteria that had been converted into a superb restaurant catering to a crowd that ranged from Wall Street lawyers to a rock star or two. I'd gotten there first, so I wouldn't miss seeing her arrive. And it was worth it.

She sailed in at 9:13, slightly breathless and forty-three minutes late, wrapped in a fur that looked like it must have belonged to a Renaissance prince. She confessed it was the most expensive single garment she'd ever owned, bought on a whim in Milan from Fendi. She had gotten very thin, and her hair was cut short and spiky, punk-influenced for the movie role, but it gave her a wonderful gamine air. Even across the room, the purity of her heart-shaped face, the perfection of the slightly turned-up nose, the lusciously vital green eyes, and the rosebud mouth made her look like an animated portrait by a master artist. I saw every eye in the room turn in her direction, apparently without her noticing, as she directed all her star quality at the maitre d', on whom it wasn't lost, then allowed herself to be escorted over to me. It was a great performance, a sight all the other customers could tell their friends about. We kissed and hugged, while thousands watched, then the maître d' helped her off with her coat, and I held out her chair for her, and she sat.

Captured, like everybody else, in her mystique, I grinned a foolish grin. It was only when she attempted to return it and faltered that I looked into her eyes and realized she was high as a kite on something—and that she'd been weeping.

chapter 33

Miranda
Los Angeles, 1983

LA ALWAYS DEPRESSED her because it made her think of Jay. Which was why New York depressed her. And London. There was nowhere, really, that she was safe from memories of him. It had been two years now, since they'd parted in the flat in Notting Hill, since she'd sent him away to save him.

And she had saved him, she was sure she had, though at the possible expense of saving herself. It was torture being without him, had been torture from the moment she'd made up her mind what had to be, and the torture had not relented in the course of time.

He was always in her thoughts, a permanent part of her life and her taste and her judgment, and she wouldn't have known how to banish him if she'd wanted to. But sometimes she felt she simply couldn't stand it. Ironically, her personal anguish seemed to have had a positive effect on her work. On the stage, on the set, her pent-up feelings of misery and loss fueled her, provided a deeper intensity to her performances, even if it meant being always on the edge of panic. If she was coming to be considered a greater, more serious actress than her mother, she had won the competition at a tragically high price. And it tired her; she was always tired.

She dreamed of getting Jay back, of being able to

rest, at last, in his arms, but she realized as she dreamed that it would never happen. She could never ask, and he would never come to her. She had made a decision, and either out of hatred or out of decency, he would abide by it. She had known that day in London how she had wounded him, and she wondered if he knew how badly she had wounded herself in doing so. Clearly, she would never know. But in the times when the public's acclaim, society's adulation, Anthony's loving bossiness, and Jack's staunch amiability couldn't make even a dent in her ironclad loneliness, she'd hoped he knew how hard it was for her.

Sometimes she thought she would settle for seeing him in a crowd, even with Stephanie, or for telephoning him, hearing him say hello, and then hanging up, the sound of his voice being reward enough. Other times, she was certain that so chance or so surreptitious a connection would have driven her mad. So she did her work, and went out with men who didn't interest her, no matter who or what they were, and thought and thought of him.

She was finished with the film—thank God—finished with the terrible hours and the shakiness and the fear that she was losing control. It would be heaven to get out of LA and back to London and rest, but she hadn't seen Jack for over four months, so she'd decided she'd hold out on relaxation a little longer and stop in New York.

As she packed, looking around the rented house in Coldwater Canyon, with no sadness at parting, she'd worked out her schedule. Arrive New York at three in the afternoon, have the waiting limo drive her to the Parker Meridien, rest for a few hours, and meet Jack for dinner. Get some sleep. Catch the *Concorde* to London the next morning.

It was seven in the evening, and she'd sent the maid home. Dinner was waiting in the kitchen, but she wasn't hungry. The speed she'd come to depend on for energy during the rough shooting was working. With no appetite, she'd opened a bottle of white wine and set to work organizing her departure.

When the phone rang, she'd decided not to bother answering it; after all, there was no one she was expecting to hear from. Very determinedly, it rang ten times before the caller disconnected. Half an hour later it rang again, ten times, as it was to ring every half hour for the next few. By ten o'clock, she was giddy from the wine and feeling good from the pill, and she decided, when the phone rang again, to give the person a break and answer it.

Flinging herself on the soft coverlet of the bed, in the small free section that wasn't covered with clothes to be packed, she snatched up the receiver on the ninth ring.

"Hi there!" she said breezily to the person on the other end. There was a moment's pause, as if the caller was debating, after so many tries, whether he or she really wanted to talk to her after all.

"Hello?" she said again, and this time the caller answered, and her heart stopped, as Jay Harrington very somberly said, "Miranda. I'm sorry to bother you at home, but I had to get in touch with you."

She was suddenly, utterly numb. "How did you get my number?" she asked distractedly.

"From Jack." There was not so much as a hint of warmth in his voice. "Something urgent's come up, Miranda. I've got to meet with you."

He wanted to see her! For whatever reason, from whatever motive, he wanted to see her! She couldn't believe it. After her baroque fantasies, it had resolved itself so simply: He wanted to see her!

She was too stunned to care why, too relieved to even consider disappointment, for she had rediscovered anticipation. His call had made her high—higher than the wine, speedier than the speed—and it was wonderful. She didn't want to sleep, but took a tranquilizer and forced herself, so she'd be as rested as possible when they met. The flight had seemed endless, but she'd endured it because, at the end of the trip, she'd see him, not in a newspaper photo, not in a magazine, but sitting beside her.

By the time the plane landed and she'd been picked up in the car ordered by Jack and was rushing toward Manhattan, she felt the onset of stage fright. As her bags were deposited in her hotel room and her watch informed her she would confront him in less than an hour, downstairs in the bar, she was shuddering inside with excitement and dread.

Jet lag was forgotten in the crucial decisions of what to wear and how to walk and what to say. Finally, it was Armani taupe pants and an oversized peach cashmere sweater set, and the amulet he had given her and that she had treasured but not worn, never worn, until this afternoon. A little perfume, no need for a purse—the futuristic card that opened her hotel room door slipped easily into a pocket—and it was time, and her head was throbbing.

Floating through the Disneyland Renaissance of the pillared lobby, through the wood-paneled and brocaded outer lounge, she was for once oblivious to all the people who stared at her and motioned in her direction. And when she reached the bar, practically empty at four-fifteen, she saw him first in a mirror, seated in a banquette at the back of the room.

He was wearing gray flannel, a blue shirt, and a navy-and-yellow striped tie, and his glasses were tinted and rimless; the overhead lights picked up what had to be a smattering of silver in his hair. He was the most beautiful thing she had ever seen. Something happened inside her, like her heart bursting, as she walked toward his table and watched him rise to greet her. He was smiling, but not the smile she remembered, and as she approached, he grabbed both her hands and kissed her, ever so politely, on the cheek.

"Miranda," he said with an easy amiability that didn't match her breathlessness. His palms burned hers, the touch more than enough to thrill her, but they pressed for no greater contact. "What are you drinking?" he asked when they were seated.

"I think . . . I . . . " She didn't really know, but it seemed not to matter, for he'd already motioned the waiter over and ordered her a dry *kir royale*; she noticed he was having Perrier. That he remembered what she used to drink, that he acknowledged the memory, gave her hope of something she wanted more than understood. She noticed, as he ordered, that he seemed older, and that it was due to more than the gray in his hair. It wasn't his face, which was tanned despite the season, and relatively unlined—very much the same as it had looked before. No, it was something more ineffable, a change of manner. He had not lost his graciousness, but she sensed an inner coldness that made the graciousness appear more style than actuality. The boyishness had vanished, gone with the mischief in his gaze.

"That's some haircut." He smiled, betraying not a hint of the nervousness he had to be feeling. "And you're so thin."

"Oh," she laughed, as if she were playing out a scene. "Both for a movie. You're looking . . . terrific."

"Thanks. At my age, that's comforting."

"Hey, you just had a birthday!" she chirped, in a half-baked attempt to make him think she'd only just remembered.

"Don't remind me." He grinned, as warm as could be, as distant as the moon.

"How's Jonathan?" she asked, and he replied, smiling for real. "Great! The most exceptional little kid in New York. Always was. Right from the start. His first word was *hutt*. But how're things with you?"

She wanted to ask him why they had to pretend that what had happened hadn't, why they had to behave like former business associates who'd had a falling out, but she couldn't. She was afraid to ask why he was here because the sooner she found out, the sooner he would be gone again. So, pursuing their absurdly polite course, she asked, "You're still with Stephanie?"

"Yeah."

"Things any better?"

"Things are . . . I guess, after London, I came to my senses and stopped expecting so much," he finished, his voice flat.

They were looking at each other, neither's glance betraying any hint of what they were, she hoped, feeling. He was a master, and it was his lead she was forced to follow—pleasant as a flower-covered field, steely as a sheet of ice.

"You still see Jack?" she asked idly, then answered, as if to herself, "Of course you do, I forgot. You're producing his new play!"

"It's his best. I really mean it."

"You ought to know. How many things have you done together?" She remembered, as she said it, a night at Sardi's years before when they had had to use Jack as an icebreaker.

"Seems like hundreds, doesn't it?" His gaze softened, with nostalgia or regret or longing, but even the softening was self-contained. To her dismay, she found she couldn't read him anymore. To her confusion, she could only guess his thoughts. With a dawning horror, she knew that what had happened in Notting Hill two years before was a break that hadn't healed, might never heal. And the knowledge made her heart plummet under the weight of her grief; whatever he wanted from her was nothing like her fantasies of reconciliation and forgiveness. Somehow she had counted on his having figured a way out of their bind. With his immense talent for negotiations, for strategizing, he had found the way to bring them happily together. And now she doubted that, and the doubt made her say, "Jay, this is pretty painful for me. It's hard for me to pretend with you. So, please, just tell me what you want."

"Yeah." He sighed, casting his gaze toward his untouched glass, then raising it to meet her questioning stare. "Miranda"—and suddenly she could see the strain in his eyes—"let me just give it to you straight. I'm splitting with Dad."

"You're what?" She was dumbfounded.

"Surprise, isn't it? I still can't believe I found the guts to do it. Want another drink?"

"After that, I could use one."

He signaled the waiter, and she was silent until the man had departed.

"What happened?" she demanded then. "Why?"

"Why?" He smiled bitterly. "So many reasons. Too many reasons. But the bottom line is that he feels I'm a dreamer, and a fool, and I think he's a cynical old capitalist who's selling out the theatre and all it represents to make a buck."

"Oh," she said quietly.

"It started over ticket prices. At a forty or forty-five top, he can make a fortune, even with union scale to pay. The only people who are hurting, in fact, are the dedicated theatregoers who can't afford to go anymore. And this is only the beginning. My father's is the kind of greed that feeds on itself, because audiences are getting smaller and smaller, and shows that could run if the top were twenty-five or thirty dollars aren't making it. So in essence, what my dad and the other theatre barons are doing is chasing the theatre away from Broadway. The theatre won't die, but Broadway might. My father certainly will, but he'll die rich."

He was speaking now with an intensity that evoked the Jay she had first known years ago, and as the bad memories evaporated and the old, good ones arose, she ached with regret. For the passing of their youth. For the passing of innocence and the freedom of careless passions merrily indulged.

"But what . . . um . . . provoked you to . . . " she

asked, as she started her second drink.

"It would have happened sooner or later anyway. Our paths and our philosophies, if that's the word, were radically diverging. But. Okay. Briefly . . ."

He told her about his father's plans to raze the two adjoining Broadway houses to make way for a huge hotel. Miranda already knew about that, there'd been such an uproar. According to Jay, that was when the disagreements between him and his father flared into more serious trouble.

"I couldn't see us tearing down theatres—just couldn't see it. So Broadway would lose two more legit houses, fine old buildings, and we'd make a fortune in a depressed economy."

By the time Sam was preparing to sit down to close the deal, Jay and he weren't even speaking, and Jay had made up his mind to leave Harrington's. But when he left, he wanted to take the theatres with him.

"And then the inspiration struck—I think . . . I hope." His smile was genuine. "Next week, if all goes well, I'm going to buy the theatres."

"How? What happened to the hotel chain?"

"They're getting their hotel, and I'm getting the theatres."

"Really?" she asked. "How?"

"Keep it quiet, okay?" he said earnestly, and she, slightly hurt that he had to say it, simply nodded.

"There's a real estate law in Manhattan concerning something called air rights. That means that if I own land in this city and erect a building on it, then in addition to the actual structure and the ground it stands on, I also own the space it occupies in the air, up to, in this case, forty-five to fifty stories. Which means if I owned a piece of property and wanted to construct a new hotel above an already existing building, I could do it. Which is what was done, in fact, right here. You know about the Helmsley Palace—on Fifty-first and Madison? The original structures were two beautiful Victorian man-

sions. They were sold to Helmsley, who not only preserved them, but renovated them *and* built a hotel above
them. He saved the mansions from being torn down,
and he built a big, new commercial hotel in midtown
Manhattan. So, I figured, why couldn't we do that with
the theatres?''

The next part of the plan would be to approach the
hotel chain and offer to build the hotel himself, then
rent it to them on a lease, with a possible option to buy
at the end of the lease date. It was not an unusual arrangement and was actually a more attractive deal to the
hotel people.

"But where do you get the cash for something like
that?" she asked. "And how do you know your father
will go along?"

"First of all, if he wants to sell the land, he's going to
have to sell it to me because I've knocked out his only
interest by offering them the same thing at better terms.
And, of course, I'll give him the opportunity to be one
of the investors."

"Tell me about these mysterious investors," she said,
fascinated.

He was positively glowing, totally caught up in his
dream, their star-crossed path transcended by the story
he was telling. Jay would never love a woman as much
as he loved a deal. "When I leave Harrington's, I take a
lot of money with me. I have a contract, you see. Sec-
ondly, I own the Globe outright, and that's not a lot,
but it's something. I've been doing plenty of real estate
speculation on my own, and it's been successful. But, all
that aside, I'm really functioning as producer because
what I'm doing is getting everybody I can to invest—all
the big theatre houses, some entertainment conglomer-
ates who back shows now, plus foreign money. It'll be
done like capitalizing a show. Like I said, if Dad's willing to play, he's in."

"Wow!" She shook her head. "So what's the

downside?"

"The downside," he said quietly, "is that if Broadway continues to go downhill, then the theatre district will go downhill and nobody'll want to stay there—if they do now. There are plenty of hotels around Piccadilly in London, but Times Square, one of these days, could make Piccadilly look like Buckingham Palace if the economy doesn't improve. That's the risk. But, what I'm asking these investors to do is to *invest* in the future of Broadway by investing in New York. Since we'll be banking on the income from the hotel to offset what could be deficits from the two theatres, I'm going down to a top ticket price of thirty dollars. I don't imagine the other theatre owners will be thrilled by that, but this is a special case, a historic situation in which, I hope, the hotel rental will provide an added source of income to the corporation. And saving the old structures will get us a huge tax abatement. So the theatres will be sort of underwritten."

"God, I hope it works," she said. "It sounds great," and it was then that she saw him look at his watch and realized, finally, that this was a meeting, not a rendezvous. But why? Why had he brought her here? To confide his deepest decisions to the woman he had loved? Hardly likely. She was on the verge of asking, when he said, "So it's all pretty well arranged, except for one final piece of the package."

"What's that?"

She looked at him, the shock waves hitting her only seconds after he said, "You."

She had wanted him, at least, to listen to her problems, the way he used to, when they were lovers. She had wanted to confess to him her growing exhaustion, and the overwhelming fear that had begun gripping her before every take of the last movie. She had wanted to tell him that she had gone up on her lines a couple of

times, she who never forgot anything; that she wanted
to do a play, but suddenly live theatre seemed too much
to handle. And Broadway—for the first time—now,
when she wasn't in any shape to try it . . . ? No.

She had wanted him to stroke her head and tell her it
was all right. That she was drinking much too much and
taking too many diet pills for a nature as high-strung as
hers, and that she should stop. Because she would, if he
wanted her to. She had wanted him to comfort her by
dismissing as silly her feeling that she was losing her
nerve. She had wanted him to say to her that she should
never be lonely because he loved her. But it hadn't been
that way.

Instead, he'd gone into some detail about the book-
ings with which he would open the theatre. In at least
one of them he would have to have a surefire star ve-
hicle, and the stars he wanted were her and Anthony, in
anything they wanted to do. He knew that Anthony
hadn't taken to him in the old days, but how could a
man of the theatre decline an opportunity to pay back
the debt? He was prepared to fly to London next week
to meet with Anthony, but, of course, he wanted to find
out her feelings before he went any farther.

She went cold with dread. The timing was so wrong
for her Broadway debut. To think of working again so
soon, when she'd been counting on a long rest to get
herself together, was frightening. But he didn't push
her, he didn't plead, he just looked at her, without taking her hand, and said, "Miranda, I'm not trying to use
any influence I have over you to force you to do
something you think you don't want to do. And I don't
want to force you to give me an answer now."

Ah, you've learned something, Jay, she thought. If
you'd let me have time to decide that opening night at
the Globe, none of this pain might ever have happened.

"But, when you do make up your mind," he'd told
her, reaching into his jacket pocket, pulling out a card

case and extracting a card, "here's the number where you can reach me or leave a message . . . anytime. It's private."

She took the card, noticing that the number was jotted down in pen, probably by him in preparation for the meeting, and that it was a number she didn't know.

Then he paid the check, and she walked him to the Fifty-seventh Street entrance, and he kissed her politely on the cheek, and, coatless, disappeared into a waiting limo. She'd gone up to her room and cried for a couple of hours, sipping some wine and taking a pill and wondering how she was going to tell him no. Because she couldn't do it. She just couldn't. The fear of failing was too great, and the hurt. No, she couldn't do it, but she couldn't tell him she couldn't do it. Well, she had to. And she had to do it fast. She simply wasn't strong enough. She needed to rest.

In the limo driving downtown to meet Jack, she was still crying a little, but she was fairly under control. Jack would calm her, Jack would make it easier for her to say no to Jay.

By the time she got to the restaurant, made the mandatory entrance, kissed Jack, and sat down, she really did feel better. And so it took her by complete surprise when she heard herself say to him, "Hey, guess who's coming to Broadway?"

chapter 34

Jack
1984

IF MIRANDA HAD harbored any hopes that Anthony would turn down Jay's offer to return to Broadway, she was to be disappointed—and shocked—by Jay's trump card. For the theatres were to be re-named, and the names would be The Gainsborough and The Seymour. Even she would admit it was an offer one truly couldn't refuse. As was the suggestion for the pro-duction, for it would be a revival of the last play Anthony had done on Broadway, as well as the last he'd done with Margo—a liltingly written melodrama of starcrossed love called *Goodbye Again*.

Jay's deal, of course, went through, although his father walked away with only a token investment and an enormous amount of bad feeling. Jay was on his own, saddled with a project more than one person considered suicidal.

Ground for the hotel would be broken in May of '83, concomitant with the opening of *Goodbye Again*. The other house would continue to play a hit—mine, I'm pleased to say—which had opened to great reviews and equally great business.

My further contribution to Jay's grand enterprise would be to work with Anthony, who would direct the play, but who had wisely suggested bringing the script

up-to-date. So, come spring, we were together again—
Miranda, I, Anthony, and Jay—in a climate and a situation that we never could have predicted that night in
Jay's loft nearly a decade before. We had fame and
money and celebrity, just as Miranda and Jay and I had
dreamed of way back then, but what had happened in
the interim had left us shy with each other and lonely. I,
for one, had eased in and out of countless encounters,
and nothing, no one, held me. Jay's obsession with
his business left little room for normal friendships.
Anthony, too, seemed a little lost, especially now,
because of what Miranda was too obviously becoming,
despite his dedication.

To Anthony's horror, and finally to mine, she was
imitating the wildly erratic and self-destructive patterns
that Margo had lived out in her last years. I could see it
in rehearsals, when she'd show up late, frenetic with
nerves, or not show up at all. And too often she either
hadn't bothered to learn her lines or couldn't remember
them. We all partied a fair amount, but Miranda stayed
out all night, driving herself to a point of exhaustion
where her concentration was totally blown. I'd heard
via in-house rumors that she was having a wild affair
with some rock star who was also doing his first show in
New York and missing as many rehearsals as she was.
Maybe it was true, maybe not, because Miranda no
longer shared her confidences with Anthony or me. And
certainly not with Jay. I was sure now of the dissolution
of their relationship, could, looking back, date it from
the beginning of her decline. From London. I was sure
of it from her inability to be around him without talking
too much or drinking too much or making too many
mistakes during rehearsal. I was sure of it from the pain
I felt radiating from her when he was present in a room.
In him, I could read nothing, could pick up not even a
hint of what had finally driven them apart, only the fi-
nality of that parting. And now, as Miranda's deteriora-
tion threatened this crucial project, I felt his anger.

It all came to a head one afternoon, at the conclusion of a rehearsal during which Miranda had not only arrived an hour late but had blown her scenes. The rest of the cast had been putting up with it, since movie people were famous for behaving like stars, not actors, but I know they were disappointed, because she had always been touted for her professionalism. And now even they were getting fed up. Granted, she always apologized, but three weeks away from preview, her apologies struck everyone as meaningless.

After several hours, Anthony had finally gotten her through the play without a missed cue or a forgotten line, but as soon as she got it right, she said she had an appointment and left. Everyone was furious, but no one was more furious than Jay. I saw him sitting in the audience, brooding, then, as soon as Miranda had split, watched him walk to the proscenium, call Anthony, and beckon him over to a couple of seats halfway down the aisle.

I couldn't hear what they were saying, but I could guess, and I waited the ten minutes until Jay abruptly rose and walked out, then met Anthony as he was walking slowly back up the aisle. At sixty-five, Anthony had more vitality and drive than most men do at twenty-eight, but the struggle with Miranda and his overwhelming concern for her had aged him. It wasn't the lines in his face; it was the world-weariness and the awesome sense of disappointment; it was his failure to prevent Miranda from following in her mother's tragic path.

"Anthony . . . " I said simply.

"Oh, Jack." He patted my shoulder, ever courtly despite his preoccupation. "Glad you're here, my boy."

"She's in trouble, isn't she?"

He looked up at me, deeply saddened. "Yes, she's in trouble. She's in dire trouble, Jack. And God knows I'd do anything to help her, but I can't. There's nothing . . . nothing I can do!"

There was a quality to his pain that touched me in a

new, tender place, in—I suppose—my spirit, brought to birth by all our sadness and loneliness, strengthened by the regret that comes when you start to move past youth. For the first time, I perceived the ignorance of my ways, the wrongheadedness of my rebellion, which had made me shrink from—and resent—love. And it was then that I truly came to realize how much I'd injured the two people I loved most. Resenting their intimacy, I'd set out to hurt them, set out to make them suffer. To me, then, the real world had been as make-believe as the stage, and nobody really bled. But they'd bled, all right, more than they would have had to if I'd told Miranda long ago that I knew their secret, or if I'd not suggested that Stephanie go to London.

And once I knew that, I had to face a different truth: that it was I, not my long-time, sometime lover, the shrink, who had been behaving like an adolescent. Foolishly proud of my bogus independence, insisting I needed no one, I had turned lonely and bitter, lashing out when I saw my buddies moving on to deeper feelings. I had done enough to hurt my friends; I wasn't going to do any more. Praying it wasn't much too late, I said, "Anthony, we've got to talk."

He agreed, of course—he was at his wits' end—and so we walked from the theatre district up Broadway, and through the park, toward home.

Anthony looked old, in his tweed balmacaan, like a park character, the type who reserves his spot on the bench and shows up every day, and who, when he doesn't, becomes cause for concern. We sat on a bench, with the spring afternoon turning cool, and it was then that he asked me, "When we were all in London, remember, Jack? They were lovers, weren't they?"

And I answered, "Yes. They were." And I hastened to add, "Anthony, she didn't tell me. I found out in a way I'm not so proud of that I want to repeat it. But, yes, they were."

"You know, Jack, I didn't really suspect—she's very

talented—until that night when we planned the trip to the country. Then I knew. But . . . after London, I think . . . they weren't seeing each other anymore. I can't imagine what could happen to shatter that kind of bond, but something did. Do you agree?''

I turned up the collar of my jacket against the growing chill. "Yes, I agree. It's what's killing her. I only realized that today.''

"Jack,'' he said, as much to himself as to me, "I've come to know her very well—her fidelity, and her willfulness and her tenacity. Whatever caused their break, she'll live with it. That's what she's like. She's so damned proud. Like her mother. She'll never go to him. Oh, Jack, I did my damnedest to keep them apart, because he was so like his father, because he seemed so ruthless. But I should have realized that it didn't matter, that the first time they met, it was already too late. I should have known that, from personal experience. But I didn't. She's falling apart, Jack, just like Margo. It's a waking nightmare seeing it happen again, losing Margo a second time. I've spent a decade, Jack, trying to prevent it. And I've failed!''

We rose from the bench and took a path heading east, as I lit a cigarette and Anthony continued. "So you know what I did, Jack? This is what I did. I went to Jay, anticipating he'd soon be visiting me on the subject of dismissing her. But I beat him to it. I went to him, and I told him I knew how she had loved him, and how I regretted coming between them, and that I'd been wrong and shortsighted. And I told him I thought it was her agonizing loneliness without him that was pushing her over the edge . . . '' He was heartbreaking, transcending tears, King Lear, and I was his Fool. "And I begged him, Jack, I actually *begged* him to go to her and tell her he loved her . . . even if he didn't anymore, just for now, just to save her now. And I promised him that, once we'd opened the show and she was past the crisis, I'd find some way—and I could, you know, I could find some way to break the truth to her quietly. So I begged him, Jack, just for that one thing, just for her salvation, to perjure himself. And I stopped speaking, and I stared at that incredibly handsome, totally immobile face, unable to read his thoughts, and begging to have influenced them. And you know what he finally said to me, Jack? Without altering his expression, without unfolding his hands placed so neatly before him on the desk, he looked at me and said, 'Anthony, let me put it this way: Either she gets it together—or she's out.' ''

chapter 35

Miranda
Manhattan, 1983

SHE HAD FELT the fear from a half hour before showtime till the first-act curtain, through intermission, and into the second act. Instead of diminishing in the first twenty minutes of performance, it had built, making her feel totally alone and utterly vulnerable in the midst of the bright lights and the celebrity-packed house. The smell of her own makeup suffocated her, and all sense of anticipation of her lines was suppressed by the panic; that she got them right was a miracle. She knew she was missing beats, throwing off the rhythm, making it adjust to the pounding of her heart, but she couldn't get back on the track. The constriction in her throat hurt when she spoke, the groping for lines made her dizzy. She was trying, trying harder than she'd ever tried, but it wasn't helping. Even having learned, from Anthony, that Jay had warned him she'd be out of the show if she didn't shape up made no difference. But she had missed only one of the five previews. There were only three more—tonight, which was Friday, and the two performances on Saturday, then the gala opening on Sunday night. She was trying too hard, but the fear and the exhaustion kept gnawing at her, interfering with her concern for the others, for all the others, who were depending on her.

And the second act was always a nightmare. A nightmare that had recurred since childhood, when she had been in the audience and her mother had been playing the scene. That scene. The last time she had seen her mother alive. And here she was, onstage, dressed like her, in ermine—a long ermine mantle arranged about her shoulders like a princess in a fairy tale. Ermine and diamonds—diamonds at her ears, at her throat, sparkling on her fingers as she dismissed the servant. Her gown was the color of young cherries, molded to her waist, spilling from waist to hem like the cascade of a waterfall.

Thinking herself unobserved, she let the ermine cape drop carelessly from her shoulders, just as her mother had done, but shaking inside, blessing the fact that all she had to do was remember the blocking. Even that was hard with all the terrible memories forcing their way into her mind. Of her mother. And the scandal. And all the misery. And Jay. And Jay. Who now hated her, and with reason. And what could have been. And the best times they were together. And the worst. And her mother, blowing her kisses during the curtain call, and then disappearing into distance and then madness and then death. And Anthony, whom she had first loved, then hated, and then loved, but who would soon appear onstage and make her say the lines her mother'd said, lines that had led to her ruination. She was going through the moves by rote, thank God, dashing to a mirror, arranging her auburn curls, straightening her necklace, obviously pleased with the way the ice-glow of the jewels and the bright cerise of her gown highlighted the flawless skin and the swan's neck.

She tried out her expressions, rehearsing for a rendezvous to come, but in her thoughts, there would be no rendezvous. No peace. No love. Only the roiling fear and the sense of empty panic. Even the awareness of her own beauty in the mirror was a stage effect, for beauty, now, was meaningless in the face of her despair and dread.

Crossing the room and pulling back the draperies, but

seeing no one arrive, she marched over to a brocade love seat and hurled herself into it, almost immediately jumping up and pacing again, her steps luring her to the window. Maybe—she felt a slight thrill of hope—maybe she could do it, maybe she was strong enough to get through it, maybe she would be perfect, be wonderful, would earn back Jay's approval, even his love. Maybe her panic would even help the performance, as it sometimes had—after all, that intensity in Margo had always been exciting. That edge of hysteria.

She was peering out the window when the door opened, and she whirled around. Oh, God, Anthony. Anthony, hair grayer, but as tall and manly in actuality as in memory. Resplendent in evening clothes, he raised a hand to smooth his thick lustrous hair, then made a fist, which moved to his hip in a pose of absolute challenge. "Madam"—his magnificent voice enchanted as his eyes fixed her in a wondrous gaze—"despite all, madam, I have come. Despite all, I have kept my word!"

She dropped her gaze, yet still kept silent.

"And so, my darling," he continued, "despite all, I expect you will keep yours."

And it was then that it hit her, the impact of all the lies and deceptions, the word not kept, the pain, the desire to be freed. And it was then, with a stab of sorrow because she knew it was the end, that she froze.

chapter 36

Jack
1984

IT WAS THE SATURDAY evening before opening, only a couple of hours after the curtain had fallen, and Miranda hadn't shown up since Friday night. She'd apparently gotten dressed after the performance, left to meet some people, and that was that. Everyone else was worried sick, but Jay, the new, heartless Jay, was furious: He was the guy stuck with making the decision of whether to open with the understudy, in case Miranda didn't reappear, or to try—if it was possible at such a late date—to postpone the opening in case she did. The opening was to be a huge benefit, followed the next day by the ground-breaking ceremony for the hotel, and all had been going perfectly—with the exception of Miranda, who had progressed from being difficult to being disastrous.

Apparently, Jay had wrestled with himself and his principal backers and had made a decision, for he asked to meet with Anthony and me at Anthony's apartment very late that night, after we'd all made an appearance at the supper held after the final preview. I had wanted to see Anthony before we saw Jay, for many reasons, but one in particular: some inaccuracy in everybody's histories as I knew them that had been plaguing me since the afternoon I'd talked with Anthony about Miranda and Jay. He'd blanched, that afternoon, sick with the revelation, and then murmured, over and over, "It's just like Margo. Just like her mother," and I'd bought it, but in the days since, through the sick dismay at Miranda's behavior and Anthony's dread of the worst, this had hit me: Why was Miranda just like her mother? Her mother had left her husband and child to go with the man she loved, and it hadn't stopped the onrush of her sad destiny. But Miranda hadn't. Maybe, if she had gone with Jay, none of this would have happened. And, as I mused, a strange thought struck me, and I had to know, had to know the truth, had to have it from Anthony.

And so, as we waited for Jay, in that same penthouse hideaway in which I'd first been bamboozled by the great man's charms, looking out over a skyline that had shone much brighter almost ten years before, I asked him.

"Anthony?" He had just handed me a refill of my brandy and soda and was sipping his own, distractedly. "Why do you think Margo continued to get worse, after she was with you?"

He looked up, startled.

"Excuse the cruelty of the question. I've a reason for asking."

"Jack. I don't know what to say. The loss of Miranda . . . "

"But I thought her trouble started before the loss of Miranda. What was it?"

I glimpsed a slight evasion in his eyes. "God, what a question, Jack. Especially now."

"No, Anthony, especially *now* is when I want to know."

"Jack, please . . . " He looked every bit of his age as he pleaded with me. "Please . . . "

"Anthony, tell me. If you care about Miranda, tell me. Did Margo have another lover—a secret lover—that no one ever knew about, except maybe you? Did she?"

"Jack!" He was begging me not to press him, but I couldn't. It was too important to know, important for Miranda, crucial for all of us.

"Anthony, did she have a lover?"

"Jack, Jay will be here in—" and he checked his watch "—in less than half an hour."

"She did, didn't she, Anthony?"

"Yes." He sighed, defeated. "But, Jack, you must never, ever reveal what I'm going to tell you because . . . well, you'll see why. But promise me, Jack, not a word. Not to Miranda. Miranda must never know. Never. Have I your word, Jack?"

And I gave it, and I meant it.

"Margo did have a lover," he began. "Someone she adored in a way she never adored her husband and never adored me, although she grew to depend on me. This . . . lover . . . she had known him since she'd started out on the stage, had wanted to leave her husband for him, but he was married, and he refused to divorce his wife. The affair started and stopped, started and stopped. At one point, she told him she wanted a child by him; after that, he refused to make love to her. So she went back to her husband, and to spite this lover, she had Miranda. I was around then—I was her cover, as much as anything, but it didn't matter to me. All that mattered was being near her. And you know, Jack, she *didn't want* to love Miranda once she had her, because Miranda wasn't her lover's child. I wanted her, though, Margo's little girl. *I* treasured her. Right from the first, when she was a baby, I loved her.

"There was a time, when Miranda must have been about ten, that Margo tried to start it up with the lover again, because, you see, she couldn't get over him; he was her life. She had long been trying to make him jealous with me, as I've said, and I was all too aware of it, but it didn't work, and she was left with her husband, whom she despised, and Miranda, whom she resented, and with me. I was the best of the bad choices. So, lovers on screen, we became, for all the world, lovers in real life, scandalous, adulterous lovers. And off we ran, she already half-crazed and I just happy to have her. And I—I fought for Miranda, wanting her with me so much, since she'd become like my own child. But I didn't win her . . . and I didn't win Margo. I think I knew, but it didn't matter, that I could never cure her of that passion, that awful, punishing passion, that ruled her like a curse and ultimately killed her. And now, seeing Miranda, seeing it happen again . . . I . . . ''

"Happen again? Anthony, what do you mean? Who was Margo's lover?''

And he looked up at me with a smile that both acknowledged and scorned the gods. "Don't you know, Jack? Haven't you guessed? Haven't you unpuzzled the truth that has made me act the way I have for all these years? Haven't you even suspected the secret that's been torturing me for more time than I can remember? Jack, Margo's lover was Jay Harrington's father.''

chapter 37

Miranda
Montauk, 1983

SHE'D BEEN WALKING on the beach for hours, the last hours of the night, when, gradually, the sky had brightened to the color of silver satin and then warmed to rose. Since Jack had called late the night before, she'd tossed and turned, unable to lie still, much less sleep; finally, her restlessness had driven her to the beach, which lay only a few steps below the terrace.

Early May in Montauk was before the beginning of the season, and many of the houses along the strip of private beach were still closed, but Jack's house was heated, and he kept it open all year long. Some time ago, he'd given her a key, and she'd used the house before when she needed to get away. After that disastrous Friday night performance, she'd told him she was going there, had promised she wouldn't do anything to hurt herself in exchange for his word that he wouldn't reveal where she was. Her disappearance was cruel to Anthony and irresponsible to everyone; she knew it wasn't fair to make him promise, but she no longer cared. Anyway, she'd sworn up and down that she'd let him know on Sunday morning whether she'd be able to open. And after all, her understudy *had* done the part enough times in previews to step in if she couldn't be there; the young actress was talented and could use a break like that; it could make her career. Jack had been afraid of her making the long drive to Long Island alone, but she swore she'd be fine and had convinced him to lend her his car, reminding him she always felt better when she was behind the wheel. And he had. He trusted her. He was the last one who did.

He'd called her only minutes after she'd arrived, worried because he'd been trying for the last half hour, but relieved when she'd said she was fine. She'd almost immediately gone to bed in the back bedroom of the cheerfully comfortable clapboard house. The room opened onto a side porch that joined the terrace, beautifully weathered from the salt spray, and it had, from two sets of windows, a marvelous view of the ocean. In May you needed a coverlet, but you could catch the ocean breezes if you just left the windows opened a fraction, and she'd slept almost around the clock, thinking about nothing, blissfully freed of any memories or decisions. When Jack had called at three o'clock Sunday morning, she'd been startled, but not surprised by the urgency in his voice. "Miranda, Anthony and I are driving out. Now. We have to talk to you. We've got to do something about this show . . ."

"But I took your car," she told him.

"I rented one. We'll be there about . . . I don't know . . . dawn, I guess. All right?"

"Sure," she said, not meaning it.

"Hey," he said finally, his voice softening, "how're you doing?"

"Sleeping, mostly," she told him. "But I'm calming down."

"Good. Keep it up, and I'll see you soon."

So the dawn was here, and with it would come Jack and Anthony, and the making of a decision she wasn't sure she could make. Because she didn't know if she could go back, even if she wanted to. She just didn't know. She didn't know what she wanted. Except Jay, and she couldn't have him. Because he hated her. She was sickened by the way she'd let everybody down, Anthony especially, but she hadn't wished this to happen; anyway, she was probably doing the play more damage in her present state than if she didn't show at all.

As she walked down the deserted beach, in that farthest part of the South Fork that reminded her so of Malibu, she heard a car pull up in front of the house. Not bothering to hurry back, not relishing the conversation to come, she slowed her pace, wrapping her heavy cardigan more tightly around her, strolling along the surf, listening to the peaceful hiss of the water washing against the sand. But even walking slowly, she was too soon in front of the house, climbing the steps to the terrace, calling "Jack! Anthony!" She entered through the back door, drawn to the kitchen by clattering sounds and the aroma of coffee.

"What in the world are you guys doing? It sounds like—"

"Hello, Miranda," Jay said.

He was standing in the middle of the big white kitchen, dressed in a tuxedo and evening shirt with his tie and satin vest undone; she saw the jacket slung over a chair.

"Here." He handed her a mug of steaming coffee, the product of an incredible amount of disarray; every cupboard in the kitchen was ajar. "Drink this. We've got to talk."

Stunned to see him, she obediently took the cup and, lost for words, sipped the strange, semitransparent liquid. It tasted like very bad tea.

"Okay, where do you want to talk?"

"Jay, I . . . I'm sorry—"

"I said, where do you want to talk? Oh, for Christ's sake, what's down this way?" he asked, stomping out of the kitchen. "What's in here?"

"My bedroom," she said. "The bed's not made or—"

"It'll do." He sat down on a white wicker piece, too

314 • CAROLYN FIRESIDE

delicate for him by far. "You can sit over there, on the bed."

"All right," she said, sighing. She perched on the edge of the bed, waiting for him to start. He looked exhausted, exhausted and angry.

"All right, Miranda. This won't take long. You're fired."

"Fired?"

"You're fired. You're out of the show."

"Yes. Of course." She found, to her astonishment, that she was fighting back tears. "Of course, you had to."

"That's right, Miranda, I had to."

"And why . . . " she asked, feelng the faint stirrings of some growing emotion, " . . . why did you have to come all the way out here to tell me? Why didn't you call? Or why didn't you just let Jack and Anthony come? Why did you have to do it yourself?"

"Because I felt it was the only professional thing to do. You're probably not familiar with the word *professional*. It means—"

"I know what it means." She could feel the searing ball of tears in her throat as she avoided his gaze.

"Says who?" he asked.

"Jay," she said, and all of a sudden, tears were coursing down her cheeks. "Jay, I didn't *want* this to happen. I didn't. I've been so . . . so . . . "

"Let me say once again, Miranda"—he sat calmly, with his legs crossed, watching her weep—"I'm not falling for your tears."

"You're not supposed to *fall* for them. God!" She bowed her head, trying to wipe away the tears faster than they came. "I feel so bad about this."

"Feel bad, Miranda. Feel real bad. Feel bad because it's your irresponsibility that's endangering not only the people you're working with, not only me, but the people you love."

"But I love *you*, Jay."

"You love me, huh? You sure have an unusual way of showing it. You do this to me when I've staked everything I'm worth, including my reputation, on some *meshuggeneh* project that even I wonder about in the wee hours of the night. You do this just when my father and I are finished. And you do it to me when my wife's in the middle of leaving me! You call that love!"

"She's leaving you? Stephanie?"

"Yeah."

"When?" She sat up, amazed. "When did it happen?"

He grinned. "About three days before I called you in California."

"You mean you knew when we met in New York? Why didn't you tell me?"

"Because I didn't want you to know, just then. But I wanted you within seeing distance—I needed you within seeing distance. And because I'd been hearing some . . . disturbing . . . things about you. I didn't believe them, you see, but I had to find out for sure."

"About my being . . . um . . . a bad risk?"

"Something like that."

"So *Goodbye Again* was cooked up just to test me? Well, I certainly flunked."

"You certainly did. But I didn't do it just to test you. Renaming the theatres and opening with that particular show was an inspiration, you've got to admit. Anyway, you're a tough one to catch, whether you know it or not, darling. I had to be devilishly clever. Miranda, I've been so lonely without you . . ."

She was dazed. "You are absolutely one of the . . . " But the words failed her.

"So don't you care what happened with Stephanie?" he went on.

"Oh, yes, yes. God, I do!"

"Well, for your information, things went great.

Really great. She's even agreed to shared custody. See, she's got a guy, and they're serious. Name's Alan Jessel, he's the chairman of—''

"The man with the department store!" she chimed in. "Of course, I met him in Paris, with—"

"You got it. She'd met him when she was an assistant buyer at Bloomingdale's. Then she married me, and he went on to his own store. He's been in love with her for years."

"So in Paris . . . ''

"Stephanie said that was the first time they had consummated their affair. In Paris. Novel idea! Which brings to mind, Miranda—Paris, you remember, was when Stephanie supposedly sent you the warning about us. Except she didn't. She didn't have a clue. She was putting up a smoke screen so I wouldn't find out about them!"

"Oh, Lord." The tears, suddenly, had stopped as she stared at him. "You mean . . . ''

"I mean," he said, meeting her gaze with his own stern one, "with your usual flair for imagining the worst, you misinterpreted the whole evening. And look how far you carried it, Miranda. Look how many people you hurt—especially yourself—because you were so afraid of hurting somebody. You were too chicken to find out that the past, which you worship and use as an excuse for everything, might *not* repeat itself. You just weren't willing to take that risk."

"Jay, the risk was yours."

"No, Miranda, the risk was ours, as separate people and together. And, frankly, until you saw that, I don't think we *would* have lasted."

"And now?" she asked.

"Now what?" He uncoiled himself from the little chair, walked to the bed, and sat beside her.

"How do you feel now?"

"How do *you* feel?" He countered her question with

his own, removing the mug from her hand, placing it on a table, and replacing it with his own hand. "What do *you* want from me?"

"Right now?" She looked at him shyly.

"Sure, right now."

"I want you to hold me." And she reached out for him, and he held her tight as she talked. "And I want you to tell me that I *can* get control of my life. And that I'm a tremendous actress. And that I'm not my mother . . . And—" It took her courage to say it. "—and I want you to stop believing that everything you feel is true just because *you* feel it. And I want you to listen to *me* sometimes . . . And I don't want you always to be so damned brave. And if you can, I want you to tell me that Jack doesn't despise me. Or Anthony—Anthony most of all."

"Miranda," he murmured, "they don't despise you. They love you. Jack told me where you were in under three seconds. And Anthony actually urged me to come."

"They did? He did?" She pulled back from his embrace to confront him, "Why? They couldn't have known about us. Why?"

"I don't know." He stroked her hair, so gently. "Maybe they're both romantics who can imagine two people carrying a torch all these years. Or maybe that isn't even the point. Maybe we all get to a place in our lives when our respect for the past is a luxury we can't afford. When we start concentrating on the future, on people's ability to change. Maybe we start realizing we didn't know as much about the world as we thought we did . . . and about the people we love. Maybe we've got to take a chance on ourselves and hope we're not wrong."

"And you feel like taking that chance?"

"I don't have a choice anymore, Miranda. I've got to. And so do you."

And she said softly, "At last we're in the same place."

"And Miranda—" He took both her hands in his. "—if we take the chance, with each other and with our work and with our fears, and we win, we'll have it as good as it gets, including lots of time with Jonathan, who already is showing a marked propensity for excitable redheads. You'll see. It'll work like a charm." He nodded toward the platinum symbol around her neck. "Like that charm. Forever."

"And if it doesn't . . . work like a charm?"

"We'll still have each other, on a daily basis."

"Jay, I'm a mess . . . I don't know if I can promise to—"

"Miranda! You're not a mess anymore. Right? I can't afford for you to be. I need you to be strong for me. Remember, I'm every bit as crazy as you think you are, and now it's my turn to need you. Okay? Besides, I may have to live off your income."

"Sounds fair," she said with mock solemnity.

"Oh, one more thing. For the last time, will you marry me?"

She thought it over, then said calmly, "I might . . . "

"You might? What kind of answer is that? You might . . . ?"

She smiled demurely.

"If you expect me to get down on my knees, Miranda, forget it. I did something to my back playing tennis the other day"—he massaged a spot near his spine—"and if I kneel, I'll never get up. So could we settle for a simple, civilized yes or no?" He sat back, folding his arms, waiting.

"Well, okay . . . " she announced. "Okay."

"Okay? I'm assuming that means yes."

She nodded.

"So that means we have a deal?" He smiled at her.

"We have a deal," she agreed.

"Well, let's shake on it." He took her hand and

shook it firmly, then opened it and kissed the palm, then hugged her tight. "Oh, Miranda, thank God! Thank God, it's over!"

Her heart leapt, really leapt. But with such joy, a joy that outshone the sun pouring in the windows, outshone the jewels she would wear that night. Outshone the marquee with her name in lights. Suddenly, she could do anything. Suddenly, she was ready for Broadway. "Oh, God, Jay. What time is it? We have to get back to town."

He withdrew his arms and sat back. "No, *you* don't. *I* have to get back and change my tuxedo. *I* open tonight."

"*We* open tonight!"

"Um, Miranda, darling. I love you, but I'm still the boss, and you're still out of the show."

"What?" She simply stared at him.

"I told you. You're fired."

"Fired?" All of a sudden, she was ablaze. "Fired? You must be kidding! Who in hell do you think you're going to get to replace a name like mine? Just tell me who!"

"I figure we'll open with the understudy—for a while . . . Then, well, to tell you the truth, I've been talking to Meryl Streep."

"Meryl Streep!" She was on her feet, stalking over to the windows, then turning to emphasize her point. "Meryl Streep! My God, I went to school with her! I know her work! She's totally wrong for the part. Any actor or director could tell you that." She began pacing angrily and had turned away from him so she didn't hear him, shoeless, approaching her.

"I knew that would get you on your feet in a hurry," he murmured into her hair. "Maybe I'll reconsider." But she was oblivious to his words and to his turning her around until she faced him.

"Meryl Streep! My God, of all the people to replace . . . I mean, Anthony couldn't possibly work with her, and her hair's the wrong color, and besides, she's a movie actress now, for heaven's sake, and utterly . . . I mean, you'll be laughed out of—Maybe she can do it with a Polish accent! Anthony'll love that! And, besides, if you're talking—''

There was nothing to do but shut her up the only effective way—with a kiss.

chapter 38

Jack
1984

So, AS IT TURNED out, Jay believed in Miranda more than I did, more than Anthony did, more than *she* believed in herself. And he believed in her all along, even to that midnight meeting with Anthony and me. Expecting that he'd heartlessly and cruelly dismiss her, we were shocked when he told us he had guaranteed his investors that Miranda would open, that he knew she was at a crisis point, but it was necessary in order for her to prove something to herself, and that he had no doubt she would weather the crisis, for many reasons, he continued, chief among them, Anthony; she'd never let Anthony down. And Anthony had beamed at that. And I knew, then, that everything would be fine, for when Anthony Gainsborough beamed, the sun came out like Shakespeare.

Jay, of course, was right. Facing the opening night was what it took, for Miranda. She confessed, however, that the best thing about a lavish private dressing room —not in the English tradition, you know—was that you had your own private bathroom, which afforded you the luxury of throwing up at will: fabulous for stage fright, after all.

And the evening was history—an antique theatre not only preserved but renamed, it and its mate, so that their passion would shine as long as the Great White

Way. The evening was about risks of Elizabethan proportions and glamorous chances, with a damned good bet for a happy ending.

And when the curtain fell, and the crowd bravoed, and Anthony came to the edge of the stage, insisting Miranda come with him, I thrilled with the rest of the audience.

And as Sir Anthony Gainsborough enchanted everyone in every seat—the master wizard, the magical charmer, speaking in his own Shakespearean style of orotund speechmaking—tears came to my eyes.

And then he ended with, ''I want to thank Margo, who, wherever she is, I know to be wonderfully joyous tonight. And I must thank you from the depth of my own humility, and . . . '' He paused, pressing Miranda's hand and turning toward her, looking at her with such extraordinary love that it shook me. ''And I'm . . . I'm . . . so . . . proud of this young lady!''

And as she, without thinking, drunk on the warmth of the evening, simply came into his arms, and the crowd rose to its feet and cheered, I thought of the one question about the past I hadn't dared ask him, would never ask him, but would always wonder about. A question concerning honorable lies, and the nature of his love for Miranda. About whether fathers are born or made. About a most profound secret, which would never be disclosed.

As they parted, with the crowd still on its feet, and took their final curtain call, Jay and I, hovering in the back of the theatre as we had eight years earlier, shook hands and then embraced, too. For we knew that the curse had been lifted and the past laid to rest, that we would all prevail, somehow, and that we had inherited a future, for better or worse, that would show us what we were; that the hotel tower would rise, and Broadway would maybe triumph, maybe not, but that we would be there, lost in our myriad loves, believing, hoping, believing . . .

ABOUT THE AUTHOR

CAROLYN FIRESIDE is a well-known figure in New York publishing and has held leading positions at major houses. At Dell Publishing Company she was Executive Editor of the mass-market division before resigning to become Editor-in-Chief of Berkley Books. Although she remains as Editorial Consultant to the Putnam Publishing Group, she devotes full time to writing and has published criticism as well as fiction. GOODBYE AGAIN is Carolyn Fireside's second novel, following publication of ANYTHING BUT LOVE. She lives in New York City.

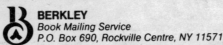